MY FIFTH SEASON

Discard

MY FIFTH SEASON

A Novel

Rebecca Clifford

iUniverse, Inc.
New York Lincoln Shanghai

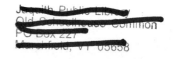

MY FIFTH SEASON

iUniverse books may be ordered through booksellers or by contacting:

iUniverse
2021 Pine Lake Road, Suite 100
Lincoln, NE 68512
www.iuniverse.com
1-800-Authors (1-800-288-4677)

This is a work of fiction. All of the characters, names, incidents, organizations, and dialogue in this novel are either the products of the author's imagination or are used fictitiously.

ISBN: 978-0-595-40429-2 (pbk)
ISBN: 978-0-595-84805-8 (ebk)

Printed in the United States of America

To Alessandro

Contents

CHAPTER 1

Should I Stay or Should I Go?

On a very warm mid-September afternoon, as Dad drove me up the winding road of Fieldings Academy's main entrance, something uncomfortable twinged in my gut. I suddenly felt thrust into this Connecticut landscape of graceful lawns and brick buildings with white trim and oxidized copper roofs. Everything looked unfamiliar to me, even though I had been here the previous December for a tour and an interview and subsequently fell in love with the place. I felt as though Dad and I were supposed to be dropping someone else off, and I was going to head back to my hometown of Cross River, New York, and to Katonah High.

There it stood: my future home, a turreted, brick building that looked like an overgrown, turn-of-the-century railway station, standing in front of me as though it were giving me this stiff, imposing welcome. Kurtzman, named after some alumnus. My roommate, Suzie Hodges, wasn't going to arrive until after orientation week because she had to go to a cousin's wedding. That's what her mom told my mom over the phone a couple of weeks ago. I never got a chance to speak to Mrs. Hodges since she called while I was in the city doing last-minute school shopping. I knew nothing of Suzie except that she was from Los Angeles, and a little excitement stirred in me whenever I thought of that. It was so far away, so different, and therefore glamorous. My piano teacher of five years, Chris Hershfeld, had just moved out there this past summer to be with his new wife, so that only added to the emotion it brought up in me. I sort of knew I was buying into that whole Hollywood myth by assuming Suzie was the daughter of some studio mogul who made big, summer blockbusters. Her parents probably thought Fieldings, with its small student body, bucolic, well-tended campus, and turreted dorms, was the ideal place for their daughter because it was right out of a movie.

And I had to admit that was one of the reasons I chose to come here. When my mom and I visited the place last December, I gazed at the pulled-together look of the campus with its classic Georgian buildings, the sprawling playing fields, and the large quad framed by oak trees. Katonah High felt dull, suburban, and anonymous in comparison. As I chatted with the head of admissions about my piano playing, love of music, favorite books, and favorite films, I felt a cheeriness in my voice that I didn't recall having before. "Perrrfect!" Mom said, clasping her hands together and grinning after a campus tour by a pretty, athletic, and chatty junior named Perry, who had wavy, blond hair, radiant green eyes, and whose last words to me were, "So, I hope you get in! You seem like a pretty cool chick." To this day, I don't know what it was about me that made her say that, and at the time, I had a sneaking suspicion it had to do with my mom being a TV soap star. But something about the way Perry looked right into my eyes made me turn so warm, I thought I was going to melt right there beside our car, despite the December chill. Somebody actually thought I was cool. It was like another reality was offered to me. So I had to come here because it was at this place that I could be the new-and-improved Jessica Thurwell. And maybe I could be friends with this Perry.

Dad parked near the steps of the dorm, and I stepped out of the car and into the blazing sunlight. The sky was so clear; it looked like it would shatter if I threw a stone at it. The grass was a kind of deep green I didn't recall seeing before.

I glanced over at Dad, hoping to exchange a comforting smile, but I only saw him staring up at the dorm. I didn't know what he was thinking, nor could I see much through his glasses or the graying beard and mustache that covered most of his face.

"Here I am!" I tried to announce but only warbled as the thought *So do I really want to be here?* nagged at me. I wondered if I was just prematurely homesick.

"Yup, here we are," Dad finally said, looking at me with a forced smile. His eyes weren't saying much. "I guess we should go register, huh?" He sounded as hesitant as I was feeling. It was weird because he and Mom wanted me to go here.

"Yeah, I guess." As I slammed the car door shut, images flooded back to me of the whitewashed, nondescript room where I had my lessons at the music school in the city every Saturday morning, and Chris demonstrating a key change in some Mozart piece with his hands flying off the keys. My throat pinched, and I swallowed. I tried to take a step forward to my new home, my new self, but I only felt my knees start to shake. The smell of my Grandma Cunningham's perfume, Calèche, seemed to pass under my nose just at that moment, and there I was back in New York, but it was evening this time, and I was settling into the red velvet seat of a lavish Broadway house with Grandma by my side. I could hear her gossipy tales of her days as a costume designer for Broadway shows and I felt her pull me close to her on her couch with pink and green satin stripes and call me her little lamby, telling me that being thirteen was just something I had to get through, and that I'd be OK. Everything about her, the weathered face underneath her powder, the white hair with its blond tint curled gently around her face and neck like something out of the 1950s, felt secure and comforting. I remember staring up at a picture on her living room wall that was a watercolor of her villa in Florence and imagining another life there once I got out of junior high. And now here I was, a sophomore in high school. I wasn't in Italy, I was in Connecticut, but it was another life. I just wondered if it was going to be the one I wanted.

I didn't get it. All throughout the summer, I counted down the days until I would arrive at Fieldings. While initially the idea of boarding school wasn't mine so much as it was my parents', it was clear that when things started to fall apart for me my freshman year at Katonah—when Chris announced his departure and Grandma died of a stroke—a change was needed. My parents saw me as lost at that school with its enormous student body, and maybe they were right. "It's a great school but much too big for you, Jess," Mom would crisply announce to me over and over again, whenever I complained about feeling left out and friendless. My brother, Tom, who, as a senior, won Best All Around, certainly had no problem there, but it was clear to all that I wasn't like him. And it didn't help that my best friend, Kim, in all her bubbly sociability, eased into the cool crowd, while I stood by the sidelines, with my long, stringy, dark blond hair, prepubescent body, and bovine, brown eyes gawping at her. I couldn't understand how she could be with a group of girls who all dressed alike in their cashmere sweaters, jeans faded just so, and who had an innate inability to do anything completely on their own. That just wasn't who she and I were. For us it was vintage clothes and 1960s music. She was still nice to me, but all our after-school afternoons spent listening to the Beatles and Burt Bacharach began to bore her. "Jess, there are so many other things to do! And maybe it's time you kind of get with the 1980s, you know?" she'd exclaim, her dark blue eyes wandering over to her herd of new friends, who were talking about what a blast last weekend's party was and how they could barely remember it.

Dad and I walked over to the gymnasium to register, my mind buzzing with the past. We waited in a line on a soft, pitch-black asphalt path that led down a little hill to the back door of the building. Neither of us said anything, and I didn't feel uncomfortable with him because unlike Mom and her constant need for chatter, Dad and I had relaxed silences. It was the other new students around me who made me thrust my hands into the pockets of the green and white culottes I had bought back in June at the Canal Street flea market and wore all summer long. I wore them on this day, thinking I could display some New York cool, but I just felt dorky. No one seemed to care. Some looked as wide-eyed and bewildered as I felt, and others cast their faces down at the ground, shuffling their feet. A few chatted with each other as though they'd known one another before, and I stared at them, wondering how they could make friends so fast. Or did everyone already know everyone?

It all seemed a blur of brilliant sunlight, unfamiliar bodies, and smells: B.O., too much perfume, and hair spray. When we entered the fluorescent-lit staleness of the gymnasium, first came the flash of the Polaroid camera for my ID. I came out thin and pale, my dark blond hair fading against the blue cloth background while my lost gaze made me look like a starved cow heading for slaughter; it was as if I'd already disappeared even before school began. Placed next to the school logo on the ID were the numbers "85" and "86" connoting the academic year. Then came the smiling teachers' faces, greeting me as though they already knew me, making me feel invaded instead of at home. They pointed to tables across the varnished floor of the echoey basketball court where we were to fill out and pick up other forms. I messed up filling in the blanks, putting in my last name when I was supposed to put in my first, my birth date as opposed to today's date. And, of course, all that were provided were short, eraserless pencils. *What's the point of having a pencil if there's no eraser?* I thought as I pressed down harder on the graphite to get my name down. All the while, people's voices—shouts, giggles, and questions—bounced off the floor and the walls.

About fifteen minutes later, we were back outside, shading our eyes from the sunshine. I thought of the coolest sunglasses I could have worn, but like an idiot, I forgot to bring them with me. Big, white, wide-rimmed things that would have horrified Kim's popular clique back at Katonah. Kim, because she'd be too nice to say otherwise, would swallow and act embarrassed, even if I knew that she kind of liked them. Fieldings would be different and more open-minded. *And* the sunglasses would have hid every emotion on my face.

"I need some water," I whined to Dad as we headed up another small asphalt path by another brick dorm to Kurtzman. I heard an electric guitar playing along with a frantic-sounding orchestra as a voice sang about the Apocalypse. *Trevor Horn,* I told myself, thinking how proud Chris would be that I recognized a music producer's signature sound. I refused to think that hearing the song was some kind of omen. A guy with jet-black hair marked with scarlet tufts poked his head out of the window where the music was playing and talked to his cherubic-looking friend outside, who kept pushing his glasses up against his nose and hiking up his jeans.

To get away from the music, I leaned into Dad and smelled his familiar dad smell of pipe tobacco and soap. He put his arm around me but didn't clutch me in closer like he used to when I was younger. He just hung there like he didn't know what to do, and, in a fit of spontaneous anger, I pulled away. All of sudden, I wanted Mom because at least she'd respond somehow. I pictured her, tried to imagine what she was thinking, if she was even thinking of me as she stood in an over-air-conditioned soundstage of her soap, *Sunset on Tomorrow,* in a former armory in Manhattan, a thick layer of makeup on her face, waiting for her cue from the director, watching from the sidelines with the TV crew and the extras, who hungered for the long table of underripe fruit and stale Danishes. And water.

My heart pounded, and I wanted to be back there with her.

Kurtzman's porch was now filled with a group of sunny, summery-looking people sitting on the railings, looking prep-school cool in their casual, raggle-taggle fashion of plain T-shirts, shorts, ancient sneakers, and hair carelessly pushed away from their faces in what-the-hell-looking ponytails and banana clips. I suddenly felt like a loser on parade with cartoonish daisies plastered all over my culottes and my brand-spanking-new white high-tops. Everyone looked like college students. Somehow I thought people at boarding school dressed more interestingly and less like a pack of lemmings. Tom had a friend who went to boarding school, and I remember looking through his yearbook the day after my grandma died, immersing myself in the various pictures of laughing students of different races, different clothing styles, all in some vain attempt to take myself away from a life that was changing too fast for me. I puffed out my cheeks and let out a long sigh.

"What?" Dad asked. He whipped his head around at me. He was reading my mind. I could tell by the anxious nature of his voice, something rare in him when he was the picture of calm, steadiness, and thoughtfulness. That was part of his job as a psychiatrist, but I think it was also there to counteract Mom's constant hum of anxiety.

"Nothing," I returned, curling my hair around my fingers. Maybe I should have worn it up. I would have at least looked more mature.

After getting some of my stuff out of the car, I tried to race up ahead of Dad with as much as I could carry, my mouth feeling like a cotton ball. And then I caught sight of a small, pretty, golden-haired girl wearing a tidy, bright blue T-shirt and cut-off jean shorts, leaning against the white porch railing, her arms crossed in front of her and her head thrown back. A husky cackle came out of her pearly pink, lipstick-coated lips. It was that girl, Perry, and a cool breath of relief tinged with fear went through me. *No,* I said to myself, *I will not slump back and gape like I usually do. Be cheerful and outgoing. Be like Kim.*

"Hi," I blurted out to the group, accidentally interrupting Perry and yet wondering in pulsating fear if she remembered me. At that moment, my lips, which had a nice full yet very defined shape, felt swollen. My chest felt concave yet tender, and it was as if my butt started getting bigger while the rest of my five-foot-four-inch frame shrank. All the other girls stopped fidgeting and chewing gum, staring in my direction while Perry fixed her green, kitty-cat eyes on me in almost a glare. My heart was ready to explode when I realized first that I had made a huge faux pas in interrupting her, and then secondly, and worse, when I realized she had no idea who I was. She studied our dark blue Volvo, at which point Dad yelled up to me, "Jessica, we're going to get the trunk out last." I nodded to him, my head feeling separate from my neck, and turned back to the group. "Is there a water fountain here?" I squeaked. Didn't she remember me?

Perry answered just as I finished the sentence, as if expecting this question all along. "Yeah, inside, let me show you." She slid off the railing. We were almost the same height, although she was a little shorter. She gave me a once over that made me almost shiver, her eyes were so distant and appraising. "Cool outfit," she remarked, tapping one of the daisies on my culottes. "Where'd ya get it?" Her voice sounded calm, like we were already friends, or at least familiar with each other, which would have been fine had she at least remembered who I was.

I tried to swallow, but there was no saliva to wet my throat. "Flea market." Another attempt at swallowing. "New York."

Her eyebrows lifted, and she said, "Oh! I was there last summer." I almost wanted to ask her about her internship at the public relations firm that I remembered her mentioning back in December, but something stopped me.

She reached down and grabbed one of my suitcases. Just from the brief touch of our hands, I noticed hers were sweaty, which was odd because she seemed so … cool. Maybe it was the heat of the day, although it wasn't that hot. She pushed away a wavy strand of hair and smiled at me, her eyes disappearing into her face, leaving only the freckles I'd always wanted. I heard Dad coming up behind me and a faint "hi" from another one of the girls. Perry looked over my head to see him.

"Sorry, guys. Student leader duties beckon," she said over her shoulder to the rest of the girls on the porch as she led me inside. She clomped ahead of us in a pair of worn-out, white Dr. Scholls. Her legs looked like they were sculpted out of marble. I recalled the gymnast conversation she had with Mom in front of the music building, Perry saying how strong the school team was, how she was probably going to be made captain for next year, and Mom saying how she wanted to try it growing up but was too busy with ballet, and there I was, skin and bones and not a muscle to speak of except in my fingers.

We entered the cool, dark commons room, filled with blocky, orange-cushioned chairs and sofas that were supported by simple varnished slabs of pine. The large windows had Gothic arches. There was a big, color TV on top of a cabinet surrounded by a bunch of chairs and sofas along with a low, thick coffee table made of the same wood. We came to a metal water fountain humming near the stairwell. I lunged at it, and the delicious, icy water slid down my throat.

Meanwhile, Perry introduced herself. "I'm Perry, by the way. You're Jessica Thurwell, right?"

I jerked up, wiping my dribbling mouth, and blurted, "You *do* remember me!" I felt enveloped in dorkiness. It would have been great to have my big white sunglasses on my head, pushing away my hair. There was something sophisticated about that look, even if my sunglasses were kind of big and would probably keep falling off at inopportune moments. But they said something—like I had been around and was known to utter offhandedly, "It's casual. No prob."

She cocked her head and asked, "From?"

"From … um," I stammered through the stunned feeling. My face was bright hot, and to hide it, I bent down to retrieve two suitcases. "Last year. You showed me around." *And you said I was a pretty cool chick.*

She squinted her eyes at me, as if driving the point home that even though I was pretty there was nothing in me she would find memorable. But then her face opened up into a large smile, her teeth white against her pink lips, and her eyes glistening as the corners seemed to stretch up to her temples. Everything inside of me sighed with relief.

"Wait a second! Sorry! I showed so many people around last year, they all became a blur. Of course I should remember you!" She let out a chuckle. "Before I just knew who you were because I heard your dad call your name." She gestured behind me, smiling at Dad who had found us and set two milk crates on the ground, arms akimbo.

Giggles came out of me before I could stop them.

Perry extended her hand out to Dad. "I take it you're her father." She grinned at him, showing the whitest teeth I had ever seen.

"You took that right," Dad replied with a smile, and he shook her hand briefly and then put his hands right back on his hips.

"I'm good at making educated guesses." She turned and pointed a finger at my neck almost causing me to jump. "You are so lucky! You're Suzie's roommate! How great!" Her face lit up with a thousand watts, and I tried not to giggle again, but her exclamation seemed to come out so suddenly, that I didn't know what else to do.

"You know her?"

She rolled her eyes as we picked up the luggage and ascended the staircase. I felt like I was asking one dumb question after another while I noticed Perry seemed to be having a very easy time lifting the suitcases. "We're old friends from gymnastics camp. She's awesome! You're gonna love her. Plus, I'm your student leader, so that's totally great!"

I looked back at Dad with a large grin as if he could somehow read my mind once again. Seeing *St. Elmo's Fire* five times over the summer fueled my fantasies about what school was going to be like into something which felt like some kind of mission. I spent countless afternoons by our pool imagining that it was actually a crisp, colorful autumn, and I was with a gorgeous-looking, cozy group of friends, (all looking uncannily like the recent college graduates in the film) who stood by each other no matter what. But there was something odd and frozen about Dad's smile. I wanted to scream at him to loosen up, but instead I spun around and just tromped up the stairs behind Perry.

We got to the third floor and walked down the carpeted hallway, passing several dark wooden doors with names on them, an alcove with a black phone, a wooden chair, and a white refrigerator that looked like it had a lot of old food stains on it. Then we stopped at the door that said "302" in tarnished bronze, and taped on the wood were two balloon shapes with my name on the yellow and Suzie's on the red. So at that moment, all Suzie was to me was a red, dry piece of construction paper. Dry. I needed water again as a piece of dust flew into my throat, and I started to cough. Perry opened the door, and I chokingly looked behind me and saw a bathroom, dropped my stuff, and ran in. I turned on the faucet in the white sink and slurped some more cold water.

"Thirsty much?" Perry chuckled at me from inside my room when I returned. The sunlight from the window behind her caused her hair to glisten as she crossed her arms and leaned against one of the bureaus.

"Sorry," I gasped.

"I know it's a shoe box, but that comes with being a new student." Perry explained, gesturing with her hand like a game-show hostess.

I gazed at my room. The first thing I saw was the large window at the opposite end from where I stood. There was the smell of stale heat, as though the door had been shut tight all summer long. The walls seemed too close together with two beds, one on each side, along with desks, dressers, and a closet, all mirroring each other. I thought of my room at home with its dormer windows and relatively gargantuan size, its huge, sliding-door closet, and another door that led out onto a small porch and fire escape. I was suffocating in my new room. I could feel my face develop tiny stings that hinted the onset of tears. I wanted to turn to Dad, throw myself against him, and have him give me a bear hug and say, "OK, I understand, we'll go home." But I could just feel his stiff presence behind me and hoped that maybe it was because he was going to miss me.

Yet when I looked at Perry's easy smile, I told myself I'd be OK if I remained with her. *As long as I'm with her*, I thought. I couldn't figure that out. I didn't even know her, but I liked her, even if she didn't quite remember me. She was going to be my student leader. She was friends with my roommate. She liked the way I dressed.

Dad announced that he had to leave because he was meeting Mom at the studio and had a rush hour to contend with. I felt the sting return to my eyes, knowing he had a point, but suddenly fantasizing that he could spend the rest of the afternoon with me and that Mom could wait. But he just looked at me, a picture of tense resignation as if to say, without any conviction, "Well, that's life."

I hugged him, hoping he would do the same this time. If I hugged him hard enough, he'd have to respond, or else he'd look like an idiot indecisively holding me. And he returned that grasp fully, and I inhaled his smell as much as I could, so it would be fresh in my mind. He mussed up my hair, something he hadn't done since I was eleven, and then put his hands on my shoulders and looked at me. His brown eyes seemed a bit bigger than normal under his glasses. "You'll be fine, but you also have to write, OK?" I nodded, because in the midst of already missing him, I felt much better. I stood for a moment in the threshold of the doorway and watched him as he headed down the hall. My eyes continued to sting as something in my chest grew heavy, and I knew it wasn't just my ace bandage–like bra that was already a bit too tight. Once he was out of sight, I had this sudden urge to see his car drive away.

I heard Perry's clear voice asking, "You need help unpacking?"

CHAPTER 2

That's Not Me

She actually wanted to stay with me. Maybe she felt bad for not recognizing me before. More grateful than necessary, I said, "Sure!" as she unzipped a big maroon suitcase.

As we unpacked, I sat on my new bed, just a striped mattress, as Perry launched into conversation with me. Perry Wagner. It was like the name of a little bird or periwinkle, the color crayon I always used for dresses in coloring books. I wanted to relax, but my whole body was buzzing. I imagined Dad at this point a mile away from campus, ready to get back onto I-95.

Names tumbled out of Perry, names that meant nothing to me except the hope of future friendships. Our dorm head, Marcie Segal, who, Perry announced, was "one of the coolest on campus." She was once a student here and was the best person to talk to if you had problems. Her husband, Ben, was the head cook in the dining hall. "He makes school food edible and sometimes does a special dessert for our dorm." She mentioned Pepa, which sounded like "pepper" in Spanish, Perry's roommate from Madrid, Pepa's boyfriend, Hassan, from Morocco, and Perry's boyfriend, Marcus. And Suzie. "You are going to *love* her. She's not coming 'til after orientation 'cause she's at a wedding. But she's the sweetest thing. She competed in figure skating for the longest time and is amazing. You guys are going to be perfect for each other."

How did she know that? I couldn't skate. Maybe Perry saw something in me that I had never recognized before, some latent jock or a girlishness so often associated with skaters. I shifted on my mattress, looking forward to when it would be made up with my big, black-and-white polka-dotted comforter on top, and I could sink into it and escape into my music.

"So we're going to have to show her around," Perry interrupted my thoughts. "Or maybe you could show her around since by the end of the week, you'll know this place like the back of your hand."

The husky voice and the assurances about Suzie's and my future here made me sigh and the corners of my mouth turn up. Giggles spilled out of me, and at the same time, I wanted to sink into a hole and hide.

Perry put my clothes in the drawer, sometimes refolding the shirts and sweaters with a straight back and a calm gaze in her eyes. She knew where to put everything and smoothed out all my pants and skirts before putting them in the closet. "I see we share an interest in flea market finds."

I gasped, "You like that stuff too?" She didn't seem to, judging by what she was wearing.

"I worked for a fashion PR firm this summer—"

"I remember you saying that," I said and then stopped, realizing I must sound like an obsessed lunatic. I remembered her mentioning it during my visit last year and Mom adding she had an old friend at the firm, even though I didn't know who she was talking about. But it still made me wonder when I was in town every Saturday that summer if I was going to run into Perry.

Perry smiled at me with half-shut eyes. "And my friend who I worked with would take me to the Canal Street flea market every weekend—"

"I go there too! That's where I got these!" *God, interrupt much?*

But Perry was unperturbed. "It's like a bargain hunter's paradise. OK, a lot of it is really weird. Like, who would wear some of that stuff?" *Uh, me,* I thought. "I totally like to mix it with other stuff. Not go too overboard." I almost winced at that dart thrown in my direction. And she must have noticed, because then she said, "You must look really great in this stuff, though."

"My mom's not crazy about it," I shrugged, feeling a lot better. Mom thought it too sloppy and wished I dressed in a more pulled-together manner, like Kim's new friends or preppy Tom who always had the right oxford, right jeans, and a belt if the shirt was tucked in. Perfect Tom with the perfect, gleaming blue eyes like Mom.

Perry looked up at me and squinted. "Wait a sec. You're the daughter of that actress," she said. I nodded, feeling my eyes go dead. "Sorry, you're probably so sick of that. It's just that Pepa and Suzie love that show. I don't watch it. Pepa's obsessed with it, and so she told me about your mom after I met you. So sorry. That was tacky."

"Oh no, that's OK!" My voice jumped all around. Was she sorry my mom was a soap actress or sorry for remembering me because of her and not just for myself?

Her speech sped up. "There are a couple of kids of famous people here. I mean, Marcus's dad is David Feld."

"Oh." I panicked because I knew I was supposed to know who that was, and the name was vaguely familiar. I recalled seeing it a number of times in boldface type in *New York* magazine regarding big real estate deals.

Perry saw the look of confusion on my face. "He's one of the biggest corporate lawyers in the city." Her tone of voice suggested I should have known all along, even though I didn't, so I nodded and rolled my eyes.

"Not to brag," Perry added quickly, and I shook my head as if to tell her not to worry.

"Right," I said, nodding again. There was a heavy pause, and I decided to change the subject, so I asked her if she lived in New York, kind of knowing she didn't.

"No, New London, right near here."

"My brother goes to school there!"

"Coast Guard Academy?"

I jerked my head back at this. How could she assume that my brother would go to a military academy? Is that how I came across—really conservative and straitlaced? I pursed my lips and said, "Connecticut College?" like I was venturing a guess.

"Really? What year is he?"

"Freshman."

"Oh, well, then I wouldn't know him."

Oh my god, she hangs out with college kids. "Do you know people who go there?"

"Yeah, my parents teach there." Again a look that told me I should have known that all along.

"What do they teach?" I had hardly done any unpacking, and all I could do was fiddle with the straps of a new bra.

"Well, Dad teaches philosophy. He's this Nietzsche nut." No questions asked, although I almost wanted to because I didn't know who or what that was. "And Mom is an English lit professor."

"You have any brothers and sisters?"

"An older sister, Alison. She's twenty-two and getting married to some investment banker, and of course my parents are thrilled, even though she only graduated from college last year. She just wants to be a housewife in the suburbs. We are totally different."

"That's like me and my brother!" I exclaimed.

She asked if there was anything else to unpack, and I pointed to a suitcase that held my tape collection. All my records were already placed where they were to remain: in their red plastic record holders. I was proud of my collection because I thought it was really eclectic. Rock, classical, musical theater, and even some jazz. It was all there. I wondered what Perry would say about them.

She said nothing as she unpacked, barely glancing at the tape titles. I felt everything in me plunge to the floor. Then she swung her head up at me with wide eyes and asked, "You into Prince and Madonna?"

"I guess," I said. I liked Prince's music but not as much as Chris, who had seen him live and thought he was great as long as he stayed away from his Little Richard and Jimi Hendrix impressions. Madonna, however, I could do without. Every time I heard her petulant voice singing against a background of tinny synthesizers, I cringed. Chris thought some of her singles were well-crafted pop tunes, but I figured he just had a crush on her and her big green eyes and endless eyelashes that she'd bat into the camera. Besides, I associated her with twelve-year-old girls, mimicking her trashy, bratty style of big hair bows, rubber bracelets, and loose-fitting, lacy camisoles.

"Well, get used to it, because we all are. My boyfriend Marcus is so into Prince, it's nuts."

"Wow," was all I managed to say.

She poked through my record collection and said nothing about the Beatles and continued on about her part-time collegiate life back in New London. "Anyway, that's how I know a lot of the students there. They're awesome. They have this co-op dorm off campus, and sometimes I hang out there. I'm younger than they are, but they're always saying I'm pretty mature for my age."

"Are you thinking of going there?"

She frowned. "I'm applying to Princeton, early decision."

Early decision. Here I was with this person who was probably going to Princeton. She was bright, pretty, totally grown-up, and she was hanging out with me. "That's great!" I let out a small giggle. Oh brother. I sounded *unconscionably* dorky. You didn't giggle in the company of someone like this; it sounded way too wishy-washy. Laughing was defiant and confident.

Perry didn't take any notice of my reaction and, as if reciting a speech she had given a number of times, she launched into her gymnastics career. She was supposed to train down in Texas with some big coach, "because everyone said I had Olympic potential" but got a scholarship to come here instead. "Education is a little more important and that guy was supposed to be a monster. They continued to bug me for months, even after I arrived here. Phone calls all the time. It was insane. And you?" She dragged out the last word, sounding like a slide whistle.

For a moment, I had nothing to say. What could I say? Was there something about me that came off as successful as Perry? Is that why she chose to hang out with me? An image of Mom's face on TV swam in my brain. "Composing stuff, you know," I said as I shrugged my shoulders.

"I noticed you have quite the collection of music," she said, glancing down at my tapes and records.

"Thanks. I don't know if I want to be a songwriter or write musicals or what. But sometimes I listen to that stuff and think it'd be fun to write that kind of thing." I paused thinking I had no awards to show her, no teachers from Julliard begging me to study with them. I added hopefully, with a small nod, "I studied at the Manhattan Music Studio." I tried to make it sound like Julliard, but I doubt that came across.

"Huh." It was clear she had never heard of it. "Maybe you can compose something for my gymnastics programs. Everyone always performs to the same shit. And I always like to do something to make me stand out. You can be my weapon." She raised her eyebrows at me.

I burst out laughing, thinking she was kidding. Or maybe it was another release of nerves. It was like she wanted to beat up every other gymnast, and something poked in me, making me only more nervous. Maybe now we were sisters in arms.

She asked me if I had a boyfriend. Was she kidding? I'd only briefly dated one guy with whom I exchanged a slobbery kiss in the parking lot of a mall after seeing *Ghostbusters* last spring. It was one of my many attempts to be a part of Kim's cool crowd. He was a football player, and we had nothing in common. We kissed like it was an obligation because everyone else was pairing off in separate areas of the parking lot, leaning against strangers' cars. It was so pathetic and suburban. Meanwhile Perry had Marcus, a senior like her, and they'd been seeing each other for the four years they'd been here. "He's a total babe," Perry said, shaking her head with a soft smile. *Naturally*, I thought.

"Uh huh," I replied as I scrambled onto my bed to hang up my posters. As Perry blabbed on about what a great wrestler Marcus was, I hung up two big posters of my favorite movies of all time over my bed: the *Breakfast at Tiffany's* one that Grandma Cunningham gave for me for Christmas two years ago was at the head of my bed, right next to the window, and on the side was the oversized *Yellow Submarine* poster Mom and Dad bought for me.

Perry gasped when I was almost done. "No!"

I almost jumped out of my skin. Had I done something wrong?

"I loved that movie!" She pointed to *Breakfast at Tiffany's*. "How did you know? It's my favorite."

"That's great," I said, almost tripping over my words in excitement, "because none of my other friends know what it is just because it came out before they were born." Except Kim. It was her favorite movie as well.

"They're just uncultured, Jess," Perry sniffed as she got on my bed to take a closer look. "But I gotta warn you. Suzie kind of falls into that camp. I mean, she's great but quite the teeny bopper. She was going on about *St. Elmo's Fire* this summer like it was some sort of masterpiece."

"Actually, it wasn't bad," I said, quelling my enthusiasm and the crush I had on one of the stars of the film, Rob Lowe.

"Never saw it." End of discussion.

She later took me downstairs to meet Marcie, who seemed a lot younger than I imagined. She greeted me with a wide, thin-lipped smile, her straight brown hair caught up in a ponytail. "Hi, Jessica," she said. "Welcome to Fieldings. Are you making out OK?"

I could only nod quickly.

"Well, you're in really good hands with Perry. But if you need anything, don't hesitate. Door's always open." She winked at me, and for some reason, that made me cringe.

I knew I was supposed to go out and meet other new students, but all I wanted to do was hang out with Perry and compare notes on our lives. Apparently, she did too, and so we were glued to each other during orientation week. We ate every meal together and talked about how much we hated our public schools and how our mothers seemed to like our older siblings better than us.

Perry's stories always seemed to be worse or more exciting than mine. "I do so much for my mom," she told me one night at dinner. "Always calling her, always there for her if she's having a fight with Dad—and then she turns all her attention onto my sister, Alison, like I don't exist."

My heart melted for her. But what I loved hearing most were the stories from her summer at the PR firm. I was a willing audience, because she was doing everything I dreamed of but was too young to do—and God forbid my parents would even allow it. Especially the part about going to clubs every night in clothes she and her friend stole from the office. "My friend's a model now," Perry told me, "and she can fit into anything!" How they'd crawl home, sometimes at the crack of dawn, like a pair of Holly Golightlys.

She told me about a twenty-one-year-old painter from NYU with whom she had make-out sessions in the bathroom of some club. Of course, I was so bewitched by these stories that it only dimly occurred to me that her boyfriend Marcus was lurking in the background.

But she later showed me pictures of Marcus. I felt a pinch of jealousy when I gazed at his jaw and wavy, light brown hair that seemed to be all over the place. Squinting eyes. Big sweaters. Wrestler's hands that grappled Perry's shoulder. I didn't want to admit it to myself, but the truth was inescapable: he looked like Rob Lowe with lighter hair.

"What about the painter guy?" I asked in a voice that echoed my fidgeting fingers.

"Please, a few drunken evenings don't count," Perry snorted back. "Besides, Marcus was always off in the Hamptons with his family, and I don't get along with his mother because she's really jealous and competitive, so I was never invited. And Marcus and I would fight about it, and so the painter guy didn't even count."

"Right." I pretended to get it even though I didn't. I chose not to question Perry any further since I didn't know her well, nor had I had a boyfriend for four years. Maybe this was the sort of thing that happened in a relationship like that. I knew of parents, not my own, but like Kim's mom for example, who weren't exactly faithful. So I just figured this was normal, and at the same time, I put it out of my head.

At the end of orientation week, on a gray, muggy day, spitting with rain and wet, falling leaves, a new bunch of cars were parked all over campus, overstuffed with blankets, trunks, crates, and stereos. I saw a girl step out of a car with a squealing "Heyyy!" as she ran up to a long-lost friend. They hugged, their faces turning red as they shut their eyes and grinned, like they were almost about to cry. I marched back to Kurtzman to look for Perry.

The halls, once filled with small, chattering packs who fell into silent pauses, were now echoing with "Hey, Vanessa!" and "Caroooliiine!" and the sound of trunks hitting the floor. Parents helped carry big rolls of carpet, boxes, bunches of posters, and lamps. Doors slammed, and I heard the sound of running feet in the hall. There were lulls, then outbursts of laughter and shrieks. Everyone looked bigger or older or both. And we new students just gazed at them with bewildered eyes.

I kept losing Perry because she was boomeranging back and forth between our dorm and our "brother" dorm, Hilliman. I knew Marcus had arrived because I overheard one of the other student leaders talking about it. At one point, I decided to head over there, and I saw, in the bushes between Hilliman and the library, a silhouetted couple very close to one another, looking as though they had just finished kissing. There were low voices, and I was sure one of them was Perry's. A tremor went down my spine, and I started running over toward Hilliman thinking that would make it go away. I tried to convince myself that I'd find the real Perry over there, but I didn't see her, so I took a longer route back to Kurtzman, staying far away from the bushes.

Half an hour later, back in my room, I looked out my window and saw her walking toward Hilliman. Shooting down the stairs, I ran out the door to catch up with her. I tried to hide my breathlessness as I greeted her, and she exclaimed, "Hey! I was looking for you!" At first I didn't believe her, but I mentioned nothing about the bushes.

"You never came to my room. I was there," I gasped.

But I got no answer, and she continued, "Come on! I want you to meet some of my guy friends."

The guys towered over us with hair that looked like it hadn't been brushed that morning. I listened in on chatter I knew nothing about, but now I knew to laugh when they laughed. It was automatic. I didn't know what they were saying, but what else could I do? I thought I'd get a joke better if I laughed along with everyone else. I found it worked a lot more easily here than in the cafeteria at Katonah.

And then I met Marcus. He still looked like Rob Lowe, which I had hoped he wouldn't. His hair was darker than it was in the photos, but he was a Rob facsimile nonetheless: the pointed chin, high cheekbones, long mouth. His eyes were a clear, intense hazel, and his voice even had the same tenorlike timbre as Rob's. *He and Perry are a couple*, I kept repeating as a mantra in my head.

When I was introduced to him, I said, "Hi!" my face stretched into a grin. I was beginning to get a headache from smiling this much. My eyes were wide open, like I needed to see absolutely everything. The response from all the guys was a wave of the hand and a "hey" with a small smile, then they returned their gaze to Perry as she rapidly told them about her summer and names kept coming up that made them all nod and laugh. I hoped I'd get a little more from Marcus, and I thought I did see an extra glimmer in his eye. He made some kind of joke that was miles over my head. Even when all I could muster was a small giggle, my head hurt even more.

The female friends of Perry ran up to her and hugged her when they saw her. I noticed she never ran up to them. They'd greet me with very brief, very cheery hellos, reminding me of jack-in-the-boxes. They blabbed about the summer, Perry's story dominating everyone else's since it was obvious hers was the most exciting. They broke out into laughter at the right places, always with their heads thrown back, saying, "That is *so* funny!" Still trying to keep up with the cheeriness, I continued to grin. My face was really beginning to hurt now. My eyes weren't as wide as they were earlier because I needed to rest them. At one point, I was literally pushed aside as one tall redhead, who seemed to interrupt Perry more than I did on that first day, went to put her arm around Perry, and another shorter Asian girl with dyed-blond hair cut asymmetrically, who sounded like she was on helium, followed suit. They were sandwiched together, and I was the piece of parsley. But I still paid rapt attention. Some details from last year always finished up with, "Oh, it's too bad she's graduated. They were all so cool." It sounded like last year was so great and filled with so many cool people this year would never measure up.

I shifted my gaze ahead of us to the porch of our dorm and noticed a tall girl with masses of dark, wavy hair and lots of makeup standing near the entrance of our dorm waving to us. She was very buxom but not overweight—she looked like she was in her twenties. It was Pepa, who I also recognized from my visit last year. First Perry squealed, then the redhead and the Asian, and, after a small pause and a quick glance at each other, they followed Perry as she ran up to hug her. Pepa greeted me in a high-pitched operatic version of, "Hi!" We pranced into the dorm though I hardly felt light and airy. Scrambling up the stairs, I was the last in the flock. I almost ran into Pepa's brand-new, white, high-top Reebok sneakers.

"Oops! Sorry!" I said. She smiled back at me, her eyes looking down her nose. She had very long lashes. Or maybe it was lots of mascara.

"Jess is going to be Suzie's roommate!" Perry pointed to me.

"Great!" Pepa barely answered, the same smile stuck on her face.

Right before dinner, Suzie arrived. In the commons room with Perry and a group of seniors. I was gazing about at the other sophomores, who were now making friends with one another. A voice inside me told me I was missing out on something, but I ignored it because at that moment they looked too young for me, and I resumed listening to my new friends gossiping at rapid-fire speed. And yet I wondered if I didn't look like a useless mascot, but I ignored that thought, too, as I heard the front door open and saw a small girl enter. She and Perry saw each other across the crowded, noisy room, and they screamed so loudly at each other, the whole room, jammed with reunited chattering students, stopped for a moment to look at them. I noticed the girls' faces, including Pepa's, go still, their eyes level as they stared at the pair running up to each other. The sudden silence was heavy and dead, enough to squelch the noise from the rest of the room.

"Huh," the Asian remarked.

"That's her?" asked the redhead.

"Yes," Pepa said, looking at each of them.

"Ohhh," they lifted their chins and slowly brought them down.

I stood next to Pepa, trying to think of what to say. My stomach tightened until I saw the guys from Hilliman enter. Marcus kissed Perry on the mouth, and my face turned warm and tingly. Pepa rushed past me, stepping on my toes, her arms outstretched, and one of her bony fingers almost poking my eyes out as she waved and yelled. I felt skinny and alone. I noticed Hassan, the guy with dark, curly hair from this afternoon, giving me a small wave and a shy smile. I returned the same, still rooted in place as my two other companions started talking about someone else. Suzie kept sticking her gold chain necklace in her mouth. Perry saw me and turned to Suzie to say something, and the two headed in my direction. I let out a huge breath, realizing I had been holding it for a while. The rest of the girls dispersed.

Suzie was short, like Perry, but a little skinnier with brown, myopic-looking eyes and short, dark brown, wavy hair. She continued to put her necklace in her mouth as she greeted me with a smile and a slight bounce in her body. I looked down at her chest and noticed that she, too, along with Pepa and Perry, was well developed. Everything about their bodies was curvy, symmetrical, and perfect. I wondered if there was anything else I could do, aside from crossing my arms in front of me, to hide my junior-high body.

The doors of the dining hall opened, and we rushed in. Suzie and Perry talked as though they were running out of time. My jaw clenched as I kept thinking how much better it would be if Suzie had decided not to go here. She was a figure skater and Perry was a gymnast. Suzie even made it to junior nationals last year, so why didn't she just stick with it? "Top ten." Perry announced as she put her arm around her and smiled at me, once again reminding me of my lack of athleticism. *What am I doing with these guys?*

But that thought vanished as Perry took my elbow, and we arrived at a table while she whispered, "Come on, you sit next to Suzie." She patted the chair next to the top-ten skater who settled on Perry's left. But then I looked at Pepa, who, despite her large chest, did not have the sinewy looks her friends had and seemed as out of shape as I was. Marcus and I caught each others' eyes, and I thought I saw his lips curl up a bit. Something inside of me cracked, but it was so imperceptible, I ignored it. Everyone was yapping, guffawing, and pointing. Perry reached over, squeezed my shoulder, and winked. It appeared I finally belonged somewhere.

CHAPTER 3

Fixing a Hole

Once classes started, I realized that my romantic ideas about boarding school—a beautiful New England autumn settling over the campus while my cool friends (including my roommate, who I'd be best friends with) and I cavorted about, free and easy—weren't going to materialize. First of all, when classes started, it was still very much like midsummer in Westchester, hot and steamy. I wanted a sheltered environment complete with its own weather system, even though I was only two-and-a-half hours from home. I wanted to breathe crisp autumnal air, see trees bursting into leafy, red fire. I expected to wake up to misty, cool mornings that would make me skip off to class with anticipation.

Instead, I walked to classes in one of the three boring cotton culottes I brought to school, the thick heat making the ancient cotton feel like burlap. The dark green leaves hung from the trees in the muggy deadness as though they, too, were suffering from the humidity. Even as close as we were to Long Island Sound, the breezes did little to take away the heavy heat, and I could almost hear the collective *thwack* of bare thighs, from those of us wearing shorts and miniskirts, unsticking themselves from our seats at the end of class.

And my classes. Maybe I was being too judgmental, but I thought that in boarding school and with smaller classes, I would have teachers who'd make even something as dull as a paramecium interesting. But instead, my biology teacher, a small woman with limp, gray hair in a 1950s-style bob, droned on in a monotone about the life of the cell and gazed at us with beady, brown eyes. In religion, we read the book of *Genesis,* which I felt I had read a million times. My geometry teacher directed everything to the guys in the class. Italian and English looked promising, however, even though I already knew some Italian words from music. Just the sound of the language was rhythmic and musical, and it reminded me of Grandma and her house in Italy. My English teacher was a guy with scruffy, blond hair who laughed easily and listened to what each of us said with rapt attention. We were studying the theme of Romance and I was surprised that *Sir Gawain and the Green Knight* swept me off my feet, causing me to envision a world with a more nuanced beauty than all the Disney movies I had grown up with.

But the biggest blow was piano. I had only had two lessons, yet I knew right away I had the wrong teacher. The former concert pianist responsible for the school's great reputation, Anna McGowan, I didn't end up with. Instead, I had a young, blousy woman named Molly Hanson, whose frizzy, brown hair flecked with gray seemed to have a life of its own. It seemed as though every time she looked at me it was as if she were trying to remember who I was, but it obviously took her too much effort. We studied the most basic exercises in the Hanon workbook. In an airy, Thumbelina-like voice, she said, "Good!" when I finished playing. Sometimes I messed up on purpose just to see what she'd say, which was usually, "Oops! Let's try that again. You need to work on your pinkie a bit more!" Then she flipped through the book, distracted, and said, "Ummm, let's try this!" All the while, she smelled overpoweringly of patchouli.

So the year was off to slow start. Maybe it was the heat that dragged everyone down. And the oppressiveness only brought up memories of the summer and Grandma's death. Suzie and I slept on top of our comforters almost every night. Suzie fell asleep immediately. Was that because she was from L.A. and therefore so laid back she didn't care about the heat? I lay tossing and turning in the thick air, enduring the nightly thunderstorms, shielding my eyes from the white lightening flashes outside, and then bracing myself for the imminent clap of thunder. Because of the lack of sleep, I would roam from class to class the next day as though I were under warm water.

Sleep patterns aside, I knew that Suzie and I were very different, and it would always hit me the minute I hung out with her. We hadn't really spoken that much the first night when we went up to Perry and Pepa's room. Suzie and Perry regaled us with stories from gymnastics camp while Madonna and Rosanna Arquette stared down snottily at us from a large poster of the film *Desperately Seeking Susan* and Prince groaned from the stereo speakers. Eleven-thirty rolled around and my yawns became so frequent, I left to go to bed, followed by a chorus of cheery good nights from my three new friends. I lay in bed, unable to sleep and listened to the muffled gabbing through the walls, wondering what I was missing.

When I returned from classes the following afternoon and swung open the door, I saw Suzie sitting on her bed singing along to a bland pop tune on the radio. "Hey, Jessie!" she yelled, eyes disappearing underneath her lashes.

I allow no one to call me Jessie, but I told myself that coming from her it sounded adorable. Just as long as it wasn't contagious, and everyone else started to call me that. "Hey!" I answered, glancing at my bed to see Pepa sprawled on it. She gave me a small, "Hi," and sat up. She told Suzie she should put her Rob Lowe poster over her bed.

"I loved *St. Elmo's Fire!*" I exclaimed, feeling Pepa's eyes turn to me and drip in disapproval. *What did I do?*

"I saw it five times. It was amazing!" Suzie said. She stood up on her bed and proceeded to unroll the poster. "Pepa still hasn't seen it."

I looked at her, wanting to tell her in the friendliest way possible, "You must!" But instead all I could muster was, "Really?" in a weak voice.

Pepa shrugged and replied to the stereo that she almost did but never got around to it.

The poster of Rob unfurled, showing him sulking next to his saxophone. I noticed that it was autographed. "You met him?" I barely got the words out.

"No!" Suzie sighed and both our faces fell. "I was away at skating camp. Dad got him to autograph it since Rob is one of his patients." Her dad, I had discovered earlier, was a dentist to the stars. "He's a fox, huh?"

I nodded, not caring what Pepa thought. I even considered placing my pillow at the other end of the bed so I could fall asleep with Rob gazing at me.

"He looks like Marcus," Pepa observed.

"Yeah!" Suzie replied. I tried to remain cool as a nerve in me buzzed and heat crawled up my face.

Pepa changed the subject. She and Suzie talked about the Madonna concert they went to over the summer and about how "*unbelievably* talented" she was. I said nothing.

I turned my attention to the room and considered the glaring differences between my side and Suzie's. There was my bed, which despite Pepa's sprawled-out body, was neatly made up with my black-and-white comforter on top. I had a small nightstand with a white lamp and a frosty, peach-colored box of Kleenex. Next to that, piled on top of one another, sat two milk crates—one white and one blue—with my tapes and records inside. My trunk was settled at the end of my bed, where sheet music and notebooks commanded one side, while on the other, a ministereo, consisting of a small amp, turntable, tape deck, and speakers sat ready to faithfully play my music. The bureau, right next to the trunk, I had covered with cases I had received for Christmases and birthdays: a brown leather one for my jewelry; a brushed silver metal one for my makeup; and a blue, clear plastic one that held my accessories. Even though we all had mirrors above our bureaus, I placed the glass-framed Italian mirror from Grandma Cunningham's old dressing table at the corner. Between my bureau and closet was a solid, pine-colored, but clearly Formica, desk on which my electric typewriter sat dead center, guarded by pictures of my family. Tidy, tidy, tidy.

Suzie's side, though, consisted of a cool teenage sloppiness that indicated she was a rebel. A lot of the clothes she wore—bras, T-shirts, and the omnipresent designer jeans that all the girls at school seemed to be wearing—were left flung over her chair and bed. A sleek, black stereo system included, much to my jealousy, a CD player. I learned later her parents gave it to her after she won the Pacific Sectionals or something like that. She had a puffy, baby blue duvet swallowing her bed, along with various pillows in shiny, polished cotton. A huge, stuffed Garfield cat stared at me from his round, goofy bug eyes, a Garfield poster was on the wall next to her bed, Garfield figurines patrolled her bureau, and a Garfield message board had been secured to the outside of our door. Suzie really liked Garfield as did Pepa, who, when Suzie was unpacking earlier, cooed with each Garfield curio Suzie brought out. "He's sooo funny!" she cried, and I wanted to say something, too, but I wasn't a big fan, so I remained mute, hoping Perry wasn't a Garfield fan.

And then Suzie's record collection: generic, overproduced top forty. Stuff so innocuous that it was used as Muzak at the supermarket. There was some New Age, which I couldn't disagree with, and when Suzie noticed me looking at it again that afternoon, she said, "That's some of the music I used for my skating programs."

"What is?" Pepa asked.

"This classical music," Suzie replied.

The words came out before I could stop them. "Actually, it's New Age, not classical."

"Whatever," Suzie rolled her eyes, and I knew I committed a faux pas once again. Pepa cleared her throat, and then I hunched my shoulders.

The girls continued talking about some island both had been to, but I hadn't. I looked at Suzie's bulletin board. Several cheery photos of aging, overly tanned stars, whom I remembered from TV shows I'd watched during my childhood, along with a snapshot of Suzie's short, stout, balding dad smiled down at me, all displaying fluorescent white grins. Alongside there were dozens of pictures of Suzie and her heavily made-up friends in sparkly costumes or sweats, and the occasional skating celebrity, grinning right next to them—people even I recognized. The picture of her goofing off with some adorable boy, a state champion or something, whom she later told me she had "a stupid fling" with, caught my eye. Suzie splashing around in a pool with her friends, Suzie and her coach, who looked like a big mamma bear with too much lipstick and a fur coat that seemed ridiculous in the Southern California heat. A medal hung around Suzie's neck as she stood on a podium, a bouquet of flowers in her arms.

We were from two different planets.

Pepa looked at her watch. "Hey, the show's almost on!" It was three o'clock, and I knew they were talking about *Sunset*. I was both nauseated and excited. It reminded me of all those afternoons when Tom and his Theater Club friends from high school would be hanging out in our living room, his friends clearly wanting to get a glimpse of Mom if she was coming back from the studio early. I now wondered if Pepa would finally say something nice to me.

Instead, Suzie turned to me flashing another grin. "When Perry told me about your mom, I was like, 'That is so cool!' Isn't that cool?" She looked at Pepa.

Pepa nodded and said, "Yeah, Perry told me all about it. Your mother's very good." Something in her voice made it sound more approving than admiring. The two girls picked up their Diet Cokes and packets of Marlboro Lights and headed down to the commons room, assuming, I suppose, that I'd follow. Instead, I gathered my books and headed to the library to memorize geometry theorems, wondering when Perry was getting back from the math tutorials she gave at the local elementary school. When I walked through the commons room, I was relieved not to hear Mom's voice. A group of girls had gathered around the TV watching the new actress who played Mom's conniving stepdaughter. Suzie turned to me and whispered, "Bye, sweetie!" I waved back, grateful for her friendliness, but feeling like I was walking unsteadily on a balance beam. Pepa never turned around.

I reasoned that it couldn't all be perfect, and in terms of our little group, two out of three wasn't bad. But I still mentioned it to Perry when we ran into each other after my English class the following morning.

When she saw me she put her arm around me and asked, "Hey, sweetie, how's it goin'?" Her eyes danced around my outfit and my face. I smelled the Bazooka bubblegum that she was loudly chomping on.

"Pretty good." I wanted to say everything was terrific, but I was more concerned about Pepa. "Uh, I don't think Pepa likes me." And the minute it came out, I felt I had just gone up to a teacher in the playground and complained about someone throwing sand in my face.

She cocked her head. "Really? Aw, don't think that." She squeezed my shoulder. "I haven't noticed anything. You're probably just imagining it." She shook her head quickly and snapped her gum with a loud *sok!* "Listen, gotta go. I'll be late for dinner tonight because we have an editorial meeting at the paper," she said. She stuck her middle finger in her mouth. "My coeditor, Mitch, is a total dictator. Anyway, meet me in the butt room later!" she called out as she headed down the hallway. The butt room was in the basement of the dorm, where students with smoking privileges were allowed to smoke. I had no such privileges, as my mother pointed out to me when we were filling out the forms for school.

I forgot about Pepa for a moment. A warm jitteriness lifted me up off the ground. I never had a senior greet me in a crowded school hallway like that, all smiles and squeezing of shoulders. *She is probably right about Pepa*, I thought, once the buxom brunette crawled back into my head. I imagined Dad in the nether regions of my brain saying, "You're just projecting," or Grandma telling me that European women, especially Latin ones, could be a little strange with other women. "But it doesn't mean a damn thing," she'd say, shaking her head at me with a weary look. During biology class, I occasionally fantasized about Pepa joking with me the way she joked with Perry and Suzie, showing an interest in my music or telling me she was sorry about how cold she had been; she was just really shy around me. "I just got intimidated because of your mom. It's stupid, I know!" An embarrassed chuckle would follow.

And at the end of the day, there was dinner, which always sent a thrill through me. It was the same group every night and for some reason, jokes were funnier, stories more interesting. I never really said much because I was so afraid that whatever I would say would be met with some kind of awkward silence. I still had to gain my bearings. But I joined in the laughter, which at times was so loud we'd all spring away from the table causing everyone to turn around and look at us. It felt wonderful to look so happy and to let everyone know how happy we were. We laughed at the same jokes. The fact that everyone looked so attractive made me feel prettier, like my skin had an extra glow. I always sat next to Perry. She practically demanded it of me. I tried not to look at Marcus, who always sat opposite me. I knew then a time would come when Suzie and I would stay up most of the night talking and talking about stuff we realized we had in common. Pepa and I would be friends. I didn't know when, but I believed the time would arrive.

Two weeks into classes, Hurricane Gloria hit southeastern Connecticut. Every day the air pressure seemed to intensify as though some big monster were headed our way to eat this helpless human population alive. This was not right. It was fall term at prep school. We weren't supposed to be deluged with something from the tropics. Where were those crisp fall days? How could a major hurricane try to blast me out of here when I'd just arrived? I remembered the nuclear war song I heard coming out of a dorm window that first day and realized that was what the omen was for.

We were hyper with anticipation. There was an increased buzz on campus and U2's song "Gloria" blared out of everyone's speakers. Classes were going to be canceled, which meant we could goof off all day, watching Mother Nature's destruction as she ripped the campus to shreds. Just the very thought of it filled us with a rush of adrenaline. Even when Marcie addressed us at the weekly dorm meeting that night and told us all the rules we had to follow for the storm, people were restless. Marcie, whose sleepy, hazel eyes gazed at us from behind her glasses, held her six-month-old son, Bryan, over her shoulder and listed the emergency plans to her fidgeting, whispering students. But even Bryan wouldn't keep quiet, letting out gurgles and loud "anhhhs" as he yanked at his mother's long, brown hair. The storm was to make landfall that Friday, the 27th, with the eye of the storm going over New London. I had to call Tom. I knew he would be OK, he had told me the dorm he lived in was built to withstand a nuclear attack. I wasn't too worried about him.

I couldn't help but be swept up in the excitement. I thought about what it might be like to snuggle with a guy during the storm, which would have added a much-needed romance to the whole thing. I fantasized that Rob Lowe was filming his new movie in the nearby town of Mystic, and that he'd come by to introduce himself to Suzie, since he had met her dad. They'd discuss something boring like how many fillings he had done or root canals or whatever—I always breezed over this part. And then he'd turn his attention to me. Things would be friendly and flirtatious between us in the beginning, and then later when the storm hit, the two of us would be alone in a darkened room with only a candle for light, and he'd protect me from the storm by holding me in his arms. Then slowly but surely (if I hadn't fallen asleep in real life by this time) we'd kiss, ending up in a passionate tangle. Other nights, the scene would play out in one of the practice rooms in the music building. We'd somehow escaped to there, and I'd play a song I just wrote. He'd be so impressed that he'd want it as the theme song to his new movie, and we'd get into the whole heavy petting deal on the worn carpeting. I really had to focus on his dark hair so as not to confuse him with Marcus, who managed to make a couple of appearances in these fantasies.

I called Tom the night before the storm, right after a study session of memorizing theorems and a new chapter in biology. He was just about as excited as I was, hopping from keg party to keg party in anticipation of the storm but complaining he was getting really sick of hearing "Gloria" being played all over campus, so he and his friends blasted The Association's "Windy" in revolt. I never got around to asking him about Perry's parents. Something held me back even though it was on the tip of my tongue. So we just talked about the storm.

After that, I went to find my three friends in the butt room. "I don't know what to do with myself! This storm is totally preoccupying me!" I said as I plopped myself down on the bench next to Pepa.

Perry rolled her eyes at her humming typewriter. "You should hear my parents! Boarding up their house, putting masking tape on all the windows, and stocking up on supplies. They're expecting major power outages, flooding. At least our house is near the college, which is elevated and not by the beach. But my parents are so out of control. I was trying to talk about other stuff, like what was going on in my life, and all Mom could talk about was how the shelves at Stop 'n' Shop were virtually empty this afternoon. It's like, 'Yes, Mom, I know the hurricane is a big deal, but there are other things going on!' She has this total one-track mind."

"I haven't even spoken to my mother," I said. "For some reason, whenever I call she's always out and yet she always manages to talk to my brother." And that was true, since Tom just told me he had spoken to her at least a couple of times. Every time I called, she was working late or had just gone to do some food shopping, reporting back to Dad, who reported back to me, on the emptying of the shelves at the supermarket. Just to make conversation and to hide the pang of disappointment about not talking to Mom, I told him it all sounded just like our campus store, where the four of us frantically ran earlier that afternoon. All the batteries, instant soup, cigarettes, and junk food disappeared in mere hours. And, because of the predicted power outages, every soda machine on campus was depleted of soda. I had cans of Coke lining my desk, while Suzie and Pepa had Diet Cokes lining theirs. (I was relieved to find that Perry was a regular Coke drinker who found, like me, diet soda to be "nasty.") We were all set for Armageddon.

Suzie looked up from her notebook and widened her eyes. "It's like preparing for an earthquake, only you don't prepare for them."

Perry burst out laughing. "You're such a ditz, Suzie!"

"It's all those Zamboni fumes you've been inhaling," I remarked with a wink. Finally some form of wit managed to come out of me.

And no one laughed. Instead, Perry's eyes narrowed as she said, "Along with other inhalants." She jabbed Suzie with her elbow. I couldn't tell if she was joking with her or at her.

Suzie fluttered her eyelids. "Along with other inhalants," she sighed.

Drugs. Great. Another gap between us. Did Suzie snort glue? Or coke? I knew kids at Katonah who did that and wondered if Suzie could be a part of their sniffly crowd. But she was a successful athlete, so it didn't make any sense.

"Just be careful, darling," Pepa said as she looked up, exhaling some smoke from a freshly lit cigarette, and pointed to Perry. "You have friends in high places." Her dark hair was caught up in the usual half bun-half ponytail, making her looked relaxed and experienced.

"High friends in high places," I blurted out, trying once again.

Perry gave me a look of mixed wonder and suspicion, and then resumed her typing. I froze until Suzie guffawed and then tickled Perry, making her yelp. *It's all going to be OK now. Just relax.*

The next morning at breakfast, Suzie slurped on her coffee and kept looking at her watch. "It's going to arrive any minute!" She exclaimed over and over.

"What?" I laughed at her. "You expect everything to go *bang* at the time of landfall?"

"It's not like an earthquake. It happens gradually," Marcus, sitting across from us, drawled in his sleepy, sexy tenor. I tried not to look at him for too long.

Through the windows, we saw the wind pick up speed. The smaller trees arched further with each gust. It could have been just a blustery morning, but the air pressure felt way too heavy. We had visiting hours all day, meaning we could visit the guys' rooms and vice versa as long as we signed in and had permission from dorm faculty. Of course, it all depended on how strong the storm got. So, after breakfast, before things were supposed to get rough, Perry, Pepa, Suzie, and I signed out of the dorm and traipsed over to Hilliman to hang out in Marcus's room.

Marcus had a single. It was small with that slight acrid boy smell of sweat and something else. My bother Tom's room had the same smell. When I sank onto his bed that was covered in a deep green duvet, the words *fabulous* and *sexy* came to my mind. I didn't want them to, but they did. He had an over-sized poster of *A Clockwork Orange,* which Perry pointed out they both saw and loved. It struck me as pretty cutting edge of them to love a movie that was so violent and yet a classic. I told myself I had to see it and like it at the next opportunity, despite the fact that I never before had any intention of seeing it because it was so violent.

"I love your room," I said.

"Thanks." I couldn't help but detect a note of pride in his voice, like he knew he had the best taste on campus.

When I sat down on the bed, I was happy that Perry and Suzie sandwiched me. Pepa sat on Hassan's lap in a butterfly chair and whispered into his neck. His clear eyes lit up against his olive-skinned face. I felt like the little kid who walked in on an adult party. Marcus put a Prince album on a stereo, the same one that Suzie had.

As the music started, Perry yelled out, "Whoo hoo!" and rubbed my arm, and I wanted to do the same, but I felt too self-conscious at that point. I looked for pictures of Perry since she had so many of Marcus in her room, but there was only one in a silver frame. It was a candid profile. She was looking down with a small, bashful smile on her face. I thought I should have been relieved at only seeing one and not a million, but given the Spartan quality of the room, it made me realize this one lone photo was like a gem to him. There was a hairbrush, books, shampoo, various records, and a mirror—that was it. Marcus sat in a chair and tipped it back while bouncing his head to the beat. I wondered if he had any Beatles in his collection. He *must*.

Suzie and Perry leaped off the bed when the last song on the album began. With the storm picking up outside, the fast beat against the grinding guitars, and the fact that Perry and Suzie were dancing and shouting the lyrics out at each other, I had no choice but to join them.

But then Prince's yelp warped to a halt and, except for the rush of wind outside, a sudden silence fell all over the campus. We had lost power. We were on our own against the storm.

Marcus cursed as he lunged over to his stereo. "Of course this happens right during my favorite song!" It was as if he felt the storm was doing this to him on purpose. I made a mental note that this was his favorite song, and that the next time I heard it, I would pay attention to it and, of course, like it.

But everyone else cried out in a mixture of joy and disappointment. "The storm is taking over!" Perry yelled out, shaking her boyfriend's big, grumpy shoulders in an effort to cheer him up.

"Hey! Let's see if we can go outside!" whispered Hassan, as he hugged Pepa.

"Yeah!" I replied, though I was terrified to face those elements and, worse, of getting caught. I didn't know if we would be suspended, but I knew there would be repercussions.

"Cool!" Perry cooed and grabbed Marcus's hand as she got up to leave the room. The rest of us followed.

"We have to sneak out through the butt room door," Marcus whispered.

I smiled back at him in an effort to cheer him up. He looked at me, a slow smile developing on his lips. I swallowed hard and wondered if anyone, particularly Perry, noticed. But she was already out the door.

Nothing more was said as we sauntered down to the butt room as if to go grab a smoke, smiling at passing faculty. Mr. Salk, the dorm head of Hilliman, was in the commons room. Once in the butt room, we escaped out the door and into the wild wind. It was impossible for us not to get caught, yet I didn't care if we got kicked out for this; I didn't care about anything. My blood rushed through me like a white-water river, and I hollered, "Gloria, come and take us!" spreading my arms out to greet the force of the wind, which I let knock me backwards and onto the grass.

Perry giggled and shushed me. Suzie tried dancing around, but she, too, fell down with a scream and a laugh. The warm rain splashed against our faces, and my light blue T-shirt clung to me, showing off my embarrassing mosquito-bite breasts. A roaring gust pushed against us again. Pepa clung to Hassan's stocky body for protection.

"Let's all try and spin!" Perry called out, and she, Pepa, Suzie, and I spun around, our hands reaching far out into the wind, which pushed us into each other. Pepa and Perry's grins were broad, larger than life. Suzie's laughing eyes disappeared into her cheeks. Marcus and Hassan were both lying splayed out on the ground, mouths open to catch the rain, which was almost blowing horizontally. Suddenly, a powerful gust flattened the six of us, me on top of Marcus's wet, T-shirt-clad abdomen. I tried to savor the moment but then I heard a loud creaking and groaning sound behind us as though God was opening a large, rusty door. A slow, deep sounding *whoosh!* followed and ended with a rustling thud as the large elm that shaded part of Fletcher Hall, the biggest dorm on campus, lay across the quad twenty feet away.

We stared at the massive, uprooted tree as the wind thundered and pushed against us.

"C'mon, we better head back," Marcus hoisted himself up on his elbow, and the rest of us followed suit. We ran as fast as we could back to Hilliman, our paths zigzagging. This time we were silent, and there were no screams of anticipation. We entered the butt room in a rush, breathless. It occurred to me Mr. Salk could be standing there waiting for us, and my knees jiggled in fear.

But he wasn't there. Apparently he was busy patrolling the halls, making sure no one was doing anything illicit behind closed doors. There was a group of guys sitting on the benches, red-eyed and smiling, who greeted us with, "*Duuudes!* You actually went out there? Whoa. Hope Salk didn't see you!" One of them grabbed an enormous piece of a quickly deteriorating store-bought coffeecake that sat on a table.

We stayed there until the storm died down. I grabbed a few crumbs, but wasn't hungry. Perry sat next to Marcus, dominating the conversation, and every so often I caught Marcus looking at me, his eyes a little soft, his mouth curling up. I stiffened, and as Perry went on about the falling tree, I distracted myself by glancing up at the ceiling every time I heard footsteps creaking along the floors above us. I was trying to be as nonchalant and cool as everyone else, kicking my feet back and forth and letting out yawns as though I were tired and bored. But Marcus kept glancing at me, and I was positive someone must have seen us earlier. I waited for the inevitable, clomp, clomp, clomp down the stairs to reveal Mr. Salk's angry face.

But nothing happened. Even when Perry, Pepa, Suzie, and I left the dorm once the storm died down, we saw Mr. Salk in the front lounge, his back to us as he was talking to three other students. "Yeah, I heard it. I can't believe the wind knocked that elm down. Thank God it didn't fall on Fletcher Hall." My heart raced as we went out the main door.

That evening a bright moon hung in the sky amidst swirling clouds, and the electricity returned with the familiar buzz we were used to and which had been absent all day long. The air was clean for the first time since I arrived, and breathing was a lot easier. We four girls ended up in Perry and Pepa's room, listening to Madonna once again. I wanted to suggest something, else but it was clear that I was too new to this group to voice dissent. And I kept wondering if Perry noticed Marcus's glances toward me. Even if she did, I wanted to make sure she knew I didn't care and that her friendship was more of a priority. So whatever music they chose was fine with me.

The whole room was like a warmly lit, perfumed (thanks to the Obsession that Perry and Pepa sprayed on themselves) womb. There wasn't the strong demarcation line down the middle like what Suzie and I had in our room. The beds were pushed together next to a wall with Pepa's big, pouffy lavender duvet thrown on top. They had an old, grayish white shag covering most of the floor, a poster of a Jessie Wilcox Smith illustration of a small girl in a peach dress pouring sand through her fingers, and another poster of a Manet painting of a Victorian barmaid staring wearily ahead. And, like Suzie, they had a huge bulletin board covered with photos, a gallery of their past years here. There were photos of Perry and Pepa sliding down a snowy hill, Perry and some other rosy-cheeked girls sipping drinks, a blushing Pepa and Hassan with red pupils holding two plastic cups, a pyramid of them with Perry on top. Perry dangling a daddy longlegs in front of her open mouth. Everyone looked pretty and healthy, and I was proud to be accepted into this close-knit, lovely looking group.

Madonna squealed from the speakers about an angel, and I bounced my crossed legs to the beat. It was a happy, light song. The bell-like synthesizers that made their way along the four notes between the stanzas were OK. So it was cheesy; it was also kind of cute. I had new friends and had just spent an exciting day with them battling the elements. We needed something mindless and bubbly like this.

"I ran into," Suzie said, paused, and looked up at Perry with a devious smile, "that *guy*."

Perry grimaced. "Oh, please, don't remind me." But then she asked, "Did he say anything to you?"

"I just looked at him!" Suzie cried. "I couldn't take my eyes off his red and black hair. It's all over the place."

"Who's that?" I asked, recalling a tall, lanky guy with black and red hair bounding across campus and shouting to his friends in an accent that sounded somewhat foreign. He was the same guy I saw that first day poking his head out the window while the apocalypse song played.

"This guy," Perry sighed. "He's a moron."

"He's Italiano," Suzie said to me in an exaggerated Valley Girl accent. "Leonardo the Italiano."

Pepa added, "He's a total womanizer. A walking cliché of the Italian male."

"He's just some guy." Perry waved her hand dismissively, explaining, "He's a senior in Fletcher. We had a thing a while ago." She adjusted her shirt, and her cheeks became a bit pinker. "Last year when Marcus and I broke up for, like, two seconds."

"I think I saw him," I said. "Isn't he a student leader?"

"Yeah, don't ask me how he got *that*," Perry said as she adjusted her shirt again. She went over to the stereo. "I wanna put something else on. I'm getting really sick of this." She turned Madonna off in midchirp.

"You have to tell these two how he compares to Marcus," Pepa said, beaming at Perry, who just snorted but then giggled.

"Yeah, bigger or smaller?" Suzie said, readjusting a pillow under her chest.

"He seems a lot taller than Marcus," I said.

They all burst out laughing. "Oh, right, Jess," Perry replied in a voice that was a bit too loud for me, "Like height has anything to do with it!"

"Duh," I shrugged, despite the heat burning my face. "But you never know."

"You might have a point." She sounded distracted as she went through various cassettes.

"So," Suzie looked up at her friend. "Gherkin or cucumber?"

We all laughed.

"You guys, it's totally not worth it," Perry whined as she flopped back on the bed.

"You said cucumber!" cried Pepa.

"Whatever. But that's all he's got going for him," Perry sneered. Then she smiled at me. "Marcus ain't bad either, but he's a bit ... " she pinched her mouth, "skinnier."

My chest tightened. Why did she smile at me? She saw those glances. She definitely saw them.

"More the pepper variety," Pepa chuckled.

"Ooh!" shrieked Suzie.

"Strawberry Twizzler," I said, surprising myself. Thank God everyone doubled over, even Pepa. The roomed seemed to dance around me in my relief. "Do he and Marcus know each other?"

"Duh!" chorused the girls.

"I'm sure it got around," Perry shook her head. "Leo is a total loudmouth."

"He's kind of cute, though," Suzie said with a shrug.

"He's nothing like Marcus," Perry sniffed.

"I remember when I was first with Hassan, and I was like, 'It's so small!' But when I sucked on it, it totally grew!" Pepa redid the bun in her hair. It was like she was talking about last week's chemistry lab.

"Well, he was your first one, right?" Perry said, turning to her, and Pepa nodded. Perry said, "OK, let's all talk about our first time!"

My stomach churned. This was not how I wanted to divulge that I was a virgin. The football player in the parking lot of the mall last spring was about the farthest I had gone, French kissing and his hand under my shirt, touching my stomach. I kept telling myself I was really into it, but I couldn't get over how sloppy we were. We had to keep wiping our mouths on each others' jean jackets.

I stood up and forced a yawn. "I gotta go to bed. I'm wiped."

All eyes looked up at me. "Oh, OK," Perry said quietly.

So this is what brought them all together, why they bonded. They were adults and had sex. I didn't want to embarrass myself further by partaking in conversation that proved what a little kid I still was.

The following evening, Perry and I were down in the butt room doing our homework while Pepa was helping Suzie out with her geometry upstairs.

"It's so nice and quiet when you're down here," Perry said at one point. "When Suzie and Pepa are here it's like, 'Yap, yap, yap,' and I have to keep telling them to shut up. They're always fighting for my attention. I hope you spend more time down here with us, so you can help calm things down."

There was a pause. I didn't feel like reading any more of the chapter on chromosomes and DNA and the wild ways of cell life that was due the next day in biology. I watched Perry, bent over her typewriter, typing out her AP history paper, with a nagging thought that my grades were going to be pretty mediocre at midterm. Whereas at Katonah, I was always one B away from high honors, here I was barely applying myself and receiving only Bs when I knew with more effort, I could be doing a lot better. But at the moment, I didn't care.

"Actually, I always feel like I'm missing out on a lot when you guys are down here, and I'm up in bed." I tried to make my voice sound as though I was just musing, but it came out like a whine.

Perry looked at me with her eyes that now looked like two green pools. "Oh, honey! Believe me, you aren't. It's just mindless gossip."

I wanted to tell her I was still a virgin. I had to. She would understand. Pepa and Suzie wouldn't. Well, maybe Suzie would, but then she'd tell Pepa. Or was Pepa still a virgin? The way they talked about sex made it seem like a normal, everyday occurrence. Perry was more bashful about it, and therefore, would be more understanding. And I wanted her to know, maybe as some kind of protection against further incidents like last Friday. "Like the other night? When you guys were talking about sex? I felt so left out."

"Why?" I knew right away she knew the answer, because that was a pretty stupid question.

"'Cause I've never been with a guy like that." I fiddled with the jagged white sole of my sneaker.

"You mean you're still a virgin?" Perry sounded unsurprised and cheery. "You're still" seemed to say a lot though, as if I waited way too long.

I nodded. I could not come out and say, "Yes, and I'm still a good person," the way those magazines tell you to. Please.

"That's OK. I think it's totally cool you've waited. Believe me, going around and screwing every guy in sight the way Suzie does is not the way to go." I guessed Perry didn't want to call her a slut. "Seriously, guys respect you so much more. I mean, Pepa waited for Hassan. That was last year, even."

"Huh." It wasn't like I was in any kind of rush. Even next year seemed too soon.

"I mean, I lost mine when I was fifteen, with Marcus." Perry stretched with a yawn. "That doesn't mean you have to. I just felt ready, and I was with the right person. But don't feel pressured. You're too sweet to go out and lose it just for the hell of it. There are guys out there that could rip you to shreds. But you'll know when you meet the right person. I did, and it was worth it."

"What was it like?" I asked this way too fast. I know I sounded stupid and desperate. I wanted to be as casual as they had been about it the other night.

"Marcus?" *Who else?* "Beautiful. It was at his parents' apartment in New York during Christmas break when I was visiting him. Snow was falling outside. We had dinner at this restaurant down in Tribeca where his dad knew the owner. It was way romantic, and we even got served. I know it sounds so lame, but at the time we thought it was cool. I mean, we were only fifteen, right? Then we got back to his place, totally buzzed on this amazing wine and food, we went out onto the terrace and snuggled, and then he led me into his bedroom. He has this wonderful downy mattress, and he was like this god taking me in his arms. It was his first time, too, and it was funny because it was like I had to show him what to do, you know? I think I was ready because I was aware of my sexuality since I was really little, so it all came so naturally to me. I was like an expert from the start."

"Wow," the word eeked out of my mouth. My heart pounded, and I realized my jaw was clenched, pushing my teeth into my gums. I felt a jealous ache in me. Marcus naked. The feel of his warm skin. I wondered if he had any chest hair. I tried to look appreciative toward Perry. Well, I had to ask, didn't I?

"It was basically my Christmas present to him that year. And we've been together ever since."

I wanted to say, except for Leo and the painter at the club last summer, but a strong voice in me told me to shut my trap. It must be normal after seeing someone for so long. I guess it put Perry on a more human level for me knowing she strayed. And maybe that meant Marcus did too. Maybe they just knew each other, and so what happened in the butt room of Hilliman the previous afternoon wasn't such a big deal. "Cool," was all I could say, and I think I sounded like I meant it.

CHAPTER 4

Girl, Don't Tell Me

The first night home for Thanksgiving break, I finally asked my brother if he had heard of Perry's parents. It was after dinner, and Tom and I were in the kitchen cleaning up while Mom and Dad were in the living room drinking coffee. I washed the dishes, which I always enjoyed more than drying. There was something therapeutic about the feeling of hot water and soap against my hands and seeing pots and pans go from being filthy dirty to shiny clean. I was scrubbing away on a black cast-iron pan with the salt we used to clean it, when I asked Tom if he had heard of any professors by the name of Wagner. It was weird, because I had to brace myself for his response. I was afraid he'd say something negative about them, or worse, her.

He nodded, "Yeah, I'm not taking any classes with them, though. His Nietzsche course is supposed to be amazing." He then gave me this sideways glance and a smile as he dried the large wooden salad bowl. His dark brown hair was beginning to obscure his eyes. I wondered if he was letting it grow shaggy on purpose. "Why? Their daughter goes to your school, you've obviously met her?"

"Yeah! She's my student leader!" I said with all the enthusiasm I could muster in order to push away the smirk on my brother's face. I rinsed the heavy pan and put it in the drying rack.

"You're kidding! She's supposed to be this totally obnoxious, pretentious teenager. Apparently she's tried to sleep with every guy she can get near. You're not friends with her, are you?" He made a face as he put the salad bowl in the cupboard above the refrigerator.

This was why I waited so long to ask him, and I should have waited longer. Now what was I supposed to say? My whole face turned hot and tingly, and all I could do was shrug and reply, "She's been really nice to me." I concentrated on washing the pot that had bits of white rice still clinging to the sides. I poured way too much gooey yellow dishwashing detergent into the scrubbing pad and went to work on the petrified rice.

Tom snorted and then leaned in with an exasperated whisper, "I bet you anything it's because of Mom." He shook his head and resumed the dish drying.

"Tom, that's so untrue! She doesn't even watch the show. And besides, you've never met her!"

"Damn! You don't have to get so defensive!"

"You're criticizing a friend of mine!" With blazing hot water that I usually could not withstand, I rinsed the pot.

"It's what I heard, OK? The kid's kind of notorious."

The kid. Like she was so much younger than Tom. Freshman-itis was hitting him hard, I could tell. Plus, he landed a role in a production of *Cowboy Mouth*. It was being directed by a junior, but Tom made it sound like it was Sam Shepard himself. To make things worse, he was getting all method actor–like. I discovered tobacco and rolling papers in his room and couldn't believe it since he was only used to Marlboro Lights. And then he showed me some really repulsive chewing tobacco that he started using. "Actor's Studio rears its ugly head," was my reply.

I glared at Tom as he finished his drying and went to the living room. I noticed a slight swagger in his step, which was all the more annoying. All for the sake of his "art." I poured the powdery detergent into the dishwasher and slammed the door shut. What right did he have to criticize Perry? He never met her. My parents had, though. When I had told them I was friends with her and her little crowd, Mom sounded happy for me. "Maybe she'll bring you out of your shell," her voice bounced on the phone during one of our regular Sunday night phone calls.

"I think she already has," I replied.

And during break, I wanted my parents, particularly Mom, to see how much I had changed in those two and a half months at Fieldings. I explained away my fall from grace as an honor student to the string of Bs and a lone C+ in religion by saying the work was really hard. "Hmm," was the reply I got, along with two sets of furrowed brows. But both of them were too busy to see the new me, or so I thought. Dad was in emergency sessions with patients, it being holiday season, and was getting ready for a conference on personality disorders. Mom was doing overtime at the studio, shooting the big Christmas episode that Tom managed to get extra work for, meaning at least I'd have less of the Westchester cowboy to deal with.

So I hung out in my room and tried to start a letter to Chris. But I couldn't finish it. What was there to say about my piano? Nothing. I hadn't sat down and composed a piece since I'd arrived at school. I hadn't listened to any of my music since I was so bombarded with top 40 and Madonna. It made me wonder what the other girls would say about my taste in music, and I figured it was too soon to let them really know. Besides, part of me was convinced I was opening myself up. I remembered Chris comparing music to ice cream flavors and that before you could understand something like Heath Bar crunch, you had to understand vanilla. So that's what I was trying to do now—understand the vanilla Madonna.

Although they weren't around much, my parents managed to discover my piano playing was taking a back seat. "How did you end up with someone like *that?*" Mom interrogated me one evening when I told them about dreary Molly Hanson. She made it sound like it was my fault I was with her and not the school's. "I mean, you went there to study with that wonderful Mrs. Whatser-name!" That was Mrs. McGowan, a tall, reedy woman who looked like an angry pigeon. It seemed as though every time I was in the music building, I could hear her barking down the hallway, "No! Watch the timing on this! How many bloody times do I have to tell you!" Leo studied with her, but he always swooped out of his lessons in his black trench coat, laughing and blowing her kisses. He probably spent his lessons milking that Italian charm.

So I didn't practice, which for me was like not eating and breathing. If I didn't do it, I felt unbalanced. Yet that fall any enthusiasm I had for it was transferred onto my new friends, and besides, it wasn't like I had a teacher like Chris or Mrs. McGowan breathing down my neck.

I decided the one person who could see the new me was Kim. She sent me two postcards asking me about school, and I had sent her one back filled with cheery superlatives on how great my life was. She seemed happy, still entrenched in the cool crowd and getting straight As, which made me a little jealous. When I got around to calling her, she shrieked into the phone with joy, "You're back! We have to get together now! We gotta go into the city and everything!"

I laughed back, feeling a comfortable giddiness that I hadn't had in a long time. She told me all about her classes and how they were much more interesting this year than the last. "Our choir is singing the *Magnificat* at St. Thomas in the city over Christmas. I'm so psyched. Plus, I just met this guy, Andy, who wants to form a band and he asked me to sing."

"Wow," I said, having nothing to tell her except the fact that I had more than one friend at school.

"So tell me about boarding school. I heard Fieldings is pretty white bread."

"What do you mean by that?" I felt defensive and twisted the phone cord around my fingers as I gazed at the stairs that led directly up to my room.

"You know, that it's really conservative, like a white, Young Republican training ground."

"That's bull. And like Katonah doesn't have that?"

"I know, right? But this was what I heard."

I assured her it was nothing of the sort although I pounded my brain to tell her something exciting in my life. I told myself it'd be easier once we were face to face. We made plans to see each other the following day.

When Dad dropped me off at the train platform, there was Kim, looking the same, her wild, red, curly hair flying in the wind. She wore a bomber jacket, gold hoop earrings, and high-top sneakers. I broke into a run toward her, and we gave each other bear hugs. "I am so glad to see you!" we said in unison and then laughed. I felt something in me, which had been away all fall, return. It was like a familiarity and comfort that settled itself in the pit of my stomach.

We spent the train ride talking about music, what Broadway shows she had seen, and what we wanted to buy.

"I think I want to get some Madonna," I ventured. "And maybe Prince."

"*Prince*? What happened to you? I thought you didn't like Prince. You kept saying he was kind of sleazy."

"I know, but my friends listen to him so much, I kind of like him." An image popped into my head of last Christmas when Mom and Dad threw their annual party. I was dressed in a blue angora sweater dress, a dusting of makeup on my face, and my hair gently curled. It was one of those moments of feeling like I went from being fourteen to twenty-one in a matter of hours—both heady and scary. I looked lovely, but I didn't know how to carry myself. And Leif, the soap's resident hunk, spent the party leering at me right in front of his girlfriend of the month. It was the same sort of feeling I had about Prince.

"Jess is waking up," Kim said with a look of bemusement. "Although the Madonna part, honey, where did that come from? Are your friends wannabes?"

"No!" *Yes, they are, actually.* "She's light and fun." I shrugged.

"I definitely agree with the former."

We got into town and first headed to Bloomingdale's because I wanted to buy a pair of the snug designer jeans everyone else, including Kim, was wearing. "I'm sick of the baggy look," I announced. "Maybe it's time to show off my legs."

Kim still had a smile on her face, but her jaw dropped all the same. "So this is what boarding school does to people. I thought you got more serious about work? I mean, not that *you* needed to, but still."

"I just, you know, need a makeover."

After that, we took the subway to Astor Place, and then, after a lunch at Cozy Burger, we headed down to our regular haunts. After the amount I spent on my jeans, I didn't have enough money left except to buy some junky jewelry.

Towards the end of the afternoon, we walked up north on lower Broadway in the chill that was filled with the smell of roasted chestnuts and honey-covered peanuts. The sky was cloudy and a bit threatening.

"So it sounds like you like your new friends," Kim said.

"They're great," I nodded, realizing I was using that word a lot to describe them.

"You're lucky," she sighed and stared ahead.

"What do you mean? You sounded so happy in your letters."

"Believe me; I was making it sound a lot better than it was. It's all backstabbing crap, having to kowtow to the right people, feeling like you're on the verge of being out of favor. And the weekends! It's the same crap. Parties where everyone is getting completely wasted, and the less memory you have of the weekend, the better. And then hanging out at the mall. Sometimes I wonder if I should go off to boarding school."

I glanced at the various window displays as a little bit of hope sprung up in me. It would be perfect to have her join. Sort of like Perry and Suzie. "That would be great!" I replied, hoping she'd then talk to her mom, fill out the application, get in, and go.

"Yeah, I dunno. I'd miss my mom a lot. It's weird, because hanging out with these so-called friends without having you around makes me miss you. At one point, I thought I wanted to be a part of that whole crowd, but I just feel anonymous." She smirked. "A wannabe."

And then I realized I missed Kim in a way that felt profound and heavy as if I had somehow lost her and our time together before high school. The feeling I had that first day at Fieldings, like I wasn't supposed to be there, rose up in me. But I pushed it back by reminding myself of the grim realities of Katonah High freshman year.

The Sunday after Thanksgiving break, I was ready to go back to Field-ings. The problem was, I arrived in the middle of the afternoon, and no one was there. I looked like a total loser who had nothing better to do than to go back to school while the cooler students would wait until the last minute to set foot on campus. Because Dad had to go down to DC that morning, and Mom was at a mall in New Jersey with the rest of the cast signing auto-graphs, Tom took me back to school. And he had to go back that afternoon because he had play rehearsals.

The car ride was smoky with Tom puffing away on his hand-rolled cigarettes. Since he was "chauffeuring" me, he demanded that we listen to the growly, yowl-ing voice of Tom Waits.

"Sounds like he's being put through a meat grinder," I sneered as I opened my window to let out the smoke and let in the sound of the wind.

"Better than that helium-voiced tramp you've taken a liking to," he replied, cigarette dangling out of his mouth. He then held his cigarette between his thumb and forefinger to get one last toke before chucking it out the window. "Ahhh," after it was all done, like it was the most satisfying thing in the world. With his flawless, clean-shaven skin, a mouth that fell easily into a boyish pout, and a voice that was somewhere between an alto and a tenor, he hardly passed for the rough cowboy type.

We exchanged no further words. He dropped me off in front of Kurtzman, staring out of the windshield, his eyes steely and mean and then tore off once I got out of the car. And there I was, alone on a desolate campus with my duffel bag.

Except for the occasional distant purr of a car and the glimpse of a lone faculty member, it was silent and chilly. I wanted to be home. I wanted to smell Mom's Diorissimo perfume and the tobacco from Dad's pipe. I wanted to be in my own room, under the comforter, a mug of hot chocolate in my hand and listening to my records.

I walked up the gray-painted, wooden steps to the veranda of Kurtzman, thinking of the day I first visited this place and saw Perry singing, "We're off to see the wizard," with her friends, all arm in arm, skipping down this very road I was standing on. And then I thought, with a twinge of wistful-ness that was so deep it seemed to be coming from the center of my gut, of that cloudy, brisk afternoon with Kim. I imagined her right next to me, on our way to my room to listen to the *Abbey Road* album the way we always did during junior high.

"You're back!" That was Perry's voice, crackling with a slight huskiness, making me jump like a popping corn kernel. I turned around to see her in her red, down vest and perfectly fitted jeans, bouncing over to me to give me a hug. Tom's comment about her came roaring back into my head, and I froze momentarily.

"Hiiii!" I replied, trying to relax. "I'm so glad you're here! I was—"

"Are you kidding?" She flashed her eyes at me as her body twitched. "I have this huge paper to write for AP English, and I wanted to get back early to work on it. Come on, let's go to my room." She ran up ahead of me, unaware that I was carrying a heavy duffel and therefore would be trailing behind.

In her room, she turned on the radio, and we plunked down on her bed.

"How was break?" I asked.

"Sucked," she shrugged. I was glad to hear that. "It was all about my sister, Alison, and her new fiancé, Buddy, this total good ol' southern boy from Charleston whom she met at Tulane. He's got this obsession with Jimmy Buffet songs. Drove me crazy." I laughed, thinking of when I visited a boarding school down in Virginia, and how I heard his lazy voice rambling from speakers all over campus.

She continued, "Meanwhile, there's my Princeton admission, and no one seemed to be interested. It was all about Alison." Perry's legs were banging against the mattress of the bed, making tiny earthquakes. As she rattled on about family life, her eyes zoomed around the room, and she barely looked at me as she shoved two pieces of Bazooka gum into her mouth.

I wanted to be miserable with her, to let her know that she was in good company. "I know, my vacation was crappy too. Tom and I were just—"

"Now I've got this paper that I'm freaking out about," she threw me a piece of gum. "I hear from Princeton on the fifteenth. I can't deal."

I opened up the wrapper of the gum, sank my teeth into the heavy pink sweetness, and continued listening to her. When she paused, I started to talk about Tom and his method acting. At one point, I chucked the wrapper into the wastebasket.

"Jess! What the hell are you doing?" Perry screamed at me as she scrambled to save the wrapper. "You know I keep those!" She pointed to the growing collection of Bazooka comics which she recently started pasting above the door.

"Sorry!"

She threw herself on the bed, almost knocking me off with her force, and then let out a loud sigh. "I'm sorry. It's also because I haven't slept, either. I've been so busy and stuff."

Perry's room felt cramped, like everything—the walls with posters of street-tough Madonna, the innocent girl in the peach colored dress, Perry's flaming-green eyes, and the freckles speckling her nose—was pummeling down on me. I wanted to get out of there.

"I just remembered!" I gasped. "I gotta practice this Chopin piece for tomorrow." There was no Chopin. Molly gave me no homework.

"Oh. Just thought you'd want to go to the library with me."

"I didn't practice at all during break."

"I'll come get you at dinner."

I went over to the music building, Bartlett Hall, to my regular practice room with its high ceilings and worn beige carpet. It was nice to be the only one there, and I played scales and exercises, trying to get my fingers to warm up in their own time. It had been a while, and I wasn't used to that cold, stiff feeling. I just wanted to hear the logical succession of notes over again to maintain some order in my head. The arpeggios, the way my two hands coordinated together as though they were talking to one another. And listening. It seemed as if only half an hour had passed, when I heard Perry's knocks on the door.

"C'mon!" She said. Her bright eyes were sparkling in a way that didn't make her look pretty; just anxious and overtired. "Marcie and Ben are offering to take a bunch of us to Friendly's for an early dinner, so you gotta come because I'm going."

Part of me wanted to protest against her bossiness, but as if on cue, my stomach rumbled. The thought of a cheeseburger, fries, and a coke temporarily made me forget about my piece.

We bounded out of the music building, arm in arm. I wanted to think it was nice to have Perry all to myself and not have Pepa shoving me out of the way or Suzie distracting us. But she was too hyper for me to enjoy this.

I sat squashed in the front of the car between Marcie and Perry while three freshman were in the back seat, cooing over Bryan strapped in his car seat. Marcie asked everyone about their vacations as Perry's arm slithered into mine, and she made snickering remarks into my ear. "Those girls are so public high school!" The ultimate put down, and yet I didn't know what these girls did to deserve that comment. Perry's breath was like a warm paring knife going into my ear. I looked straight ahead, not reacting.

"You find out about Princeton soon, Per, right?" Marcie said with a sidelong glance and a smile to Perry. I wondered if she knew how malicious Perry's comment was.

"I'm *obsessed*," Perry replied.

"Ohhh, don't lose sleep over it!" Marcie chided. "If they don't accept you, it's their loss." She looked out the windshield and smiled as if satisfied with her platitude. I wondered how helpful she would be if I knocked on her door wanting to discuss a problem with Pepa. "Ohhh, you're just overreacting!" She'd say.

But Perry seemed to agree with her. "You're right," she announced loud enough for all to hear. "It's their loss."

I could have sworn I saw one of the girls behind us roll her eyes.

When we entered the restaurant and sat in a booth on brown, slippery vinyl banquet seats, we were handed laminated menus with pictures of larger-than-life burgers and sundaes. All the flames went out of Perry's eyes, and her body steadied itself. It looked deliberate and studied like she was telling herself she had to behave this way in front of Marcie. She chewed her gum slowly, mouth shut. She was relaxed in a way Dad described people's reaction to antipsychotic drugs. There was something synthetic about it, like it didn't come from inside of her, but that it was something on the outside making her pose like this.

As Perry spoke vaguely about Princeton, her paper, and Thanksgiving, Marcie nodded back at her. Everything was smooth about Marcie, her long, brown hair falling straight at her face, her soft, hazel eyes framed by the straightest lashes. She patted Bryan's blue and white blanketed back as she held him to her shoulder, waiting for the waitress to attach the high chair onto the table. I looked at Bryan's blue doe eyes and his drool-covered lips as Marcie placed him in his seat. I wanted to slow down and relax but couldn't because something told me Perry was still jumping around inside.

"So," Marcie leaned on the table, her chin in her hands and gazed at Perry. "You're sister's actually getting married?" Her voice resonated like the singer Karen Carpenter's when she sang—a voice that fell out of the speakers and into your lap.

Perry snorted. "I know Marce, you should see this guy."

Marcie laughed, "I used to date a guy from the south. He was a total gentleman. Give this guy some time, Perry. Besides, *you're* not marrying him." Her eyes lit up, her mouth had an eager grin. It was easy to see her as a student here doing the same thing with her dorm head, and I was struck by that because I could never see adults as being younger. Especially around my age.

"Do you know Alison?" I asked Marcie.

She shook her head and the two of them said no in unison as though my question were an annoying distraction. They continued chatting like two close sisters catching up. Perry's eyes were mostly averted, and she sighed a lot as if to calm herself down while Marcie chuckled at her sarcastic asides about Alison and Buddy and remarked, "Perry, *honestly*! You're so judgmental!"

Then Marcie turned to me, and her tone of voice completely changed. She was a faculty member again. "So Jess, Perry tells me you've got quite a collection of Beatles records." It looked like she was trying to smile at me.

"Yeah, they're my favorite." What else could I say? I bit into my cheeseburger, which seemed tinged with a metallic taste. "They're really inspiring. My piano teacher from last year would have me go through and analyze their compositions." I continued on, showing off my composition knowledge: the way timeless melodies are constructed with question-and-answer phrasing; the importance of rhythm and how strong it has to be in order to be memorable. Marcie kept blinking at me as though trying to stay awake, and I could feel Perry's eyes glaze over. Marcie added that *The White Album* was her favorite album and Perry chimed in, "Me too!" I wanted to agree, but instead stayed loyal to *Abbey Road*.

When we arrived back at school, we passed a large Greyhound bus pulling out of the main school entrance onto the road. I wondered if it was Suzie's bus. I glanced at Perry, who remained still and looked out the windshield with almost glassy eyes. Wasn't she interested in seeing Suzie? Or maybe she knew this wasn't her bus.

When we entered the dorm, the whole place seemed slanted sideways, as Debbie Cochrane, the faculty member on duty, marched straight towards us, eyes on fire. Strands of gray hair had fallen and framed her clenched jaw.

"We have a problem," she nodded to Marcie. Bryan wailed, and Marcie kissed him on the head before she handed him over to Ben, standing nearby. "Come upstairs. It's um," Debbie scratched her nose, "Suzie Hodges."

The room stopped tilting. I swung my head around to Perry, but she ignored me. She swallowed. Everything in my body withered to a wrinkled, prunelike mass, a million nerves sticking out, prickling my skin, which turned clammy and warm.

We followed Marcie and Debbie upstairs, all eyes in the dorm lounge following us, along with whispers of "She was drunk off her ass," and "I heard it was pot," reaching my ears.

The hallway seemed endless, and when we reached my door, I could hear Suzie sobbing. Celia, the student leader from the second floor, was in the room, keeping an eye on Suzie so that Debbie could go downstairs to retrieve Marcie.

"Can I go in with you?" Perry demanded to Marcie. Already there was a group of interested students gathered around the door, all craning their necks to listen better to what was going on in the room. The air felt thick, like those days before the hurricane.

"You guys stay outside," Marcie said in a hard voice. I wondered why she directed this to me and not Perry. "And everyone, go back to your room. This is none of your business, OK?"

"Except me, Marce. I'm her student leader, remember?" Perry raised her eyebrows and crossed her arms, but the nervous energy from this afternoon had returned.

Marcie sounded almost apologetic to her as she shook her head and put a hand on her shoulder. "Perry, relax. Debbie and I just have to go in and talk to her and then you'll get your chance, OK? Can you hang on for two minutes?"

"So fucking unfair!" Perry's stage whisper hissed out, and she looked at me as though this were all my idea. At that moment, I wanted to be back in the music building working on my arpeggios, strengthening my pinky.

Celia came out, and the crowd of girls dispersed. She was about Perry's height only plumper and with black, ringletted hair that never looked combed. Perry once told me she was a stoner, and now greeted her with a nasty glare

Celia turned to her with a sigh, "Excuse me for taking over your duties. But I just happened to be around, and you weren't, OK?" She glanced at me as if to say, "What are you doing with her?" and shuffled down the hall, her flip-flops making gentle clapping noises.

Perry rolled her eyes and gave a well-manicured finger to Celia's back. "Bitch." Her mouth, her whole face, made me think of sour milk. I tried to give her a sympathetic look and roll my eyes, but Perry didn't appear to notice.

"I didn't mean it! I didn't do anything …" Suzie cried out, slurring her words. I didn't know how much of it was sobbing and how much was actual drunkenness. Perry glared at the closed door with the shiny memo board filled with old scribbles and Garfield bouncing all over the place.

She had stopped twitching and was now a fortress of neatly pressed jeans, a fitted sweater, and a shiny, red down vest covering the muscles she spent years developing for gymnastics. Her mouth was clamped shut, but I knew her tongue was working up a storm of curse words I wouldn't hear until we were in the room with Suzie. That is, if I was allowed in.

Then, as if out of nowhere, I was given my order. "Go downstairs," she commanded. "Now."

"She's my roommate!" I shot back.

"*She* is none of your business right now, got it? Get your butt downstairs." Her voice shook underneath all her effort to maintain its steeliness.

Just as I turned around to obey her, a screech came out. "*I can't believe I'm busted*!!!!" Suzie's sobs sounded like they were falling down the same staircase I was on, and I paused.

"Go," snarled Perry, and I clicked my tongue at her in response.

"We need to talk to Perry," Marcie remarked as she opened the door.

It was no accident that Perry ended up as Suzie's student leader. It was one of her duties to keep an eye on Suzie, so she wouldn't get into trouble, like now. I remembered Perry telling me early in November, when the rink opened, and Suzie was spending most of her time there, that Suzie, although an extremely talented skater, wasn't exactly "all there in the discipline department" and that despite having made it to junior nationals, she also had a reputation for partying, and the more successful she had become, the more rebellious, too. Her parents felt she needed a break from the world of competition, and that was why she came to Fieldings, where she could be with an older, more stable friend. So I made myself accept that Perry wanted to be alone with her.

But once I entered the commons room, which hummed with gossip, one head turned and saw me, and then everyone seemed to lunge at me. "Ohmigod, what did they say? What happened? Is she busted? Is she gonna get kicked out?"

"She's busted," I replied feeling both powerful and betraying. "I think she was drinking."

Their questions answered, the girls turned back to watch Andy Rooney whining about something on *Sixty Minutes*. Some who had been on the bus and witnessed the whole thing murmured, "She was so totally trashed!"

But I couldn't stay put. Marcie came downstairs and opened the screen door of her apartment. When we caught each other's eyes, I asked her if I could go upstairs.

Her eyes slanted down at the sides, and she let out a deep sigh. "Yeah, I guess. But it's up to Perry. OK?" And she let the screen door slam behind her.

My knock on my door was answered with Perry's, "Come in," which sounded unusually pleasant. When I opened it, there she was, sitting on my bed, her back perfectly straight, hands folded in her lap, clutching a plastic baggy. Suzie crouched on her bed, her face swollen, giant tears spilling out of her eyes which looked bigger than ever. But the rest of her was tiny. Her red turtleneck was fraying at the sleeves. I saw her as a five-year-old, not fifteen. Instinctively, I went over to her and put my arms around her hunched, shaking shoulders. The corners of her mouth went up as her eyes overflowed once again.

Perry announced, "She was doing shots of rum on the bus with two other people. They offered." It was as if Suzie had done something utterly clumsy like spill her Diet Coke all over Perry's pillow. Nothing more than a stupid inconvenience.

A long, thick pause followed, cut by Perry's sigh. Why on earth did she sound so relieved? "They got busted too?" I asked, not knowing what else to say.

Suzie nodded with a hiccup.

"Uhhh," Perry let out a fake sigh. "We thought it was gonna be a lot worse, right Suze?" Her fingers tightened around the baggy, which I had a hard time taking my eyes off of.

Another nod and another hiccup.

"What's in the bag?" I asked, walking over to my bed. I knew it wasn't any of my business.

Perry shook her head, her eyes heavy lidded. "Nothing that would interest you. Don't worry." She slid off my bed as I sat down on it. "I think it's safe to leave you two alone." With an almost proud smile, she headed out the door shutting it quietly, her back ramrod straight.

Suzie leaped toward the door and kicked it. "Stupid bitch!" She whispered. "She was supposed to be here when I got back. And now she's totally turned on me!"

"What are you talking about?"

She stopped, her back to me, everything suspended in her body. "No," she said as she turned around to me slowly. Her face was set. The hysteria gone. "I just wanted some protection, that's all." She collapsed on her bed, face to the ceiling, and spoke in deliberate, practiced tones. "I know I was dumb about getting drunk, but I thought if Perry sees me, she'll protect me. 'Cause she said she was going to wait for me and stuff." An edge seeped into her voice. "Like meet me at the bus. And she didn't"

I had the image of Perry's grip on the baggy. "Just to meet you, just to welcome you back?"

"Yeah." Suzie looked like the little girl who knew she had done something bad. I thought of her gum chewing, the gold necklace she was always playing with against her lips, her jumpy way of running over to me to throw her arms around my neck.

"It was about that bag, right?" I hoped beyond hope, though, that all that was in there was a leftover cookie. *Right.* Drugs held this dark, creepy terror for me with the whole idea of a substance turning you into something you weren't and the numerous horror stories from my parents about strung-out actors and what acid and mushrooms did to the brain.

"It was nothing," she mumbled and chewed her nails.

I knew I should have been angry, but I pushed it down. So what if there was something between Perry and Suzie and it involved drugs? I had to admit, though, that creeped me out, but I was sure Perry would tell me later. Like it was something I really wanted to know, anyway.

CHAPTER 5

Anyone Who Had a Heart

On Sunday night, two weeks after Suzie got busted, Perry and I were in the library doing our homework. I was recopying my biology lab report that was due the next day, and Perry was studying AP calculus while chewing furiously on her Bazooka gum and blowing an occasional luminous pink bubble out of her mouth, sending an overly sweet candy smell up through my nostrils.

"How's Suzie?" Perry asked me in a whisper. Her eyes were on some formula, making it sound like the question was an afterthought, but I knew it wasn't.

"Fine," I shrugged. Suzie was not talking to Perry these days. Perry still said hi to her when they passed in the hallways, waved to her, smiled, and all that, but Suzie continued to look through her, flaring her nostrils.

Perry smirked. "Has she been saying anything nasty about me?"

"She doesn't really talk about you." That sounded a lot less diplomatic than intended, and my face turned warm.

For a mere second, Perry's mouth fell, just a millimeter, but it was noticeable. She flicked her eyebrows up. "Figures. Oh well, she'll get over it. I mean, I've known Suzie for awhile. She's really moody. And young, in case you haven't noticed."

I nodded, although I didn't think *young* was the right word. More like *irresponsible*. She was an idiot to get drunk on the bus while carrying around a stash of ecstasy for her friend. The night she got busted, it only took about one hour after Perry left the room for Suzie to blurt out the whole story to me even though she wasn't supposed to. She explained that Marcus asked her to buy some ecstasy for him and Perry from a dealer friend of his out in L.A. "If Perry finds out you know this, I am dead," she had told me.

"Why?" I asked. Underneath my placid façade, I was shaking. On the one hand, I never had a desire to do the stuff, yet on the other hand, it gave me a bit of a thrill to be vicariously living on the edge. There was also the jealousy factor: Perry and Marcus, who were already pretty glamorous in my mind, doing something dark and glamorous together.

"She's afraid you'll tell everyone else, and then she'll get into trouble."

"*Who* else am I going to tell?" I had no idea what I'd done in the span of our short friendship that would lead her to believe I'd be a blabbermouth. She should have been more worried about Suzie. It was like my Mom, who never told me any soap gossip because she was afraid I would tell Kim, and Kim would tell the world, and it would get back to Mom, and there would go Mom's career. There was no trust. "What does she think I am?" I said to myself more than to Suzie.

"She's paranoid."

"Duh." I tried to tell myself that it was maybe because Perry and I hadn't been friends for that long, and so she just didn't know me well enough. But the idea stung me. I thought of saying something to her, but that meant betraying Suzie. So I chose coldness which lasted until breakfast the following morning when Perry sat down next to me with her bowl of cereal and patted me on the back. The corner of her eyes tilted down, her freckles speckled over her pug nose. "Hey," she said. Her voice was shy and contrite.

"Hi!" Cheeriness flooded me.

But Perry kept her voice low. "Listen, I'm so sorry you had to get involved in this mess. Suzie really screwed up on me even though I guess it could have been so much worse."

"Screwed up how?" I cocked my head at her, hoping my feigning ignorance convinced her.

She paused, her mouth open but no words came out. Her eyes were hard, and she leaned in and whispered with that warm paring-knife breath that smelled of toothpaste. "You have to promise not to tell anyone, OK?"

I nodded with a look that told her to get on with it.

She relayed the entire story, true to Suzie's. "Then like a jerk she gets drunk on the bus. But thank God, when she got caught, no one was the wiser."

"But why would you think I would tell anyone this?"

She took a spoonful of cereal and said in between crunches, "I dunno. It's drugs. People can ask questions. Stuff can slip out in situations like this. You have to realize that."

That made sense especially given what Suzie let slip the night before, but I knew there was more. "But how come Suzie said you two were supposed to meet?"

Perry gulped, her eyes widening. "We never made that plan! I don't know where she came up with that! I mean, I just said *maybe* I'd be there. Besides, Suzie was the one who got drunk. If she were sober, none of this would have happened!"

True. But Suzie was pissed off at Perry and decided not to talk to her, which meant they were no longer hanging out. In the meantime, Pepa and Hassan were glued together, so Pepa had no time to play diplomat, either. Yet I wondered if it was also because hanging out with Perry meant hanging out with me. No Suzie to act as a buffer.

Perry and Pepa were still using the butt room late at night to do their homework, but Suzie remained with me in our room. As a result, she went through fewer packs of Marlboro Lights and Diet Cokes. Together, we memorized our theorems on flash cards, compared my Italian with her Spanish, and sometimes read aloud from *All Quiet on the Western Front* together. Then we'd go though the campus directory which had people's ID shots next to their home and school addresses, and we'd talk about who looked geeky, totally cute, what gossip we had heard. When we came across Marcus's picture, squinty-eyed and smirky, we concluded that he was a god but an arrogant one. In Suzie's words, "a dickhead." "He didn't even thank me for getting the ecstasy," she snarled. "He just handed me the money, and that was that."

"What an asshole!" Yet this only made him more attractive to me.

And as if reading my mind, Suzie asked slyly, "You still have a crush on him, right?"

It was like someone turned on a thermostat in my body, and I felt everything in me bake. "It's that obvious?"

"Jess! Everybody knows! It's so clear when you look at him. We all noticed during the hurricane. And it wasn't like he didn't reciprocate, you know?" She giggled.

My heart started pounding. "I hope Perry didn't notice!"

"Who cares if she did? She probably gets off on it. It's a challenge for her. She knows he's hot shit, and of course being with him makes it rub off on her."

Out of my peripheral vision, Rob Lowe sulked down at me. My jaw tightened. "I dunno, Suze." I didn't want to think that about Perry, that she was that superficial. But there was the story of them losing their virginity to each other and the eagerness with which she told me. Well, I *did* ask.

I didn't just feel disloyal talking behind Perry's back but also afraid that once the two girls were friends again, this conversation would be repeated, and I didn't want my words twisted.

But that was all that Suzie said about Perry. She seemed much more interested in asking about my mom, and even though I wanted to know what celebrities she'd met, she answered dismissively, saying they were nice, and that was it. She complained about her parents and how Republican they were, how they thought Reagan was so great, even though she thought he was just an ageing cowboy, and I had to agree.

"He scares me," I said. "I am so convinced there's gonna be a nuclear war in the next couple of years."

"It's like he thinks everything's a movie. That's what's so weird about L.A. No one has any sense of reality. It's all fantasy."

There was a pause. "Are you close with your parents?" I asked.

She shrugged. "I dunno. It's not like I see them all the time. I'm closer to my coach, Daniella. She's like my real mom because I saw her every day all the time."

"Then why'd you stop skating?"

"I got sick of it, Jess. It was all about preparing for the next competition, and that was it. I got tired of spending my life in an ice rink, always having to win a competition or pass a test. I felt like a gerbil on one of those wheelie things. I couldn't have any fun." She sighed, a deep heavy sigh that seemed to say so much more than what she had just told me. "Do you get along with your parents?"

"I guess. But I just feel like my mom prefers my brother to me just because he likes acting and is more outgoing. And my dad doesn't know what to do with me. When I was growing up, he was always so affectionate with me, always holding me. But now he's freaked out."

"It's like parents have no idea what to do with teenagers."

"Totally."

During the time we spent together, I found out that Suzie was no dummy. She started handing in her assignments on time, instead of constantly asking for extensions, which used to lower her grade because of lateness. After neglecting most of her geometry theorems throughout the term, in just a week, she was caught up, and that Friday she waved a pop quiz in front of my face that displayed a big red A-. She breezed through *All Quiet on the Western Front* and finished her essay on time, also getting an A- on that. In biology, which we took together that term and were lab partners, I no longer had to cover for her, and she no longer stared back out at our teacher blankly with a wavering pen-to-mouth—"Uhhh, dunno ..." when asked a question. In just two weeks, Suzie's academic apathy had disappeared, and she was already rivaling me in my own grades, which were finally improving as well.

"Her grades have really shot up," I was now telling Perry that Sunday night in the library.

She shut her calculus textbook with a *whoosh!* delivering a fresh wood pulp smelling breeze of paper, a relief from the Bazooka. Then she looked up at me, hands folded on the wooden table that separated us and twitched her mouth. "Well, I knew something good would come of this whole trauma. It may make life more uncomfortable for you because you have to split your time between her and me, but trust me, she'll come around, and we'll all be together again." She gave me a reassuring smile, stood up, and announced that she wanted to go visit Marcus.

And then I wondered if I wanted the group back together again even though I had no say in the whole thing. I liked having the two girls on an individual basis. It erased all that competition for Perry's attention, and Perry didn't appear bothered by the fact that I was spending time alone with Suzie, so the whole situation was ideal as long as they didn't criticize each other to my face. But you can't have everything. Perry had Pepa and I had Suzie and Perry, and it was like finding new friends. And, when I was hanging out with Perry, Pepa was hardly around, so even that barrier was gone.

Weekends were divided between Suzie and Perry. Friday nights Perry and I went to whatever movie was playing on campus. It had been a ritual with our group all term, but since Thanksgiving, Pepa had been hanging out in Hassan's room on Friday nights, and Suzie skated at the rink. So every Friday night after a dinner of spaghetti and ice cream, Perry would grab me and say, "Let's go and get good seats." And then afterwards, we'd go to the student center for milkshakes and fries and gossip. I showed her how I dipped my fries into the shake, and she tried it out and loved the combination. It was like our own private party.

"How's Marcus?" I asked one night after we had seen *The Godfather*. He was supposed to come with us, but decided on bongs and bootleg tapes of a Grateful Dead concert with some other friends in his dorm. I knew bringing him up was a bit dangerous, but I was tired of listening to Perry rattle on about her dictatorial coeditor, Mitch, and the weekly crisis at the school paper. So I found a convenient pause when Perry let out an exhausted sigh after ten minutes of nonstop chatter. I kept my eyes peeled for any sign of suspicion on her part.

But all she did was shrug. "Ehhh, OK. We were supposed to spend Christmas together, but now his mom says they're all going on a family ski trip to Vermont. And of course I won't be invited because the woman can't stand me."

"Why?"

"She's threatened by me. She ignored Marcus throughout his childhood, you know, nannies and everything. And now that he has this serious girlfriend, she wants him all to herself. She's such a hypocrite. She's been like this with me ever since Marcus and I first started going out." She popped an ice-cream-laced french fry into her mouth, her nose slightly tilted in the air as if to say she found the whole situation tiresome. "Marcus says she's been like this with all his girlfriends, but let's face it, I'm the first serious one he's had, and the longer the relationship lasts, the less she wants to see of me. She wants to be the center of his attention. She's really narcissistic."

Out of the corner of my eye, I saw a tall, dark figure barrel through the doors, laughing with a full, hearty sound that echoed throughout the center. I looked up to see Leo Borghi and his trademark trench coat and Doc Marten boots. The red spots in his black hair seemed brighter than ever.

"Oh, God," Perry said. "Look who's here."

Leo and I caught each other's eyes, and I realized that he recognized me from the music building. I smiled faintly at him. Perry glared at me. "What are you doing?" she whispered. "I mean, not to be all high school-y but—"

Before she could finish, Leo came over to us, his stride so great it seemed like he only had to take two steps. "Hey. You take piano, right?" I noticed his accent, despite a slightly foreign-sounding lilt, was pretty Americanized.

"Yeah. I see you all the time."

He smiled at me, ignoring Perry, whose face became stony and prim. "I heard you play a couple of times. You sound really good." He had bright blue eyes that were framed by light brown lashes, making me realize that underneath the mass of black and red locks lurked a guy with my hair color.

I swallowed, grinning back at him. A warmth went through me, something I hadn't felt since I had been with Kim over Thanksgiving.

Two girls over by the snack bar called out to him. I immediately recognized them from my visit here almost exactly a year ago, when I saw them, along with Pepa and Perry, all arm in arm skipping up to the administration building singing, "We're off to see the wizard." Even at that time they seemed to be such a contrast to Perry and Pepa since they were more sloppily dressed, clad in crazy-colored leggings, thick, black Doc Martens on their feet, and their hair all over the place. I always heard British dance music blaring out of their window from the girls' side of Fletcher. Neither Perry nor Pepa ever mentioned them, and I had a sense that they weren't ever friends except for that one day.

Leo waved a big hand up to me. "I'll see you later." For a split second, I wanted to join him and his friends, and when I turned back to a sullen-faced Perry, something in me felt trapped and gray. I ignored it.

Perry gave me a level-eyed look, both exasperated and hard.

"What?" I asked. "I'm not supposed to talk to him?"

"Oh, come on! I'm not that childish! He's just a total jerk. Watch out for him, that's all. Besides, those guys are nothing but a bunch of trendy poseurs."

"What happened between you two?"

She straightened up. "Nothing! We just had a stupid fling." She shook her head. "He has a really bad reputation, Jess. He's a total Lothario."

A defensiveness rose up in me. "He just said hi to me. We take piano around the same time."

"I know! I'm just warning you, that's all. I saw that look in your eyes." A small smile crept on her face.

"What look?" My mind raced, trying to go over every reaction I had. All I did was smile at him.

"I've seen that look before."

I managed to make a face despite the fact that the rest of my body froze. "Whatever." I sipped my cold, creamy milkshake with its hint of coffee flavor. Suzie's comment about Marcus and me was now confirmed. I dipped my fries with a lost appetite, now knowing Perry knew.

"And of course he hangs out with those two girls because they pose no threat," Perry leaned in and whispered to me in a delicate voice. "They're so skanky! They're like wannabe club kids, but they totally don't get it." She looked pert, pretty, and mean. I watched as Leo and the two girls giggled. They didn't look nasty or conspiratorial. They weren't glancing around the room the way we sometimes did in the dining hall. And the way we were doing now. They were just with each other. It dawned on me that Perry didn't have nice things to say about other people, and I felt cloaked in her negative damp cloud. I swallowed, steeling myself before I asked, "Why do you always criticize other people so much?"

Perry looked as though I had just slapped her across the face. Which I kind of had, and I started to regret it.

"Jess!" Her voice became soft and foreign, something I'd never heard before. "I don't!" Her eyes were shiny, and yet her unexpected vulnerability pushed me on.

"No, you do. It's like you never have anything nice to say about anyone outside our group."

I was half expecting her to bounce back with a nasty comment. Instead, she stared at me with a look like a child who had lost her mom in a department store. "That's not true! I can't believe you think that about me! Jess, it's not like you know me well enough to say that kind of stuff." She shook her head, and then her voice became a little stronger while she focused her attention on shredding a napkin. "It's just those people. OK, I tried to be friends with them last year, and they totally turned on me. I don't know what I did."

"What do you mean?"

She crumpled a fry into her mouth. "It's just I knew they had something against me for a long time even though I have no idea what it is. It was like they just spit me out. I don't want to talk about it. And anyway, I'm sorry you think I'm a bitch." I could barely hear her voice.

"I'm sorry." And I was. I thought of the way Perry took me under her wing and how she was so nice in the beginning. She was probably that way with everyone, and maybe they became jealous of her. Her smarts, her talents, Marcus.

She stood up with a sigh and one more glance over at the trio. "Well, you can't be friends with everyone."

Perry continued to sulk on our silent walk back to the dorm in the dark night, and I wanted to comfort her, but I didn't know how. I was a sophomore who had told a senior off. That was like breaking a cardinal rule. And I became not a little afraid that I had just jeopardized my friendship with Perry. "I didn't mean to tell you off like that," I said.

No response.

The next day at breakfast as I sat down next to a silent, still-sullen Perry, I blurted out, "I'm sorry I told you off last night."

"No, you're right, I can be a real bitch," she replied to her cereal. "I guess I'm just going through a rough time with Suzie not talking to me and Marcus and Christmas. I just have a lot on my mind. I mean, I'm super nervous about Princeton. I find out in a few days, and it's driving me nuts. I've got this major AP English paper on Bleak House, and I have no idea what to write. Plus, I know I'm bitching about someone else, but Mitch is such an asshole. Every suggestion I make, he ignores. He killed an article that I wanted to keep. It's like he's the only editor!" She threw her spoon into her cereal and then sat back with her arms crossed, glaring at the table. "You're lucky. You don't have to worry about these things. What I wouldn't give to be a sophomore again and not have to worry about this whole college insanity." She resumed eating her cereal. "It's really going to change for you next year, Jess. Enjoy it while it lasts."

I hadn't thought about that. How selfish and unaware could I have been? "Perry, I had no idea! It's OK. I didn't really think about that." There was a pause as Perry remained silent. I guess I was supposed to say some more. "Listen, I'm meeting Suzie at the rink this afternoon. You want me to say something to her?"

"That would be great," Perry nodded, her voice a little weak. Noticing the shadows under her dull eyes, I wondered if she had slept at all that night.

Suzie usually went to the rink right after her weekly drug and alcohol workshops that took place every Saturday and Sunday. I had never seen her skate before, and this time we made a date to go together so she could teach me. I was determined to tell her to make peace with Perry.

"It's been a week since I skated! I feel so out of it!" Suzie said as she came up to me breathlessly after doing what she called a warmup, and I called a phenomenal bit of skating.

"Do something amazing!" I said, hopping up and down on a pair of floppy skates that I got last year. They looked like pretend skates next to Suzie's scuffed, sturdy ones. She burst out laughing, and it sounded so full and rich that it fell over me and bounced off the walls.

She skated backwards, crossing one foot in front of the other, her feet barely leaving the ice as if she were knitting with her feet. She cut a circle with one foot on the ice, the other trailing behind it at a forty-five degree angle, and she stepped into a fast spin. I heard a swishing noise that sounded satisfying and delicious as her blade took her around in a dizzying circle. Her back arched to the point where it looked like her head could almost touch her butt, and her other leg was held in a perfect attitude.

"How did you do that without falling backwards?" I gasped at her.

"It's all illusion," she shrugged with a smile. "You push your hips really far forward to balance yourself, and you actually don't go back that far."

"No, you were going back really far!" I shook my head, refusing to believe that Suzie was hardly arching her back.

"Illusion!" she sang out. "Come on!" she gestured. "Let's skate." She grabbed my mittened hand and led me around the rink, telling me to bend my knees and to watch out for the toe picks.

I told her about Perry wanting to make peace, saying, "I think this is really getting to her."

Suzie just stared straight ahead and sighed.

"I kind of told her off last night," I added.

She swung her head around so fast that it would have knocked me off my feet had I done it. "Ohmigod! What did you say?"

"She was just criticizing everybody left, right, and center, and I told her to stop it." It came out sounding so much easier than it actually was. "And then this morning she apologized, and said she did it in part because she was upset that you weren't talking to her."

Suzie put her hands on her hips, looked down at her skates, and started to glide around, making small half circles and said, "It's funny, she never said anything to me."

I looked around the vast, white, cold rink with its mottled and scuffed barriers from so many years of hockey games and bad skating. "Maybe she was afraid to or something."

"Why?"

I shook my head. "It's weird. Perry seems so fearless but maybe ..." My thoughts started to drift. Dad's oft-heard phrase "intimacy fears" popped into my head, but that seemed too large a label to put on Perry. After all, she'd been with the same guy for four years. OK, she cheated on him, but she was still with him. And who's to say he hadn't cheated on her? "Well, I think she's going through a lot now. And she is only human, after all."

Suzie skid to a stop and gave me a look that made her appear years older. "Jess, sometimes you're a little too good to be true."

"What do you mean by that?"

"A little suspicion wouldn't hurt."

And that's all she said to me, but I figured it was because she was still mad at Perry.

When I told Perry about asking Suzie to make peace (and not Suzie's failure to respond), Perry called me her "little diplomat" and gave me a squeeze on the shoulders. I wanted to be happy with her praise, feeling like I was an integral part of the group. But there was something distracted about it; it was a little too fast, and she didn't give me any eye contact. Nor did she ask any further questions about Suzie.

It was mid-December and we had Secret Santas where we had to secretly give small gifts to whoever's name we each pulled out of a hat, the whole week culminating in a Christmas party right before finals. I hoped beyond hope that I would get someone in our group, particularly Perry or Pepa. During the dorm meeting when the hat was passed around, there were squeals when it was obvious someone picked a good friend, and Suzie and I rolled our eyes at each other, mine more in despair than anything else. Then the hat was passed to her. She sighed, reached in, and opened the little scrap of paper. With a grimace she showed me the name: Perry. I was both relieved and insanely jealous. I knew she wasn't going to do anything, and when I got a fellow sophomore whom I barely even said hi to, Suzie asked me if I wanted to switch, but she was interrupted by Marcie's declaration, "No switching!" and a subsequent glare at Suzie.

"It's like fate or something," she grumbled to me.

I looked over to Perry, who was looking right at Suzie in a calm, almost hopeful manner.

CHAPTER 6

Dancing with Tears in My Eyes

When Perry got accepted into Princeton, it was pretty clear to me that she and Suzie were not going to make up before Christmas break. While the rest of us were discovering Hershey Kisses on our beds at night, or a surprise mug of hot chocolate delivered by one of "Santa's elves," Suzie did nothing, which gave her away to Perry. "She's making it so obvious!" Perry giggled to me.

I was trying my best, in the meantime, to figure out who I had, matching the handwriting to what I had seen on memo boards outside everyone's door. I knew right away I had neither Perry nor Pepa, and I resigned myself to the fact that it was all OK despite the enormous disappointment that I felt. Besides, I was pretty lucky in that I was getting something every day—treats from the campus store, a set of colored pens, fashion magazines. Suzie wasn't doing too badly either. She shrieked when she discovered a pack of Marlboro Lights and an icy cold Diet Coke one night on her desk. "Someone knows me very well!" But just as quickly her tone darkened, "As long as it isn't—" and she indicated our next door neighbors with a slant of her head.

I knew it. The look Perry gave her during that dorm meeting said it all. It *was* like fate, or something.

Perry had already reported during a very moody dinner on Thursday that Mitch Greene had been accepted at Harvard, which sucked because, as she said,

"You just know he's gonna ask me at the editorial meeting tonight whether I heard. Just to rub it in." But on Saturday morning as we were watching cartoons in the lounge, the front door opened, and in came the mail carrier. Our heads swung around to watch him march over to the mailboxes near the stairwell, a gray, bulky bag in hand.

Perry grabbed Pepa's knee, and they let out yelps. I slurped loudly on the hot chocolate that I was drinking, almost to drown out their camaraderie.

"Where's Marcus?" Perry demanded, a sudden change of mood sweeping over her. "He said he was going to be here." She clicked her tongue, shook her head, and sighed. "He's such a flake."

"Call him," I replied, nudging her elbow.

Pepa snapped, "No, he should just *know* to be here."

I began to wonder, with a small amount of hope, if he just wasn't interested.

The mail carrier finished and strode out the door and the three of us scrambled, Perry in the middle holding our hands, over to the mailboxes.

"Oh, please, do not be a small envelope!" Perry cried.

And there in her mailbox was a big, thick envelope from Princeton. We all screamed. Perry grabbed it, tore it open, and pulled out the letter. She read it aloud as we jumped up and down, hugging her. I couldn't help but notice that her hug to me was brief and loose, and the one to Pepa was much tighter. *They've known each other longer*, my voice reprimanded me.

As if on cue, in came Marcus, wearing his dark blue, down jacket giving him a sensual, husky look. Everything seemed to stop for a moment as he and Perry looked at each other, small smiles growing into huge grins and ending with a bear hug. I told myself I really had to get over this crush on him, but given the fact that my heart was racing, I knew I wasn't getting anywhere. I made an excuse to go to the library or do something. I couldn't stand there in the lounge with these guys any longer.

That afternoon, as I was in my room writing a paper on *The Great Gatsby*, Suzie came in, and I told her the news.

She shrugged. "Not surprising. I guess she's just the Queen for the Day or queen every day." She plunked down on her bed. "What are you doing?"

"I'm working on my *Gatsby* paper."

"What are you writing about?" she yawned.

"Romance and loss." Although I was swept away by the romantic imagery in all the books we read that fall, *Gatsby's* tragic glamour hit me hardest. The observer who gets caught up in the world of big parties, big houses, and a lost group of people. Everything we read that term seemed to tie romance into loss.

Which made me wonder: Was that all romance led to? Is that why we were study-ing it in the autumn because that's when everything basically dies, and we roman-ticize the past and the things we can no longer have?

And reading about Jay Gatsby reminded me of Marcus, so of course I wanted to write a paper about him. Although I refused to let him enter any kind of fan-tasy (those were still saved for Rob Lowe) my pillow would miraculously become Marcus's face every now and then. Actually, all the time, and my efforts to wipe him away by chanting "Oh, Rob" in my head over and over again weren't work-ing. "Oh Marcus" managed to slip in on several occasions, and a warm embar-rassment went through me.

Ever since I told Perry off, I could tell that she was distancing herself from me, but it wasn't in a way that was obvious, so it wasn't like I could confront her on it. And say what? "I don't feel like you're giving me as much eye contact as you used to. You hardly hugged me when you got into Princeton." How paranoid and picky can you get? Besides, I was still sitting next to her during meals, going to the library with her every now and then (although I noticed I had to invite myself along), and one Friday I went to a movie and the student center with her, only this time we were accompanied by Marcus. She spent most of the time gig-gling with him and complaining about Mitch the Dictator (to which Marcus made obscure references to *Citizen Kane,* and, having never seen the movie, it all went over my head). And while Marcus asked me a few questions about my piano like he was trying not to be interested in me, but I could tell he was (looking around the room in distracted manner, but when his eyes got back to me they smiled), I made bored replies like he was the last person I wanted to talk to. Perry said nothing and asked me nothing, even in regards to Suzie. I was kind of hop-ing Leo and his two friends would come in, giving me an excuse to back off from Perry and Marcus, but they never showed up.

I still liked having Suzie to myself. We studied well together for finals, and she dished out gossip that her mother had given her in her latest phone calls and let-ters. Both parents thought the bust was good for Suzie since she was clearly doing much better in her classes. They had no idea about the silent treatment to Perry, however. I didn't push Suzie to make up with her, either, because I knew some-thing was going to happen at the Christmas party.

But it was all lukewarm. The night of the party, two nights before finals began, we all gathered in the lounge, decorated a limp-looking tree that we weighed down with lights and tinsel. There were cookies, brownies, hot choco-late, the Supremes singing Christmas carols, and everyone was red-faced and cheery.

When it came time to open the presents, just as it happened during the name picking, Suzie unwrapped her present before I did. She read the card, and I leaned over, seeing Pepa's handwriting. "Ohmigod!" I exclaimed as she let out a gasp and looked up at a grinning Pepa, standing in the other part of the room with Perry by her side. They looked lovely and flushed, and I wanted to shrink. The gift was a set of makeup enclosed in a shiny blue case.

"Wow!" she said, her face looking like it was trying to find an expression. "Thanks, Pepa!"

"You're welcome." They didn't hug each other as happened with everyone else. In fact the person I chose engulfed me with a squeeze when she opened a bottle of her favorite perfume I gave her.

Then it was my turn. I was handed my present, ready to receive something I knew I'd never use. Except that it was big and flat and wrapped in light blue tissue. A record. Wow. I opened the card, and there in the handwriting I recognized from our memo board, but certainly not from all the messages I had gotten that week, was written:

For having been such an angel this fall, it is only right that you receive this gift that will remind you of Saturdays in New York and our friendship. Love, your-no-longer Secret Santa, Perry.

All the breath went out of me, and I looked over at her. "I had no idea!" I giggled. All that distancing which had been going on for so long and now this.

"Open the present, silly!" she giggled back along with everyone else except a silent Suzie.

It was an LP soundtrack of *Breakfast at Tiffany's*.

"Thank youuu!" I leaped up and ran over to hug her.

"You're welcome!" she mimicked back. Pepa even managed a smile at me, her arms crossed in front of her.

"I had no idea!" I repeated.

Perry laughed, "That was kind of the point!"

But she knew Suzie, who had given her a white scarf with a matching headband, had her name. I remembered Suzie grabbing it at the Accessory Place when we went shopping together at the mall, and she sniffed, "This'll have to do. It's all acrylic, so there."

"Thank you, Suzie," Perry said loud enough for all to hear. Everyone looked at the two of them in anticipation of some scene.

"You're welcome, Perry," Suzie said without looking at her.

I focused on the album cover of Audrey Hepburn, cigarette holder in hand, sitting amidst a display of Tiffany finery, her brown eyes looking large and elfin-like. It was out of print, so Perry must have gotten it at a used record store. Going through all that trouble. Nothing in me could stay still.

And the break couldn't have come soon enough. I knew Perry, Pepa, and Suzie were going to New York, and I had images of us walking down lower Broadway, shopping bags in our hands, the smell of chestnuts and honey-roasted peanuts in the air. Or maybe even coming to my house for a sleepover. The only niggling thought was how things were going to be on the family front, this being the first Christmas without Grandma. But I kept pushing it aside as I looked at Perry sitting next to me on the bed, her teeth nibbling on her thumbnails while she talked a mile a minute about the upcoming break.

"You *have* to meet my friend Andrea from last summer," she told Pepa and me. "She's like the coolest person. She just finished doing a shoot for *Seventeen* and lives in this really great apartment with all these other people. Plus she told me she can get us on the guest list at almost any club!"

"Cool!" I replied like an overeager teenybopper.

Perry continued, "And, she's got some great drugs." She said this as if she were talking about her clothes.

"Cool," I repeated. The two girls glanced at me for a moment, and then Perry continued on about Andrea and that maybe we'd meet Joel the painter from NYU and various make-out sessions. "But I haven't spoken to him in ages," she said, clearing her throat.

When Christmas break arrived, I gave everyone my number. Suzie was staying at the Plaza and promised to call. Pepa and her parents were staying with some family friends on Central Park West, and Perry, when not in New London, would be staying with Andrea down on East Fourteenth Street. She gave me her number. "I'll let you know when we can all go out," Perry said, her green eyes direct and alert. And then she left without saying goodbye to me. I figured it was because at the time I was taking my bio exam in the gym. But there wasn't even a note on the Garfield memo board on our door even though that could have had something to do with Suzie's continued silent treatment toward Perry. I returned home the next day, a knot of unease in my stomach.

Kim and her family were in London, so there went any plans for her to meet my new friends and see my new life. There was a Christmas card from Chris, who wondered how school was. He loved Los Angeles, was living in Hollywood with his wife. He had gotten a couple of gigs working in the studio with some big name artists, and his life sounded very cool far away from his life in New York.

His questions nagged me. How's you're teacher? (*Wasted*). What are you working on? (*The same Telemann from what feels like ages ago.*) How's you're composing? (*Composing? I need to look that word up.*) I knew I was supposed to write him, but I felt like I had nothing to say except talk about my social life, and I didn't think that would interest him.

Unable to contain the excitement in my voice, I told Mom and Dad that all my friends from school would be in the city and that they had invited me to visit them. Mom's eyes lit up in a way I had hardly seen before. "That's terrific! I was so afraid, with Kim gone, you'd just shut yourself up in your room." She then trilled on about how wonderful Fieldings was for me, wasn't it just kismet that Perry was my Secret Santa, and once we changed my piano teacher for the following term, life at Fieldings would be perfect. Despite the daunting feeling of working with Mrs. McGowan this winter, I grinned back at Mom, knowing that finally she was happy for me. In all this exhilaration, I called Perry, but she wasn't home, and so I left a message. I wanted to invite them out to my house for a slumber party, knowing Pepa would have no choice but to accept, and then if she saw where I came from, maybe she'd warm up to me, see me for who I really was. Plus, how could she not want to meet my mom?

But the phone remained silent and still for me. I leaped, of course, every time it rang. The day before Christmas Eve, I tried again, leaving a message with either her mother or her sister, who had a voice so familiar it almost made me think I was talking to Perry, who was trying to pretend to be someone else. They told me she was "visiting some friends in New York" and would be back the following day. I was given the number where I could reach her.

So she went into town without me. She said she'd call. Maybe it was a last minute thing, a problem with Andrea, which was none of my business. I called the number, the 212 area code making it sound like Perry was in the midst of a fast-paced, noisy life. And here I was in the quiet dullness of 914 Westchester County.

"Hello!" came a half giggly, too-loud female voice over the receiver.

I swallowed. "Yeah, is Perry there?"

"No, she's not!" The voice remained giggly, and I heard her chastise whoever else was with her. "Gimme that!"

"Uh, when is she coming back?"

"I have noooo idea!"

"Can you tell her Jess called?" I left the number but it was greeted with such quick "uh huhs" that I wondered if this person had written anything down. She hung up before I could say goodbye.

I had a vision of Perry out on the wet, cold streets, banging around town with the rest of the holiday crowds. Was she shopping? Seeing Pepa? I figured that could have been it, and maybe that was why she didn't invite me. But I only felt worse.

Dad was smart not to ask me about my friends. Mom, not so much. And when I grumbled my *nos* at her, she tried to comfort me by saying, "Well, this is a crazy time of year," echoed by a quick smile and glittering eyes, which made me wonder if she hadn't been crying recently over Grandma. I wanted to go and hug her, feeling thrown by her vulnerability and yet wanting to be close, but she always gently pushed me away saying she didn't need any emotional scenes, thanks. And then there was the nervous laugh.

But on Christmas Eve, as we all sat in the living room after dinner, the knot in my stomach grew larger and tighter. I looked at the tree, large and heavy by the sliding-glass doors, its tackiness oppressive with all its tinsel and primary-color lights. I usually loved staring at it. Now it just looked like a big bug.

"Jess," Dad said from the couch in front of the fireplace decorated with a garland of pine boughs and a crèche. "Chin up, OK? They'll call." I could barely see his eyes for all the twinkling lights reflected in his glasses. Mom was snuggled up next to him, encased by large, beige pillows. Her face had a wistful happiness with her eyes slightly tilted down, her platinum blond pageboy gracing her jawbone. Grandma's lack of physical presence hung in the air along with the dry heat in the house. This was one of those moments, like the ones I had that past summer, of wondering what it'd be like to lose a parent. It always stopped me in my tracks whenever that thought came to mind, and it was too uncomfortable to seriously contemplate. My brother, though past his Westchester cowboy act of this fall, didn't help matters with his penetrating gaze toward me. I knew what he was thinking, wondering how I could have mixed myself up with Professor Wagner's daughter. *You don't know what she's really like,* I wanted to hiss at him, *so stop staring at me like that.*

Christmas was quiet. It was just the four of us and a little snow to cover the brown-and-gray landscape, but not enough to make it look like the mythical Christmas I was expecting. The phone rang off the hook, but most of the calls were for Mom and Dad. It all made me want to rewind our lives and go back to when we went to the city to spend Christmas with Grandma, or go up to Massachusetts to visit Dad's parents. But we were in Cross River. Mom and Dad were alone together a lot, laughing softly in the kitchen as they prepared the meal, or sitting, as I so often found them, on the couch in front of the fire, silent and pensive. In the meantime I was filled with desperate, hushed anticipation.

The day after Christmas, Tom took me into the city with him to visit a friend of his who lived in Chelsea. Either Mom and Dad had said something to him or else he genuinely felt the need to cheer me up. On the drive in, he comforted me, avoiding any snide references to Perry. "Jess, this happens all the time. People rarely keep their promises about getting together over break. If we lived in the city, it'd be different, but it's kind of hard when you live out of town. It all gets screwed up and inconvenient."

I wanted to take him at his word, but deep down I knew something else was going on. And I had a feeling so did he.

We got to his friend's brownstone, and Tom introduced me to his college friend whose name went right through my head and out the window the minute I heard it. I was too distracted, wondering if we were going to run into Perry when they started talking about where we were going to go. What movie we were going to see? Would she be in the theater? I asked Tom's cherubic, olive-skinned friend with the most beautiful black, wavy hair I had ever seen, if I could make some local calls.

I flew to the phone, pounded out Perry's New York number, kind of hoping she would be in Connecticut. It also occurred to me that this friend of Tom's might know Perry. I hoped not.

The same loud voice answered, "Yeah?"

"Hi, Andrea," I thought I'd impress her by knowing her name. "Is Perry there?"

"Nope, she's gone out to see some friends!" The voice banged in my ear. There was something about her energy level that made it seem everything in her life was an exclamation point.

My heart thudded to the ground. "Do you know when she's going back to Connecticut?"

"Uh, not until next week. Who's this?"

"Jess. I called earlier."

"You got a number? I can leave her a message."

"She has it. Thanks." I hung up, too afraid to call Suzie at the Plaza to find out she was out as well.

I attempted to put on a good face when it was announced we were going to play pool. I never played it before and didn't think much of it. But the idea of being that concentrated and focused and sharp would help get my mind off my so-called friends. The pool hall was dark with the clacking sound of pool cues, a loud, pop rock–sounding band playing on the jukebox, and the smell of cigarette smoke. I watched these tall, older guys, muscular and T-shirted, at a nearby table take easy shots, knocking the desired ball into the pocket and saunter around their table as though playing pool were like breathing. It was the same way with Tom's friend, and Tom wasn't so bad either. Both helped me out with my shots, and I found I enjoyed the smooth precision of the game.

I had just finished shooting a red ball into a pocket when I felt a light tap on my shoulder. I jumped a bit, turned around expecting to see Perry, but instead there was a tall, dark figure with black-and-red hair. He grinned at me, his blue eyes shining in the fluorescent lights over each of the tables.

"Hey!" He sounded somewhat more Italian.

"Hi!" An absolute yet inexplicable thrill went through me.

He kissed me on both cheeks, smelling of cigarette smoke and some kind of aftershave, and pointed to our table, shrinking cigarette in hand. "What are you doing here?"

"Playing pool! Why aren't you in Italy?"

He laughed, and it sounded nice and full like a hug. "My family is here for the holidays. Florence gets too touristy, and we have relatives who live here, so we decided to be here." He put the cigarette back in his mouth, took a drag, and then offered it to me.

I never smoked, but I wanted to learn. Except not in a public place where my inexperience would make me look dorky. I shook my head.

I introduced Leo to Tom and his friend, realizing I sounded breathless. "I'm just learning how to play. I suck."

"Me too," Leo replied. "I don't know what I'm doing. My brothers do, though." He pointed to two brooding guys across the room—one with brown hair, the other blond—who saw us and showed me their hands in greeting, their intense eyes piercing me. "Tiziano and Pietro. They are older."

"Are you the youngest?"

"Yes."

"Me too! Plus I wanted to tell you this, and I always forgot. My grandmother had a villa in Florence. We still have it. I mean, she died and left it to my mom." The words were tumbling out helplessly; I had no control over what I was saying. And I hated the way I mentioned Grandma's death in such a blithe manner.

"Really? That's great! So then you have to come to Florence. It's the best city in Italy."

"My Italian teacher, Mr. Mazzi, said the same thing about Bologna. Everyone says that."

He nodded with a smile. "Yeah, but Florence is where it all began—the language, the culture. Even Rome has nothing on us!" He chuckled as he took another drag and let out a white trail of smoke. "How was your Christmas?"

I shrugged. "Yours?"

"Good. A few nights ago I saw Perry and Pepa and that other girl at a party, and I was wondering where you were."

I froze and it took me a few moments to get the words out of my mouth. "You saw them? Did you talk to them?"

He pulled out another cigarette and offered me one, somehow knowing I was ready, and I accepted. He said, "I'm not really friends with them, so it was, hi and then bye!"

He lit our cigarettes and told me in a whisper to inhale as he held the flame up to mine. He knew I was a virgin smoker.

I inhaled, but not too much. I didn't want to OD on the sharp-tasting smoke. It slightly burned the back of my throat, and I vowed not to cough, but my eyes welled up. He must have seen the look in my eyes because all he said next was, "Don't worry, you'll get used to it," gesturing to the cigarette.

I gave a sheepish smile.

"You want to come hang out with us?"

"Yeah! Hang on." I ran over to Tom.

"Call Mom and Dad," he said. As he nodded his head to the cigarette, he asked, "How do you like it?" He took it from me and inhaled to show me how it was really done, and I pretended to ignore him.

"It's OK."

To Mom I made it sound like I saw Perry without saying her name. I figured if I told her I was to spend the day in the big, bad city with three Italian men, she wouldn't be that permissive.

I left the rest of the game to Tom and his friend, and Leo did the same with his brothers, and we hung out by the bar drinking cokes. When Tom was about to leave, he asked for Leo's number in case of an emergency, and, being the great master of subtlety he was, slapped me on the back, winked with a smirk, and left with his friend. People talk about how parents are embarrassing, but you never hear about older brothers.

Leo taught me how to French inhale. I noticed how droopy his eyes were, and it was kind of sexy. His nose was big, but it looked noble. I watched the wisp of white smoke fly up from his small, curly lips and into his nostrils. I couldn't wait to learn.

I wanted to talk about Perry, but never got the chance. All Leo said about the party was that it was thrown by someone who graduated from Fieldings the year before, and there were a lot of drugs, and, "It was really boring. Everybody was on ecstasy, and I wasn't because I hate that stuff. As we say in Italian, *due palle*, which literally means, two balls."

I burst out laughing. "I study Italian. We haven't learned that yet."

"Great! I am leading a conversation class in the spring, and so I can teach you all that stuff! Those are the important things to learn, you know." And he went on reciting other phrases, all Florentine slang, making me laugh harder. I gazed at his eyes, the long lashes, the way the bottom of his eyes sagged just a bit, as if they were weighed down by emotion.

His brothers finished their game, and we all went to a restaurant to meet their cousin Sylvia, a makeup artist, for a late lunch. Dark, small, and pretty in a way that reminded me of the garnets my mom sometimes wore, she greeted me with two kisses on my cheeks and told me, in her slightly accented English, how pretty I was. We settled into lunch, and discussion flipped between Italian and English midsentence. I loved listening to all of them speak. I couldn't understand anything of their indecipherable accents filled with lispy *t*'s and devoid of hard *c*'s. But I didn't care. Just being surrounded by them in a restaurant that served French-American food and feeling my head swim with red wine the brothers slipped me and cigarette smoke made me lose contact with the rest of the world. They all teased me as I tried to recite the slang they taught me. Tiziano promised by the end of the evening, I would be speaking like a true Florentine. "It is the best dialect in Italy."

"What's the worst?"

"Roman," they all chorused and they all ended up mimicking an accent that sounded like a guttural barnyard.

By the time we got out of the restaurant, it was late afternoon, and I knew it was time to head home. But Leo wouldn't hear of it, and Pietro looked at me with disdain and demanded, "Why do you want to go back home? It's boring!" He took a drag off his twentieth cigarette.

I tried to explain that my parents were expecting me, but all I got in response was, "They expect you tomorrow."

"Go call them," Sylvia patted my back. "You can spend the night at my apartment. You can sleep in my room!"

I called Dad, who was taken aback when he found out I wasn't with Perry. Assuring him everything was OK, that Leo was a friend from Italy who studied with Mrs. McGowan, that there would be older females around (I handed the phone to Sylvia), I got his OK and a request to speak to Leo.

He told Dad who he was, how we knew each other, making it sound like we were best friends and yes, there would be parents around, beefing up the story to convince Dad that everything would be OK. He then gave the phone back to me.

"Is it OK?"

"Sure," Dad replied. I felt a smile in his voice. "Call me tomorrow to let me know what train you're getting in on. Have a great time, but don't stay out too late, OK? Even though I have a feeling you're going to." We said good-bye, and I looked up at the three Borghi brothers and Sylvia, and felt like I had just grown two inches and that something inside of me, once closed and cramped and taking up too much space, had opened up and escaped. I was lighter and freer.

That evening we went out first for a late dinner at a sort of bistro-y place down in Soho called I Tre Merli. Sylvia loaned me a black silk tank top and a jean jacket to wear for the evening along with a pair of worn, but elegant flats. She put makeup on my face and made me look older but not too old, with my eyes bigger and my mouth more sensuous. I couldn't help but stare at myself in the mirror. It was like an ideal version of me at twenty-one. I flashed forward to a future life I would have here in the city at that age—almost done with college, living in a small apartment somewhere downtown, writing songs for some funky off-Broadway musical or jingles for commercials that left everyone humming. That sounded nice and comforting. I'd have a boyfriend, and for a second, I thought of Leo, but then wiped that out of my head. I already knew him, and it wasn't like I had a crush on him or anything.

All the guys greeted me with, "Mamma mia!" (I didn't know Italians really said that. I thought it was some cliché). I felt adored, not like prey. At the restaurant, I sat at a table, squeezed between Leo and his cousins and brothers as they all yapped back and forth to each other, Leo trying to translate whatever they said to me and occasionally putting a big, trench-coated arm around me, as we sipped red wine and smoked cigarettes. I only smoked one since it was all I could handle. I looked around the dark, high-ceilinged place where everyone was dressed in black and the women wore big, dangly earrings, while the men wore ponytails. Loud, Latin-inspired music played over the speakers, curly cigarette smoke rose from the tables and bar. I sat there, legs crossed, sipping my red wine and practicing my French inhale. *This is how my life is going to be*, I thought and smiled to myself. Later, we headed off to the club Limelight, where we swooped in like birds and settled ourselves (well, Leo and I did; the rest hung out at the bar) onto the pounding dance floor. Loosened up by the alcohol, it took me no time to move to the music that was a lot cooler than what I heard at dances at Fieldings.

And then I saw her. She stood next to an oblivious Sylvia and Pietro, who were talking to each other at the same time. Perry was with a tall girl with short, bleached-blond hair, a very large mouth, and a very skinny body clad in skin-tight black-and-white striped pants and a mock sleeveless turtleneck. Perry, looking short and almost squat, was in an oversized, black oxford, black and yellow striped leggings, and black boots. I slowed my pace down as I watched them. The two were gazing around the room, making occasional comments, looking jaded and pissed off. Then Perry and I locked eyes, but just for a moment, a look of horror crossing her face before she caught sight of Leo, who was too concentrated on bouncing around to even notice. I turned away as I saw Perry lean in to her friend Andrea, the human exclamation point, who had answered the phone the two times I called.

I grabbed Leo's arm, "She's here."

"What?"

I guided him off the dance floor and over to a corner at the opposite end of the cavernous, black space. "I saw Perry."

"Go say hi!"

He was so oblivious. "I can't. She looked at me like I was ..." In that very moment, every emotion that I had been holding back escaped in a rage of sobs. Everything—Perry deliberately blowing me off, the realization that my friends weren't really my friends, and at the bottom of it all, Grandma. I wanted to be back in her apartment, telling her everything that happened, listening to her commiserations laced with wit. I wanted Mom to be happy again, or at least accept my hugs. I only had one large crying session in the bathroom for about two hours a week after Grandma's funeral. But this was the only time since then I had allowed myself to cry.

Leo's face became confused and he pulled me towards him, holding me as I sobbed into his sweaty, warm T-shirt. He guided me to a nearby chair, sat me down on his lap, held me while I sobbed, and asked me why I was crying. He patted my hair, rubbed my back, tried to get me to look at him and explain.

But I couldn't answer. I sobbed as loud as I could, hoping Perry would see me, come over, and apologize. But she didn't because it was a ridiculous fantasy. I knew it was over.

*   *   *   *

I told Dad what happened when he came to pick me up at the train station the next day. I was heavy and bleary from too much crying, wine, and the two cigarettes. We had woken up late, Leo falling asleep on the floor right beside my bed after holding me. My ears rang from the music, and I could still feel the memory of Leo's sweaty T-shirt against my face. My eyes were swollen, my head exhausted.

"I had some wine at dinner, we went to a club to go dancing," I explained to Dad. "The Borghis are really nice." My voice was hoarse and weary. I stared straight out the window.

"Hey, what's going on?" Dad asked. "Did you have fun?"

"I did until I saw Perry at the club. She just looked at me, and then started talking to her friend, and I cried." I made it sound so simple, even the act of crying.

Dad bit his lower lip. I wanted him to give me something, some kind of psychological insight at the very least. Instead, he put his arm around my shoulders, drew me to him, and said in a calm voice, "Jess, I think it's time you look for some new friends. That Leo guy seemed to show you more respect than any of your three friends. You need people like that in your life."

"Dad, it's not like I can just stop being friends with Perry."

We were in our driveway now. He parked the car and turned to me and said, "You need to ask her what happened. You do not get treated like that." His jaw was set, and his eyes bore into mine.

That was all he said, and he got out of the car. On the one hand, it was the first time Dad was that direct and affectionate with me. *You do not get treated like that.* The fact that my dad actually was actually telling me I was worth more was a new thing.

And yet, it was so short. A few words, a caress, and then *bang!* it was over. We were out of the car, and Dad was talking about plans for New Year's Eve—dinner in the city with the director of *Sunrise* and his family. It was the same old Dad, the one I had known from when I turned thirteen, all anxious and distant, hiding behind his glasses after a brief moment of tenderness.

CHAPTER 7

I've Got a Feeling

The night I returned to Fieldings, the campus looked as though some giant came along over vacation and decided to stretch everything out and flatten it. The air had a solid, January chill, but there was no snow, just frozen, brown ground. It reminded me of my images of the Siberian tundra, and I wanted to be back in my warm room at home on my bed listening to my music. A damp breeze from Long Island Sound went right through my bones, and I stared at Kurtzman, which stared back at me with its turrets and lit windows, sternly telling me to go inside this instant. It made me think of my first lesson with Mrs. McGowan, which was to start the following day. I hadn't practiced that much, if at all, over vacation.

An icy prickliness crawled through my chest. I had returned from break without ever having heard from Perry. Leo called on New Year's Eve to wish me a Happy 1986, which made me a lot happier than I'd expected. Just the thought of going into a year that ended on an even number made me feel like things were going to get better. Yet the image of Perry looking at me in the club stayed in my head even as I tried to rationalize it away. Maybe she was drunk and didn't recognize me, or she was really looking at Leo. Maybe she was appalled that I was hanging out with him, and therefore didn't want to come up and say hi. We'd talk about it and clear it up once we saw each other. I had a scenario going on in my head where I'd tell her, "Hey, I think I saw you at Limelight." Then she'd say, "That *was* you! I'm so sorry. I was completely wasted that night, and I didn't want to embarrass you. I was so rude!" We'd talk about break, why she was unable to call me. Everything would be fine.

I marched up the steps of Kurtzman and into the commons room to see if my friends were among the girls who were splayed out on the orange couches watching a program about the space shuttle *Challenger*. I rushed up the stairs (as best I could with a big duffle), threw my stuff in our room, and knocked on Perry and Pepa's door, through which I could hear a falsetto, male voice singing against a pounding base.

The voice sang out about making girls go crazy as I swung open the door and saw Perry, Pepa, and Suzie in a tight circle on the pushed-together beds. The only light on in the room was Perry's white desk lamp, twisted up so that the bulb shone directly onto the ceiling giving the room a pastel, yellowy-pink glow. The three girls looked up at me at once with unsmiling faces, and my heart almost crashed through the floor. Perry and Suzie had clearly mended their ways.

"Hey," Perry said. No smile. No surprise. Pepa turned the corners of her mouth up to show me she was trying to smile but her eyes looked flat, and Suzie, too, gave me a small smile, but at least her sleepy brown eyes looked warm.

I could feel fear in the room. Everything was just a bit too still, the girls' bodies a bit too frozen. A bell went off in me. It was as if a piece of me was in the room before I arrived, a piece they could criticize and dig their nails into.

I plopped down on the bed, disrupting their little meeting and tried to ignore the growing lump in my throat. "How were your vacations?"

"Fine," they chorused. Glances flew all around, and then there was silence.

"What'd you guys do?" It came out like a demand, my lips pursed.

Perry let out an audible sigh. "Kind of boring. My whole family is going crazy over my sister Alison's wedding. My interview went well, though."

"Interview?" I asked.

"Internship at a magazine."

"Did you get it?"

"Yup."

"That's great!" It was as if we were running lines for a play. I didn't bother to ask what magazine and turned to Suzie. "How was yours?"

She took a breath. "Really busy. We went to see a lot of museums and stuff."

"What about Marcus?" I turned back to Perry.

"He was up in Vermont with his family. I told you. No outsiders allowed." She then added quickly, "I did see him right before he left, though only for two seconds."

Everything was heavy and suffocating, thanks in part to the invisible cloud of Obsession hanging over the room. In an effort to push it all away, I looked right into Perry's eyes and said, "I think I saw you at Limelight."

"Really?" Her heavy-lidded eyes were insulting. I knew one of my scenarios was not going to play out.

"Yeah, I was with Leo, and I thought I saw you next to this tall, blond girl."

She sneered, "What were you doing with Leo?"

"We ran into each other in town, and he invited me out with his brothers and his cousin." My eyes and throat stung, and it was almost too hard to talk.

All three girls exchanged looks, and Perry remarked, "You must have been really desperate to have someone hit on you."

It was all I could do to keep myself under control. "He's a really nice guy, Perry."

"Sorry, Jess. I wouldn't trust him as far as I could see. You don't know him like I do."

"I didn't know you knew him that well," I replied primly.

Pepa then burst in, "OK can we just stop it with the little drama here? It's so boring!"

"Exactly," Perry nodded to her friend.

I had no reason to stay, so I announced, "Gotta go unpack. Leave you guys to your business."

There were no objections as I headed out the door, feeling all eyes on me. I went downstairs because how the hell was I supposed to unpack, knowing next door I was being slandered? The purple-gray linoleum danced in front of me as I trotted over to the phone near the lounge and called Leo's extension, but he wasn't around. I decided to watch some TV.

Christa McAuliffe, the teacher and the first civilian to go into space, was being interviewed, and I sat in an empty chair to fix all my energy (and suppress all my tears) right onto her. I didn't listen to a word she said because my mind was in a little spin cycle of Perry, Pepa, and Suzie.

Christa's face was clear eyed, enthusiastic, and pretty. *She is probably one of those teachers everybody loves,* I thought. *Allowing her students to call her by her first name. Maybe she pushes them in their studies, but she isn't a bitch.* It was so funny how her face on TV grounded me like that. Looking at Mom's face on TV, whether as her characters, the twins Sheila and Shelby, or as a supermom spraying blue window cleaner in her sunny kitchen, was bizarre. I never got used to it because I would remember the days of those long shoots, and how I missed her and wanted her to be home. There was always the knowledge of the real Mom as I watched the fake one on TV, and I couldn't separate the two.

When the interview was over, I got up and knocked on the Segals' door. Marcie knew Perry the best. She could help me out with her.

I breathed in the smell of baby food and baking bread in their apartment, as Marcie, who had just put Bryan to sleep, let me in. "Hey, what's up?" she asked. I wanted to think she was my Christa. "How was break?"

I sat down on the couch that was covered with a white sheet. "OK."

"Yeah?" She tilted her head towards me and sat down near me.

I swallowed. "I'm having a weird time with my friends. It's like they don't like me anymore, and I don't know what I did." I explained about break, although carefully leaving out the scene at Limelight.

Marcie sat back in the chair, the baby monitor on the coffee table in front of us making a whirring sound. It reminded me of the kind of sound I would hear in the lobby of Dad's office from the noise maker lying on the floor, preventing anyone from hearing whatever troubles his patients were pouring out. She kept biting the corner of her lips, and every so often would glance around the room, like someone was listening. When I was done, she shrugged and said, "Well, I think you're reading too much into this. Perry may just be in a bad mood. I don't think it's worth it to get all paranoid."

"I'm not getting paranoid!" Or was I?

"Jess, just because you're their friend doesn't mean you need to be included in everything." She stretched and yawned. "You have no idea what they might be going through. After all, they've known each other a lot longer than you have."

She had a point, but still it was all a slap in the face, this unsympathetic response from her. My cheeks burned, my jaw hung open, and I tried to nod.

"I mean if you want, you can talk to her, but just don't be clingy. Nobody likes clingy."

I got up to leave with a small, "Thanks," feeling worse than I did before.

The trip up to my room was long and dreaded. When I walked in, there was Suzie, unpacking. *Nobody likes clingy.*

"So, you and Perry made up!" Already I got off on the wrong foot with the forced cheeriness in my voice.

"In a sense," Suzie gave me a timorous smile. "We all just got together over break, and at first had this fight, and then we made up, and we were just talking about that when you came in."

"Leo said he saw you guys at a party."

Suzie stopped for a second and then continued unpacking. "Huh. Really? Was he sure it was us?"

"Yeah," I nodded slowly as I watched Suzie slam her drawer shut.

Pepa barged in and announced that she and Perry were heading over to Hilliman before dorm closing. She directed this all to Suzie, who grabbed her coat and said, "Bye!" Pepa slammed the door shut behind them.

I wanted to have big, heaving sobs so that Perry would hear me and come in to comfort me. But my eyes were dry, my throat less tight. And there was nothing for me to do except go to bed early.

It took me a good two hours before I fell asleep.

"That's so great you and Suzie are friends again," I told Perry the next day as I caught up with her after first period. I wanted her to believe I was really happy for them.

"Well, you know what a little ecstasy can do to a girl," Perry said, smiling to herself.

I should have known. "She told me about the party and stuff."

"Yeah, it was fun," Perry said, with no eye contact with me.

I took a breath and launched into my prepared speech. "I can't help but get the feeling that you're pissed off at me for something. I tried getting in touch with you over break, and I never heard from you."

Perry stopped in her tracks and turned to me. "Would you stop being so self-centered? God, you gotta take everything so personally!"

My mouth fell open, but I was too stunned to respond.

She continued, "I had a lot going on over break, OK? Don't think that everything I do is because of you. That's your problem. You have to take every slight and turn it into something personal. Jesus Christ, the world doesn't revolve around you!"

"I'm sorry," I managed to whisper. We were silent as we marched up to the math and science building. "I still ... want to be your friend," I said, having a hard time getting that phrase out.

Perry turned to me and gave me a withering look. "You're so dramatic!" And then she stormed on ahead of me to her class.

She was absolutely right. I knew it. If I had a tail, it would have been stuck between my legs for the rest of the day, at least. I figured my selfishness ultimately put Perry off and besides, I had no idea what happened with her over break. She'd tell me when she was ready—when I wasn't so clingy. At least she didn't say we were *not* friends.

And then, to top off my whole afternoon of shame, was my first piano lesson with Mrs. McGowan. I walked to Bartlett Hall that cold, cloudy day, feeling my feet heavy in the wet snow that had just fallen. I opened the door to the practice room I was instructed to go to, and saw her next to the piano. She greeted me with a little more warmth than I expected. She wore a beige turtleneck sweater with a jade necklace dangling around the neck, her black-and-white hair pulled back into a tight little bun. She was as tall and thin as ever and commanded the room in a way that reminded me of Katharine Hepburn in *The Philadelphia Story* very patrician.

"Welcome back," she said to me, smiling, and then opened a notebook and started writing in it. She motioned to the piano bench. "You can sit down and begin your scales."

I crept over, sitting down on the bench as if it were some valuable heirloom. I knew things weren't right. Whenever I met with Chris, I felt like the bench was as familiar and comfortable as an old armchair, that it was mine, and I belonged there. Now I felt disconnected and shifted around to feel more secure, but it did no good. The lack of practice over break haunted me as I started on my scales, and my hands stiffened up the minute they hit the keys. In fact, every muscle in my body clenched into a tight little fist. I flubbed up on the first round, shouting out these desperate, "Sorry's!" until Mrs. McGowan told me to "Stop, stop, stop!"

I did. I stared at the shiny, black key cover perched above my fingers.

"First of all, relax," she said. "You'll get nowhere if you play like that. They're just scales. You're not tackling Rachmaninoff. And secondly," she paused, her face all inquisitive angles. "Did you practice over break?"

"A bit," I answered, turning warm.

"Do you have a piano at home?"

"Yeah."

Her voice was frighteningly quiet. "OK. I know vacation time is for getting away from your studies, and that's fine. However, I do not believe that it carries over into your piano playing. You need to do at least half an hour every day in order to keep those engines running. Once you stop, it takes that much longer to start back up again. If you really want to learn, you must practice. It's as simple as that. You cannot use vacation as an excuse." Every sentence was said with the same tone: going up a bit in the beginning and then coming down at the end.

I wanted to cry out for those rainy Saturday mornings with Chris, and all the improvisations we did. "That's OK, Jess. Keep going. Don't think so much!" Firm corrections. "Don't plunk your hands down like dead weights in this section. Light! Gentle! There you go, kiddo!" But that was also because I had practiced a lot then.

She got me started again on the scales, slowing me down, and then had me do finger exercises the likes of which I hadn't done since I worked with Chris. I remembered being able to handle them when I was with him, but it had been so long ago that my fingers had no idea what to do anymore.

"I'm sorry," I said every time I messed up.

"*Don't* apologize!" Mrs. McGowan's famous bark finally came out. "Just go back and do it again. We have a lot of work to do, but we'll get through it as long as you are willing to."

She pulled out Chopin's *Waltz in A Flat Major*. I knew this piece by heart, I'd heard it so many times, but I had never played it. I was about to place my finger on the first A, when I was interrupted. "Hang on. Before you start pounding away, let's go through the beginning and hum it out loud." And so I tried, but my voice came out all wobbly and weak.

"I can't hear you. A little louder, please."

I was about to say, "I'm sorry," but stopped short and hummed again. It was tempting to just hum along by memory, and it took some willpower to follow the uneven tempo, the *pianissimos* and *fortes*.

"Good," she mumbled when I finished. "Now take a good look at what's written. Don't just see the notes, but everything else." She had me repeat what I saw, and as I kept talking, my voice got stronger. I kept my eyes glued to what I was doing as Mrs. McGowan leaned over me with rapt intensity.

"OK," she nodded and gave me the corrections, which weren't as nasty as I had imagined.

It wasn't until the end of the lesson that I realized I was still at Fieldings, and that I had forgotten about Perry and company. I was loaded down with homework and wondered if I was going to be able to get through it all. But when I walked out of Bartlett, I felt almost giddy, and the ground felt light underfoot as I walked over to Kurtzman.

That feeling, along with the gentle waves of Chopin's piece that sang softly to me in my head, stayed with me until I entered the commons room. *Sunset* was on, Pepa and Suzie, along with the regular soap crowd, were watching a scene that had just ended with a closeup of Mom's face looking pensive, and then a cheery commercial for diapers came on. It was probably a scene she had shot over Christmas which brought back a rush of memories, the thrust of which clenched my whole being: being blown off and then saved, so to speak, by Leo. My mother and missing my grandmother. Playing pool and smoking. Looking twenty-one and then bawling my eyes out in Leo's sweaty T-shirt. I never really liked seeing Mom on TV, anyway, so I went upstairs to do my homework. Anything to get my mind off what was going on.

Nobody likes clingy, Marcie's words echoed in my head.

At dinner, I made a concerted effort to relax by slumping in my chair, maintaining a small smile on my face with my eyes hooded. I listened to the gossip about people I didn't know. I noticed Perry sat up straight and barely looked at Marcus. She was probably still pissed off at him. *Oh well, that's their problem.* I had nothing to contribute and instead became the laid-back listener, the easy-going member of the bunch. Soon everyone wouldn't see me as clingy but as the cool, independently minded friend whom everyone looked up to because I dealt with everything that came my way with total equanimity. I would surprise them all. I paid attention to my breathing because Dad told me that was a great way to relax. Marcus looked at me, his eyes twinkled, and happiness flooded over me, but I tried not to show it. And for the first time, I thought about my piano playing, and how one day, I wanted all of them to hear how good I was.

With this in mind, I ran over to Bartlett after dinner and got straight to work on the Chopin, making sure I barely touched that first note before gradually sliding into the rest of the piece. I tried to let the tricky tempo take me instead of making everything sound forced, feeling as though in the beginning I was holding my breath and then letting go, like riding a wave.

CHAPTER 8

You Still Believe in Me

Soon after I decided on this new attitude, Perry got sick. I knew there was a stomach bug going around, but she was sick for more than the usual twenty-four to forty-eight hours. I couldn't blame her for the horrific mood in which she ensconced herself. Despite saying to her, "You'll get over it soon. It's just a really harsh bug," in my best quasi-stoner voice, I felt like I was talking to a grumpy cloud who refused to acknowledge my presence.

Throughout what seemed like weeks, Perry was exhausted. She hardly ate, complained of nausea, and slept a lot. The only thing she managed to communicate to any of us was A) "I feel sooo gross" and B) "I'm gonna take a nap, so *nobody* bother me." She sat through dinners stirring tea and not making eye contact with anyone, not even a confused-looking Marcus.

Suzie said Perry probably had mononucleosis and that she should go to the infirmary. Perry groaned at her, and Pepa sighed like a nervous mother and gave her roommate worried looks. Gymnastics practice didn't go so well either. Perry was captain of the team, the season just starting, but she slept through two practices. And when she did make it, she complained she wasn't able to do anything with any grace at all.

Then it all fell apart. It was a clear, crystalline, freezing day. Suzie, Marcus, and I sat in the Fletcher dining room, finishing up our pizza slices while some people were gathered around the TV in the commons room watching the *Challenger* take off. I was desperate to see it, but Suzie was taking her sweet time on her after-lunch orange pekoe tea. Perry had gone to the infirmary after spending the morning in the bathroom barfing and then moaning on her bed.

I nudged Suzie to get up so we could watch the *Challenger* lift off. I glanced at Marcus to see if he was going to join us, but he was talking to a tall brunette about skiing in Vermont, and he asked her how it felt to be captain of the cross-country ski team this year. As he continued grinning up at this girl, Suzie and I left to go watch the TV.

The sun poured into the commons room. I made my way over to the group gathered around the TV and saw the two girl pals of Leo's. They were on the floor, the Asian girl peeling an orange, nodding to the frizzy brown-haired girl, who was laughing. I looked around to see if Leo was in the room, but there was no sign of him. Suzie and I sat next to Mitch Greene, Perry's editorial nemesis, whose glasses showed the reflection of the windows behind the TV. He greeted us and asked where Perry had been, but we were interrupted by a gasp.

And there it was. It looked like this strange firework that had billowing clouds of white smoke against the deep blue Florida sky. I thought it was an unusual sight for a takeoff, although I had never seen one before. The room was silent except for a dull boom on the TV and the shuffling students coming in for lunch. Everything just stood still for one moment. The room was filled with widened eyes and dropped jaws. The frizzy-haired girl, who had been clutching a can of Sprite, let it slip out of her hands, and it made a *thunk* on the floor.

"Something happened," Suzie muttered, and she sat down on a chair behind me.

"What was it?" I asked Mitch, the sun-filled windows reflecting in his glasses, so I couldn't see his eyes.

His cherubic mouth opened, and he was silent for a second. "It just exploded." He looked over at me for help.

The room remained still except for the occasional "What happened?" and "Ohmigod" from latecomers. I swallowed, everything in me going quiet.

I knew I had witnessed an historical event the enormity of which made me feel like I didn't know what to do. I looked at my watch and slowly realized English was starting in five minutes. I told Suzie I was leaving, and she nodded, saying, "Yeah. I gotta go smoke a butt. I'll see you later."

The campus was subdued, and the sky was too bright. It didn't feel real. I wasn't in Florida, I didn't know Christa. I saw it happen on TV, so maybe it didn't happen, but I saw it on TV, so therefore it did happen. Maybe no one was in the shuttle. Maybe Christa missed the flight. I had a vision of her running out to the launch pad, all suited up in her heavy gear, helmet in hand, waving to the rocket as steam and smoke billowed out from underneath. And then it went away. Since I didn't see her, and I didn't see her get in, maybe she wasn't in it. Maybe she went back home to Maine with a huge, "Whew! Glad I missed that!"

But she was on it. Special reports aired throughout the day on TVs all over campus. I skipped religion to watch the constant replaying of the explosion, the spectacular white cloud, with a tail shooting high into the sky like some kind of disorganized comet. But after a few minutes, I'd had enough and decided to go to the infirmary.

Just as I was about to leave, in walked Perry, her face all swollen and haggard. "Perry," I said, but she passed by me and up the stairs. I followed her asking if everything was OK.

"Does it look like it?" she snarled at me and slammed her door in my face.

I went to my room and lay on my bed, hoping for a knock on my door but knowing it wasn't going to happen. Maybe she, too, had heard the news, and it was all she could take. I heard soft knocking and sat up like a bolt only to hear Suzie's muffled voice and Perry's door shut. I couldn't make out what they were saying. I knew that going in would only give me the same reaction I got the night after Christmas break.

I couldn't taste my food during the quiet dinner and tried to ignore the dark looks Pepa and Suzie, sitting on either side of Perry, were giving everyone else. Perry mumbled something about having to go outside to think. Pepa, Suzie, and I went up to our rooms.

In the stairwell, I asked, "Suzie, what's up with Perry?"

But before she could answer, Pepa roared from behind, "Don't you *ever* sit there and stare at Perry like that again! You are the most nosey, insensitive person I've ever met."

A shock wave went through me before I uttered, "I was just asking. I'm her friend, and I have no idea what's going on."

"It's OK," Suzie said, not looking at either one of us. "She's just going through a hard time. Pepa, you didn't have to yell at Jess like that. She *was* only asking." I wanted to hug Suzie.

Pepa snorted and ran up the stairs ahead of us.

"Thanks for standing up for me," I said to Suzie as we entered our room and threw ourselves down on our beds.

"She's just upset about what's going on with Perry. Don't worry about it," Suzie replied to the ceiling, her hands behind her head.

"Can you tell me what's going on?"

Suzie put her gold necklace into her mouth and started to gnaw on it. "I think Perry's gonna have to tell you."

"Why?"

"'Cause she's pregnant." Then Suzie gasped when she realized what she had done. "Damn! OK, now you know."

I had this image of Perry's belly with a prone little Perry inside. At Katonah, there were plenty of rumors about pregnant girls, but this was the very first time I had actually known someone who really was pregnant. To me, Perry had taken yet another giant step into adulthood, and I didn't know whether I felt younger or older.

"Do you think I can talk to her?" I asked.

"Why are you asking for my permission?" Suzie picked up one of her stuffed Garfields and started poking it in the eye.

Whatever had been swirling around me now settled into a sort of resolve, and without a word, I got my parka and left the room.

Perry was outside, sitting on the bench nearby the bus shed, hunched over and staring at the ground in front of her. A streetlamp illuminated her like a spotlight.

"Hi," I said as I reached her. I sat down, and the bench felt chilly and splintery.

"Hi."

"What's up?"

"Just going through a rough time."

"You can't tell me?" *Clingy, don't be clingy.*

She looked up and met my eyes. I was trying to find something familiar about her, something that would remind me of last autumn. But I realized, seeing Perry's pale face, her dead, hollowed-out eyes, that something had broken between us. I didn't want to believe it though, and so I pushed it out of my mind.

"I, um, got myself into some pretty deep shit over break, Jess. And I don't think you'll understand." Her voice was lower and hoarser than I had ever heard it before.

"Why?"

"Because this is something that I don't think you've ever encountered before with a friend. Maybe I'm wrong, but I don't think so."

"Try me." I kept my voice steady.

"Jess, you need to realize that a lot of things in this world don't work out the way we want them—"

"Just tell me."

She continued to look out into the dark night. "I'm pregnant. It happened over break." There was a long pause as she made circles in the dirt with her foot. "We were being really dumb."

There it was, this image of her and Marcus in the midst of this sexual embrace. An icy warmth went through me. "I'm really sorry, Perry." I put my arm around her, thoroughly confused by my feelings because I also felt her admission to this grave mistake put her on a human level with me. "So what are you gonna do?"

She clicked her tongue, indicating I had asked some insipid, unnecessary question. "Get an abortion, obviously."

I tried to ignore her tone. "Marcus knows, right?"

After a moment she turned her head up to me and said, "Yeah. He figured it out. But it's not his. That's the part he hasn't figured out."

I opened my mouth, and it took a long time for the, "Ohh," to come out. "So whose is it?"

She cleared her throat. "Joel's. The painter I told you about from last summer. We got together over break. And we didn't think." Click, click, click went her sentences like some telegram.

"Does he know?" It took forever for the words to come out, I guess because I wanted to sound like something other than those hushed actors on *Sunset* when they were talking about this.

"Nope."

"You're gonna tell him, right?" But I already knew the answer.

"Nope. He'd kill me." Her voice shook, and it made me wonder just what kind of character this guy was. Street-tough and sadistic in his paint-spattered jeans and distressed-leather jacket, his artistic temperament raging while Perry cowered in the corner of his dark studio apartment or his cavernous loft. Perry, small and vulnerable. "I just want to get an abortion to get it over with."

We were silent. Is that how easy it was? I couldn't imagine an abortion to be anything less than traumatic. Just "get it over with"? How could you do that with something that was alive in you? That you helped to create, albeit accidentally? Perry's nonchalance had me looking at her, trying once again to find something familiar about her, but all I got were the lyrics to the Beatles song that talked about looking through the person they thought they knew, like a little life sound track.

"But I'm gonna need some help." Her voice interrupted the song.

"If you want me to accompany you to the hospital or wherever, absolutely!" Maybe then I'd see the trauma in her surface. She was in too much shock now to think about it.

"That'd be great, Jess, but um, I was actually talking about financial help." Then she looked right at me, and part of the old Perry returned. She was squinting at me, her mouth swollen. I felt my jaw open, and my mind raced.

She took a breath. "The thing is, I do not have the money for this, and there is no way I'm going to tell my parents because then they'll forbid me from seeing Marcus or even going to the city this summer. We tried Pepa's parents, and you'd think they'd have all this money to throw around, but they are total nitpickers with her, and her mother must be psychic or something. It's like she knew it was abortion money, for some reason she knew it was for me, and since they're super Catholic, forget it. And, Suzie's parents are away on a cruise, so we can't get in touch with them."

"I'll try my parents. I can't guarantee anything." Except a firm *no*.

"Cool." She nodded, sounding more secure. Was she expecting this answer all along?

If I were pregnant, I would have been terrified to call my parents. It also occurred to me that Dad wasn't going to be too hip to the idea of helping to pay for Perry's abortion especially after what happened over break. Of course I wanted to be the one to come to Perry's rescue. To be crass about it, it would gain some points for me. But I also wanted to see her indifference towards the whole situation go away. I knew she couldn't have the baby, yet to say it felt weird to help pay for killing something was an understatement. I lay in bed that night, staring up at my *Breakfast at Tiffany's* poster in the dim light, the muscles in my mouth so contracted, my tongue took up my whole mouth.

But I steeled myself nonetheless, and Sunday night, with Perry by my side, I called my parents, instead of having them call me, which was their usual pattern.

"Oh! Hi!" Mom sounded surprised as she answered the phone.

"How's it going?" I started casually.

"Fine! We saw your friend Kim. She says hello. She seems very happy."

I had just gotten a letter from her Friday wailing about her banishment from her group just because she made a comment about a girl's sweater that was completely misinterpreted.

"Yeah, I got a letter from her."

"Good. Write back."

"Jess?" It was Dad, and I didn't know whether to be relieved or scared. "Is everything OK?"

He knew right away. Whereas Mom remained in her own world, this man saw right through everything.

"Yeah," I made small talk about piano, classes. And then an idea hit me. "My piano teacher wants me to work with this woman who's really good at teaching composition because she said I have a lot of promise, and she wanted me to develop a piece."

Perry's stare jumped out at me as I waited for one of my parents' responses.

"Mrs. McGowan can't teach you?" Dad asked.

"No," I said too quickly. "She really wants me to do this, and so do I." I made up the name of the teacher, where she studied.

Mom made noises of curbed enthusiasm. Dad continued in a voice loaded with doubt. "Well, this is great, but, um, how much will this cost?"

I gave them the price, and told them to mail it to my account here at school. That would be more convenient. The phone receiver became sweaty under my palm as I had to deal with the long pauses in conversation. I had never lied to my parents before so why should they doubt me now? And they agreed to it. The money would be sent as soon as possible. I hung up the receiver, which felt heavier than before.

"You're a really good liar, Jess," Perry said with a slow nod yet a look of disbelief.

"I think it was the only way." I scratched my left thumb just to give myself something to do.

She gave me a small smile. "When's the money coming in?"

I continued to fidget. "Soon. They're gonna wire it."

"Awesome."

"Jess, pay attention! What is wrong with you?" snapped Mrs. McGowan during my lesson the following afternoon. I almost fell out of my seat. I was going through the Chopin, my mind on the money, the phone call, the lie, and the abortion instead of the keys, the pedals, and the notes. My hands shook. All the work I had done pretty much disappeared, and it sounded as if I was playing the piece note by note, and that was it.

"Sorry," I looked up to see Mrs. McGowan give me a look that was a mix of worry and irritation. "I'm distracted." *I'm guilty*, I wanted to say. When I walked into my lesson and saw her at the piano waiting for me, the reality of what I had done the night before, including her in my lie, hit me.

"I can see that! Now please, let's not waste each other's time! You've got a lot of work to do on this, and you can't have your mind wandering."

That was when I wanted to tell her everything that was happening. I knew my lessons demanded every ounce of strength, and I was somewhat surprised to find that aside from that afternoon, I usually managed. The focus, the concentration, the ability to leave the rest of the world behind once I darkened the doors of the practice room was the rule I stuck to for every lesson and practice. Mrs. McGowan wasn't as enthusiastic about my playing as Chris was, who threw around praise almost every Saturday, while pushing me harder. She was more of a drill instructor, having me play each note over and over again until I got just the right touch, and I thought I was about to go crazy. She wasn't nearly as mean to me as I was afraid she'd be, but this was the first time she snapped at me.

I continued with a rather uneventful interpretation of what we had worked on so far with the piece, and then she went through the exercise books and assigned next week's homework and snatched the Chopin to make further notes. When finished, she put down her pencil. "OK. Sermon on the Mount Time." Dread sprang up in me. "I know things in school aren't easy, and you have a lot of other stuff going on. But that doesn't mean you can come in here and fall apart. Maybe other teachers let you get away with spacing out in class or not doing your homework—"

"I *was* doing my homework," I peeped.

She shook her head slowly, and her eyes widened. "You're not focusing as much as you can. And I am not going to let you get away with it. It's not going to help you either, Jess. My feeling is that you're in this room not just because your parents said so, but because there's a large part of you that wants to be here. Am I right?' She leaned forward and waited for an answer, which came as a lame nod from me. She was right, and I was mute, either because I was entranced by her interest or scared by what she was going to say next.

"I've been teaching for a long time, and I can tell the difference between the students who want to play and the ones who are told to, and you are the former. Therefore, you cannot be lazy. The music needs to feed you, and even though a lot of it feels like a chore, and you'd rather dwell on your other problems, this," she tapped her fingers on the black mahogany, "is something you cannot lose. Sermon over."

I never got a lecture like that from Chris. I sat stock still, staring at the keys. They seemed like the voices of various people in my life, particularly my parents. "I lied to my parents." It came out even before I was aware of it.

"Oh yeah? About what?"

"I lied to them about money a friend needed for an abortion." There was no way in hell I was going to mention the phantom teacher, whoever her name was. I had already forgotten it.

The silence was like the silence that greeted me over the phone the day before with my parents. I couldn't even hear Mrs. McGowan breathe.

"You know, if you tell the truth, it will take a lot off your shoulders." She was calm, controlled, and deliberate. Neutral.

And now that I had told her, I knew there was no way I was going to be able to get through future lessons, much less practice, without telling my parents. I had a hard time getting up from my seat, collecting my books, and leaving.

"I'll see you next time," she called after me as I left the room. She sounded gentle, yet timid, as though there were something else she wanted to tell me but didn't know how.

I called Dad at his office once I got back to Kurtzman. I was so zoned out, yet focused on my job at hand, that I just went to the phone in the lounge without considering the importance of privacy in this matter. I waited until it was ten minutes to the hour so I knew that he would have some free time between appointments.

"It's Jess," I said when he picked up the phone.

"Hi, sweet pea. You want to tell me something?"

There it was again. He just knew.

"I lied."

I wanted, but didn't want, to know what was going on with his face at that point. "So what's going on, honey?"

"It was for Perry, not for me. There is no other teacher."

"What's up with Perry?" It came out like a grumble.

"She got pregnant, needed money for an abortion, and didn't have it. No one else could help her, so she asked me."

I could just feel all this information going over the wires and settling into Dad's brain. Finally he said, "Look, Jess that's very generous of you, but you didn't have to lie about it. But it's not like your mother and I can throw money like that around. And an abortion. I mean, you know what a big deal that is."

"I know, I'm totally aware." But I was having a hard time conceptualizing the whole thing. Pregnancy was one thing. But an abortion? I barely knew what the process was.

"And the important thing is, I hope you aren't doing this to save the relationship."

Of course I am, I thought, and at the same time also thought, *Are you kidding? I'm not that stupid.* "No! She was just in a lot of trouble."

"So why'd you lie? You were afraid we weren't going to give you the money if you told the truth?"

"Well, obviously."

"No, we would have. Look, it's great that you want to help others out, and if she really is in trouble, and no one else can help her, fine. But don't expect a lot in return for this from her. Things like this are more complicated than just handing out a check. You see what I'm saying?"

"Yeah, I know." Even though I couldn't articulate it, it was like the word *abortion* and the actual event itself hung like a heavy shadow over me. While Dad was describing the emotional outcome of all of this to me, I couldn't help but feel a little angry that Perry got herself into this kind of trouble.

After telling me he'd have the money wired that afternoon, he said, "And I'm glad you came around and told the truth, Jess. Thank you."

"Thank you, Dad. I really mean it. I'm sorry."

"It's OK. Let me know how it goes, OK? I want you to call me as soon as you can."

When I hung up, there was Pepa only a few feet away on one of the couches, nursing a Diet Coke and eyeing me. She had heard the entire thing, and after that, it was clear she was going to refuse to speak to me. Later on, even if she did glance at me, it looked like something in her was about to break if she were to hold her gaze for more than a few seconds.

I was all set to go to the clinic with Perry early Saturday afternoon. I had gotten the money out of my account piecemeal throughout the week so that the bursar wouldn't be too suspicious as to why I was withdrawing all this cash. By Friday, it was all in an envelope on my bureau with Perry's name on it. And that night Perry swiped it off, saying, "Fan*tas*tic," and nothing else. And then, when I went to meet Perry on the porch, she was nowhere to be found. Neither was Suzie. I heard Marcie's voice in her apartment and bolted over to the door and knocked a little harder than necessary. Marcie arrived, her forehead looking tense.

"I was wondering where Perry was because I was supposed to meet her."

"She went into town." I knew Marcie knew the truth, and I couldn't understand why she could not at least admit it to me.

"Oh, right. I forgot." I waved at Marcie, whose eyes went through me, and walked away. Craving a cigarette, I ran down to the butt room, far away from her.

Not before checking the sign-out sheet, however, to find Suzie and Perry's names. Pepa's was not on it. I wondered where she was and figured the most logical place would be the butt room, giving me second thoughts about going down there. But then I figured it would look cowardly if I didn't at least go see her given Perry's dilemma. Maybe she needed someone to talk to, but I kind of knew I wouldn't have been her first choice.

I entered the room where whitewashed walls were covered with graffiti and saw Pepa, puffing away on one of her Marlboro Lights.

"Hey," I said as I walked in.

She took a drag and gave me a stony look. Her hair was caught up in a lazy bun, strands of dark brown wavy hair framing her face. She was wearing a tight, mauve turtleneck sweater that showed off her curves.

"How come you're not at the clinic with them?" I was trying to sound casual, but the image of Perry lying in a hospital bed getting rid of a baby with my parents' money made it impossible. I swallowed a couple of times to try and relax the muscles in my mouth.

"I have to work on a chem lab project with someone in half an hour, and I couldn't get out of it." Her voice was prim as she took another drag, her pinkie slightly raised from her hand holding the cigarette.

I sat down, my nerves jangling, dying to bum a cigarette and knowing I shouldn't. "Pepa, are you mad at me because I paid for the abortion and you couldn't?" The minute that came out I wanted to inhale it back again. My whole face pulsated with my heartbeats.

Pepa let out a mirthless laugh, and then her eyes flashed at me like two wild, brown dots. "Jess, you kill me!" I never got used to hearing Pepa's use of slang in her lilting accent. It seemed to make it harsher, less glib than it would if it had come from an American. She uncrossed, then recrossed, her legs the other way, tilting back a bit. "That is so base! It's not that. What you did was such a form of brown nosing—"

"Perry *asked* me to, Pepa. What was I supposed to say? No?"

She lasered her eyes into me, her mouth pinched like she wanted to smile, but she couldn't. "But I'm sure you were happy to be the one, weren't you?"

"God! Why do you hate me so much? You've always resented me. I've tried to be your friend, and you just turn your nose up in the air. I haven't done anything to you!"

I heard the hum of electricity, running footsteps overhead, and muffled voices. They carried over to the stairwell and came closer and closer, and I prayed they wouldn't enter our lair. Thankfully, they didn't, they just headed out the door to the parking lot.

"I don't know," Pepa said, shaking her head. "I never felt like you're really who you are. You're just pretending to be someone who you think we'll approve of, and I hate that. I hate people who pretend just to be a part of a group. And I also feel like you want to have Perry all to yourself. I mean, I really think you helped Perry out just for her to be on your good side because you knew that you had hurt her feelings." She stubbed her cigarette out in an ashtray.

I almost wanted to heave either with shame or defensiveness. "How did I hurt her feelings?"

A new cigarette was in her mouth and she lit it. The sharp smell of the lit match and tobacco hit my nose. "You accused her of being a bitch, and then there was that total flirting that went on between you and Marcus during the hurricane."

I sat still trying to think of what to say next. It all seemed ages ago. "I called her a bitch because she was being one. What, we're not supposed to criticize Perry? And I couldn't help that Marcus flirted with me! You try having someone that gorgeous flirt with you and not do anything back. And besides, nothing happened between us, OK?"

"Maybe next time you should exercise some self-control." She shrugged.

"Look, I apologized to her for calling her out. And the whole thing about Marcus, well, she sure didn't act pissed. And besides, that baby isn't even his." We might as well have been in an ice-cold soundstage, three different cameras on us, lights burning down on the set. I imagined a director calling out orders from the intercom and a stage manager pushing us around. Cut to a close-up and then a commercial break.

She just looked at me, puffing away on her cigarette, refusing to budge. I stood up and looked at her olive-skinned, slightly acne-scarred face. "Forget it, Pepa. I don't think I'll ever get through to you." I left the room.

CHAPTER 9

I Just Don't Know
What to Do with Myself

When I first saw Perry right after she returned from the hospital, she and Pepa were in Marcie's apartment talking to her in hushed tones. I saw Marcie give Perry a hug, and I went to Bartlett to go practice. If Perry wanted to see me, she could come find me.

But instead, that evening I went to the library with her, hoping she'd at least mention something. "How are you feeling?" I asked on the walk over. It was just the two of us.

"Ehh, you know. Not great. But whatever. It's over with, thank God." Her eyes traveled around campus as if she were trying to look for someone else.

"I'm so sorry you had to go through something like that." *I wish you invited me along. Why didn't you?* The unspoken words hung on my tongue.

"Well, just remember, whenever you have sex, *if* you ever do, don't be stupid."

I looked right at her. "What's that supposed to mean, *if* I ever do?"

"Oh, God, Jess! I'm just kidding!" She elbowed me, and I tried to smile. "I'm sure you'll get more men than you know what to do with." Her voice was sing-songy and rehearsed.

"Well, I'm glad I could help you out." How many cues did I have to give her in order to hear a simple thank you?

Apparently she didn't need any because it just wasn't going to happen.

Dad called me, wondering how it went. I told him Perry seemed OK and left out the part about her standing me up and her ungratefulness. I tried to make it sound as if everything was fine, which clearly, it wasn't. Dad gave his spiel about her maybe seeing a counselor.

"Yeah, I'll mention it to her," I replied, envisioning her ripping my head off.

I threw myself into my work. It was as if I had no place else to turn. But sometimes, my concentration was lost. For English, I wrote what I thought was a pretty stellar paper on *Othello* about betrayal and jealousy, but when I came to typing it up, my mind must have been someplace else, because I handed in a paper filled with typos galore, and I got a B+ instead of an A+ with the sole comment from my teacher: *This is a Tiffany jewel wrapped in Kmart packaging.* Italian fared no better because the irregular verbs, the transitive and intransitives, just became a maze to me. But I pushed through; the trick questions on the geometry pop quizzes, the uninspired run-through of Judaism in religion, and the sour smell of formaldehyde from the fetal pig in biology. For gym, I was taking ballet and felt like a robot at the barre. I didn't even care to look at myself in the mirror.

I went to Bartlett every chance I could get. As I played the Chopin piece with its begging quality and constantly changing tempo, I realized it reflected a lot of what I was going through. There were the happy major chords that lasted only a few seconds before the melancholy theme of the piece took over. The notes entered into me measure by measure, and a trance took over in a way that I had never felt before. I loved the question-and-answer quality of the piece, the tension the scales brought to the melody. Sometimes I got a little too carried away with the progression of angrier sounding chords, wondering how many other fellow musicians in the building could hear me. I remembered Chris telling me about watching Keith Jarrett get so caught up in his piano playing that he barely sat down on the bench nor stayed in the same position for more than one note. At the time, I hadn't really understood it. But during those weeks I worked on the Chopin, that image came back to me, clearer than ever.

In English we started *The House of Mirth,* and reading about the plight of the social-climbing protagonist, Lily Bart, made me think that spring couldn't come soon enough when we'd move on to comedy. But I was glued to it, and one evening, having become completely frustrated with the Italian verb disorder that was my homework, I read ahead. I was tucked away in one of the carrels on the first floor of the library, when the bell of the chapel chimed announcing it was ten o'clock and the end of study hall. I gathered my books and left the library only to hear a big voice call out to me. It was Leo, giving me a wide grin, and something inside me let go, like some sort of release. I remembered hearing that he was on the ski team, and that every weekend, he was away at some race, which was why we had hardly seen each other since Christmas break.

I went up to him, not knowing whether to hug him, but before I could decide, he wrapped me up in a hug filled with the smell of cigarettes and cologne. He introduced me to the two girls I had seen with him around campus. Lally was the frizzy-haired girl, and Alicia was the Amerasian. They gave me distracted hellos.

We talked about piano, what it was like working with Mrs. McGowan, whom he called "Anna," and what we were working on. I wanted to forget about my homework and just sit and talk with him forever.

"You have to hang with us sometime." Something in his eyes seemed to crackle with light.

"That'd be great!" I looked at the two girls, who seemed oblivious, wrapped up in two large volumes of *The Reader's Guide to Periodical Literature*. He told me to call him, or to stop by anytime. I didn't care what Perry thought of him; Dad was right. It was time for me to make new friends.

And that's when the shift happened. After our confrontation in the butt room, Pepa smiled at me now. Not big, gushing grins, but the corners of her mouth did go up whenever she said hi to me. But it left me confused, and, although I was friendly back, I was too angry at Perry to make much of an effort over any of these girls.

I was walking through the doors of Kurtzman, thinking about making friends with Lally and Alicia through Leo when all of a sudden, an arm grabbed me around the shoulders, and there was a shriek.

"Whoa!" I exclaimed and saw Perry's face too close to mine with a huge grin and wild, green eyes. "You scared me!"

"I did it! Come on!" Without allowing me to answer, she grabbed my hand, and we went down to the butt room. There, among a few other girls, were Pepa and Suzie.

Perry then gathered the three of us into a little huddle. "It's over, you guys. I finally broke up with him."

Gasps all around, even from the other girls who overheard. I guess I should have expected this given what was going on. I found out through Suzie that Marcus, too, had cheated on her over break. No big surprise there.

Perry's words spun out of her mouth. "I totally had it. He was all upset because I got pregnant, and he knew it wasn't his, and he wanted to know whose it was, and I was like, 'I'm not saying anything. You screwed around with that piece of trash up in Stowe so don't give me the third degree.' And I *know* it wasn't the first time he was unfaithful to me."

"Totally," chorused the two other girls. I bummed a cigarette from Suzie, hoping I wouldn't cough while I tried to light it.

"So now you're a swingin' single!" Suzie raised her hands in the air and snapped her fingers.

"Whoo hoo!" Perry's eyes danced, but there was something tired about them.

The cigarette tasted stale. Quite frankly, smoking wasn't really all that it was cracked up to be. But it gave me something to do, and, superficially speaking, it looked good. It was a cover for these feelings that were creeping up in me; feelings of ambivalence that I realized I had always had about these girls, but now, in light of what was happening at that moment, it was all becoming clearer. And the ironic part was, during this whole conversation, Pepa kept giving me little smiles as if asking for my approval. So this was really the trick to winning them over: acting like I didn't care.

The next evening before dinner, Perry, all sweaty from her gymnastics practice, put her arm around me while I was sitting in one of the chairs watching TV.

"Hey," she said in a creamy voice.

"Hi!" Her greetings of late always surprised me.

She came over and sat on my lap, arm still around me, smile on her face, eyes disappearing, and her voice low. "Listen, I've been doing a lot of thinking, and I am really sorry for the way I've been treating you lately. I was such a shit to you. You've done so much for me, and I kept turning my back on you. Please forgive me, Jess. I also want to write your parents and thank them for their help. I know it's been a long time, but better late than never. So, friends?"

I looked up at her. There was nothing about her that was bouncing around in that frenetic energy. She actually looked OK, calm, and serious. I answered, "When were we not?" *Over Christmas.*

She hugged me. "See? You're so good to me. Thanks, Jess."

And there we were, a quartet. Marcus and Hassan sat at another table (Pepa and Hassan giving each other meaningful looks and reattaching after dinner to make sure the Marcus/Perry split wasn't affecting them). There was no eye contact between Perry and Marcus, even when he was talking to some willowy blond or brunette who always managed to sidle up to his chair now that he was a free agent. I was getting a lot of compliments on my wardrobe from both Perry and Pepa, and in the evenings when we gathered in their room, Perry insisted we play *Breakfast at Tiffany's.* We walked across campus with our arms around each other, making me feel like I was at summer camp. I wanted to ask Perry if she had written my parents, but I didn't want to badger her. Pepa and Suzie automatically offered cigarettes to me without my asking, and I always said yes, just to give me something to do.

And every other Saturday when there were home meets for the gymnastics team, Pepa, Suzie, and I went as faithfully as if we were going to class. Marcie also came along and watched Perry with a pleased look on her face. Marcie, I soon found out, was a gymnast herself here at Fieldings, and when she said, "although nothing compared to Perry," I had a feeling she was going to say that. As I sat next to Suzie on the bleachers at every meet, I was unable to cheer Perry on with the same gusto as everyone else. I tried to clap, to yell out her name, but everything felt forced, my hands barely touching, my voice sounding fuzzy. The meets were like a three-ring circus. One girl on the unevens, one on the beam, the vault, or the floor. I thought about how much more fun I'd be having if I were alone in Bartlett practicing my Chopin waltz, cleaning up, perfecting every phrase.

But even when she wasn't doing anything, it was hard to take my eyes off Perry. She seemed more electric than ever. Her blond, wavy ponytail bounced with every nod and gesture. Her eyes were bright. She moved quickly, with a kind of focus that was so strong, it pulled my attention away from all the other swinging, leaping bodies around her.

She rubbed chalky, white resin between bandaged palms before she mounted the unevens. Her black leotard, with its white-and-blue stripes climbing from her hips, under her arms, and then out to her wrists, gave a false sense of elongation. Even standing motionless on the mat, arms extended over a slightly tipped-back head, she seemed even shorter. Muscles bulged in her thighs as she landed her aerials, flips, and her beam and unevens dismounts, her back arched making her resemble a human banana. She sometimes seemed so solid as to appear inanimate. Her movements were quick and reminded me of one of those squirrels in a Disney cartoon with little, overstylized hand flicks and curled toes as she prepared for each new trick. She was still pretty, but her jaw was too set, and her eyes glinted at the judges in an almost conspiratorial way. As soon as we had congratulated Perry, I ran off to the music building and settled into the piano. I banged out scales and arpeggios, trying to drown out any thoughts. And once I was thoroughly warmed up, I was ready to tackle Chopin like a surgeon.

And during those weeks before spring break, my time was taken up with work, piano, and hanging out with the girls. I only caught fleeting glances of Leo, and we always promised we would see each other, and it always fell through. He was away for races, I was with my little group. Always ending up in Perry and Pepa's room every Friday and Saturday night, listening to the same music, drinking soda, making plans to make margaritas, and go to one of the dances trashed, which never happened because Perry was too exhausted, sometimes saying she was still nervous about running into Marcus. That would lead us to talking about guys and sex. Suzie was "hanging out" and fooling around with a wrestler named Matt, who seemed to be more into playing hackey sack and listening to tinny Grateful Dead bootlegs than anything else. Pepa was still cozy with Hassan, and Perry wanted one last fling before she graduated.

"I know someone who has a crush on you!" Suzie cooed to me one evening.

"Who?" I was hoping in vain to hear the name of a friend of Marcus's or even Leo, but I knew those names would never be mentioned.

It turned out to be a fellow wrestler named Eric, who was friends with Matt and had the same penchant for hackey sack and The Grateful Dead. He was squat, stocky, and not bad looking, but his eyes always looked half shut, and his lips were always wet. *Eww.*

"You guys would make such a cute couple!" Perry cried.

"He's not my type."

"You don't know him!" said Pepa. "I think it would be great if you went out with him!"

"Exactly!" Suzie followed. "Then it'd be me and Matt and you and Eric." Matt was a lot cuter than Eric and a lot taller, and even though he wasn't my type either, I'd still be mooning after him.

"Aww," said Perry, and she rubbed my back. "Jess, I think it'd be good for you!"

So the four of us, that following Friday evening, went to see a movie playing on campus. My conversation with Eric was filled with, "Wow," and, "That's cool," and talking about wrestling meets and how I had to see The Dead in concert. Meanwhile, Matt tickled Suzie, which led to long, messy kisses that seemed to happen out of nowhere. And, like a déjà vu from the year before in the mall parking lot, when the film was over, we went out in pairs, and Eric planted a slobbery kiss on me, his hands almost patting my back, like he didn't know what to do.

On Monday morning, I saw him walk to class with his arm around a girl from my geometry class. He was off my hands.

But Perry and Pepa thought it was terrible. "What happened? I thought you guys would be perfect for each other!" Perry exclaimed in the butt room after study hall.

"How? We have nothing in common."

"Yeah, but you both like music," Pepa said, and I looked at her nonplussed.

"Those guys are kind of boring," Suzie interjected. "All Matt wants to do is get stoned and have sex."

"And that's a problem because …?" Perry said sarcastically.

"There's more to life than that," I said.

"Not much," Perry murmured.

"Frankly, I cannot take hanging out and listening to The Dead and watching these guys play hackey sack," Suzie said. "Matt's cute, but please. And I don't think Jess was all that thrilled with Eric."

I chuckled, "Thank you, Suzie."

Pepa and Perry looked at us, their bodies still. "Well, that sucks," Perry replied almost more to herself than to us.

Talk turned to college. Pepa was nervous about Cornell and Amherst, wondering what she was going to do if she didn't get into either one. "It would be so embarrassing to end up at my safety school!" she groaned. Her safety school was Connecticut College.

I was painting a vine on the wall, and when I heard this, I lifted up my brush and stared at Pepa. "It's a good school, Pepa. So what? I mean, my brother goes there and loves it." I looked over at Perry, waiting for her to admonish Pepa for her tackiness.

But Perry just exhaled cigarette smoke, leaned against the wall, and said, "You're getting way too neurotic about it. I mean, you'll find out when you find out." She sounded weary and hoarse. Unlike the rest of us, she had no books surrounding her, which I thought was a little odd.

"Well, it's easy for you to say. You have your future all wrapped up. Everything's settled."

"Whatever." Perry took another drag.

"I'd be really excited to go to a place like Princeton," I said. "You sound like you could care less." I knew next year was the year that counted, so to speak, for colleges and wondered if Princeton was going to be an option for me. But somehow I felt pulled to NYU or Barnard/Columbia, seeing myself more in the throngs of New York City than on some lovely campus with elm trees and Gothic buildings.

"I'm just looking forward to getting out of this place," Perry spat the words out. "I mean, Pepa, this is our last spring break! We're going to Florida. It's gonna be awesome, but all you can talk about is college acceptances. That's like a month or so away. Relax." She leaned back against the wall and sighed. Her face looked pale and hollowed out, even her freckles seemed faded.

CHAPTER 10

Wouldn't It Be Nice?

I went home for vacation high on the compliments Mrs. McGowan gave me on my Chopin piece when I played the whole thing for her the day before I left. I kept summoning up Keith Jarrett as a sort of muse as I went through the piece with all its waves of emotion, and let the rest of the world, and at times the watchful eye of my teacher, melt away. When I was done, she smiled and said, "Nice." That was it, but it was enough to let me know I didn't wrap the Tiffany jewel of Chopin's composition in Kmart packaging, and I was so overcome with satisfaction, I continued grinning on my way out of Bartlett.

In the safety and solitude of my own room at home, the memory of the piece floated through me, and I started thinking about Marcus. Not just flitting thoughts, but all out obsessions that put me in a sort of alternate reality. It probably helped that my friends were far, far away this time. Suzie was three thousand miles away in California, Perry and Pepa were way down south in Fort Lauderdale. It all helped make my fantasies come alive in a way they hadn't all year. No sooner was I under the covers the first night home, then my mind jumped right over to what it would feel like to kiss those lips, soft and passionate in the way his mouth would just take over mine. It never felt the same way twice when I imagined it, and that was why it was so much fun. Then the following night, "we" moved on to fooling around. But something always stopped me short before I could really get into my fantasies. Every time my hands ventured down between my legs (my hands pretending to be Marcus's) Perry's face would light up in front of me, and all the lust, excitement, and rushing blood came to a halt. So I had to do the rest in my head.

I felt like I was in some kind of odd dream state at home. I was going to be turning sixteen years old at the end of vacation, and just as I felt at the start of the new year, I thought there was something magical in turning sixteen—sweet sixteen, sixteen candles. It was as though I were about to climb out of the dingy, smelly start of adolescence and go into the more romantic, mature part. I started a poem, albeit only three lines: *You find yourself an open road/in front of you seems paved with gold/ What once was green has now grown old.* And then I fell back into fantasizing about Marcus. It was so much easier, and it felt a lot better.

I listened to endless amounts of Beatles on my Walkman, while in my fantasies, I ran into Marcus in Greenwich Village. He'd see me first, call out my name, completely surprising me. His outfit always changed, sometimes he was in a jean jacket and white T-shirt, other times a big, off-white, cotton fisherman's sweater. We'd be a little shy with each other at first, not knowing what to say, and then he'd invite me to have a cappuccino with him. We'd sit and talk for hours at some café, finally getting to know one another. He'd tell me how much he loved *Abbey Road,* and how as a kid, he spent time alone in his room listening to it, which was exactly what I used to do.

The conversation didn't really go anywhere beyond that. Every time I listened to "Something" and the hazy, lovely "Across the Universe" I was sent off into a neverland of being in Marcus's arms while John Lennon's dreamy voice sang about how nothing was going to change his world. I started composing a piece, a homework assignment from Mrs. McGowan for spring break. Even though the last time I really worked on composition was with Chris, I knew that given all the work we were doing on improvising with exercises and pieces of music, Mrs. McGowan was nudging me toward working on a piece. As I improvised on the chord progressions of the major scale to get me started, along came the Lennon and McCartney rip-offs I had begun ages ago. I wondered if I really wanted to go back to all that old stuff, feeling chagrined at hearing what were surely juvenile-sounding melodies.

Given my state, and imagining having Marcus right there next to me as I was writing, our legs brushing up against one another, gave me inspiration. The first and the last line of the poem I started came back to me along with their rhythm. The piece started off with a bass line in a minor key, very simple, like a launching pad. And then my left hand started with a progression of chords playing against the bass, which gave the piece a begging, wistful quality, something I seemed to play a lot of lately. The lines of the poem fit right in: *You find yourself an open road/in front of you seems paved with gold.* But I didn't want the whole piece to sound like that, so I immediately played some major chords that gave the piece a more determined mood.

I spent little time in the city. Katonah was having their spring break as well, and Kim was down in DC on tour with the school choir. Ever the loyal letter writer, she told me all the exciting stuff they were doing in the choir, in the theater. They were doing *West Side Story.* Fieldings would never do a musical because it wasn't "real theater." She told me how in her bio class they went to a hospital and saw a real cadaver, and about all the projects she was doing for her other classes. There was a vitality to her descriptions of school that I couldn't compete with. It was why I never wrote back, which made me feel guiltier with each postcard, letter, or card.

My birthday fell on a particularly blustery March day, towards the end of break, the kind of day where winter is just beginning to give way to the little warm gasps of spring. I arranged to meet Mom for lunch and then spend the day wandering around town. Then we'd go home and celebrate my birthday. Tom's vacation didn't coincide with mine, so he was still at school. As I headed across town to meet Mom at the TV studio for lunch, I suddenly had the sensation of being home. I was sitting in the big blue and white cross-town bus, with its tinted windows and blue, slippery fiberglass seats as the bus rocked and rolled gently on its way through Central Park to the Upper West Side. Everything felt comfortable and easy. The trees with their buds beginning to show at the tip of their branches, bending over the big stone walls on either side of the street as we passed by Tavern on the Green. *I am now sixteen years old,* I thought as I saw the majestic-looking apartment buildings lining Central Park West and imagined my future here in the city. This time I'd be living in a sprawling apartment in the very neighborhood we were driving through. I'd have written a number of pop songs for successful artists, and Marcus would be my live-in boyfriend. I wasn't sure what he'd be doing, but that wasn't the point. Evenings would be spent going to openings, screenings, and whatnot, weekends wandering around downtown, checking out flea markets.

Suddenly I stopped fantasizing. I didn't want to go back to school. Fieldings felt more like a vise on my awakening than anything else.

When I arrived at the TV studio, there was a thin, bespectacled security guy at the front desk. He greeted me, saying Mom was on the soundstage. I went downstairs to the overly air-conditioned green room to wait for her, and no sooner had I entered, then busty, blond Karen, who played Mom's slutty daughter, bounced over to me in a pink, fuzzy bathrobe and gave me a squeal and a hug. At the

Christmas party last year, she had been decked out in a light blue angora sweater that matched my sweaterdress so much she shrieked, "We're like the Bobbsey Twins!" In her tight leather mini to match, she led my deliriously happy brother to an embarrassing (for me) make-out session in the freezing December night.

"Jessica!" She sounded like a dog whistle. "Happy Birthday! Look at you! How's boarding school?" Her face was caked with stage makeup, but I could tell she had been out late the night before since her eyes looked a tad puffy.

"Great," I responded, sounding as though I meant it.

"I hear you've made a bunch of grrreat friends! I'm so happy for you!" She sort of jerked my shoulder around.

"Yeah, I like it there." I tried to give her a serene smile to make her relax, since she was grasping me a bit too hard. Then, with great relief on my part, Karen's scene was announced over the intercom, and in an instant, she bounced away from me, quickly saying, "Gotta go!" and blew me a kiss.

"Jesss." I heard a greasy, familiar drawl. Ewww. It was Leif, *Sunrise*'s hunk. He sauntered out of the makeup room, his wavy, brown locks lacquered in place and his powdered face a rather unnatural tan. A leering smile crept around his lips and eyes. I thought about Pepa and Suzie and wondered what they thought of him. They never mentioned him because it was *verboten* to talk about *Sunrise* in front of me, a rule Perry made.

He approached me, slowly putting his arm around my waist. "Can I give you a birthday kiss, my Sweet Sixteen?" and before I could answer, he gave me a light, cool kiss on the cheek. Everything inside me revolted. There are guys who just feel *dirty*, no matter how little you know about them.

"Thanks," I said, trying to politely pry myself away from him. I looked around for Mom, who was supposed to be finishing her scene any moment.

"We missed you."

"Wow," was all I could say. Some of the extras who were sitting on the couch in front of the TV looked up and snickered in commiseration with me.

"Did you miss us?" He almost whispered in my ear.

I stretched my arms and yawned in an effort to push him away. "I really missed my mom."

"Awww."

I wanted to toss my breakfast. I made myself look at him, straight faced and no nonsense, and said, "I think your scene has just been called. If I were you, I'd get your ass onto the soundstage."

He raised his big, mousy brown eyebrows at me in shock like he had just been caught doing an illegal act, which in a sense, was not too far off.

"Right," he said as he rushed off, practically bumping into Mom, her hair and shoulder pads all pouffey. She kissed me, giving off the powdery flowery smell of makeup, and brought me into the makeup room where she reclined on a big black chair as Helga, one of the makeup artists, spread cream all over her face. Helga wished me a happy birthday and congratulated me on my treatment of Leif. Mom gasped, "What happened?"

"Nothing for you to worry about. Your daughter just knows how to take care of herself," Helga replied, wiping off the cream.

"Well, I knew that," Mom chuckled as she patted my arm. I watched her in the mirror, which was framed by big moonlike lightbulbs. I wasn't entirely convinced by her response; she sounded too distracted by wanting to have her makeup off and get out of the studio.

When she was done with everything—wardrobe, getting her script for the next day, a last minute chat with the director—we walked over to the Saloon, a restaurant right across from Lincoln Center. Mom liked it because of the Caesar salads, and I liked it because all the staff members wore roller skates. We sat at a table near the window and ordered lunch from a tall waitress with stringy, dark hair and a rushed, businesslike manner. "This is New York," she seemed to say to us, "and I don't care if you're a soap star. I don't have time to make a big deal about it." Although I bet anything she kept the charge receipt with my mom's signature and posted it up on her fridge for all her friends to see (an extra on the soap told me about her "collection" of celebrity charge receipts).

Generic-sounding jazz was playing over the loudspeakers—a saxophone destroying some Motown tune—as the lunchtime crowd bustled along with the occasional soft whir of roller-skate wheels.

"Happy to be home?" Mom clasped her hands under her chin.

"Yeah, I am," I said, nodding back, and this time I meant it. I inhaled the smell of burgers that were just delivered to a nearby table. "I miss it here."

"Well, I doubt you miss Katonah!" Mom said as she let out a little laugh, and I thought of Kim and the familiar scent of the crowded hallways.

"I kind of do," I replied. The waitress came back and plunked down our iced teas.

Mom's head jerked back. "Really? But you seem to enjoy Fieldings! By the way, are you going to get to see any friends who may be around?"

I stabbed the lemon floating around in my tea with my fork and watched various bits of pulp rise in the amber liquid. "Perry and Pepa are down in Florida, and Suzie's home." I poured some packets of sugar into my tea.

"Don't overdo it, honey," Mom said, watching the white grains fall into my glass.

I ignored her and poured away.

"So you're still friends with those girls?" The way Mom said this, I could tell she was trying to sound neutral.

"Yeah, Pepa's been nicer to me, which is a change. And Perry apologized for the way she treated me before, you know, over break and stuff. She appreciated I helped her out with her whole thing."

Mom looked somewhat surprised and nodded her head. "Well, that's great." I watched her lips turn up. "You know, your father and I are so happy you're there. I think it's such a good school for you. You've got a lot of interesting, intelligent people there, and yes, there are people like that at Katonah, but you got so lost. What I like about Fieldings is that it's smaller and more manageable." Mom tucked in a salad made up of prehistoric size romaine lettuce leaves.

I stared at my mother and wondered if she was saying this because she wanted me to stay away at school. And besides, it wasn't as if my reports from school were all that effusive. I only talked about some of my classes and piano. Hardly any mention was made about my friends. In fact, Mom made no mention of the piano playing I had done over break, unlike Dad who told me the night before that I sounded better and asked about the piece I was composing. I sighed. "I don't know. Compared to what Kim is telling me about what she's doing at Katonah, everything at Fieldings, aside from piano, seems kind of dull."

"Believe me, if you were back at Katonah, you'd be saying the same thing. You expect everything to be perfect, and it can't be." She shook her head and took a sip of her iced tea.

Everything seemed spiky about her—the way she stabbed the crisp lettuce, her gleaming blue eyes, even her hair, pulled back in that super tight, little ponytail. I felt like I was talking to a porcupine. She was direct and to the point without any soft edges like I thought a mother was supposed to have. I looked at her, her face that looked a bit too smooth for someone her age, and although I could forgive her for getting work done given her profession, it only made her appear like she had a hard shell. I thought, *This is my mom. She actually gave birth to me.* I continued eating my hamburger as she changed the subject and talked about this summer and going to Florence and to my grandmother's villa that was about to be sold. It was like having a conversation with an acquaintance. I wanted to burst into tears over the whole thing, the realization that this woman sitting across from me who was my mother was really nothing more than a foreigner. I was alone, but maybe I had always been that way.

"Can't wait to go," I managed to reply. Of course, part of me wanted to jump up and scream with joy, "We're going to the villa this summer! I actually get to see it!" I thought about Leo, everything in me gearing up in excitement. "I have a friend who lives there."

"Oh?"

"That guy I hung out with over Christmas break."

"When?"

She didn't remember? "Mom, that time I went into town with Tom and ran into this guy, Leo!"

"Is he nice?"

"Yeah," I nodded with a smile, more to myself than to her. "He is."

And that was all I said about him.

When we finished lunch, Mom had a hair appointment, and I went to the movie *Pretty in Pink*, which was playing nearby. I had seen almost every other one of these teen films and loved them, particularly their star, Molly Ringwald, who Kim and I agreed could just stand in a school hallway, draped in burlap, and be utterly cool. And in this film, decked out head to toe in vintage, she went way off the meter for me. Her carrot top bob, bee-stung lips, her ability to talk back and handle every situation that came her way with total aplomb made me wonder if I couldn't try and adopt that kind of an attitude. She did not care what people thought, and she had a fabulous wardrobe. Every time she appeared in one of her many pink-themed outfits, I became aware of the skin-tight designer jeans I bought last fall with Kim, now enclosing my legs. I was once sort of like that—maybe not as accessorized or feminine. And one of the bitchy girls in the movie bore a resemblance to Perry, especially her feline green eyes. The character was a lot boozier and sluttier, but it was like watching a creepy facsimile.

And the school in the film reminded me of Katonah—big, busy, and diverse. If Molly Ringwald could find her way through there, well, so could I. She had a caring—if confused—father and a nonexistent mother, and despite all this, she walked across the screen, shoulders back, head held high, the word *capable* written all over her. How she managed to be the breadwinner for her and her father while working after school at a trendy record store was beyond me, but that was Hollywood, and I didn't really care. The fact of the matter was that she could stand on her own two feet a lot more easily than I could. She never sold herself out, even when she was dating Mr. Popularity. As superficial as it sounded, I realized how much I wanted to look like her, have that kind of individuality, and not let anyone, particularly my current group of friends, step all over me. I was now sixteen, and I was not going to be the subject of their whims anymore. Now it was time to stand out on my own. Yet I felt trapped. I was here in the middle of New York City, and I felt a profound ache, a homesickness for the place, even though I hadn't left it.

I came out of the movie, my mind spinning, and headed over to Bendel's to meet Mom. As I made my way through the throng of people on the city streets that late, cloudy afternoon, I got a slightly panicked, strangled feeling in my throat. There was Mom again, sitting across from me at the Saloon, looking like a familiar stranger, negating everything I said. She seemed happy, no, *relieved*, when I seemed happy and frustrated, and uncaring when I wasn't.

What would it be like to go back to Katonah and live at home again? Knowing full well my mother didn't want me there, that she would be much happier if I were away at school? What about Dad? But when I thought of him, there was a small seed of comfort in me. I saw his glasses reflecting the Christmas tree lights on Christmas Eve. *If I were home*, I thought, *I'd have him. And Kim.*

There was Mom smiling, her hair looking more natural than before, under the awning of the entrance at Bendel's. She asked me in a businesslike manner how the film was, and I replied in a small voice, "Good." I felt stabbed in the stomach. I wanted her to take me in her arms and tell me how much she missed having me, missed those Saturdays in the city when I would meet her at the studio. I wanted her to say, as she played with my hair, the smell of her Diorissimo perfume caressing my nose, "I've thought about it, and if you want to go back to Katonah, by all means. OK?" And there would be the smile, the eyes like the blue part of a flame.

But there was nothing, and I asked her if, for my birthday, I could get some of those amazing floral tights that Molly wore in the film, and some dangly earrings—something to make me more feminine without looking like a preppy clone. We found the earrings at Bendel's and then ended up at Bloomingdale's, where we got tights that were somewhat similar to what I wanted and headed back home. I put *Abbey Road* on the car stereo, fantasizing that it was I who had composed the ultimate love song, "Something," a song inspired by Marcus, written for him.

As the end of break drew near, I consoled myself with thoughts of seeing Marcus's face, adding fuel to my fantasies, and carrying me through the rest of the school year.

CHAPTER 11

I'm Looking through You

Once again, I was the first of my friends to return to school. As I stretched out on my bed with my new issues of *Seventeen* and *Rolling Stone*, I felt comfort in my solitude, which was weird given that I expected to feel like the loser who had come back to school too early. A tape that my brother gave me for Christmas played on the stereo. I heard knocks on doors, names called out, and the thumping of feet down the carpeted hallway as more students returned, and the dorm began to fill up. I felt tucked away and safe. No pressure to socialize.

I was reading an article on a girl group's new LP when I heard loud laughter and shouting down the hall. I recognized Pepa and Perry's voices that had a ring of hysteria to them.

"Suzie said her flight may not get in on time. I can't wait to show her this!" Perry exclaimed. I stayed put. *Let them come and find me,* I thought, as I tried to focus on the article. My heart pounded, as I waited for what seemed like ages.

"I have to go see Hassan. Be back soon!" Pepa called out, and then there was silence.

I flipped the pages of the magazine, trying to find an article that I could lose myself in, so I wouldn't have to worry whether or not Perry was going to come in.

And then she burst through the door.

"Fort Lauderdale was awesome!" she yelled at me as she threw her hands up into the air. Her eyes were as wide as her grin, and every muscle in me tensed up.

She looked utterly transformed. Like me, she wore a white oxford shirt, only hers was tucked into a brand-new pair of Levi's, an outfit that fit her curvy body perfectly and only made me feel wispy with the little curves I had that were all so asymmetric to each other. Gold hoop earrings peeked out from her platinum-dyed blond, wavy hair, some of which she caught in a fluorescent green banana clip. The outfit was simple and classic—nothing trashy, nothing cheap. Her skin was darker, like creamy coffee, making her eyes an iridescent green and more feline than ever. But it was her hair—so blond that it didn't seem to be part of her body, it stood out so much—that made me jerk back my head in surprise. She looked years older.

She leapt onto my bed, gave me a kiss, and, noticing I was still gawking at her hair, said, "I got it dyed." *Apparently.* "You like?" she giggled, and her eyes darted from my face to the magazine, to the speakers, and back to me, perusing my out-fit. It reminded me of the nerviness she had after Thanksgiving break, but there was more here.

"It's great," I said meekly, still immobile, unable to take my eyes off her. She was the lightbulb to my moth. "Florida was fun?"

"*Un*believable! We had such a blast! We hung out on the beach, as you can see, met a ton of guys, went out to these clubs, and didn't come home until five in the morning." She readjusted her banana clip. "Not a lot of sober memories! I still feel kind of messed up!"

"No kidding." I could barely laugh with her.

"Jess, you should have been there! We met this guy who scored some really good coke for us, and then one day we spent the entire time on the beach 'shrooming our asses off. And then I had, like, all these guys after me. One guy even told me he was, like, in love with me, and I was like, 'Right, whatever.'" She let out a high-pitched giggle that made her sound like Woody Woodpecker; I never heard her laugh like that before. I imagined her picking it up from someone she had met down there, someone she deemed cooler than herself.

"Sounds wild," I replied, unable to muster any enthusiasm and wishing I had a leash to keep her under control.

"So how was break?" She slapped me on the back with a bit too much force.

"OK. I turned sixteen."

She threw her arms around me, exclaiming, "Happy Birthday, sweetie! We gotta celebrate!" She shook my shoulders.

"Perry, I'd love to, but I know by tomorrow, you'll forget all about it."

"You gotta remind me! We still have to make margaritas and stuff. We'll have a blast."

I crossed my arms and looked at her, trying to steady myself. I had to ask her. What could I lose?

"What?" She squinched up her face. "What's your problem? Are we dealing with moody Jess again?"

"What are you on?"

"Oh, that! Jesus!" She leaned in and whispered, "We had some coke left over from the trip and just did a few lines." She made a mock puppy-dog face. "Are you mad at me? Does this make us no longer friends?" Before I could answer, she leaped up from the bed, shouting, "I gotta pee!" and ran out of the room.

Jim Kerr from the Simple Minds moaned over the speakers in his guttural voice about an age of thundering rage. I always loved this song for its hymnlike sound; it was powerful and commanding. "*Set yourself freeee!*" came the final wail, and I thought that was exactly what I had to do.

But I didn't know how to go about doing it. I felt like a stranger had just flown into my room, shouted into my ear for a few seconds, and then left. I felt useless. I couldn't read any more, but just looked down at the pictures in *Rolling Stone* of wild-haired musicians at various benefits, concerts, and openings. I had already unpacked. Do I go out for a walk? But dorm closing was imminent. I envisioned myself going up to Leo's dorm, maybe making friends with those two girls, Lally and Alicia. But I decided I had nothing better to do than to go to bed. Sleep did not come quickly, however.

When Suzie returned, I feigned a slight snore and listened to her plunk her bags down and run into Perry and Pepa's room, slamming our door as she left. I listened to the pounding beat of the Supremes' "You Keep Me Hanging On," played over and over again, coming through the walls, the girls talking all at once. I wondered what the thing was that Perry had to show Suzie. They didn't miss me. If it were Suzie lying in bed, Perry and Pepa would have woken her up and insisted that she come in and be with them. It was like I wanted to be needed, but I didn't want to be with them. But if I was jealous of their supposed preference of Suzie over me, didn't that mean I wanted to still be their friend?

I wanted to feel liberated, but instead, I felt oddly trapped. I didn't know where to go, except back to Katonah and make a fresh start like I had hoped to here. Always new and improved, but this time I really felt that would be the case. I'd learned to talk back, and I had the experience of hanging out with a fast crowd at boarding school; a crowd that was far from virginal. And people would regard me the way I regarded Molly Ringwald: independent and self-assured. I was no longer the soap star's shy, nerdy daughter, I was my own person who'd seen it all and was tired of it because I had already "been through that phase."

Except that wasn't really the case. I was still a virgin with no intention of losing it any time soon. I hadn't broken any rule, not even one sip of anything closely approaching alcohol—having wine with Leo in New York didn't count. I only dressed slightly more sexy than I had when I first arrived, that is, I wore tighter jeans. And I wore makeup, something I never did at Katonah.

But if I did decide to go back to Katonah, it wouldn't look good going backwards. And could I go back to the cold, gray linoleum-lined disinfectant-smelling hallways, where everything was under one roof? Where you ate in a *cafeteria*, where there were pep rallies and cheerleaders and prom? That was so *high school*. At Fieldings, everyone seemed to have a sense of pride at being at boarding school, particularly a small, prestigious one. Almost like being away at college. It was so above public high school.

But was it? The only difference was that at Fieldings you spent the night and your classes were in different buildings. There seemed to be so much more going on at Katonah, so many more clubs, so many different kinds of students, which was strange because it was right in the middle of wealthy Westchester County. And yes, Fieldings had students from all over. Pepa was from Spain, Hassan was from Morocco, Leo from Italy. Yet it was small. That was it. It was just too small. I thought that's what I wanted. And it wasn't.

I still ate with my group but was plotting my escape. I kept looking around the dining hall to find groups that were more like me. But all the girls dressed the same, the same jeans, the same fluffy, asymmetrical haircuts, lip gloss. No one in my dorm listened to the music that I liked, and I was getting a little tired of hearing the local top-40 station blare out from every room. I loved pop, but I also liked other things.

One gusty Friday afternoon the following week, I came out of the music building from my lesson knowing that this was the moment I had to change. To help me continue with my piece, Mrs. McGowan had me improvise on the melody, along with a couple of other exercises. I wondered if the middle of my piece wasn't going to sound like pure Lennon and McCartney. As I played, I thought they had probably written the tune themselves. Even though I felt like it had come out of my imagination, parts of it ended up sounding an awful lot like Lennon's pleading melody, "Julia." So I tried something happier, which ended up like McCartney's "Martha, My Dear." Ever since I heard that was his favorite piece, I felt like I had to emulate it somehow, and the jaunty chords of the melody kept making their way into almost everything I tried to write.

"I feel like this stuff has been written before!" I cried.

"Don't worry about it, and don't even think," Mrs. McGowan said. "Remember that everything has already been written. Just let it go. Don't let your brain get in the way."

I tried to just let my fingers do whatever they needed to do over the keys, and what came out was a lot happier, if a little more confusing-sounding than I had expected.

As I walked out of the building, my fingers, arms, and brain all slightly buzzing from the work I had done, I looked up at the sky filled with gray and white clouds moving swiftly over patches of baby blue. I felt the balmy spring wind brush against my face, and I smiled. My first inclination was to head back to Kurtzman, but instead my feet led me up the hill near the chapel and then over to Fletcher. As I approached the vast dorm, the wind carried the sound of some Indian singer trilling against a pounding disco beat. Alicia poked her head out of a window, and I realized the music was coming from there. She looked down and saw me. I waved up to her.

"Hey! Jennifer, right?"

"No, Jess." *Well, she was close.*

"Sorry! What's up?"

"Nothing. I love that song!"

"Oh, thanks! Wanna come up?"

I skipped into their dorm up the stairs to the third floor.

The music greeted me as I entered into a very cool, if messy, room. A huge blue-and-black poster with the words *Cabaret Voltaire* covered one wall. The wall by their bunk bed held drawings, corny, 3-D postcards of guardian angels, the Virgin Mary praying with her blue eyes heavenward, and concert posters of bands I had heard of but never really listened to. The rug on the floor had once been baby blue but now was dingy, scattered with socks, old jeans, graying sneakers, and pink, fuzzy slippers. Alicia sat on the floor drawing a cartoon figure that looked like it had a lightbulb for a head. Lally was going through records in one of the many milk crates the roommates had. "Hey, Jess," she said.

"Hey. I love this song."

"It's the East India Company." I had no idea who that was as I watched a bright green 12-inch LP spin on the turntable. "We have to deejay the after-hours toga party tonight," Lally said.

"Cool," I replied, hoping to get an invite.

I sat cross-legged on the floor, watching Alicia hunched over her drawing. "What are you working on?"

"Oh, it's an idea for a cartoon," she said, squinting her eyes at me. "Hey, aren't you the one who has that *Yellow Submarine* poster?"

I nodded. "How'd you know that?"

"I remember seeing it when I was in your dorm last fall. It was incredible. I love that movie." She reached for a purple Craypas.

"It's one of my favorites," I said.

"The music is great, even though I haven't listened to the Beatles since I was a kid."

"You should. They've influenced so many people." I gestured to the turntable, "Like these guys."

"You sound like Leo. He loves to say that," Lally replied, pulling out more LPs.

And, as if on cue, a male voice called out to them. "Owooh! Lahlee!" I recognized it immediately and scrambled to the window along with Lally and Alicia.

"Speak of the devil!" Alicia said.

"Leo!" Lally cried out.

"Jess!" He exclaimed when he saw me. "*How* are you?" His hair, the tufts looking redder and blacker than ever, whipped about in the wind.

"Good!" I replied, almost jumping up and down.

"We're getting the music ready, but we need to see what you have. We wanna borrow some of your records," said Lally.

"You have to play Madonna!" He yelled. He pronounced her name with a soft *d*, making it sound beautiful and holy as opposed to snotty and obnoxious the way it had always sounded before.

"Nooo!" we all cried out in unison.

Leo stamped his enormous Timberland boot on the worn grass. "Siii!!" he whined and pouted, but moments later the expression was gone, and he pointed to me. "Jess, you have to come to our party tonight."

Lally and Alicia looked at me, Alicia nodding, Lally with her eyebrows raised.

"Really?" I squeaked. "That would be great!"

"And you have to have dinner with us," Leo boomed out. "We'll practice Italian." There was something equine about him, the stamping of the feet, the large nose and big teeth.

I giggled and nodded back. "'Kay."

I spent the rest of the afternoon with Lally and Alicia, listening to what the two of them were going to play that night, songs I had never heard and whose liveliness was such a nice change from the repetitiveness of Pepa and Perry's music. I was kind of bothered by the fact that Leo insisted on Madonna, but told myself not to be so judgmental. I watched the evolution of Alicia's art project, which she said was based on a song by a band named the Beat Farmers, something else I'd never heard of.

We then went downstairs and ate a dinner of spaghetti and ice cream. Leo, clad in a big, black turtleneck, sat next to me and stuck his fork into my spaghetti, saying, "*Scusa*, I'm hungry like a beast!" and then doing the same with my ice cream. When he pinched my cheek and winked with his clear blue eyes, he caused a flurry of giggles to come out of me. He argued with Lally and Alicia about what music to play, waving his spoon at them and pressing his point of view as if his was the final word. Lally rolled her eyes and snorted a lot while Alicia whined, sounding like a strong-willed mouse. "Forget it, Leesh, he's never gonna listen," Lally said over and over again. Leo never stopped moving, constantly readjusting himself in his seat, randomly putting his endless arms around either me or Alicia, who was sitting on his other side. He was like a big, restless bear, and yet at the same time there was something easy about him. His movements were large and graceful. It felt nice to have a big, warm arm around me.

"*Guarda che bellina sei!*" He complimented me on my looks in the middle of a discussion, giving me his big grin as his hands brushed my cheek. His eyes, framed by his long, curly lashes, contrasted sharply with his dyed-black-and-red hair. I barely had time to respond before he launched into another argument with the two girls about the lead singer of yet another band unknown to me.

I felt like someone had thrown me into one of those large inflatable tents they have at fairs where you bounce around for hours, bumping into people and helplessly laughing the entire time. It was in that spirit I called Marcie after dinner and told her I was spending the night with Lally and Alicia and going to the dorm's toga party only to be greeted by a distracted and slightly peeved, "Yeah, OK. Fine." I refused to stop and wonder what was going on. I didn't want anyone to disturb my mood.

That evening, before going to the dance, we hung out in Leo's room, his walls covered with posters of British bands. A large Beatles poster form their *Sgt. Pepper* days, with something written in Italian underneath, covered another wall. Where did they find these cool posters? Like Marcus, he had a single. Like Lally and Alicia's room, it was messy and overcrowded, with clothes strewn everywhere. Then out came the vodka, and I clenched up. I wanted to do it but at the same time flipped out at the thought of getting caught and then being busted just like Suzie and explaining all to my parents. But I braced myself and went ahead with it, doing shots out of black film containers, followed by chasers of 7 Up, my eyes always on the closed door and every footfall sounding like impending doom. The buzz came quickly, and that, on top of my adrenaline, gave me an enormous amount of energy. We talked about bands, what music we would put on the "ultimate" mixed tape, and I had no resistance to mentioning what I liked, all the Burt Bacharach, the Beatles, classical. My three companions told me I had to hang out with them more often, just based on my taste in music. Meanwhile, the stereo played a happy, jazzy melody as a smoky-voiced singer sang about his ever-changing moods.

Drunk, or at least feeling that way, and laughing, we all bounded over to the student center and barely paused to catch our breath as we danced to one song after another. Leo lifted his arms up to greet the millions of friends he seemed to have. Girls ran up and hugged him like he was their savior, and he smiled down at them, his blue eyes benevolent like the guardian angels in the 3D postcards I saw earlier. He invented dance moves which we all copied: loony arm waving and shouting that would never even have occurred to my former friends, who were now feeling very far away. I didn't even look around the room to see if they were there, because I knew they would never show up at a dance to begin with despite all their talk.

It continued into the toga party, where Lally and Alicia, swathed in floral-printed sheets, manned the turntables in businesslike fashion while Leo and I, dressed in his dark purple sheets, ("The color of the Florentine soccer team!" he announced to me as though I were about to don sacred material), danced close by. Even some of the faculty members were dressed in makeshift togas, adding a whole carefree element to the school I'd never seen before.

Maybe I'm just in the wrong dorm, I thought.

Leo leaped over to the turntable every other song to tell the girls what to play. If they shook their head, he'd wag his long fingers at them. This in turn would start yet another argument until Lally would gently guide him back to me on the dance floor where all was forgotten. He'd smile, pinch my cheek, and start hollering out to his friends who would come over and join us.

At around 1:00 AM, I collapsed onto Lally's bed. She demanded I sleep there since I was a guest. Leo offered me his bed earlier, saying it was big enough for the two of us. I smiled, feeling like my blush matched his sheets, and said, "Yeah, I don't think so."

"You can sneak over!" he yelled.

"And get kicked out!" yelled back their dorm head, Mrs. Elton.

"I'm kidding! Ha ha!" He barked into her face and then nodded at me.

"Can't do it! She's staying with us!" Lally grabbed my hand and dragged me towards the stairwell.

After a momentary puppy-dog look, he waved and called out, "*Buona notte!* Nighty night!" He blew kisses while yet another female came up and hugged him as if in desperate need of Leo vibes. He was like another kind of lightbulb to all us moths. Whereas Perry seemed almost fluorescent, he was a warm yellow, the kind I saw in the cabins at summer camp.

Up in Lally and Alicia's room, we didn't go to sleep right away. Instead we started talking.

"I never did this with Perry and those guys," I said. "We'd always talk about it but it'd never happen."

Alicia looked at me. "Did what?"

"You know, partying and then going to a dance. We're always in her room gossiping." I stopped myself because I didn't want to say anything bad. This was a small place.

Lally rearranged her pillow to get into a comfortable position and made a face at me. "Why are you friends with those guys? You totally don't seem like their type."

A few months ago, I would have been insulted by this. Now I didn't know how to take it. "In what sense?" I ventured.

But Lally just shrugged her shoulders. "You're nice." The two girls giggled.

I swallowed. "And they're not?" *Obviously.*

"Please. You ever heard of the word *manipulative*?" Lally replied dryly.

Alicia mumbled, "Perry's middle name. And Pepa's not exactly …"

"No, that girl goes way off the meter!" Lally's voice was so loud, I wondered if the rest of the dorm was going to hear her, or worse, if any of the noise was going to travel out the window.

"It's strange, because in the beginning, Perry was so nice to me and then—"

Lally laughed and adjusted her pillow once again. She seemed determined to divulge more information. "Look, I've known her since freshman year. We were in the same dorm, and back then, she was friends with everyone. She was really funny, smart, and doing favors for everyone. But looking back on it, it was like she had to be friends with everyone. Everyone had to say nice things about her in return."

"Like the Mafia," Alicia added. In contrast to Lally's bark, Alicia's voice sounded silky and gentle, gliding easily on a groove.

"And it started getting weird because I remember she started dating Marcus, and if he, in her eyes, flirted with any of her friends, that was it. The friendship was done. But she'd stick with him."

"She's possessive," Alicia added.

"I remember when I first came here for my interview," I said. "I saw you two with her and Pepa. You guys were singing arm in arm, like you were all buddies."

The two girls exchanged glances. "I remember that day. That was in the winter," Alicia replied.

Lally pointed to me. "I remember you! You were with your mom. And we all recognized her. Sorry!"

"That's OK." I shook my head. "It's not a crime to mention her." I paused. "But weren't you friends with Perry then?"

They shook their heads, and Alicia grimaced. "No, it was just one of those moments where we had class together, and we were all excited about Christmas break. And Perry decided to be nice." She put her head down on her pillow. "She never liked me. But then again, I came last year. She had already made that dividing line between who were her friends and who weren't."

I pursued further. "She dated Leo, right?"

"Dated?" Lally exclaimed. "If you can call it that. Yeah, it was last year. He was totally not into her, and she had broken up with Marcus for two seconds, which she essentially does every year. So she and Leo went out once or something, and then he pulled away from her, and she tried to blackmail him by trying to get him kicked out for dealing drugs." She snorted. "It didn't work."

Alicia smiled, adding, "And then Leo goes and moves on to the next girl in two seconds."

"Leo, in case you haven't noticed, has a way with the ladies," Lally raised an eyebrow at me. "Perry couldn't deal with it."

My face turned icy warm as shame went through me. I pictured Perry in my mind, and she seemed small, her green eyes losing their almond shape and becoming large and desperate, like a lonely doll. I tried to find a comfortable position in the bed and let my mind flip over to Leo and all the girls he had gone out with, which didn't make me feel better. "Is Leo like the typical Latin lover or something?" I asked, an edge catching in my voice, probably due to exhaustion. I smiled to cover it up.

"He just luuuhves girls!" Alicia giggled. "He's had two real girlfriends since he's been here, but mostly a lot of flings."

I made myself continue to smile.

"A lot of flings," followed Lally. She looked at me, the corners of her eyes turning up. "I think he likes you a lot."

I swallowed, and the smile disappeared as I felt the temperature in my face and ears get a little warmer. I thought of the night at the club, wrapped in his comforting arms, my tears and snot on his T-shirt. But I didn't want him to have a crush on me. I have a crush on Marcus, and that would be inconvenient. "Wow. I actually have a crush on Marcus." Which isn't exactly how I wanted it to come out. I felt mean.

The two girls looked at me for a few seconds making me feel worse. "Yeah, you and the rest of the female population." Alicia stretched her arms and rolled her eyes. "I wouldn't touch that guy with a ten-foot pole. I mean, he's cute, but he's so arrogant. And besides, he and Perry have something weird going on."

"They always have. They test each other with other people. That's why they break up all the time. It's like some game to see who's more desirable."

"Marcus always gets somebody else," Alicia said.

"And Perry can't deal with it. It's fucked up."

I was the last of the three to fall asleep. Hearing this about Marcus gave me an oily sensation that disappeared once I woke up the next morning. Besides, what these girls said was probably only rumors.

CHAPTER 12

Don't Make Me Over

"Where were *you* last night?" Perry asked me Sunday morning when I returned to the dorm. The three girls were hanging out by the doorway of Perry and Pepa's room.

Perry's head was cocked to the side, eyes lasering into me. Pepa and Suzie just looked questioning, almost hopeful.

I was still a bit queasy from the vodka I drank the night before, and Perry's demand was making it even harder for me to hold myself steady. "Didn't Marcie tell you?" It was all I could do to sound relaxed. "I spent the night in Fletcher. I was invited to their toga party."

"Who invited you?" Pepa asked, looking down at a chipped nail and then back up at me.

"Leo, Lally, and Alicia." I shrugged, although the names tripped off my tongue awkwardly as I continued past them into my room. The girls trailed me.

I heard Perry snicker. "Did you have a good time?"

I shrugged again. "I had a blast. They're a lot of fun."

"What'd you do? Talk about what a mean, hateful person I am?"

I wasn't going to give it to her. "Perry! Why would we do that?"

She gave me a simpering look. "Isn't that why you wanted to step over to the other side?" The two other girls giggled, and I pictured them as the munchkins next to Glinda.

"Maybe I wanted to widen my circle of friends. What's wrong with that?" I went to my desk to get my notebooks. If these guys were going to be hanging out in my room, I had to leave.

Suzie's voice came out sharp and nasal. "With those lesbians?"

I glared at her. "Really mature, Suzie."

The munchkins and Glinda giggled again. "That's how much you know," Pepa said.

"Well, you just wondered why I wasn't hanging out with you guys, and I gave you my reason." I swung the knapsack over my shoulder.

Despite the fact that her expression remained calm, there was something rumbling under the surface of Perry's skin, the tan that she was working so hard to maintain by spending fifty-degree days out on the lawn had become lighter. "I was just wondering why those guys invited you!"

"They were nice to me." I wanted that to make me feel strong, but it was a nasty slap in her face.

Her mouth opened slightly, and she raised her eyebrows.

Pepa snorted, "They're so desperate to make other friends."

"Did Leo make a pass at you?" Perry asked, composure regained, leaning against the wall, arms crossed.

"No, he was a real sweetheart." I headed out the door.

Her voice mimicked mine in a high-pitched, weasely manner. "*He was a real sweetheart.*"

Every nerve in my body stood on end. I headed down the stairs, feeling I had been scratched raw. Any sympathy I held for Perry from the previous night's discussion drained out of me.

I walked into the library and sat down to work on memorizing my Dante passage, from, appropriately enough, *The Inferno*. Although the ancient Italian that I was trying to store in my brain resembled nothing we had studied that year, I knew just working on it would remind me of Leo, and therefore Lally and Alicia, and therefore, something more positive. But then I remembered what the two girls said about him liking me, which made me feel weird. So I turned my mind to Marcus. But that made me think of Perry. I moved on to geometry.

That evening, I waited in the commons room for Sunday's dinner and scanned the room. Everyone wore their Sunday attire—skirts, dressy pants, guys from Hilliman in their jackets and ties that looked thrown on them in a reluctant manner. I sat on the couch next to a girl and a guy who were tickling each other, and if they weren't a couple, they were certainly heading in that direction. The TV was on, but I paid no attention. School just plain sucked, and it didn't make any difference where you were. In fact, because this place was smaller than Katonah, it only made things worse. At least with Katonah, you could go back home and not have to be with your enemies every single meal. Here, it was with you twenty-four hours a day.

So my plan was to sit somewhere that would take me. Not with Marcie, who was regarding me with a chilly distance. Her apparent adoration of Perry was too much for me to stand. For campus meeting, I would head straight over to Leo, Lally, and Alicia. Just pretend Perry and her duo no longer existed. Then they would just leave me be. Done. I even crossed my arms when I thought of this.

Then I felt a tap on my shoulder. And a voice saying, "I'm sorry about this morning."

I craned my neck up to look at Perry. She was leaning on the back of the couch looking down at me, her Obsession perfume wafting into my nose.

"We were being a bit out of line." She looked around the room and then back at me. "I felt like you were deserting us, or something, and it really hurt my feelings when you said they were nice to you, like we were a bunch of bitches." She let out a nervous chuckle.

I didn't want to fall for this again. "Perry, I don't always feel that comfortable with you guys, OK? It's like you're on some other level. And Pepa has made it really clear she doesn't like me."

Perry bit her lip. "Pepa's got her own stuff to deal with, so I wouldn't take it personally. But there's no reason why you shouldn't feel comfortable around us. Is it because you're still a virgin and we're not?" This she whispered in my ear and then paused with expectant eyes. "Because that is ridiculous." And then almost under her breath, and so fast I almost missed it, "There are times when I think you're more mature than all of us put together. No kidding." She didn't look at me.

I let that sink in. "Why were you so mean to me this morning, then?"

"I was upset. And when I get that way, I have a bad habit of lashing out. I'm really sorry. Friends?"

"OK."

Sitting with the three girls at dinner, I felt like the once-banished child allowed to return to the grown-ups' table. But what Perry had told me also made me feel as though I was put on a higher pedestal, and I realized that she actually looked up to me. So the girl was this thunderstorm of emotions and drama. It always blew over. It always got better. I ignored Pepa as much as I could, and Suzie mouthed a sorry to me, rubbing my arm, her eyes disappearing into her face from her smile.

At campus meeting that night, I spied Leo, Lally, and Alicia in the front and waved to them, knowing Perry was watching. "I'm not going to be a snob and just ignore them!" I said, before she could make any comment.

"I didn't say anything, Miss Defensive!" She let out a loud laugh and sat down in the pew, making room for me.

Throughout the meeting, Perry and I sent notes to each other on the back of her notebook. She started it, and I felt like I had no choice but to respond. A guest speaker, an alumnus who was now a photographer with *National Geographic*, showed slides from his trip to Papua, New Guinea. We spent more time paying attention to him than his photographs of the rain forests. His black, wavy hair hung in huge forelocks over his face. His nose was too big, but his mouth, all curly and sensuous, coupled with his sleepy voice and offhand remarks about how out of place he was in the country, made Perry and me sort of fall in love with him.

Nose a bit too big but very cute, she wrote.

Agreed, I wrote back.

He has the *sexiest voice. He's like an American Sean Connery.*

Mouth good enough to eat, I scribbled.

Down girl! Leave some for the rest of us! Perry wrote back and gave me a side-long glance.

I couldn't wait for campus meeting to be over with. I looked over at my new friends up in the front who never turned to wave at me. I wondered what they were doing afterwards. Was Leo going to Bartlett to practice? I couldn't wait for Tuesday's conversation class after dinner. I had this urge to throw myself into my piece and fantasized briefly that he would be there to help me out with it. Or maybe he could help me out with my Italian homework, memorizing a few stanzas of Dante. All friendly, of course. No romance.

Perry wrote me a note, wondering how big he was.

Can't you think of anything else? I wrote back.

She wrote: *Fuck you raw.*

I froze.

She looked at me, smiled, and continued, *Loosen up, honey. Don't take everything so seriously and STOP being so puritanical!* She bugged her eyes at me and broke into a silent laugh. I tried to do the same. It was the end of our note passing.

The next week was strange. Walking across campus on the way to class Monday morning, I was sandwiched between Suzie and Perry. Lally and Alicia glanced at me with no expression. In the evening when I went to Bartlett to practice, Leo wasn't around. I felt as though I was repeating the same bass line and chord progressions I had been playing forever with my piece while I tried to recapture some of the magic from that Friday improv session. But I couldn't let go. When the first Italian conversation class began that Tuesday evening, I sat straight in my chair, waiting for Leo to arrive. How was he going to treat me? Was he going to see me as a little pushover? Was that all I was? But when he opened the door, the breeze hit my face, the increase in my heart rate when he grinned at me with a "*Ciao topolino!*" made me realize that everything was OK. We talked about what we did that weekend in halting, painfully slow sentences as we searched for the right words to describe ultimate Frisbee, toga party, biology lab, and a trip to the mall. It all eeked out of our mouths, ending in question marks, and Leo ending up doing a lot of the talking, looking mostly at me, about Fletcher's *festa di toga*.

I wanted to catch up to him after class, to tell him that I wanted to hang out. But he had to rush to the library and told me that we'd see each other soon. "*Ciao!*" And that was that. I felt there was something a little superficial about him, that what happened that weekend meant nothing.

There was no question Perry was being nicer to me. Pepa was still cool and as much as I tried to ignore it, it still stung. Perry kept reminding me about the plans we made earlier to go to the mall that Saturday.

"Yeah, but I have to practice for spring recital!" I said. And I meant it. There was a long stretch of unknown notes waiting to be written, and I wondered if I'd ever find out what they were.

"It would be so great if you could come, though! Please?" Her eyes danced, and she was beginning to look kind of pale, the tan continuing to fade and revealing something pasty and worn underneath. I spent some study halls with her and the other girls down in the butt room, but unlike Pepa who managed to shut out the rambling nonstop conversation between Perry and Suzie and concentrate on her work, I couldn't get anything done. While it was par for the course that Suzie was, once again, falling way behind in her classes, what I was beginning to glean from the conversation between the two was that Perry was doing the same thing.

"I thought you had your editorial meeting tonight," I asked her at dinner on Wednesday.

"Ugh!" She shook her head. "I'm mad at Mitch. He's being fascist again."

"In what sense?"

"He just is." She picked at her food, talking more than she was eating.

And talking about nothing—all three of them. First it was about the show *Dynasty*, which all three wanted to see. Pepa thought Linda Evans was, "absolutely stunning. She looks so good for her age."

"Plastic surgery," I responded.

"If it works," she snipped.

But the show was on during study hall. Then they talked about *Sunset*, at which point Perry turned to me with a small gasp, "Jess, is that OK if we talk about your mom's show?"

"Yeah, I don't have a problem with it," I replied, wondering whether I did or didn't. Maybe it was an effort to make me feel included; that the fact Suzie and Pepa (and now maybe Perry) still watched it meant there were no hard feelings. Suzie talked about why the characters were "more, like, real because it's on every day, and it's from New York, which has a much more real-er mindset than L.A.—"

"Realistic," Perry interrupted her. "You're absolutely right. There really is a correlation between too much sun and escapism, you know?"

"Ugh! L.A. is sooo fake—!"

"Suzie! You've got to come to New York this summer!" Perry almost shouted at her as she slammed her hands down on the table.

"Right?" Suzie nodded her head.

"We should *all* be there this summer!" Pepa said, looking at both of them. And she meant just them. "You know what? You guys! We should all get an apartment together! That would be so cool! I need to tell my parents about this. They can definitely help us out!"

They couldn't get their words out fast enough, and it was hard not to be swept up in their excitement. Perry turned to me and said, "Jess, this would be so cool!"

"Yeah!" Suzie exclaimed. But it all felt like an afterthought.

Pepa did what she always did. She looked at me, trying to at least begin to show some enthusiasm, but her mouth never got beyond the beginnings of a smile, and her eyes remained flat.

My heart pounded. It was like the night after spring break all over again, only this time it was all three of them bouncing around me like a bunch of screeching birds.

"I'm going to Italy, remember?" I said.

"You never told me that!" Perry replied. *I did. Right after spring break.*

"Italy? That's so cool!" Suzie said.

Pepa asked what part.

"Florence."

"Of course. All the Americans go there. It's so cliché."

Before I could even begin to snap back, Perry bounced in, "You never, ever told me that, Jess!"

"Yes, I did." I wondered how I could make my way out of the dining hall and over to the music building as quickly as possible.

I raced over to Bartlett after dinner, hoping to see Leo, but he was nowhere to be found. I felt like I could finally breathe for the first time in hours and settled down to my exercises. My fingers tumbled over themselves at first, they were so tense. I stretched them out, cracked my knuckles, took a few deep breaths, and plunged right back in, forcing my concentration onto the keys, the pedals, and my fingers. I improvised on some other Hanon exercises and went straight to my piece. The middle part sounded like a happy yet confused jam of notes, yet that's what was coming out, so I stuck with it. By ten o'clock, I finished practicing but realized I had a huge chunk of other homework waiting for me, and that it was going to be a late night, which meant staying up with Perry, Pepa, and Suzie. Would I be able to concentrate working in the butt room with them? I would stay up in my room, an easy solution. I hoped it was going to be an equally late night for them, so I wouldn't be disturbed. And I wasn't.

Saturday morning arrived after a tortuously boring evening spent in Perry and Pepa's room, listening to the Supremes and gossiping. I wondered what my other friends were up to.

"So you ready?" Perry asked after lunch in Fletcher, and we were both heading back to Kurtzman.

"For what?"

"We're going to the mall, you promised!"

"No, I didn't. Perry, I have to work. I'm sorry."

"You promised, Jess, come on!"

"Perry, no, I didn't. I have to work. I am way behind on my piece."

She paused, giving me a blank look. "You know, Jess. I don't get you." Her voice was ragged and low. "It's just one afternoon. And I've watched you all week. You sit there like a little princess, expecting us to bow and scrape to you just because *you* feel like *we* wronged you. I'm beginning to think you're nothing more than a spoiled brat."

I was too taken aback to say anything. That whole week I spent with these guys, my work had languished—my half-hearted attempt at an essay on *Pride and Prejudice*, the missed questions on my bio pop quiz. Piano remained alive even if I still had a ways to go.

"Perry, I swear to God—" I started, ready to explain myself.

But she continued on in the same tired voice, "You know something? Do whatever the hell you want. You're really exhausting to be friends with sometimes." And she turned on her heel and went to the bus.

I stood there for awhile, watching the bus pull away with the roar of its diesel engine. I could have said to myself, "OK, Perry is really screwed up. It's just that she's on a lot of drugs." But her words, her about face, still took every ounce of energy out of me. I never promised, I kept trying to remind myself. Or did I? I had never been around someone as unpredictable as she, and instead of just tossing my hair and rolling my eyes, á la Molly Ringwald, I started to feel scared, scared of what, I didn't know. But my stomach became a knot.

CHAPTER 13

Knowing When to Leave

When I entered Bartlett, it was silent, and I went to the practice room and sat down to work. With every note I played, every scale and triad, every measure, I tried to push the three girls out of my head and what they were probably saying as they perused the lacy underwear at the lingerie store they loved so much. I moved on to the Chopin piece as a warmup before working on my own composition. But it didn't go as planned. Maybe it was the fact that I was imagining Marcus watching and/or listening to me and impressing him. I couldn't get my fingers to work properly. Putting emphasis where I wasn't supposed to, making awkward transitions whenever there was a key change, the stupid pedals, to say nothing of the strength that had been sapped out of my fingers.

I heard a knock on the door, it was so soft that had I been playing a little louder, I would have missed it. "Yeah?" I asked, thinking the hulky wrestler really was listening outside the door.

"*Ciao, topolino.*" Leo's black-and-scarlet head poked through the door. He winked at me. I earlier learned that *topolino* meant little mouse, and I loved that he had taken to calling me that.

"Hey!" I exclaimed, surprised at how enthusiastic I sounded given that I had hoped it was Marcus.

"You sound good." He slinked in and closed the door behind him.

"Oh, thanks, but I'm having a really hard time with this piece." I showed him what I was playing, and he nodded and whispered, "*Mamma mia,*" as he sat down beside me. He played a few notes, and I studied his profile. I noticed a gentleness to his big nose and that his lips curled up at the corners.

"I got it down perfectly last term, but I haven't played it for a while, so I'm rusty," I said.

"I remember working on this last year. It was so much torture, and Anna just refused to take it away. She's very fussy about this one." I loved hearing that modulation in his accent. It was like a small wave went through his sentences. I was also still kind of bugged by his being on a first name basis with Mrs. McGowan. He asked, "Are you playing this for the spring concert?"

"Uh, no. I'm composing my own piece."

"You're kidding! Anna must really like you."

"Well," I fiddled with the keys and tried to think of something witty to say to hide my embarrassment. "I'm not exactly on a first name basis with her."

"She's tough, but I make her laugh all the time." He gave me his toothy grin.

"Hmm."

"What?"

"I think a lot of girls worship you." I felt an odd combination of power and fear take over when I said this.

He tried to concentrate on the music in front of him, but I noticed a little redness develop in his face and a twitching around his mouth, like he was trying to suppress a smile. And then he whipped his head around to me. "What's your piece like?"

"Kind of jazzy. It started off really Lennon and McCartney–ish, because that's what I'm so used to listening to, so automatically I'd write it, you know?"

He nodded, "I started writing a piece last summer that was a copy of "Sexy Sadie." You know that piano in the beginning, the way it changes tonalities?" He played a bit of it, obviously having worked it out a number of times.

"Yeah! It seems so simple but it's not."

"Exactly. So of course, I ended up writing this," he started playing a few chords that sounded pretty similar, "and then it was the song all over again."

"Play me the rest of the piece," I said.

He laughed. "That's about all I wrote. I'm not very disciplined in writing. Playing other people's stuff, sure. But I'm not a composer. But you seem to be one. I mean, if Anna is asking you to write your own piece."

"Yeah, I guess."

"So since you're into the Beatles, you've obviously listened to *Pet Sounds?*"

"My old piano teacher was always pushing me to listen to the Beach Boys and even gave me a copy of it. I never got around to listening to it. I always have this image of guys with genetically attached beer cans whenever I hear them."

"Are you kidding?" he laughed.

"I know, it's lame."

"But that album influenced—"

"I know, *Sgt. Pepper.*" Chris had told me of the whole mutual admiration society that existed between the two bands when they were both at their peaks, *Rubber Soul* led to *Pet Sounds,* which led to *Sgt. Pepper,* which led to something called *Smile.*

"I do not understand!" Now Leo sounded like a full-blown Italian; all traces of any Americanisms he picked up were gone. "How can you ignore your teacher like that? Where is the planet you have been on?"

"He pushed them so much and then listening to David Lee Roth sing 'California Girls' didn't encourage me."

"I like his 'California Girls.'"

"Ew," I replied. "Really?"

"Plus, Eddie Van Halen is *the* rock guitarist."

Just like what Chris always said, but I couldn't get over that Leo liked Van Halen.

He nodded as if reading my mind and returned to the Chopin in front of him. His long fingers traveled over the keys with practiced fluidity. It didn't seem like he had ever struggled with it. He paid what I thought was undue concentration to the music in front of him instead of occasionally looking down at the keys to see what his hands were doing. There was something a little too stiff in most of his body. His hands were smooth, however, wholly separate from the rest of him. Then he stopped. "Play me your piece."

"I'm not even done!"

"So what? I want to guess which Beatles album influenced you." One side of his mouth tilted up, and he gave me a sly look.

I let out a deep breath, took away the Chopin music to reveal my scribblings on the staff sheet and looked down at the keys as though they were going to tell me when they were ready to be played. I tried blocking Leo out of my peripheral vision, but he was such a large presence, it wasn't easy. I started with the bass line, which I wanted to play forever before I got to the melody, and had to will myself into the arpeggio. The syncopation came out better than I thought it would. I felt more sure, more controlled.

Yet I was a bit too self-conscious to let my entire body get into it; I didn't want to come across as melodramatic because that would have been too corny. As a result, the music was a bit choppy. When I reached the end of what I had written, which was mid-phrase, I stopped. "So that's what it is so far."

Leo's eyes swallowed me whole, which made me swallow hard. "Wow," he said softly. "It's really summery. Really Brian Wilson. And it's like the Chopin Waltz, with the tension you have in that arpeggio. I don't see that much of a Beatles influence."

"Really?"

"I like it." He was looking down at the keys, the long fingers of his left hand dangling over them. "You have a title?"

"No, in fact, I never thought of one."

"It has kind of a sad sound in the beginning—"

"Yeah!"

"But then I love the way it picks up, the tempo and the chords. It's kind of playful, but you don't get too carried away and leave the melody." His voice was quiet, almost pensive, and when he looked at me, my stomach hopped. There was a pause that lasted for an interminable few seconds. Then all of a sudden, he playfully hit me on the arm and said, "You idiot, you have to listen to *Pet Sounds*. Come on, you're coming to my room!"

I agreed to go, not wanting to spend any more time alone with him in a music room where we would encounter more silent moments like the one we just had. We rushed to gather my stuff together and headed over to Fletcher.

After signing me in, we ordered a large pizza from Domino's, since it was dinnertime, and he produced the Beach Boys' album with a flourish, "Ta-da!" I had never seen the cover before, and it looked so unlike their other beachscape photographs. They were dressed in dark suits, had sideburns climbing down the sides of their faces, and were feeding a bunch of goats. It was kind of sweet. He placed the black vinyl disk with the rainbow-and-black colored Capitol label on his turntable. The needle soundlessly touched down, and a light-sounding harp played the introductory chords of "Wouldn't It Be Nice?" I had heard the song a number of times, but only from fuzzy radios. Never had I heard it come out of large speakers with such a full sound. Leo motioned with his hands as he sang along, pointing out the patterns in the melody and key changes. I was swept up in the symphonic sound, the close harmonies, and hopeful lyrics.

"It's so pretty!" I nodded. "I never heard it like that before!"

"It's amazing! And listen to this next song, the number of notes he uses for the word *cry*. It's exactly … it's just …" He faltered as the song started. "You'll see." We both looked at the stereo in anticipation.

He took me through the whole album, playing "Caroline No" three times (it was his favorite song), singing it directly to me and "God Only Knows," whose canonlike ending made my heart rate increase. We sat in silence as the song played out, aware of each other's presence but not knowing whether we should look at one another. And do what? Give each other meaningful glances? How embarrassing. It was both a relief and an annoyance when our pizza was delivered, although Leo refused to answer the door until the song was over.

When the album finished, the needle returned to its holder. There remained a few slices of the once huge pie.

"You know, I'm going to Florence this summer," I finally said. And then I remembered I had mentioned it before over Christmas vacation, but he responded like this was the first time I'd mentioned it.

He looked like he was about to explode. "Really? Great!"

"I know. Um, maybe we can get together!"

"Are you kidding? You can meet my friends! We can go to a lot of gigs together! There are all these outdoor concerts."

"Cool!" I imagined summer nights in a park somewhere, surrounded by cypress trees, stylish Italians, and the heat blanketing our skin while we watched some band play.

We looked at each other, my face stretched to its maximum width in a large grin. He was doing the same, and once again there were those endless seconds where everything stopped. I detected a look of panic in his eyes when he abruptly turned to pull out *Sgt. Pepper's* and put it on the turntable. There was a knock on the door, and we both sighed in relief.

It was Lally with a crate of records at her feet. "Jess! Hi!" She looked surprised.

"Hey! I was wondering where you guys were," I said.

"You're not with the others …" she said, shaking her head, and I did the same.

"Nahh. The mall. I could care less."

She gave me a small smile and then said to Leo, "Come on! Let's go!"

He slapped his hand to his head. "I forgot!"

"I told you to get the records ready this afternoon."

"I know, but I had a million other things to do!" His eyes pleaded. "Like, clean my room and stuff."

Lally looked around at the scattered mess. "Nice job. Get your ass in gear. We'll meet you down there. Jess, you coming tonight?"

"If you guys are deejaying, sure!"

"Cool." She picked up the crate and said good-bye.

Leo growled, "I can't believe I forgot. Come on; help me decide what to play!" It came out like a sharp demand as he lifted the needle up just as Ringo was about to start into "A Little Help from My Friends."

"I have no idea. All this stuff is so foreign to me." I wished he had left the record on, to give us some noise in the background. The abrupt silence unnerved me. I flicked through his records, pulling out the 12-inch ones with the most interesting covers.

Leo's eyebrows were furrowed together, and whatever enthusiasm he had earlier was now gone. He responded irritably to some of my choices. "No, not that. No one'll dance to that." I held up another. "Yes," he replied and snatched it out of my hands. "Sorry, but I was so stupid to forget, and now I'm late. *Vaffanculo,*" he said under his breath.

All the giddiness from before was gone, and I figured he was just preoccupied and mad at himself for not getting ready sooner. But at the same time, I felt like an intruder in his room, that although he insisted I help find some records, my presence was no longer needed. He hardly looked at me the entire time, as though giving me eye contact would destroy his concentration.

I stood up, and said I had to get ready.

He nodded, still looking at his selection.

"Thanks for inviting me," I said, willing him to at least glance up at me.

He looked up with heavy-lidded eyes, but only for a second. His shoulders went down a bit, his mouth twitched, and his eyes drooped at the corners. "It was a pleasure." He swallowed, cleared his throat, and got back to his records.

I walked to Kurtzman, trying to gauge my feelings. Did I really like him more than I wanted to admit? Why was he so irritable? What was with the sudden change in manner? Maybe he had a crush on me, and that was why he was acting all weird because that's what guys did. But *I* couldn't have a crush on him. Besides, Leo is a friend, and I couldn't wrap my mind around the idea that a friendship could turn into a romance. Thinking about it almost made me nauseated; it was too close for comfort.

As I approached my door, I could hear the Supremes' harmonies echoing out of my room and filling me with dread. I opened the door to find Pepa and Suzie on Suzie's bed, having settled themselves against the vast array of Garfield stuffed animals. They were sipping something out of their mugs, which they immediately clutched to their chests in fear as I opened the door.

"You scared the hell out of us! We thought you were Marcie!" Suzie said. "You want a margarita? Perry's gone to get limes from her room."

"Sure." I sat down on my bed, thoughts of getting ready for the dance disappearing. "How was the mall?" I asked.

The girls shrugged. "Crowded," Pepa replied.

I felt the need to apologize, and so I did with the same story I had told Perry earlier.

The girls nodded without much interest.

Perry zoomed into the room and stopped short when she saw me. "Where were you?" she asked.

"I told you I had to practice." I braced myself, the sting of our conversation from earlier returning.

"All this time? You must have had a lot to do."

"Well, I ran into Leo, and since we are both doing stuff for the spring recital …" I trailed off, wondering, by some tiny chance, if any of the girls were going to ask me what I was doing.

"So. That's why you didn't want to come to the mall with us," Perry said, raising her eyebrows. Her cheeks looked hollowed out, and she seemed much older.

"No—" I began. I had to focus on Perry's imminent nasty remarks while my faculty radar shot up, my eyes darting to the door.

Perry remained silent, focusing on making her cocktail. I gave her my mug and asked her to make me one too.

"I gotta say, he is sort of sexy," Suzie said, squinching up her nose and curling her mouth. She looked loose and floppy. She was drunk.

"Latin men have that," Pepa said, pointing her manicured finger at Suzie. "They just have this thing about them. It comes from their mothers who treat them like little princes. But you have to watch out." She sipped her margarita and tried to narrow her eyes at me but there was something too unsteady about it, like she didn't quite have the motor control.

"I wouldn't say he was sexy," I said. "He's just a cool guy."

Perry snorted and rolled her eyes. "Admit it, Jess. You have a crush on him, just as you did on Marcus. It's like you really think the shit don't stink."

I wanted to jump up and go to the dance. These guys were all wrong for me.

With a lime in one hand and a red Swiss Army knife in the other, Perry started cutting wedges on my desk. "Sorry, I know you're his so-called friend and everything but he's a total Lothario. Plus, he has more than a real penchant for heavy chemical substances." She continued, "I didn't want to say this before, but he's like the main supplier of coke and x at this school. And, I would venture to say, Connecticut College as well." She handed me my drink.

"Well, I guess you'd know, wouldn't you?" I asked in even tones, and with that, a hole had been punched in the atmosphere of the room.

She still wasn't looking at me. She grabbed her margarita and threw herself on my bed, clicking her tongue. "Please. I know some of my parents' students, so word gets around. You can bet he's turned Lally and Alicia on to the stuff. Jess, trust me, he's bad news."

When people talk about cold water being thrown on your happiness, I knew then exactly what it was like. All the warmth and hopefulness I had when I thought of Leo (despite our weird parting) vanished. I took a huge gulp of my drink, savoring the tartness of it. The alcohol burned my throat, and it felt good because I had to relax. I took another gulp. The stuff was yummy, like candy for grown-ups.

"Speaking of partying," Perry addressed her two friends. "Guess who I'm going to see next week when I go to New York?" She clutched her yellow mug between her hands and took a sip.

"You're going to New York?" I said.

She didn't look at me. "My friend Andrea invited me. You weren't around for the news."

"Will Joel be there?" Suzie said. I had a hard time imagining this painter, who, according to Perry, was a fixture in the so-called downtown scene, going to college. It was like clubs were his college.

"You bet!"

"Cool!" The girls raised their mugs to the ceiling. I took another gulp. All of a sudden, I wanted it to be that other Friday night in Lally and Alicia's room. The wistfulness in me was so heavy that tears were threatening to glaze over my eyes. The room closed in and turned oppressive.

Perry regarded my lack of enthusiasm. "Of course, Jess has to be jealous again, doesn't she?" Her smile was tight, and her voice soaked in acid and mockery. I had heard her speak this way before, and I was always terrified it would happen to me. A slow shock came over me; it was really happening now.

As she spoke, the control in which she held her voice made it seem like she was talking to a crystal glass she was careful not to break. "Jess. If you're gonna continue to hang out with us, you really have to work on getting over your jealousy and competition. It is totally the wrong vibe for this group. We're all trying to have fun and relax from all the stress of school and stuff, and it doesn't help to have you sulk every time something good happens to one of us."

Suzie and Pepa nodded their heads in agreement. Perry blinked her green eyes in such a deliberate fashion, I was reminded of Madonna in her "Like a Virgin" video, the way she blinked her eyes at the camera in a sarcastically innocent manner. There was a cool warmth in my scalp, making me think this is what animals feel like when their hackles are raised. "I'm not jealous of you, Perry. You got it all wrong."

"Oh really? Why do you have to criticize me all the time? It's really obvious to all of us, and we all agreed that you need to recognize it and get over it."

I wanted to explode but instead took another large swallow of my drink, feeling the heat of the alcohol wave up to my head. "No, Perry, that's not it at all." The old moth feeling was back.

Perry let out a grunt and replied, punctuating each word with a pause after it. Her voice continued to rise as she spoke. "You are so jealous, I cannot believe it! But if you want to deny it by pointing the finger at me, go right ahead. It's called projection, honey. Didn't you learn that from your daddy? I am so sick and tired of you raining down on me. Every time something good happens to me, you just sit there and sneer and wonder why it's not happening to you! You are one of the most self-centered people I know. You can't spend the rest of your life just wimping around, resenting other people who are actually going out and doing things like I am! You just wait for your mommy and daddy to tell you what to do. At least *I* get off my ass and do things *on my own*. I don't wait for Mommy and Daddy's approval because usually they don't care. That job last summer? I did that all on my own. God, you are so pathetic!"

Suzie and Pepa gaped at me with open mouths. Suzie let out a groan that was almost like a laugh.

I stood rooted in place, my lungs void of any air. The room rotated on its own, a jerky merry-go-round. The attack on my father. The fact her parents ignored her. I left the room, the tartness from my finished margarita still in my mouth.

I was buzzed, at the very least. I didn't want to run into a faculty member on my way outside, so I walked as fast as I could while trying to remain in control. My feet felt numb as I walked over to the student center with the muffled pounding beat from a dance that was well underway inside. I tried to figure out what Leo and Lally were playing, but I couldn't concentrate enough to figure it out. Everything in me was too stunned from Perry's roar.

I floated up the stone steps to the warm and sweaty-smelling entrance, paid my two dollars to the German Club that was sponsoring the dance, and walked into the vast student center. I recognized a song that Lally and Alicia had played before, something with the word *thieves* in the title, and a heavy symphonic sounding synthesizer adding too much mood to the background. I could have entered into the sun-shiniest place on earth while listening to this song, and it would make me feel as if I were in a dark vault. I noticed how a lot of the girls wore the same hoop earrings, sleeveless mock turtlenecks, many with long strings of fake pearls bouncing over their chests, and oversized, cotton, V-neck sweaters or oxfords belted low near the hips. Almost every guy had a variation of either a rugby shirt or tucked-in oxford. Hair gel glimmered everywhere and dripped from the humidity. Sunglasses were perched on heads like cat ears. The overall colors were black, pastel pink, and green. *The Stepford Students*, I thought to myself.

Up on a balcony that encircled the room, were Lally and Leo hunched over the turntables and flicking through the vast collection of records that lay in the milk crates. I saw a statuesque brunette, all limbs, big red lips, and a tangled mess of hair, saunter over to the duo. Leo looked up, beamed, took his earphones off, gathered her in his arms, and gave her a kiss on the cheek. They talked, she nodded, he laughed, and Lally gave her a friendly wave and returned to her duties while Leo's arm remained around the girl's waist. There was more nodding, laughing, and then he leaned over and whispered something in her ear. She nodded again, and I could tell, even in the dim lights, she was glowing. My heart almost leaped into my mouth, and over the music, I could hear, in the faintest tones in the back of my head, the bit I remembered from "God Only Knows." I scanned the room for Alicia, and when I saw her, she was heading out the back door with two other people. I started to make my way across the dance floor to join her, when I bumped into a T-shirt–clad chest.

"Oh! Sorry!" I looked up, and it was Marcus. I turned warm when I saw his face, which smiled down at me, his eyes glinting. Everything in me started to hum.

"Hey! Long time, no see!" he said. Another senior, Dan, taller and skinner than Marcus was, with a beaky nose and dark, curly hair, stood next to him and looked half asleep. He acknowledged me with a half nod.

"How are you?" I asked, surprised at how relaxed I sounded.

"Not bad," he shrugged, his smile growing broader. An image of Leif hulking over me in the green room over spring break popped into my head, and I pushed it out.

"I thought you didn't come to these things." I had to shout now, since the music became a boisterous Caribbean-sounding song. I wanted to dance.

"Ehh, needed a change of pace. You? Why aren't you with your buddies?" He nudged my elbow making my body hum even more.

"I'm banished." I started moving to the music.

"Uh, oh," Marcus started to laugh. He mumbled something to his friend.

"What?!" I demanded in a bitchy screech.

He chuckled. "Nothing. Sorry. Just joking. C'mon let's dance." And with that he grabbed my arm, led me to the dance floor with Dan. It was as if he had thrown me up into the air, my body felt so light and excited.

Even after the margarita, major self-consciousness overcame me as I tried to dance. I wanted nothing more than to just let go, swing my hips, and jump up and down, yet my feet couldn't figure out what to do first to make my body follow. But towards the end of the song, I felt warmed up, and as the Hindi/Disco song that I had first heard in Lally and Alicia's room started, I was as free as a bird. I swayed my body to the music and refused to look at the deejays, yet hoping one of them saw me. As if he'd care.

Marcus wasn't much of a dancer, not that I expected him to be. Compared to the enthusiasm that Leo had on the floor, Marcus looked like he was stuck in peanut butter. Dan was the same, only his arms seemed to have a life of their own and dangled like loose appendages from his body. At the end of the song, he saw someone by the entrance, waved to us, and left. And thank God because I was ready to be alone with Marcus. It looked so much better.

About half an hour of dancing passed before Marcus asked me if I wanted to go outside. We headed out the door.

"The air feels so good!" I exclaimed as I stretched my arms out to let the coolness of the air dry my sweat. I closed my eyes and breathed in the earthy, muddy scent of the spring night mixed with sea air. The alcoholic buzz was gone, and I was relieved to be seminormal. Perry and Kurtzman felt miles away. There was laughter and hushed rapid voices, which could only mean gossip, that grew distant as we headed away from the student center. I looked up at the sky, which was pitch black and heavy with clouds.

"You're a good dancer," Marcus said.

"Oh, thanks!" I knew I couldn't return the compliment. "I hardly ever go to these things, and I wish I went more often. They feel amazing."

"Yeah, I've sort of forgotten about their energy!" He let out this adorable, dorky chuckle, like he was seven years old.

"Did you used to go a lot?" I asked.

"During my freshman and sophomore years, and then I got sick of it. You know, spending time with Perry and all."

"Right." All of a sudden the night, like my awful room back in Kurtzman, weighed on me. I changed the subject, asking him about the ultimate Frisbee team, of which he was cocaptain.

"Great! We beat Northfield Mount Hermon last weekend!" He put his hands in his pockets and stared out at the black night.

I imagined our conversations so many times that the reality of the situation was awkward, and I was desperate to fill in the pauses. But with what? And then he turned to me, and there was a hint of a smile on his face. I crossed my arms and scratched my elbow, pretending I had a mosquito bite. *I could ask him about college.* "So, um, what schools—"

"You don't seem like their type."

"Whose?" I went cold. Was he talking about Leo, Lally, and Alicia?

"You know," he gestured towards Kurtzman with his head. "The *girrrls.*" He dragged the word out mockingly. "You seem really ..." His voice trailed off, and he looked around as if the answer was propped up somewhere on the lawn we stood on. "I don't know. Different." He sneered for two seconds, and then his smile returned.

I nodded. "Is that good?"

He looked directly at me, his hazel eyes like two big dots of ink in darkness, and moved closer. "It's great."

"Good." My shoulders tensed.

"I wanna kiss you."

"Uh," It was like my voice was falling down stairs. "Sure."

He took me in his arms, and as I leaned against his damp chest, he pressed his lips against mine. They were like soft petals. As he opened his mouth and let his tongue explore my mouth, it felt like the easiest, most natural thing in the world. His tongue was velvet. Not like the sloppy French kisses of earlier. This was like exploring a large, velvet flower.

His hands moved over every part of my backside while mine were firmly planted on his shoulders. When he slipped his hands over my butt and squeezed it, five thousand shivers and volts of electricity went through me. I could not believe this was happening. A string quartet seemed to strike a chord deep inside me.

"Let's go to my room and listen to some music," he said in a low voice that resonated in my gut.

Unable to speak, because I was shocked that he was inviting me up to his room, I nodded, and we headed over to the lit porch of his dorm. I kept reminding myself to breathe.

When I signed in on the visitor's sheet, Marcus said, "Don't use your real name. Just in case. Maybe it's stupid, but …"

"Right." My heart sped up, and I wrote the first name that came into my head: *Lisa*.

I hadn't been to his room since Hurricane Gloria, but nothing much had changed. He still had the large poster of *A Clockwork Orange* on his wall and the forest green comforter on the bed. The sleek, dark stereo and small, yet powerful speakers. There was that boy smell that every boy room had: an acrid, sweaty smell. But no pictures of Perry.

Marcus slipped a CD into the stereo. Prince whined from the speakers as his guitar followed.

"Siddown." Marcus patted the space next to him on the bed. I sat down and was consumed by the dark green cloud of his comforter.

Maybe we were going to talk. Frisbee. College. I was wondering if we'd ever talk about music. Why did he like Prince? Why did I like the Beatles? All those imagined conversations I had. But when his lips headed straight for mine, it was obvious they were not the questions to be asked.

For a while, we simply kissed. And it was nice. Not sloppy, just nice. Kind of repetitive. In fact, I wondered if there wasn't supposed to be more to it, like passion, and no matter how much I tried to spice it up by kissing his neck or playing with his tongue, everything remained the same. I reminded myself that all I had dreamed about happening was finally happening. *Yup. Here it is.* But the string quartet inside me had packed their instruments and gone. The hum wasn't even a low vibration.

My mind wandered. Leo popped up. God, it's not like I wanted to kiss him. Maybe I was wondering what he was up to. Was he still with that girl, and why did I have to be so bothered by it? And then I wondered what his lips felt like, if they felt like Marcus's. Who cares? Was the dance over with? I had to push Leo out, since he was really distracting—all those scarlet spots in his hair. I tried to be more passionate with Marcus, letting my hands explore him and slowly make their way down to his jean-clad crotch. It felt firm and warm. I massaged it, telling myself this was what I was supposed to be doing.

Marcus unzipped his fly, brought out his penis, and made me hold it and do whatever I was supposed to do, and the little string quartet started warming up as I tried to recall all the fantasies I had over spring break. It was unbelievable that they were coming true.

We kissed some more. He was very smooth, practiced, he put his hands up my shirt, unhooked my bra easily, and I felt exposed and vulnerable and closed my eyes. I thought of Rob Lowe, who then morphed into Leo, which made me feel warmer but confused my brain.

We got under his large, green comforter. Marcus's hands worked in one area and then moved on to the next. While I was excited with the newness of everything and feeling him against me, his hardness pressed right up in me, I couldn't help but think in the back of my mind that there was something very mechanical about the whole process. My thoughts veered to the scene from *St. Elmo's Fire*, where two of the characters had sex that was so spontaneous they fell out of the shower, the young woman's pearls still draped around her neck. It was as if Marcus had everything timed.

"Oh God, Perry, suck it now," he moaned.

I bounced back, almost falling off the bed. As if in an echo, Prince finished off the song with a high-pitched moan.

Marcus stared at me, eyes wide and terrified, his hand to his mouth. "Oh shit. I'm sorry!"

"No, that's OK," I said, not knowing how I was feeling. Probably disgusted. I hooked my bra back up.

"Uh, sorry, uh … Jess!" he shook his head, looking around the room as though disoriented. "I totally didn't mean that I didn't want to be with you and stuff."

I nodded, trying to make him believe that it was all cool. "Right. Totally. Don't worry about it." I looked at my watch. It was almost 11:00. "Dorm closing! I gotta run! Uh, thanks!"

Thanks? For what? I rushed out of the dorm and jogged down the small hill, past the emptying student center and over to Kurtzman. Maybe I said it because I finally got to kiss the guy. Even though it didn't come close to what I had imagined over spring break. Whatever the reason, it was a dumb thing to say. And I had to go to bed.

Luckily, my room was empty as was Perry and Pepa's. They were probably down in the butt room smoking. It took a long time for my heart to calm down. And even then, I couldn't get to sleep. His tongue traveling around my mouth and then the utterance of her name circled in my brain nonstop. I fell asleep around 5:00 AM. Suzie, I realized, never came back to the room.

CHAPTER 14

Carry that Weight

Once I opened my eyes at 9:00 AM, the proverbial tape of the previous night's events still played in my mind, along with occasional bits of Perry telling me off—the statuesque brunette making her way over to Leo, the dull feel of Marcus's lips and tongue mixing with mine, our bodies against one another, the warmth in my thighs. I held my pillow close to me, not knowing whether I wanted to recapture the sensations or somehow exorcise them. And then came Marcus's utterance of Perry's name and hearing her bark at me, and it all wound around and around in my head nonstop. I had to get up and shower, hoping the enormous amount of lather my lemony-smelling shower gel produced would somehow erase the tape. But once I was down in the dining hall, getting corn-flakes and coffee almost without thinking, I was only more bleary eyed, feeling as though a bunch of people had plunked themselves right on my forehead.

No sooner had I sat down at a table that was not our usual one, when Perry came up, placed her plate of bright yellow scrambled eggs and brown toast next to my bowl and joined me. We sat next to each other in a thick silence for a few moments.

Finally she spoke. Her voice was so controlled, it was like the slow injection of something poisonous into the air. "Have fun last night?" she asked.

For a second, everything in me contracted. I tried to continue eating as if I didn't know what she was talking about, but that was pointless. She saw us. Or at least, heard what happened. The question sped through my mind as to whether Marcus knew she was in the vicinity and did the whole thing deliberately, maybe to show her up. But I couldn't remember him looking around to catch someone's eye. Then again, I was a little buzzed by both the alcohol and by being with Marcus. "No, not really." I looked ahead while eating my tasteless and crunchy cornflakes. The degree to which they stuck to my teeth annoyed me but at the same time gave me something to concentrate on while the rest of me continued to wind itself up in fear. Why didn't I stop him?

"Right." Out of my peripheral vision, I saw her flat expression. "So, is he a good kisser?" There were tiny breaths coming out of her nostrils, and I realized she wasn't going to budge until I gave her an answer. She crossed her arms in front of her. "We saw it."

Of course.

But still, her announcement punched me in the stomach. It took a while for me to get my breath back and to answer, only this time, I looked down at her faded, scuffed-up, pink flats that were clamped to the floor. "It was nothing, Perry. He called out your name, anyway." I held on to the edge of the table.

I looked up at her face, a picture of disgusted disbelief. "When? I never heard it."

"When we were in his room." My mouth was contracted and dry.

"Yeah, nice try with 'Lisa,'" she said in a serrated voice while making quotation marks with her fingers.

"Perry, I'm sorry. I fucked up." I started running my hand up and down my thigh in an effort to calm my shaking.

"Jess, with anyone else, it would be fine. But you were my friend. Sorry is not enough. I *trusted* you! And it's common knowledge that a friend never goes behind another friend's back and kisses an ex-boyfriend. It's totally off-limits and tacky. God, what kind of world do you live in? It's like you're out of touch with everything around you!"

"He told me he wanted to kiss me. He didn't even ask." Every word came out in a steady monotone.

She started to yell. "Yeah! And you could have said no, but you grabbed the chance. Don't try to excuse yourself. It's really time you lose the sweet and innocent act, OK? You had us fooled for a bit, but it's beginning to get really tired. And when I saw you last night, I saw that you were deceiving us all this time about who you really are. All pure and virginal, when you're as sly and conniving as the worst of them. I trusted you, and you go and slap me in the face like this." She got up and picked up her tray of uneaten food, and I wondered if she just had it as a prop. As she left, she said, "I should have learned when I heard you lie to your parents like that."

I slumped in my chair, knowing in all my embarrassment that every pair of eyes in the room was either staring at me or sending messages to the other eyes about what they had just seen. I thought I heard whispers.

I was trapped. I had no idea where I was going to go once I left the dining hall. I thought of the Italian word for nightmare which was *incubo*, always reminding me of the word *incubator* and making me think the Italians thought an incubator, something to keep you warm and alive, was actually like death.

Making my way out of the dining hall and then the dorm, I sleepwalked over to Fletcher, hoping Lally and Alicia would still find me acceptable after what happened. Maybe I wanted to see Leo, see what his reaction would be after last night. If he really cared. I had to think of a backup plan if the statuesque brunette was going to be anywhere in sight. Just turn around, leave the school, and run away home.

I passed by scattered groups of people lying out on blankets, some girls in bikinis and baby oil, while their boom box blared out a song about walking on sunshine that sounded desperately hyper. The temperature was only in the sixties, but that didn't prevent them from pretending this was midsummer heat. As I approached Fletcher, I heard the singer Paul Morrissey's delicate tenor sing from the speakers in Leo's window. Lally, Alicia, and Leo sat on a blanket under the window, decked out in baggy shorts, and I gazed at the light brown hairs on Leo's legs. Textbooks and notebooks were scattered around them, pages occasionally flapping in the sun. Leo looked up, gave me a vague wave as though we were mere acquaintances. Now I really wanted to leave the school.

But when Lally shouted out, "Jess!" and Alicia waved, I had second thoughts and continued to approach them.

"Hey," I replied and then just stood there like an idiot. I didn't know where to put myself, and I didn't want to acknowledge Leo. All I seemed to be able to do was walk and stand. But then I had to look at him; he was concentrating on some chemistry formula.

Lally patted the beige blanket for me to sit down on.

"What's up?" Alicia asked.

"I had a huge fight with Perry."

"Uh oh." Lally adjusted herself on the blanket.

Leo's head shot up, his face appearing particularly Italian in his black wraparound glasses, which matched his hair. I noticed how graceful his lips were, how majestic his nose, but there was something firm and angry in all of it, making him even more handsome.

"What happened?" Alicia hugged her skinny, bare legs.

I sat down but felt like there was something between me and the ground, like I wasn't really sitting on it. "Well, I ended up dancing with Marcus." I sounded so gossipy and chatty that it undercut the turbulence I felt. I knew I was going to get no reaction, aside from stoniness, out of Leo. I swallowed and persevered. "Anyway, so we went outside, and we were just talking, and then Marcus said he wanted to kiss me, and I said OK." I shrugged like it was all no big deal while Leo's sunglasses appeared like one large, angry, black fly in my peripheral vision. "And then we went up to his room, and we just kissed, and then I was like, 'I gotta go.'"

"Wow, you *kissed* Marcus?" Lally replied in a whisper.

"It was just this stupid thing. I was kind of drunk."

"So did Perry see it?" Alicia asked.

"Yeah. But they aren't even going out. And anyway, it's totally over!" As I shook my head, I wondered if Marcus felt the same way. Maybe last night made some sort of an impact on him, made him realize who I was, that maybe he was attracted to me. Except for the fact that he called out Perry's name. I clicked my tongue and rolled my eyes only to emphasize how completely ridiculous the whole situation was.

Leo's deep voice intoned, "Is he a good kisser?"

Part of me wanted to say he was incredible, but given that Leo repeated what Perry had asked me an hour earlier, and that his voice had lost all traces of Italian as he spat these words out, I felt stuck. He sounded nastily American, like he had become someone else.

Lally and Alicia looked over at him and then at me, Alicia clutching her knees even closer to her chest.

I looked right into his glasses, trying to summon up any strength I had. "Whatever. It's not important because it's over."

I felt the intense heat of the spring sun on my back as Leo continued to study me, biting his lip. The memories of the night before with Leo making cameo appearances in my brain caused my stomach to clench in a mix of repulsion and excitement.

Lally shook her head, "You just can't take over Perry's old property."

"They just kissed, and besides, Perry and Marcus broke up two months ago!" said Alicia.

Lally shook her head. "Yeah, and so what? Do the math."

Then the words fell out of my mouth. "The thing is, we'd all been drinking margaritas in our room right before. And Perry and I had this fight because she thought I was jealous of her. 'Cause she's going to New York next weekend, and she kept talking about this guy she was going to see, this painter she had a fling with and who got her pregnant over Christmas."

"What?" All of them, including Leo, who now lifted off his glasses, exposing wide, blue eyes, gasped and leaned toward me.

I knew the longer I sat there with them, the more I was going to divulge.

Alicia's jaw dropped down, and she looked over at Lally, "She is *so* unbelievable!" I didn't know if she meant me or Perry.

Leo put his sunglasses back on. "I can't believe you were friends with her." He opened another textbook and started studying it, the light glaring on the smooth, white pages.

I let out an audible sigh in response.

"Don't worry about her," Lally put her hand on my leg. She smelled of some floral perfume that was so light and feminine it seemed contrary to her sloppy-extra-large-black-concert-T-shirted-and-Doc-Martened self. "You can hang with us."

"Thanks," I replied.

Leo shut his book, stood up, and announced he had to go to the library. I didn't know whether to be relieved or sad at this.

"Clearly jealous," Lally indicated with her head towards him. "And it's really lame because he hooked up with this girl last night, so I don't know what his deal is."

A flash of very distinct jealousy went through me. The statuesque brunette. "And he's mad at *me*?" I said through my teeth.

"He's kind of confused," Alicia said with a grimace.

"Does he really have the Lothario reputation that everyone talks about?" I tried to make my voice sound oh-what-the-hell, but I couldn't.

"I guess," Alicia shrugged.

"He's a *guy*," Lally said. "And a total Scorpio."

Like that was going to help me. I wanted to know who this girl was, and plus, I had to admit to myself I had crush on him. The previous afternoon in his room did hold an electrical charge in my memory, and it all seemed to come plunging down with his sudden change of mood. What was he thinking? "I can't like Jess like that! I have too many other girls to think about." Yet wasn't that what I had been thinking as well? Maybe the reason I kissed Marcus was also to get back at him as well. And Perry.

I sat silently with the two girls, mulling this over as I watched their index fingers trailing mathematical formulas in their notebooks. The sun continued to heat up my back, and Leo's stereo was silent. But what made me feel even worse, especially right now, was that my chances of being Leo's girlfriend were slim to none since he was clearly such a run around. Life really and truly sucked. It felt like one long string of fuckups and an overly warm, stifling *incubo*.

I spent the rest of the afternoon with Lally and Alicia, the question about the statuesque brunette ready to leap from my lips, but never doing so. First I had to make one dread-filled trip back to Kurtzman to collect my homework. Luckily, when I went back to my room, the door to Perry and Pepa's room was shut, and I could hear Suzie's voice, which meant my room was empty, and the three of them were probably talking about me. It was hard to imagine otherwise. I rushed out of the dorm, so I wouldn't have to encounter any of them.

But I couldn't concentrate on my work. I was in Lally and Alicia's room, Lally working on her history paper while Alicia was finishing up her Beat Farmers project, the chemical smell of art supplies hitting my nose every so often, reminding me of art class at Katonah and joking around with Kim.

With such a tiny glimmer that I barely noticed it, an ache of wistfulness went through me. I saw the crowded hallways filled with kids banging lockers shut, feet clomping on the linoleum floors, weekends filled with promise because I was going into the city to have my piano lessons, being with my grandmother. My eyes stung. I had put her safely in the back of my mind while I got on with my life. But now she was front and center, sitting on the couch with me in her living room or next to me in a yellow taxi telling me stories, her white hair tinged with yellow, the curls cradling her ears. I felt her hovering above me and had the memory of her Calèche perfume.

I read my Italian assignment all about Cesare and Marisa who complained about *i troppi compiti* (too much homework) and wanting to toodle around downtown Bologna on Cesare's Vespa, which led me to think about Leo and seeing his hairy legs this afternoon and wonder how they would feel. *Hairy*, I told myself. But as dinner approached, and it was Sunday night, and therefore I had to eat the Sunday sit-down dinner in Kurtzman, I toyed with the idea of feigning illness.

"Go to the infirmary," said Alicia when I told them my plan.

But Lally interjected, "No, that'll look lame. Everyone will read through it. Go back there and show them you do not care."

"Yeah, but Marcus will be there."

"You just kissed him, so what?" Lally replied.

"Actually it was a bit more than that."

"Excuse me?" Alicia said. Lally gave me a warning look.

"I couldn't tell you guys the whole story because Leo was there."

Alicia leaned toward me. "You mean you had sex?" It sounded like she was trying out new vocabulary words.

"Not exactly. We just fooled around a bit. It all happened really fast. You know, we were kissing one moment and the next his shirt's off, and then we're under the covers ..." My voice trailed off. "It's weird because once it starts happening, you don't want it to stop."

"I know, it's like something takes over," Alicia nodded at me.

"You're like, 'What's happening?'" Lally's voice sounded uncharacteristically airy.

I looked at both of them. "Wait, did you both ... you know?"

Alicia fidgeted with the paper label on her craypas. "Well, last year I was with this senior, and we were both kind of drunk. It was pretty heavy. We came close, but he didn't have protection." She smiled. "Lally's crossed that barrier."

At that moment Lally let out an embarrassed laugh, yet at the same time looked like an adult, like she had graduated from college.

"It was last summer," she replied. "I was working in this restaurant and flirting with this guy who was a waiter, and we started going out, and at the end we slept together. He was about to go to college." Her face lit up a bit. "It was kind of nice. He was really good to me. But it wasn't like I was in love with him or anything. You do feel kind of different I guess."

"I feel awful." I looked down at my legs.

"Yeah, 'cause you were with an asshole," she replied, her voice flat and frank.

I stared at my legs. "He called out Perry's name."

"You're kidding!" Alicia came over and put her arm around me. She smelled of tea rose.

I wanted to cry, but nothing came up. I felt constipated with my feelings.

Lally sat by my other side. "Jess, you gotta show them they will not get you down."

"And at campus meeting, we'll save a place for you, OK?" Lally asked, and Alicia nodded.

"Isn't Leo ...?" I started.

Lally snorted. "Don't worry about him."

I decided to wear simple black and white for dinner. I wanted to look pulled together and correct. No namby-pamby pastel crap. Black suede miniskirt, white oxford shirt, simple black pumps with a low heel, wide, black vinyl belt, and some vintage jewelry. Hair pulled back in a tight ponytail. A bit of perfume.

When Suzie came in to get dressed, neither one of us spoke. We did not exist for each other.

I went downstairs, and the phone rang. It turned out to be for me; it was Mom and Dad, picking the worst Sunday to call.

"Hello?" My voice was weak.

"Hey, honey," Dad said, and I waited a second to hear Mom's voice bounce in. It didn't.

"Hey, Dad," I said with a sigh of relief.

"Your mom's in the city and won't be back until late. So it's just me tonight. How is everything?"

"OK."

"Classes OK?"

"I suppose. It's the social side of things."

"Uh huh." He waited, giving me enough room to speak.

"I didn't want to say anything before with Mom on the phone. She always gets so defensive."

"Listen, that's just her way of being worried. I know she has some sharp edges to her, but you are her daughter, and I know she wants you to be happy. And when you're not, she gets kind of funny. Tell me what's up."

"I'm no longer friends with my old friends. Perry saw her ex-boyfriend kiss me last night." I was surprised at how comfortable I felt telling Dad this. "And it just ... it ended up being a mess."

"Oh, Jess, honey, I'm so sorry." He sounded like he really meant it; no placating. "Listen, I have to be honest with you. I always had a funny feeling about Perry, ever since I first met her. I didn't like the way she looked at you."

"What do you mean?"

"She just seemed very uptight. Guarded. It was something I picked up." A pause. "Her eyes were too cold. There was this smile, but her eyes were cold. I didn't like it."

I tried to think back on that day, but all I remember were my own rattling nerves.

"You making new friends? How about that Italian guy you hung out with over Christmas?"

"Well, he's mad at me too. But I'm friends with two of his friends. These girls."

"Good. Is he upset you kissed this guy too?"

"Yeah."

"Sweet pea, let me tell you something. I want you to hang out with your new friends as much as possible and know that although things are going to be tough with Perry, just hold your head high. Do not take the bait with them. And with this other guy, well, you never know. It could all even out. Keep me posted, OK? And also, Kim would love to hear from you."

"I started a letter to her," I lied guiltily, and then we said good-bye, but I still felt Dad next to me. It knocked me off balance, being this candid with him for the first time in ages. I wondered if he knew how uncomfortable I was here.

At dinner I looked at my usual table, and there were Marcus and Hassan like nothing had changed all these months. Perry and Marcus were together again. Whatever appetite I had when I came in, now disappeared. I was dizzy and wondered where I could sit. I chose another table and sat silently as everyone else chatted.

At campus meeting, I made a beeline for Lally and Alicia. Leo was with them, and my heart sank and beat faster at the same time. But he turned to me and said, "*Ciao,*" making me feel cooler.

"Hey," I replied as I slid in between him and Alicia, wondering which of the two girls talked to him. Probably Lally. I didn't bother to look back at the Kurtzman section, knowing full well the gang was together again.

When the meeting ended, Leo and I said nothing to each other, just exchanged shy glances. But there was so much I wanted to say. "*I'm sorry! I didn't know what I was doing! I saw you with that girl! What happened? We were having such a good time, and then you changed!*" And so did I.

Under the large oak tree by the entrance of the chapel were Perry and Marcus, standing very close together, talking intently. They were oblivious to me as I passed slowly by. I heard a sharp, "You promised it would be just one kiss. I didn't say go back to your room!" Marcus replied in almost a whine. "So I got carried away! It was your idea! Let's just move on and forget about it."

CHAPTER 15

Raindrops Keep Falling on My Head

I got little to no work done on Sunday, my mind buzzing the overheard words. All day Monday, the code of silence between myself and my old group prevailed. News of what happened that Saturday night was beginning to leak out. I had at least two different girls come up to me and ask me if I really slept with Marcus Feld, while I got the occasional leering glance from some guys. I ignored them both, or at least tried to.

I had lunch with Lally and Alicia and inhaled a pizza despite the absence of any appetite. I didn't say anything and just listened to their talk about colleges. Alicia got accepted at UC Santa Cruz while Lally was pondering Wesleyan or Oberlin. Leo was going to NYU, and judging by the screeching I heard in Kurtzman, Pepa was accepted at Cornell, her first choice. Once I finished my ice cream, again eaten with the need to swallow and put food inside of me, I stood up, said, "See you later," and rushed to Bartlett.

I heard no piano sounds and found most of the doors, aside from the ones behind which I heard trilling voices or strings, were open, but Leo was nowhere to be found. I defiantly told myself I wouldn't think about him. But as I sat there trying to practice my neglected homework, it was hard to shove him out of my thoughts.

Mrs. McGowan sailed in, tall and reedy, bringing with her the lemony scent of her perfume. Not missing a beat, she gave me a quick smile and asked, "Did you practice Saturday and Sunday?"

It was interesting how she just knew. What was it about adults? She had never asked me this question before, and yet the one weekend I didn't get anything done, she knew to ask.

"Yeah, but I had a bad weekend. I'm sorry," I grumbled back.

There was silence, which I hated because I was terrified of what was to come next.

But instead her voice was oddly quiet. "You can't let that get in the way of your work. No matter how horrible things are, you cannot use it as an excuse not to work, Jess."

More silence followed.

"What happened?" she asked, cocking her head to the side.

"I had a falling out with my friends. It was really bad." I wanted to blurt out the whole story and at the same time wanted to keep my mouth shut. Mrs. McGowan was older than my mother; forget about telling her all the nasty little things that happened. And yet, ever since the beginning of winter term, after that first terrifying lesson and the week surrounding Perry's abortion, I realized she may have known more about what was going on than I thought.

"I'm so sorry," she said as her voice wavered.

I talked to the black-and-white piano keys. "I should have never trusted those guys in the first place." I started to play some chords.

"Jess," Mrs. McGowan began, leaning on the piano with both elbows, hands clasped around each other. "What you have to remember is that while you may feel really alone right now, you're not. There is not one person on this whole earth who hasn't gone through what you're going through right now."

"My mother," I announced, surprised at the grating edge in my voice. I never once heard her speak of any lack of popularity.

"Now come on!" Her voice filled the room, and I thought of my grandmother, the way she could bark like that. "You're mother is an *actress*! You honestly believe she hasn't gone through something like this? Maybe she never told you, but in her profession?"

It was so obvious, I felt ashamed for not thinking it before. I remembered years ago, hanging out in the green room at the TV studio, and hearing her give advice to a young actress who was also an aspiring Broadway dancer. My mom told her how during dance class she had to make sure she was always in the front row for the teacher to see. "It's all an audition. Those teachers know people.

Don't let anyone get ahead of you." The glint in my mother's eye when she said it had a hardness, an anger. And then I thought of all those young ingénues prancing around in front of her day after day on those icy cold sound stages.

"Yeah, duh," I finally replied, trying to let out a small laugh, but it came out as a hiccup.

"Everybody, and I mean every last person, unless they've been a lifelong hermit, has to go through this. It happened to me in high school. I became part of the popular crowd one year, and it was *awful*! I had admired it from afar for so long, and then when I finally 'made it,' I was miserable, if not bored."

I thought about Kim and her complaints about her crowd and all those weekend nights I spent with my quartet gossiping. Just gossiping. The same music. The same cloud of Obsession.

Mrs. McGowan continued, shuffling my sheet music on the piano. "But at the worst, it was pretty humiliating. And it's like that even for the ones who seem to be in the thick of things."

I had a hard time imagining Mrs. McGowan as a teenager. It was hard enough with my mom, despite the countless pictures I saw of her. But I had no pictures of Mrs. McGowan, so it was next to impossible imagining her parading the halls of some high school in the 1940s or 1950s, laughing with her other cohorts in that confident way that made popular people all seem taller than they actually were.

"Come on, let's get to work. Let's start off with some warmups." She cut into my thoughts.

And somehow I was able to push everything aside and plunge in. Despite the fact that it had been two days since I practiced, my fingers cooperated, my mind concentrated. Even the dreaded fifth finger behaved.

We worked on my piece. She wanted me to close my eyes, not look at the keyboard, the piano, or any place else in the room, just feel where to put the notes. I started at the beginning of the piece. Something came over me, and my fingers were now led by the keys. What surprised me were the notes that came out of the middle part: a jazzy syncopated section that was defined by major chords and gave everything a bit of a determined lift as if to say, "I'm gonna do whatever the hell I wanna do." The keys seemed to tell me how to touch them. As I moved my fingers over them, I immediately got the message: *soft, soft, now sharp*. I opened my eyes. Mrs. McGowan was looking at me. "Good," was all she said for a moment, and then she nodded, "Keep at it. Keep trusting yourself." I scribbled what I remembered on the staff sheets quickly before the notes walked out of my head and into oblivion. "And I want you to think about the title. Just think about what this piece is telling you."

Those last chords echoed in my head when I got out of my lesson. That little lift that I always had stayed with me until I entered the Kurtzman commons room. Some girls sat around the TV watching none other than Mom's soap, and I prayed, as I sped through there, that her face wouldn't appear on the screen. Suzie and Pepa were absent; I supposed I had turned them off to the show. As I walked past the couch, my gaze averted from the looming TV, I could hear Leif and Karen's murmurs, followed by a melancholy phrase on the vibes, signifying the end of the scene. I saw a girl tip the red and white striped can of her Diet Coke to her mouth and glance at me. A few others did the same.

There was the ache again. It was odd how hearing Leif and Karen's voices made me homesick. Leif was greasy, and Karen was a nut. So I didn't quite get why I wanted to be home at that moment, getting off the bus from school, waving to someone whom I had sat next to and who had become a new friend.

I made the dreaded journey up to my room, praying that I would find the door locked and that the three girls would either be out or down in the butt room. I didn't know which was worse: the trip to the dorm and then my room, or else actually being there in that little cheese box called our room with all the Garfields ogling me and Rob Lowe sulking from the wall with the sax he couldn't even play.

As I opened the door, I was greeted by Suzie and Pepa's small, beady glares from Suzie's bed where they were perched, an issue of *Mademoiselle* open in front of them.

I sat down on my bed to figure out what I had to do for the rest of the afternoon. Or at least pretend that was what I was doing. I knew they didn't want me to be there.

I was right.

"How much longer are you going to be in here?" Suzie asked me.

"As long as I want. It's my room too, you know."

The two girls exchanged looks.

Maybe it was what Mrs. McGowan had said to me earlier that fortified me, made me take the plunge. "You guys, please. This is so boring." I kept running Mrs. McGowan's words through my head. *These two have also been humiliated.* At some point, but God knows when—Suzie during a competition, Pepa with a bunch of jealous Spanish aristocratic girls. What I'm going through now is what they've either already gone through or will go through in the future.

"Why should we treat you like you're our best friend?" Pepa asked.

"How about trying to be at least polite?"

"Oh, like you would know a lot about that," She replied. Her haughtiness stung through my McGowan mantra.

"Going behind friends' backs," Suzie followed.

"Right, Suzie," I said, looking over at her, slouching on her pillows. "Like you've never done that before." Her face froze.

I grabbed my English notebook, a copy of *A Midsummer Night's Dream*, shoved them in my knapsack, and left, deciding to go try and find my friends in Fletcher.

In a sense, I was lucky to have Lally and Alicia to commiserate with me. I found them at the library, and the three of us crouched around a worn, wooden table in a small corner of the second floor, protected by high, dark gray metal shelves lined with Dewey Decimal–labeled fiction, our notebooks open in front of us and me trying to explain that I probably had been set up, whether Perry and Marcus actually broke up, the confrontation earlier with Pepa and Suzie in my room. All of this they greeted with nods, refrains of, "I know!" and references to Perry freak-outs from past years. I traced a groove in the table with one of my pencils, feeling a little less alone. The girls used words like *bitch* and *psycho*, but they only made Perry sound like a dime a dozen, and maybe to others she was. To me, though, she was something else.

I stayed in the library until dinner and then notified Marcie I was eating with Lally and Alicia in Fletcher. Right after dinner, I went straight back to the library and plunged into memorizing theorems and irregular Italian verbs, agitated at the thought of having to go back to my cold, little room and try and ignore cold, little Suzie, her obnoxious Garfield curios, and her Rob Lowe poster that now looked dated and juvenile with the dumb pierced ear and prop sax. I imagined Dad saying it was just there as a phallic extension. Fortunately, she didn't get back into the room until after I fell into a thick, worried sleep preceded by a primitive ache that kept haunting me.

And then on Tuesday, it all became a mudslide. I had only seen brief glimpses of Marcus, from a distance, and that was about all I could take. My former friends were a huddled trio that stayed to the side of me, watching, whispering. To me, they were a vat of used cooking grease. The ridiculousness of every fantasy I held about my new life at boarding school was now being slapped in my face.

As I approached the marble steps of the math and science building, there was Marcus, with his lanky friend from that Saturday night, glaring at me by the door.

"You are *sick!*" his words reached my ears, and I turned to him, all my breath escaping me.

I wanted to say, "What?" but my vocal chords remained frozen as my stomach started a small revolt against that morning's English muffin and scrambled eggs.

They turned and walked into the building and down the hall, falling in with the mass of students.

I sat down at my desk in biology, my mind clicking away, going through the events of the past few days, trying to figure out what happened, what I said, what I told Lally and Alicia, and what they may have told others. Why was I sick? What did I do? Was I supposed to say something to him after Saturday night? Was there something I said to him that night, that, in all the confusion of lust and guilt, I somehow blurted out?

When class started, a pop quiz floated down onto my desk, and I had to read each question, regarding the male and female reproductive systems, about three times before I could understand what was asked. I was the last to finish.

I skipped lunch and went to Bartlett to practice, but I was too distracted. I wanted to have Leo next to me, to go through *Pet Sounds* and all the wistful feelings it brought up. I got nowhere on my piece, the arpeggios that I had improvised on earlier sounding lifeless and flat, so I ended up reading some more of *A Midsummer Night's Dream*. But Shakespeare's language only became more convoluted and nonsensical as I continued. Even the footnotes didn't seem to sink in.

That afternoon people looked at me as if my body were covered up in open sores. The Perry trio was glacial to me. It was too late to invite myself to dinner at Fletcher, so I grabbed a grilled cheese at the snack bar. Later, during conversation class, Leo directed his conversation about the school system here as opposed to Italy's, to two guys who spoke a word a minute. They made no attempt at an accent, not even bothering to roll their *r*'s, which I at least tried to do. At the end, Leo gave me a vague wave.

On Wednesday morning, whatever it was that was causing Marcus to sneer at me and the girls to glare, spread through the rest of Kurtzman. At breakfast and throughout the morning there were whispers that followed in my wake, like little lacy breaths of air. Glances that said, "Oh … mi*god!*" and frowns of disbelief. Nobody said anything to me, and I was too terrified to ask.

Well, I was no longer the cipher I was at Katonah, that much was for sure. A sleazy rumor was following me. Is this what happens when people know who you are? When you hang out with a specific group? Mom had gossip trailing her, but she appeared to never give it another thought. She learned early on, probably from loud-mouth Grandma, to keep quiet about her life, and whenever she was discussed in *Soap Digest,* her name was usually prefaced with "the painfully private."

I robotically went through the day and spent lunch with the piano and another grilled cheese accompanied by a Coke. I was beginning to feel a bit nauseous, and I didn't know if it was my snack-bar diet (that was also eating away at my allowance) or the situation I was in. I left a message for Lally and Alicia to have dinner with them, and spent the afternoon in my room waiting for a phone call from them that never came. I lay on my bed, listening to the Burt Bacharach and Hal David musical, *Promises, Promises,* whose story of betrayal and sucking up seemed apt. I had very distinct memories of hearing my mother trill in the kitchen as she prepared dinner while I sat in the living room on a big couch listening to the Broadway recording.

Actually, the song that had been in my head all day was called "Knowing When to Leave," sung in a shaky but determined manner by the female lead. The words had been echoing in my brain on and off through classes. But I didn't go when the going was good like the lyrics chimed. I stayed, remained seduced.

When dinner rolled around, I forced myself to enter the noisy hall, filled with clattering flatware, laughter, and shouts and felt like a Plexiglas shield surrounded me, isolating me from everyone else. I didn't look at anyone, but I could feel eyes on me—some from people I didn't even know. *Spinach,* I thought, as I spied a green pile of it in one of the serving trays, *I really need spinach.*

The only space available was at Marcie's table, and she gave me her brief smile as I sat down next to her. This surprised and almost comforted me since lately Marcie was, at best, chilly with me. Everyone else at the table looked at me like they didn't know who I was.

"What's up?" she asked after dinner and the others had left. "You seem, I don't know. You're acting kind of strange." Her voice tried to sound conciliatory, but it was too distant.

"You tell me," I looked right at her. "Apparently I've done something really wrong, and I have no idea what it is." My back muscles contracted and started to tremble.

Marcie searched my face for a moment as if trying to find some guilt. "You want to talk about it?"

I glanced around the room and saw the group at their table, a bunch of vultures drinking coffee. Perry's high-pitched giggles were too fast, and she was still using that Woody Woodpecker imitation.

"If you really wanna know, Marcus kissed me, I kissed him back. Perry saw it. Marcus called me sick, and I think I was set up."

Marcie's eyebrows twitched. "Huh," she replied. "Well, maybe you should confront Perry on it. Sounds like something between you and her." She closed her eyes for a moment and shook her head almost with a smile. "Jess, I don't think you were set up. Perry wouldn't do something like that. That sounds pretty ridiculous."

I responded by getting up and putting my tray in the kitchen. I then went to Bartlett.

When I saw Leo in the hallway of the music building right before study hall, a wave of hope swept right through me. It had been a while since I saw him with the statuesque brunette. Was she out of the picture? Whatever the story was, he greeted me with a small wave and then slammed the door of the practice room behind him. Something in me lurched, and my eyes became moist. I ran up and knocked on the door.

"Yeah?" He looked up at me from the piano bench.

"Hey." I tried to sound casual as I shut the door a little too loudly. I managed to blink back the tears.

"Hey there." He gave me a frightened smile and started his scales.

"I-I need," I faltered. And then he stopped and looked at me. "I need somebody to talk to," I finally uttered, and then my eyes flooded over, and I broke down.

"No, wait. Come over here." He got up and brought me over to the piano bench. But there was something in his eyes that looked bewildered, like he didn't know what to do next. It wasn't the same assured sympathy I got in the club over Christmas break; there was something hesitant about him. He held me too lightly which only made me wail louder.

"I don't know what's going on!" I said. "Everybody's treating me like I have the plague. Marcus—" I sobbed so hard I couldn't get the words out.

Leo put his hands on my shoulders and had me look at him. "Tell me!" It came out sounding like *tayl mee*.

"He called me a sick fuck this morning." Even saying it made me recoil from Leo's hands. "I don't know what I did." For a moment I didn't want to look at him. He brought me to him with such force that I thought I was going to be flattened in his embrace. But at the same time, I reveled in it, in his smell, the vague perfume of his cologne. He held me and let me sob. Once again, my snot was on his T-shirt.

Then he said, "They think you're writing the notes."

It took a few seconds for the words to sink in. "What notes?" I jerked back from him.

"Marcus has been getting these notes, and I think they are saying something bad, and everyone thinks you wrote them."

I let myself breathe hard. "Why?"

"Because you were with him." He nodded his head to indicate the direction of Hilliman.

"What did the notes say?"

"I don't know. But bad things."

"But why would people think it was me?" I know I asked the same question, but I had to keep asking it, to get a different answer. I felt like I could ask it over and over again.

He didn't answer.

"You thought it was me."

He swallowed. "For a moment. Jess, I'm sorry!" His eyes grew wide as he raised his eyebrows. "I just didn't know. It seemed weird because it's not like I know you that well, and I thought, wow, maybe there is something to this girl I don't know, and then I realized it didn't make any sense—"

"I didn't do it," I squeaked.

"I know. Whoever did it is disgusting."

I remembered the scrawls on the notebook at the campus meeting with Perry that Sunday. "It's Perry," I said.

His eyes had a look of wariness as he gazed at me. "You're probably right."

"I don't know what to do," I whispered.

"We'll figure something out," he almost whispered and put a strand of my hair that was dangling near my face, behind my shoulders.

I stood up with a suddenness that surprised both myself and him. "OK. I feel better. I gotta go study."

"Come to Fletcher after study hall."

"Uh, yeah, I will." I nodded. But I didn't know if I could.

I filled study hall with endless homework. A lengthy and convoluted geometry problem actually distracted me for a while as I made my way through it, treating it like a game. Studying comedy in English right now was ludicrous. Mr. Sullivan kept talking about the lyrical quality of the text that made *A Midsummer Night's Dream* so special, and one would have thought that I, being so into music, would have plunged right into this. But I kept confusing Hermia, Lysander, Helena, and all the rest just as they were confusing each other. They all were so happy and light despite the fact that everyone was running around in circles, trying to get the other person to fall in love with them.

When we studied Romance it made sense to me, as did Tragedy. I actually enjoyed *House of Mirth* and wrote a decent final paper on it. But now my concentration was gone. I thought about how my brother and my mom would have referred to this play as *Midsummer*, they being those annoying actors who shortened all play titles to one word because their intimacy with it made them think they had actually written the damn thing. Or that's how it always came across.

At ten on the dot, even though I thought I wasn't going to do it, I walked over to Fletcher and banged on Lally and Alicia's door, behind which I could hear a song with a synth and a jazzy piano play as a man sang about having someone under his skin where the rain couldn't get in.

Only Lally was there, lying on her bed, perusing *Rolling Stone*. She looked up to me, her eyes bulged out with that same fear Leo had, and she said, "Oh. Hi!"

"Did you hear?" I demanded as I marched in.

She sat up. "What are you talking about?" I had a feeling she knew exactly what I was talking about.

"About the notes and stuff."

She paused and looked around the room. "Oh." I glared at her, and when she finally looked at me, her mouth formed an uneasy grimace. "Yeah." Pause. And then she looked like the same adult I saw in her when she told me she lost her virginity. "I know it's not you, Jess."

We were silent for a moment as I stood there, listening to the piano fade away at the end of the song.

"When did you find out?" I snapped.

"This afternoon. Someone said that Marcus was getting these threatening notes that were from some girl he slept with, and we thought of you, and for a moment we did think it was you. I mean, to get back at Perry and Marcus." I let my mouth drop open. "I'm sorry, Jess. It's disgusting to say that to you, like we don't trust you. But I have to be honest, for a moment, we thought it was you. Just because we didn't know. And then Alicia and I were talking about it during study hall, and we were like, 'No way, this makes no sense. Perry's getting back at her.'"

"That's twisted."

"I'm sorry we doubted you." Lally played with the comforter on her bed.

Now what was I supposed to do? Every time I had to go back to Kurtzman, it was like entering some cold jail cell. Was it better that I knew what was going on?

Was it better that Lally and Alicia knew that it was Perry? I was still rooted in place, still standing.

Lally patted a spot beside her. "Come on and sit down. You are making me really nervous just by standing there."

Seemingly out of nowhere, my voice felt shrill. "I don't know what to do! I can't believe this is happening to me. I mean—"

"Sit down." She again patted the spot next to her, and I obeyed.

"How could I have screwed up like that? What the hell was I thinking by being with Marcus?"

"Come on, it could have happened to anyone! To be honest, you had the most wanted man on campus asking you to kiss him, you're drunk, what the hell do you expect? Self-control doesn't play a role in this."

"Well, I wasn't really drunk. I pretty much danced it off." I was once again in the dimly lit student center, shaking and sweating away my margarita-filled fight with Perry to the thumping bass of the music.

"Jess, you can't totally blame yourself. They set you up."

I knew Lally was supposed to make me feel better, yet I felt like someone was squeezing my insides, making everything in me feel contracted and contorted. "I don't know what to do. How to I prove that Perry wrote the notes?"

"We can spy on her."

"I know how she got my handwriting. We wrote notes to each other on the back of her notebook during campus meeting two weeks ago."

"Did you leave anything else with her?"

"No idea. Probably." I lay back on the bed and rubbed my eyes. "But how are we going to get her?"

"We're just going to have to spy on her. Follow her around." Lally nodded, but then stopped as doubt crossed her face. "Which is easier said then done. Or you could just confront her."

We looked at each other and said in unison, "Easier said than done."

I sat up. "But what if she didn't write them?"

"Well, Jess, clearly someone in that circle did. It could be Suzie or Pepa. She probably bribed someone to do it. Maybe Marcus did it. I mean, you gotta wonder why he was with someone like that for four years. And agreed to a setup. And plus, they have kind of a funky relationship."

"I wish I could talk to Marcie, but she has so much blind adoration for Perry …"

"Please, I've heard all about that," Lally muttered. "I remember last year how everyone was so surprised that Perry made student leader. She had made so many enemies, which for some reason made Marcie protect her even more."

I could see it now—plain Marcie with her long, mousy brown hair and pretty, lively Perry.

"You know she went here, right?" Lally said.

"Yeah. She said she loved it so much she never wanted to leave."

"Apparently she didn't. Maybe Perry is like someone she wanted to be, you know?"

"She's like one of those people my dad talks about, these people who never leave high school."

"And Perry is the perfect student to be blind to."

I thought of a book Dad read to me almost every night when I was a child. A book called *Wait Till the Moon Is Full*. It was about a mother raccoon and her son who kept asking her if he could go out into the night to see the moon, and she kept replying, "Wait till the moon is full." Lally reminded me of this warm, comforting mom raccoon. "I am so lucky I found you guys," I said. "Thanks."

C H A P T E R   16

Hang On to Your Ego

The hysteria from the notes traveled like a furious dirt storm from one dorm to the next over the rest of the week. As I walked around campus, and especially through Kurtzman dining hall, the glances and whispers increased every day; even Marcie gazed at me steadily whenever I saw her in the room.

I tried to imagine what the notes said, how far Perry went, how big her imagination was. And yet, I began to think it was more than one person. Maybe it was all three girls. Lally pointed out that it could be some other loony tune who, like me, had a crush on Marcus and also saw what happened and decided to get back at both him and me. "Think about it. There are a lot of people, however misguided, who see you, know who you are, and who you hang out with and are probably jealous." I was kind of hoping that was not the case. I wanted to pin the blame on Perry.

Yet how could I catch her? I tried barging into her room a couple of times without knocking only to be met with a locked door or a trio of cold looks. Once, as I swung the door open, the three of them were lying on Pepa's lavender duvet, chatting, no papers amongst them, the overpowering smell of Obsession perfume bearing down on my nose while Madonna sang in her spoiled-brat voice over the stereo speakers. "Yes?" Perry's simple question cut the air and sent a tremor of fear and helplessness right through me, leaving me mute. She looked pale and callous. There were dark circles under her eyes, and something about her whole exterior had dulled since the fall. She sniffed and wiped her nose, returning to her two fidgety, beady-eyed friends. They all looked bad, but Perry looked by far the worst.

I said nothing and shut the door.

Friday morning, the day Perry was to leave for her weekend in New York, I walked to geometry with the cloyingly warm sunlight worsening my mood. Mrs. McGowan had left a message for me saying she had to cancel the lesson because she had a cold. The one light at the end of the day was snatched away from me. And just then, Marcus's hulking figure loomed at me, and he stated, "Stop sending those fucking notes!" With his mouth redder than normal, his small, mean eyes, and his hair almost frizzy, he scared me, and the people walking past turned to look at us. All of a sudden, their lives seemed enviably simpler than mine. They discussed math problems, upcoming finals, who had gotten into what college, the ultimate Frisbee match.

When Marcus turned and walked away, I ran after him and grabbed his arm. He jerked it from my grasp. "It's not me!" I said, my voice jumping around trying to find the right timbre. His eyes were wild and scared, as he gazed down at me. Summoning up all the strength I had, I recited slowly, "I did *not* write them."

But that had no effect. He threw a piece of scrunched-up paper at me. I caught it and opened it. The handwriting could only have been mine. It said: "*Since you have chosen to ignore me, you will soon see what death feels like.*"

The full realization that it was Perry was so calm, so logical that the ridiculousness of the situation still didn't touch me. "Um, Marcus," I called out to him. "This isn't me." I sounded matter-of-fact, belying the crumbling inside of me. The words felt like they were being spoken from miles away. I noticed how Marcus's shirt was a bit looser on him and that he'd lost weight. Again, I had to jog to catch up with him as we entered the echoey math and science building. "I know it looks like my handwriting, but I swear to God, it's not me! You know who forged this!"

He grabbed the note from my hand and waved it at me. "Oh, bullshit, Jess. Perry showed me your writing."

I screamed back at him, "Try putting two and two together, Marcus! How'd she get it?" But it all fell into a void, and Marcus disappeared into the crowd of students, some of whom, I finally realized, had gathered around to witness the morning's drama. Anything else I had to say was futile, so I headed to biology class and sat at my desk, resigned to the continuation of stares that plagued me the rest of the day.

Classes zoomed by in a blur while I mentally checked out. I remained silent as the teachers droned on. I took a pop quiz in geometry and wrote proofs that were just scribbles. I was writing for the sake of leaving marks on the paper and left one question blank. I read my Italian assignment when it was my turn, on automatic, not having a clue as to what I wrote the night before. I was embarrassed at how bad my accent sounded and was glad Leo wasn't standing in the doorway, listening.

After classes, when big puffy clouds, looking about as heavy as I felt, hung in the growing humidity overhead, I skipped piano practice and ran over to Kurtzman in hopes of finding Perry before she left for the weekend. A white cab was waiting in front of the dorm, making me pick up my pace. I had to talk to her and confront her.

I flew up the stairs and into her room, not bothering to knock. It was like perfect Kismet, seeing Perry in her yellow cotton sweater, big hoop earrings, crouched over a navy blue duffel.

"Could you knock?" she asked, her voice sounding very polite.

"What the fuck is going on? Are you writing those notes to Marcus?"

She cocked her head at me. "So I take it, you're not writing them?" She resumed her packing. "And of course you think it's me, right?" She shook her head and crossed her arms. "That is so fucked up."

My face turned hot, and I wondered how long I was going to be able to keep looking at her. "You set me up with Marcus. You can't deny it, I overheard you two talking about it."

She froze for a second, her eyes bugging out, and then she resumed back to normal and nodded, saying, "Uh huh. I wanted to test how loyal you were to me, and you failed." Her mouth stretched into something like a smile. "And Marcus said you totally encouraged him. I mean, Jess, you must know by now that guys in that situation can't think straight. They just go on automatic hormone overdrive! You could have stopped it, but you didn't." The smile grew larger.

"He encouraged me, Perry. He told me to go up to his room—"

"You could have said no," she answered primly as she resumed her packing.

"OK, I didn't, and I'm sorry. I screwed up in that. But you set me up! And then you go and write these notes?"

"How do you know it was me?" she cried.

I heard a snarl come out of my body, adrenaline raced through every part of me. "You're the only one with my handwriting. It's on the back of your notebook. How sick are *you*, huh? Where do you get off on thinking, *thinking* you can get away with it? How the hell did you get such a twisted, sick mind?"

"Oh, like screwing my ex-boyfriend wasn't twisted." She was all shaky warbles.

"You hypocrite," I said, almost lunging at her. "You screwed with other guys all last summer, and this spring parading around was the most natural thing in the world. You got pregnant, then you get mad at me for sleeping not with your boyfriend but with your *ex*-boyfriend. Your *ex*, Perry. And by the way, we just fooled around, if that. I'm still a virgin; we can go to the school nurse and prove it!"

"Jess, you are so ..." Her face was white. She managed to regain enough of her composure to click her tongue. "I can't even find the right word." Her eyes skittered over the room, and she swallowed.

"You have guilt written all over you," I said, my lips tingling. "The evidence is right on the back of that notebook." I pointed to it lying on her desk in plain view.

She was silent. She had become increasingly pasty and frazzled-looking these past few weeks. Her once shiny hair was dull and streaked, making her look cheap. The tip of her nose was red, and she sniffed, as she had been doing so often, before she spoke.

"OK," she put her hands on her hips. "You wanna know why I did it? Because you piss me off, Jess. Because you're pretty, and you have everything anyone could ever want, and yet you still whine. You have a famous mom, a lot of money, and you act like you're *sooo* sweet. Everybody talks about how sweet you are. It's gross. 'Oh, Jess, she's so pretty and unpretentious.'" Perry's voice was mocking and sing-songy, and her face was disgusted. "You know how annoying it is to have people constantly tell me, 'How can Jess be friends with you? She's so nice!' Like I'm some sort of repulsive bitch! And all these guys are after you, but you pretend to be off in your own universe. Even Marcus had a crush on you, although he wouldn't admit it. And then Leo! You just walk by, and he falls in love with you! You float around, and your life is one big charm. It's *disgusting*. You are one of those people who never have to work for anything because Mommy and Daddy hand it to you. And then you have the nerve to tell me I'm a nasty, and then criticize my life! I work my ass off, unlike you." She practically punched a hole in her chest with her finger. She continued, her voice rising. "Your parents call you *every* week. My parents could care less! They're more interested in the dramas of my stupid sister! It's like I don't exist for them. And then Marcus kissing you and taking you up to his room, that was the last straw—"

"You set it up, Perry!"

"Shut up! It was a *test*, Jess. For both of you. Marcus at least knew about it beforehand." Her eyes were as wide as I'd seen them, gleaming with tears and anger. "And you both failed." She picked up her duffel, slung it over her shoulders, and marched out the door before I could say anything else. She looked smaller than I had ever seen her.

I didn't know whether to be sorry for her or furious. There was so much I wanted to say. *"I was jealous of you at one point. You think having a famous mom is a great thing? You weren't there at lunch over spring break when I realized my mom was nothing more than an acquaintance. I couldn't help it if Marcus had a crush on me, and I thought you didn't like Leo. Maybe I really am in my own universe; that's not just an act. And you were beautiful once, Perry. You seemed to have it all together. You went out and grabbed life, unlike me who got scared and hid. You were so pretty and alive. That's why I liked you."* But I remained mute and once again weakened by her force.

I wanted to have an endless arm that could reach all the way down the stairwell, grab her, and bring her back to me. Explain it all. And yet at the same time I wondered, given what I knew of Perry, even before this incident, if it was worth it since there was no friendship to salvage.

It was hard for me to make my way out of the room in a straight line. Breathing also didn't come easy as I continued to struggle downstairs. I had to hang onto the banister. It was like I'd almost forgotten the normal rhythm of my body.

And then in the stairwell, something in me shattered. It came over me so quickly that I had no time to hold myself together. My eyes stung, my face was turning warm again. It's funny how right before you really cry, your whole face seems to fill up with hot liquid. I slumped down on a stair and burst into huge, racking sobs. Two girls raced past me on the way down, their cleats clapping against the linoleum, lacrosse sticks barely missing my head, and then the stairwell remained empty.

Once all the crying subsided, I stood up and went to Fletcher, my face feeling pinched and hard, the remaining sobs echoing in me like hiccups.

But Lally and Alicia weren't there. I went to the library, and as I searched the various book-lined corridors near our usual hangout, I heard two voices whispering and giggling. With the claustrophobic feeling that comes when the horror is confirmed, I knew right away whose voices they were.

At first it was mundane chatter about plans for the weekend. The dance they were not going to. What Hassan was up to. What about Marcus? And then I listened harder.

"No! You idiot! She does the *t* like this!" It was Pepa.

"Shut up!" Suzie giggled. "I've forged a bazillion notes to coaches and judges in my time, so don't tell me what to do. 'Swy Perry gave me the frickin' job."

"Hi!" I popped into their view as cheery as the sunshine on one of my mom's commercials for household cleanser.

I could have predicted the gasps and swoosh of paper as the two girls gaped at me and shoved the note under a biology textbook.

"What are you writing?" I asked, hands on my hips. It was all I could do not to swallow in midsentence.

"None of your damn business. Leave us alone," Pepa whispered.

I walked over to their table, leaned my hands on the varnished wood and said, trying to control the shaking in my voice, "Cat's out of the bag, you guys. I caught Perry. Now I caught you. You might as well stop right there."

They stared at me, and for the first time, I felt securely situated on a very high pedestal, until Pepa said, "You have any witnesses? How will Marcie know you're not lying? And by the way, you don't know what we're writing, so what have you got to prove?" She sounded like she was critiquing a paper of mine.

Suzie pretended to read some scribbles in her notebook. It looked like doodles and names of bands. She and Pepa glanced at each other, and Suzie turned to me and said simply, "Would you please leave?"

I turned away, feeling smaller than a gnat, and at the same time, so filled with rage that I left the library and went to practice piano. There was nothing else I could do with all this energy.

It was amazing how everything that happened that afternoon was funneled into my practice, making me calm and focused, but always with the anger underneath. I worked on scales, finger exercises. I went over every little mistake with a calm determination. I was going to finish this piece that weekend, not just because Mrs. McGowan said I had to, but because at last I finally wanted to. When she had announced last week that I had to finish it up and give it a title, dread crawled through me, and I knew inspiration for composing anything was as remote as last year's Saturday mornings in New York with Chris. But now, as I relaxed my fourth and fifth fingers during a new exercise I had been assigned, a small inkling of wanting to create welled up inside of me. "*Good*," I could hear Mrs. McGowan say with a sharp shake of her head.

I grabbed a staff sheet, placed it in front of me, put a pencil in my mouth, and got to work. I knew what I wanted to do, and I was going to do it. I didn't want it to be completely sad the way it had been in the beginning. I would keep what I started on earlier, keep that question, followed by an answer. Keep a definite rhythm, so people hearing it wouldn't forget. Maintain that determination in the middle. I had heard countless stories of some of the most memorable melodies being written in the space of ten to fifteen minutes, how John or Paul would whip up what would become a legendary song while sitting in an airplane.

I don't know what it was that allowed me to churn the rest of the piece out, except that I had nowhere else to go and no one to see. As the melody came out, the questions holding the tension of the piece, followed by their answers which let it go, made me think of Leo and his hug in the club, and the hug Tuesday night. It was funny because the more I wrote, the more I thought of him. And surprisingly, it wasn't as sad as I thought it would be. The beginning six chords remained the same, wistful and set in a minor key, but then I went into a more positive section with major chords as the tempo picked up. I didn't want to make the tempo as erratic as a classical piece. I knew what I wanted to write was something closer to pop, so I tried to keep the tempo as steady as possible.

I didn't finish the song like I hoped. But the work was so intense that after only half an hour, I felt exhausted, yet happier than I had before, like I had just taken a refreshing shower after weeks of not having one. I wondered where Leo was, hoping he wasn't with the statuesque brunette. I immediately wanted to share this with him. I ran over to Fletcher, but he wasn't around, so I returned to Kurtzman for the first time in what felt like ages without feeling fearful—until Marcie called out to me from her apartment when she saw me enter the lounge.

"Um, Jess, there's something we need to discuss." Her clear voice stopped me dead in my tracks.

"What?" I asked as I turned to her, everything inside of me small with shame.

With her arms crossed, dull hazel eyes looking out at me through her large glasses, she greeted me as I came through the door of the apartment. "Come in."

She sat me down on the dreary chintz-covered couch. "I want to know what these are about." She placed five notes on the small coffee table and looked down her nose at me, her body so relaxed it only unnerved me more. "Perry told me this was your handwriting."

I didn't even dare read them, although I was curious as to what Perry had actually written, but I was too afraid.

I looked down at my jean-clad legs and smoothed my hands on the denim, my chest and throat hot, my heart pounding. "I didn't write them, Marcie. It's Perry. She told me. She copied my handwriting from the back of her notebook."

Marcie sat there, giving me the same matter-of-fact look I had gotten when I first walked in.

How threatening were the others, I wanted to ask, but couldn't. I glanced down at one of them. It had the word *death*, like the one I had seen that morning.

I still couldn't look at Marcie. "I didn't write these notes. It was Perry, and I caught Suzie and Pepa in the library a while ago doing the same thing. I swear to God. She was getting back at me."

Marcie remained still, and I wanted to slap her awake to this.

I looked straight into her eyeglasses. "I did not do this."

She bit her lip. Finally some movement. She said, "Listen, Monday, we're all going to have to go to the dean to discuss this. It's caused Marcus a lot of anxiety—it really scared—"

"*I did not write these Marcie, OK?*" I roared right at her, causing her to back off a bit, and for the second time that afternoon another rush came out of me. I thought I was too exhausted to display any more anger, but apparently I had a lot in reserve. "How about the anxiety it caused me, huh? It's all poor Marcus, poor guy. What about me? What about what this put me through?" My voice reverberated off the walls of the apartment. I sounded like Perry, that this was nothing more than one big circle of misery.

"Jess, calm down." Marcie's eyes flared up at me, and right on cue, Bryan started wailing from the other room.

I did not care but continued to rail on. "I mess around with this guy, I've had a crush on him for who knows how long, and then I'm set up by him and his ex, and he treats me like dirt because he thinks I've written these notes. Oh, not to mention the fact that while we're in his room making out, he blurts out Perry's name. Oh, poor Marcus!" Even with the onslaught of emotion, I managed to control what I was saying.

Marcie got up to get Bryan, came back with him, cradled him in her arms, and his wails simmered down. The sight of Marcie holding her son in her arms made me burst out crying. "Just go ahead and believe what the hell you want to believe. You want to kick me out? Kick me out. Here I am. Put all the blame on me! Believe your precious Perry; you don't have to believe me!"

I ran out of the apartment, brushing past her husband, Ben, as he came through the door. I ignored Marcie's calls after me and went up to my room, hoping I'd find it empty, which it was.

A couple of minutes later, I guess after she had calmed her son down, there was a knock on the door, and Marcie came in. I was lying on my bed, my pillow damp. I gave her the dirtiest look I could muster.

She stood next to my bed, arms crossed over her chest. For the first time, she appeared uneasy with me. "OK, look, I don't know who did it—"

"It was Perry!" I spat out.

She blinked slowly. "What I mean to say is, I want to believe it's not you, OK? It's just that you seemed to be the most obvious answer. I've known Perry a lot longer than you, and this isn't in her personality."

I stared at her, speechless. Where had this woman been all that time? What personality was she seeing? And what did she see in me to make it all so obvious?

She continued in her conversational tone. "So of course, I'm a little confused. It's just that, well, I'm sorry, but I have a hard time believing Perry would do this. The girl is under way too much stress right now; I don't even see her having the energy to do something like this. Plus, she's never been known to do anything like this in the past, at least not that I know of. Maybe it was someone else?"

"She admitted it to me."

Marcie stared at me for a minute. "Oh." She paused again as I stared back at her, willing her to break down. She looked around the room, refusing to give me any kind of eye contact.

"Have you really looked at her?" I demanded. "Have you noticed anything strange about her behavior? That she's more hyper than normal—?"

Marcie looked into my eyes, the steady self-assurance in hers gone. We both remained silent for awhile.

She finally said, "OK, look. I'm going to talk with Mr. Salk, and then I want to talk to you and Perry Sunday night. We're going to iron this whole thing out." She seemed to drift out of the room.

I lay there, still on my stomach, and stared at my crumpled pillow. How could this be happening? Why was Marcie being so loyal to Perry? Was it like what Lally said the other night? That Perry was who Marcie wanted to be? I thought back to fall term when Marcie was nice to me, that she at least seemed warm. But I realized as I remembered winter when things were falling apart, that she cooled off to me considerably. It seemed as long as I was tight with Perry, she was fine. But once Perry and I were no longer friends, Marcie cut me off.

For the remainder of the day, I shut myself up in the music building. I worked on my piece, occasionally wondering if Leo was going to make an appearance. I wondered if he wondered where I was. And I tried not to wonder why I was wondering about him so much.

Later, I finished my homework and decided I had to write Kim. Her cheery letter to me a month ago made me so jealous that I couldn't find the strength to respond. Yet I felt the oppressiveness of the campus, all of Fieldings, the dread of having to face yet another bunch of critical faces in another dining hall, and that no matter where I went, I could never hide. The school felt like one large incubator, that word *incubo*, an Italian nightmare. I became nostalgic, as I had since this whole thing began, for the hallways of Katonah High, for being able to escape home every afternoon, into my room, for being able to lose myself in the anonymity of New York City every weekend.

The letter came out in a rush from my fuchsia-colored pen.

Dear Kim,

I'm so sorry for not writing earlier. I feel terrible, and I am really sorry. I'm glad to hear about the band you're in. I think it's so cool, and I am so jealous! Not that I can sing, but just to be in a band. What's this guy, Andy, like? Does he write his own material? (I was careful to check myself at this point. I didn't want to make some unintentional catty remark).

I'm OK. Actually, things suck, which is one of the reasons why I didn't write to you earlier. It seemed like your life was going along really well, and mine, in comparison, is just going down the tubes. These girls, with whom I had hung out all year, have suddenly turned on me. It's nasty. One of them, Perry, has an ex-boyfriend who made a pass at me, and we ended up fooling around (OK, stupid, stupid, stupid, but I was drunk, and he is cute) and it turned out I was set up by both of them. And then she sent these threatening notes to him in my handwriting. So I confronted her and the two other girls who were in on this, too, and we had a huge fight and it turns out she was jealous of me for all these dumb reasons (like my mom? What?). And my dorm head who worships Perry, refuses to believe she did all this. Everyone here thinks I'm psycho.

I'm working on a piece that I think is pretty good. I'm almost done with it. We'll see what my piano teacher has to say. She was the one who gave me the assignment. I'll be performing it for the spring recital, and I hope you can come. Bring Andy too.

I hope everything is fine. I miss you, and I can't believe I'm saying this, but I actually miss Katonah. I don't know if I really like the boarding school experience. Maybe I just chose the wrong place.

Can't wait to see you again. I am so sorry I have been a total drag about not writing back sooner, and you are a saint not to be a bitch about it. I hope you understand.

Miss you,
Love,

Jess

I didn't bother to reread what I had written. It felt like revisiting bad memories no matter how watered down I made them. I knew that if I did sit down and write a letter that described in detail all of the events of the past year, I'd never finish it. I just knew that I needed to get back in touch with Kim. I wanted to have the connection to my old life.

But I didn't know if I wanted to go back to my life the way it was before I came to Fieldings. A part of me knew that would have been impossible because I knew something in me had changed. I had at least developed a backbone. I toyed with the idea of calling Tom, but I didn't know if he would understand and therefore be receptive, or if he wouldn't go and "accidentally" blab the news to Mom and Dad. They were the last people I wanted to tell the story to. But I also knew that I didn't want to return to Fieldings, and that subject would eventually have to be broached.

CHAPTER 17

Tomorrow Never Knows

I left the music building in the waning light of the early evening and went to Fletcher.

"Jess!" I heard Lally's voice from above as I headed toward the entrance. I looked up to their window and saw her leaning out, waving to me. "Where were you? We've been trying to get in touch with you!"

I told them I was in Bartlett, and she said to meet them in the commons room.

Soon after I came in and sat down, they trotted toward me. "Are you OK?" They asked. "What's been going on?"

I told them everything that happened. The confrontation, although reciting all that Perry said was impossible, and it came out vague and jangled.

Alicia said, "That kind of jealousy is no excuse to write those notes."

"There's no excuse," Lally retorted.

"I can't believe Pepa and Suzie were forging the notes as well," Alicia shook her head. "On the other hand, I can."

"Where's Leo?" I asked.

Lally shrugged. "He's hanging out with that Natalie person. He'll be meeting us."

I swallowed, wondering if this was the statuesque brunette. I imagined him lounging on his bed, one long leg reaching over to the wall, and then the girl on the end of the bed, facing him, both of them laughing lazily.

We went into the dining room that had filled up with people for the Friday night dinner of spaghetti and ice cream. I couldn't look at anyone because I was so confused. I thought how I had been with Marcus whom I lusted after all year, but what was it that I lusted after? Was it just that he looked like someone I had a bigger crush on? And that Saturday night. I didn't want to be with him again. I hated how he was so systematic. His kisses ended up feeling like dry Kleenex. And then he said Perry's name. I hated him. I hated them, the two of them, no, I hated the whole crowd, so much that my insides clenched just thinking about them.

I snapped back to attention when Leo appeared and plunked down next to me, his tray heaped with a mountain of spaghetti. The statuesque brunette wasn't in sight. Lally and Alicia told him what happened and he looked at me, "I am not surprised. You don't do what she wants, she goes crazy. She is worse than an Italian girl."

I didn't know what Leo meant, but it was nice to hear his confirmation of my thoughts.

Throughout dinner I said very little while Lally, Alicia, and Leo talked about the day and what the plans were for the weekend. I studied my friends, Lally and Alicia sitting side by side, Leo right next to me. I was still trying to figure out why everyone thought these two girls were freaks. Was it because of how they dressed, that it wasn't feminine enough? The dress code here was Guess? jeans and a V-neck, cotton sweater, hoop earrings, and pastel-colored mock turtlenecks, and it was followed strictly. The girls all used the same pastel shades of eye makeup, the same frosty lip gloss, and bounced around campus in their bright, white sneakers. The guys all wore oversized rugby shirts, striped oxfords, and polo shirts, (the collar always up), and had hair that was gently feathered. They probably spent their summers on Nantucket or the Vineyard working at a hotel and partying on the beach with a keg. And when they went to college they'd head straight to the Greek societies. Not that there weren't people like that at Katonah. There were plenty. But I remembered a larger group of students who were more like my new friends here. And then Kim's comment from last fall, "I heard Fieldings is really white bread." Well, she got that right.

"Do you guys like it here?" I asked, twisting some spaghetti around my fork.

They looked at me as though I interrupted them, and I realized I had been in my own world—probably a lot longer than just during this dinner table conversation.

"Yeah, it's OK," Alicia said.

"I mean, why did you guys choose to come here?"

They exchanged glances.

Lally replied, "I got a scholarship, and I hated my public school in Chicago. Then I met Leo and Alicia, and I had some great English teachers."

"The art department," Alicia nodded. She pointed to her two friends with her fork, "And these guys."

Leo said, "My brothers went here, and my parents thought I would like it too. And, you know, Anna." He placed what looked like an enormous forkful of spaghetti in his mouth and continued as he chewed. "It's OK. I got a good education, but socially it's a drag."

"Oooh," Lally narrowed her eyes. "Just a tad homogenous, I'd say. But hey, isn't high school supposed to suck?"

None of this made me feel any better. Something weighed in my chest. It was like being on a self-contained island that was disconnected from the rest of the world, and I wanted to know when I could return back to the real world, even if I had never been there before.

That night we went to see *All That Jazz* which made me miss home even more. The images of New York on a rainy afternoon, the theater district, a Broadway house filled with auditioning dancers. I thought of Mom again, this had been her environment for so many years; she had actually once worked with Bob Fosse. But thinking of Mom made me think of Grandma, having her arm wrapped protectively around me, feeling her perfumed kisses on my forehead, being her little lamby.

And then I thought of Dad, of his graying beard and mustache, which gave him a gentle, teddy-bear quality. I knew if I told him all that happened, he would understand. If I told him I didn't want to come back to Fieldings, that I wanted to go back to Katonah and back to my trips to the city on the weekends, he'd understand. Given his psychic abilities, he probably already knew.

The four of us spent Saturday together. I got through a chunk of *A Midsummer Night's Dream,* and for the first time in ages was able to concentrate on what I was reading without re-reading passages over and over again. Leo helped me with a summary I had to write of an Italian short story called, "Il Naso Che Scappa" (The Nose That Escapes) about a nose running away from its owner because he was so sick and tired of being picked by him all the time. That afternoon we watched, only for a few minutes, an ultimate Frisbee match that was on the playing field near the quad. There was no sign of Marcus, which I thought odd, and I told my friends.

A guy in a backwards baseball cap and baggy shorts threatening to fall off him, stood near us with a group of similarly dressed students. I watched them sip their sodas, and then I heard them whispering. "He got kicked out," the guy said, looking at us.

"*What?*" The three of us exclaimed at once.

"They caught him doing coke." The guy shrugged as if this were no big deal, but I could tell by the hum in the group that that's what they had been talking about.

A dark-haired girl in a pink, V-neck sweater, with a large, white belt hanging loosely around her hips, adorned with a pair of baggy, flowered shorts said, "Can you believe it? He's here four years, and they kick him out, like, a little over a month before graduation." Then she narrowed her eyes at me. "Heyyy, aren't you that weirdo who wrote the notes?" She was cute, but in a mean kind of way. Everything was slitted and small, like a paper cut.

The whole clan of baggy-shorts-wearing, soda-sipping preppies gazed at me.

"You know—" Lally was about to retort.

"No," I replied. "She wrote the notes. She and Marcus set me up, and then she flipped out." What did I have to lose at that point? The school year was almost over. I turned my attention back to the game. I had no idea what was going on, but pretended I did.

"Ohmigod!" the group exclaimed at different points followed by someone saying, "I am totally not surprised."

We decided to leave, me with the comforting thought that everyone else thought she was a bit crazy.

But the thought lasted all of two seconds when I overheard the girl say to her friends as she gestured to me, "She is such a liar. You know it's her. Kids of famous parents are, like, weird." A tingle shot up my back. Leo turned to her and said a string of words in Italian which sounded cutting and nasty. I didn't ask him what it meant, and it just left the other group confused and snickering.

"Guess Marcus's dad couldn't help him this time," he muttered.

The air was humid and heavy, just the way it was before Hurricane Gloria. I looked around to see if Pepa or Suzie, or even Hassan were there. But they were all probably with Marcus, consoling him. I took a deep breath, and then let it out. "I'm glad," I said. And I was.

That evening we were in Leo's room, the stereo blasting as we drank vodka and orange soda. Because I had hardly eaten that day, I drank very little, but it went right to my head.

Around 10:30, we saw a flash outside and ran to the window. The breeze smelled of rain and earth, the air felt tense and electric. There was a rumble.

"Yay! A thunderstorm!" Alicia cried.

The storm arrived quickly, the wind picking up and knocking over an empty coke can that stood by the windowsill. Then there was more rumbling, and another flash of lightning that seemed to take up the whole sky, and then heavy splats of rain, warning of an imminent downpour. I suddenly wanted to feel drenched in the rain and the power of the storm, as though it could wash something out of me.

"We gotta go outside to the storm!" I cried.

"Outside!" Leo said.

"Cool!" followed Alicia.

"You guys are nuts!" called out Lally. "We'll get struck by lightning!"

"Let's just go out to the steps of the dorm and watch it from there," I suggested. There was a slight overhang by the door, and I knew we'd probably be OK.

"Yeah!" cried Leo.

"Uhhh, OK," Lally said. "I don't want to get fried."

Leo put his arm around her. "We won't."

We got to the steps of the dorm and watched as the rain almost bleached out the campus with its ferocity, and the lightening flickered above us. One crash of thunder came after another, coming closer and closer after each lightning flash. We huddled together, staring up at the sky.

And then there was a really bright flash, too close, too blinding, accompanied by a *snap!* We jumped, and before we could say anything, an enormous crash descended upon us, almost shaking the dorm. We screamed and ran inside, watching the rest of the storm from Leo's room.

The window was wide open, and we let the rainy breeze, which felt cooler with every gust as it pushed away the day's humidity, brush our faces. I called Marcie to tell her I was spending the night in Fletcher, and when dorm closing arrived, and we left Leo's room to go to Lally and Alicia's, I felt like I was returning to my own room. It was a nice feeling.

CHAPTER 18

Caroline No

I woke up the next day at noon, in Alicia's sleeping bag with its slightly sweet, ropey smell of pot, on the floor. The sunlight poured through the window, the sharp rays reminding me of the thunderclaps from the night before, and I felt like an 18-wheeler had spent the entire night rumbling over me, back and forth. I was beyond bleary, and my head had a dull, heavy ache while my stomach let out a grumble telling me that I was starving. I got up to take a shower, leaving Lally and Alicia. Throwing a borrowed towel over my arm, I glanced in the mirror over Lally's bureau at my pale, saggy face.

After we each took a long shower, the three of us decided to rally Leo and make our way to the student center for omelets, fries, and coffee. I smiled as I thought that this sounded very grown-up and urban—a bunch of us going out for "brunch," so to speak, after a late night.

When we got out into the hallway, a girl from my English class popped her head out of a nearby door and said with an almost surprised look on her face, "Jess! There you are. I didn't want to wake you up. You got a message from Marcie. She wants you to call her right away." She nodded at me with a slightly crazed look on her face.

Everything in me sank as I realized Perry must be back and was unwilling to wait for the chat. And of course she had pushed Marcie into having us meet now.

I wanted to get some food into my system first. I was too hungry and worn out to face Perry, who, I was sure, had gathered her troops and planned an attack on me. Lally made a face at me, sticking her tongue out, lizardlike, in sympathy.

Alicia told us Leo had just woken up, and that he would meet us outside the dorm. The air was cleaner, the stuffiness from the past few days gone, along with the storm, and the feel of it even managed to erase a bit of the bleariness in my face. The wind pushed gray and white clouds over to the east, and I almost shivered in the coolness. Fallen branches from the trees were scattered along the quad. Leo trotted up to us, his red and black hair pointing in different directions on top of his head. "I'm destroyed," he ran his hand over his face.

"Yeah, so are we. We gotta eat," Lally said.

"The front steps of the chapel got struck by lightning," he said.

"Really?" we all replied.

He put his hand through his hair and nodded. "No one was hurt."

"That's good," Lally replied.

"That's freaky," said Alicia. "The chapel? That's like a sign or something."

Leo told her she sounded like a southern Italian.

I was so hungry I wanted to run to the student center, but my body was too drained to do anything but shuffle. I felt off kilter as we entered the building, as if everything had been perfectly balanced before and was somehow knocked sideways. Once I got my omelet and coffee, I inhaled them in two seconds. We didn't say much to each other; we sort of mumbled and giggled about the night before. There were only three other people in the center, playing video games. A Chaka Khan song came out of the jukebox.

Afterwards, we agreed to meet at our usual spot in the library. I told them I didn't know how long this meeting with Marcie and company was going to take, and they in turn wished me good luck with the confrontation. Everything that I had just eaten started to put up a bit of a fight in my stomach.

I walked into Kurtzman. Three girls sat in front of the TV, but it wasn't on, their faces glued to the blank screen as they were telling a story about a car. "I didn't know she had gone for the weekend," I heard one of them say, and something shook underneath me yet at the same time remained still. My headache was gone, replaced by this little dull thud. *I shouldn't have eaten so fast,* I thought to myself. There was something like whimpering, or laughter, coming from Marcie's apartment, and my legs walked me to the screen door, where the whimpering became louder.

Marcie appeared, huge circles under her puffy, red-rimmed eyes. I wanted to think she must have had a bad night with her son, but I knew something much worse had happened. I noticed her hair, pulled back in a half-hearted ponytail, was dull and her mouth pinched. She opened the door for me and croaked, "Come in. I have something to tell you."

For a moment, I wondered if I shouldn't stay where I was, just have time stop right there. I didn't look directly at them, but I could tell Suzie and Pepa were on the couch. They got up, brushed past me. Nothing was said. Neither one glanced at me. Maybe I should have been relieved at having them leave, but all I felt was a tightness.

"What?" I asked as I sat down on the couch, which was still warm from Pepa and Suzie.

Marcie sat down in the chair next to me. My body remained locked in place. Even my stomach had shut down.

"I'm afraid something really awful has happened." She didn't sound like herself as she played with her nails. Her voice was much lower and fuzzier. My scalp prickled, and I tried to swallow but my throat was too contracted.

"Perry was coming back from a party outside of New York last night and, I think because of the weather, she lost control of the car and hit a tree." I hoped for a moment that she was in the hospital in critical condition, and that she'd get better. Marcie swallowed, her eyes welling up. "She was killed instantly."

Even before she told me, I knew what had happened. It took a second for me to realize that my jaw had automatically dropped and just hung there. I looked down at the gray scuff on the toe of one of my white Capezio flats. It didn't seem to be on my foot. And for a second, I felt lifted off the couch.

Marcie continued, looking to the side, "Uh, we found out early this morning. I got a call from her parents. I tried calling you in Fletcher, but you were still asleep."

I remained still. I knew I was breathing, but the breaths were small, just enough to keep the oxygen going so I wouldn't pass out. The room moved around me, the dingy red, yellow, and green chintz on the couch danced in my eyes. The phone rang, and Marcie sprang up to get it. I took that as my cue to walk out of the apartment, and then out of the dorm and into the windy day. I followed my now familiar path to Fletcher, but stopped halfway when it occurred to me that my friends were in the library. And then, just as quickly, I realized I didn't want to be with them. My feet kept moving, and I found myself walking along the drive leading away from the school and onto the main road. I walked facing the traffic and let the wind from the passing cars and trucks push against me, not willing to jump off into a ditch.

My senses dulled as I concentrated on my walking; I was too afraid of what would happen if I thought of anything. Flashes from the night before, the greasy omelet from earlier, Chaka Khan belting out her proclamation, and bits of our giggles came into my thoughts but then slithered their way out. The only lingering vision was of Perry, dressed as I had last seen her, although this time she was behind the wheel of the car and driving intently in the night, a pair of headlights from a car behind her on her face and hair. Her eyes were wide open and her mouth in a determined purse. It wouldn't have surprised me one bit to come back to campus and see her getting out of the white cab she left in, her duffel on her shoulder.

I walked, feeling the thinning bottoms of my flats touch the bumpy asphalt of the road. They were designed for dance class, not for street wear, but I needed the feeling of being almost barefoot against the ground. The wind blew past me in intervals but didn't go through me. Everything felt miles away and listless, even things that were close up, like the bending tree branches and the grass, which earlier was so bright green and shiny, it made me think of the plastic-looking grass in Munchkinland in the *The Wizard of Oz*. It was as if everything became muted. A wall of Plexiglas surrounded me.

I kept walking, past woods where white-clapboard houses peeked out from their clearings. The gas station was empty and silent. As the buildings became closer together, the woods less thick, I found myself in town, the breeze off Long Island Sound hitting me in a salty, fuzzy way. I passed restaurants and cafes with their brightly colored flags flapping in the wind and small, chalkboard easels listing the rich brunch special of eggs benedict accompanied by a free mimosa or bloody Mary. People laughed as they walked out of these noisy places and into the sunlight, but it all sounded like a bunch of dogs barking territorially at each other. I looked up at the Presbyterian church that rose above the town, white clapboard like the rest of the place and saw the black-faced clock with its spindly white hands pointing to spindly white roman numerals, telling me that over one hour had passed. *Makes sense*, I thought calmly. After all, I did walk from campus all the way to town, and normally we had to take a bus there. My feet weren't tired; they actually didn't feel much of anything except the sidewalk and the occasional pebble. I saw the ferry landing not too far off in the distance and decided that would be my destination, the docks, a place to sit and rest because maybe I was getting tired, although it was hard to tell.

As I walked on and stepped up to the wooden boards that creaked with the sound of the small waves lapping underneath them, I toyed with the idea of taking one of the ferries to Montauk Point on Long Island, until I reached into my jeans and pulled out a crinkly five dollar bill, which wouldn't have even paid for a cab back to school.

But I didn't want to go back to school. The thought literally made me feel cold and dank like our cellar at home that was dark, save for one, lone lightbulb hanging from the ceiling and the humming sound of the freezer. I walked over to one of the docks, mingling with a crowd of people in sunglasses and cotton, sat down near the end, and stared across the sound to the dim, blue silhouette of Fisher's Island.

I don't really remember how much time passed before it occurred to me that people, such as Marcie, might wonder where I was, and that it would be a good idea to go back to campus. Once I arrived, this time walking a lot faster than when I had left, I went over to Fletcher to see if my friends had come back from the library.

But no one was there. I went over and knocked on Leo's window and almost burst into tears when he poked his head out. We looked at each other wordlessly for a few moments. Tufts of his hair were sticking up all over the place still, like he had just gotten out of bed. But I knew he knew the news. His eyes flashed at me in fury and disbelief.

"*Aspetta*," he told me to wait, disappeared, and then reappeared outside the door that led to the boys' side of the dorm.

I didn't have to walk up to him. He marched up and threw his arms around me, squeezing me in a desperate grasp. I knew I was supposed to cry, but I couldn't. I waited to hear sobs from him, but there was nothing. It was only breathing and the smell of his spicy cologne mixed with a slight tinge of body odor.

We stayed that way for a while, with the wind brushing past us, the birds in the tree nearby carrying on the background conversation. For some reason, I thought about Mom's description of crowd scenes on stage, and how you had to talk, but not too loudly, so as not to drown out the main actors in the scene. Something about saying, "Rhubarb, rhubarb," or "Peanut butter," over and over again to make it look like real conversation.

Leo smoothed my hair, his large hand taking up most of my head. I breathed into his gray cotton T-shirt, feeling something stir in me, something slightly warm and exciting, which also felt pretty inappropriate given the circumstances. He continued to smooth my hair, occasionally placing his lips on it in a semikiss, although I couldn't quite tell.

"There you are!" came a voice from behind me. It took me a few seconds before I realized it was Marcie. Her eyes were less puffy but even more tired looking and the lines on her forehead deeper, her green sweater hanging from her thin shoulders. "Where the hell were you? You had us so worried!"

"I walked to town," I replied like someone who had just learned how to speak. "I'm sorry."

"Jess. Don't ever do that again!" Her voice shook. "I know ..." she wiped her nose and then let out a sigh. "God, just ... *please*. Next time, please sign out. We had absolutely no idea what had happened to you!" She put a hand on my shoulder for support, and I felt Leo's grasp tighten.

"She's OK," he said to her. "She didn't mean to. She's just upset."

"I know, I know." Marcie looked around the quad and a sob caught her voice. "Everyone is." She put her arms around my free shoulder. Leo let me go as she hugged me. I hugged her back, hearing her sob into my shoulder, making it damp. It was something I never imagined happening, and I recalled the day I first met her, that wink she gave me, and how superficial it felt, like she was making some half-hearted attempt to charm me. Now as she held me, her own body shaking, I wondered if it was just Perry's death that was making her cry or her final reckoning with the truth about who this person really was. I could have been ready to burst into tears myself, but the ability to cry felt far away.

I pressed the black phone receiver to my ear as I listened to my parents console me. Somehow, I had managed to call them, my greeting too tentative, Mom's sorrowful voice like a mellow slide whistle. Dad's muffled words of, "Oh, how horrible. Oh, my Lord, are you going to be OK?" He sounded so concerned, I could see the worry lines crease right over his brow.

"I'll be fine." The lie left my lips and went through the telephone wire.

"Were you still quite close with her? I mean, were you still friends with her? I mean, your father said things were a bit ... I don't know. How was it?" Mom asked. I had never heard her sound so gentle.

I didn't want to say anything about the notes. It didn't seem worth the trouble. "We weren't ..." I tried to take a deep breath. "We weren't friends. We had a big falling out before she left for the weekend."

"Oh no," Mom replied in her slide-whistle voice.

But I wanted Dad to say something, and I waited for what was probably only two seconds but felt like ages.

"Do you have someone you can talk to?" he asked. "Anyone? Your dorm head?"

Instead of Marcie, I had a vision of Lally, Alicia, and Leo all standing there in my thoughts like guardian angels. Even Mrs. McGowan. "Yeah, I have some other friends."

Mom said, "Jess. This is so awful." I smelled the approach of Obsession perfume and looked up to see Suzie and Pepa parade by me. I was invisible to them. I opened my mouth to say something else to my parents but nothing came out.

The campus meeting was subdued. I sat with Lally, Alicia, and Leo, who were like a fortress around me. I stared straight ahead as our headmaster, Lynn Davis, went up to the pulpit. I had never actually met the woman, only seen her from afar. She was short, a little squat, with smooth white hair in a Dutch-boy haircut. She had a loud alto voice and, despite her diminutiveness, a commanding presence, a firmness in the way she stepped up to the pulpit every Sunday to lead the meeting, grasping both sides with her hands as if to endow the whole chapel with her strength. She called for a moment of silence for Perry.

The chapel became quiet and hollow, except for the occasional sniffle and cough. I wondered if the sniffing didn't come from Suzie or Pepa.

I sat through the meeting not paying any attention. We were shown a documentary about women in advertising. It looked like it was produced in the 1970s and seemed very dated and scratchy. But my mind wasn't on the various legs, glossy lips, and deep-sounding voice-overs. Besides, it seemed really tacky to talk about female objectification right now. It jarred too much against the present events. We needed the choir to sing something or someone to read aloud from *The Chronicles of Narnia* or the like.

I wondered where Marcus was. He had left Saturday afternoon. I tried to imagine his face as the news about Perry was delivered to him. I didn't know where he lived in New York, but I imagined it was one of those monolithic structures that gave you a panoramic view of the city. It would be all white, rattan, and sun drenched, and he would be in his parents' living room, on an enormous, overstuffed, white couch reading the Sunday *Times*. And then the phone call would come, from whom, I didn't know. I didn't want to imagine his face dissolved into tears or fall apart into grief, the kind of expression you rarely saw on a person.

Perry's death brought the whole note debacle to a halt. Marcie eventually spoke to Pepa and Suzie, she robotically told me later, and they confessed. They were put on a warning, in the sense that they were not allowed to leave the dorm during visiting hours during the week, much less leave campus. They never spoke to me, not that I expected them to.

I shut myself off. I didn't want to be with anyone. I went to Bartlett to practice and to do my homework. Lally, Alicia, and Leo told me to meet them in the library during study hall, but I begged off, saying I had too much piano homework to do. I didn't think I would feel protected outside the practice room, where at least I had my piano right there to lose myself in.

I tried sleeping, but usually just lay in bed, reliving the final fight, seeing Perry's pale face, the eyes that seemed to shake with anger in their sockets as she told me why she wrote the notes. I couldn't stop thinking about her crumbling throughout the term and then the car accident. How did it happen? Was she drunk? The weather was awful that night. Maybe she was stone-cold sober as she got behind the wheel, and it wasn't her fault at all. Therefore, she didn't deserve to die.

It's all for the best, I tried to tell myself. She was a mess. Maybe all of this was inevitable. Her life was spinning out of control. She never spoke about Princeton after she got in. She just slid downhill. I saw Perry, the pulled together, preppy girl who greeted me that December morning over a year ago, who had been so clean and clear eyed, so direct. And then ... was it when she dyed her hair platinum? Her tanned, yet tired-looking skin that first night back from spring break, everything about her wild and out of control, like she had lost some essential element in Fort Lauderdale that used to keep her grounded.

But it happened before that. I thought about the day I arrived, and she helped me unpack my stuff, the way she talked nonstop as if she were running out of time, and she had to give me her life story before deadline. I thought about those evenings in her room, the soft light and pastels with the musky scent of Obsession in the air and Prince or Madonna whining erotic longing on the stereo. I thought of Perry with her sly smile, while she discussed her summer fling with the painter as if it were the most normal thing in the world. The discussion about sex which was all so frank and crude it took away the romantic, gauzy mystery I had had of it.

I killed her, I thought, as I turned over to find a cooler place on my pillow. Maybe she was well on her way to destroying herself, but I was the final straw. I didn't know what happened that evening. Maybe she had a fight with someone. Maybe she was drunk or on too many drugs. And yet, I couldn't help but think that our last confrontation, and what the setup with Marcus led to, was what made her completely fall apart.

When I entered the practice room that Monday morning, foggy from lack of sleep, Mrs. McGowan was there, waiting for me. She looked the same as she always did, with her hair in a bun, her rimless glasses, and her thin, lipsticked mouth. She tried to smile, but her eyes couldn't make the effort.

"Your dorm head told me what happened. I am so sorry," she said as she shook her head and put her arm around me. "How are you doing?"

"I'm OK," I shrugged. "Tired. Really, really tired."

"I understand."

I felt her eyes on me as I plopped down on the piano bench and regarded the keys. I didn't want to talk. I flexed my fingers and wiggled them. "You want me to start?"

"You go right ahead."

The sound of the notes, and the soft, cool feeling of the keys was enough to block out everything.

Towards the end of the lesson, I mechanically went through what I had written, and ready to hear the critique from Mrs. McGowan. But instead, she asked, "How close were you with Perry?" She knew, at the very least, that I was friends with her, having seen us together on campus.

"I was close. I can't say I was her friend, though. I think I once was."

"Hmm." I don't think either one of us knew what to say. "Well, do you feel like your work is helping you in all of this?"

I looked up and nodded at her with the first smile I had on my face since Sunday morning.

"Good. I want you to keep it up." Her voice reminded me of a sip of fine red wine—warm, smooth, with a small punch to it. "I like what you've done with the piece. There's a lot of consistency to it, without being too repetitive. It's nice."

Her compliments didn't sink in, giving me the elation they normally did. I just nodded and said, "Thank you."

That whole week was a dream. All my senses had dulled. Food had very little taste. I walked without touching the ground, and I couldn't remember anything from my classes. I did my homework as if on automatic, but I had no idea what I was memorizing, what I was writing. In Italian, we studied the imperfect past, and while conjugating the verbs came easily to me, I didn't pick up when we were supposed to use this form. I skipped conversation class, knowing that Leo would understand why I couldn't come and decided instead to work on my piece. In fact, I sat through my classes imagining the keyboard in front of me. I diddled ideas on the back of my notebook, or in the margins of pages while half listening to students read aloud from *A Midsummer Night's Dream* and half listening to the chords in my head.

I ate lunch with my three friends but paid little attention to what they said. Every time I heard Perry's name from a nearby table, my ears perked up, and I tried to glean what they were saying. Mostly it was about her drug problem which, all of a sudden, everyone seemed to know about and have an opinion of. The way she screwed up at meets, her "total paranoia" at editorial meetings, and her fights with Mitch, all because of drugs. How straight she was when she first arrived four years ago and then "suddenly descended into this, like, *total* abyss." That was something I heard a fair amount of by people I'd never met before, never knew Perry knew. I wanted to simultaneously slap them and tell them to shut up and to ask them questions. Pepa and Suzie were always together. Suzie moved into Pepa's room since neither one of them wanted to be alone. Sometimes they were with Hassan, who managed to see me from a distance and give me a steely glare, or else the two girls were on the phone, talking to Marcus, the phone cord wrapped around the fingers of whoever was talking, turning her fingertips red.

And then there was Leo. I wanted to borrow *Pet Sounds* but something always stopped me when I thought about asking him. The lyrics of feeling out of place, of trying to be something one wasn't and witnessing a sad change in a close friend, like in the song "Caroline No," Leo's favorite song.

He asked me why I skipped conversation class, and I got a cloying neediness from him. Didn't he understand? "I had to be alone," I replied simply. At lunch I would look up occasionally from my meal and see him gazing at me with his dream-filled blue eyes, and I cringed. I thought I had a crush on him, and I knew he had a crush on me. But I felt too exposed being the object of someone's affection, especially when it was displayed so blatantly. I just wanted to keep everything a little distant.

And after every meal I had with them, Leo always wanted to accompany me to class or Bartlett, and I said I had to go back to my room and get some stuff and maybe go to the campus bookstore.

"Oh, OK," he replied, looking like I had slapped him in the face. And then I'd think my tone was too mean.

"But I'll see you guys," I made it a point to make the whole thing plural, "later, like maybe at dinner."

He'd nod, barely a smile on his face and walk off. I'd do exactly what I said I was going to do out of sheer guilt.

Friday evening, after piano practice, I headed over to Fletcher to meet my friends for dinner. I walked into the commons room, and as I was heading in the direction of the stairwell that led to the girls' side of the dorm, I saw Leo with her—the statuesque brunette, Natalie. They were both leaning against one of the pillars. At first I thought it was Lally because of the mass of dark curls, but this girl was too tall and gangly.

Since that infamous Saturday night, I had learned who Natalie was—a first year junior, and although I had never met her, I remembered seeing her with her endless legs, running across campus to get to class or catch up with friends. She was named, "Athlete of the Week" that week in the school paper, and there was her picture, India-ink eyes staring wide at the camera and a dark, Betty Boop mouth. She had been on the varsity field hockey team in the fall and now was doing track and field. She never had an effect on me one way or the other until that Saturday up in the balcony of the student center. She had a loud voice that came out almost in barks instead of words. When she said the word *like*, which she did often, it came out sounding like *lick*. And Leo had returned to her.

Why was he with her? Because I'd been mean. One minute I was by his side, the next running away. They tugged jokingly at each others' belt loops and laughed. She had a loud, full "ha ha!" as if announcing to the world that whatever was going on, *she* thought it was funny.

They didn't look in my direction as they continued to joke around. I couldn't make out what they were saying, everything seemed to be said in stage whispers, which made it even more intimate. Then Leo tugged her belt loops again, only this time a little more forcefully so that she came right up to him, her face against his. They kissed. He put his mouth on hers. And it wasn't just a peck, but a real groping. I felt strangled. I wanted to look away, but I couldn't. I let the coldness in me settle like some sort of punishment before I was able to turn away.

I ran upstairs to Lally and Alicia's room, my face burning and tingling. If only I hadn't been so standoffish. But I deserved it. After what happened between me and Marcus, when I could have said no but didn't, this was perfect karmic payback.

I walked into their room without bothering to knock and said, "Hey," with the brightest smile I could muster. Lally asked if I was OK.

"Yeah! Why?"

"You look flushed. Did you run over here?"

"Yeah."

"Let's head down to dinner," said Alicia, who was sitting at her desk with her electric typewriter humming in front of her. She flicked it off, put the cap back on a crusty looking bottle of Wite-Out and got up. "I'm starved."

"You guys wanna go to the snack bar?" I asked putting my hands in my back pockets. I was suddenly aware of how sloppy I was. I was wearing these stupid, faded, red and white striped pants that I once thought were cool and now seemed childish and a large red cotton sweater that had lost all its form. I felt like a weird candy cane.

"I have no money," Alicia said.

"I'll pay!" I offered.

The girls looked at each other and shook their heads. "Nahh," Lally whined. "I'm too tired to go down there."

"We can eat more here, and like I said, I am super hungry," Alicia said.

So it was down to the dining room we went, filled with its noise of early weekend excitement. I searched the room for Leo, but he was nowhere to be seen. I didn't know whether to be relieved or more upset.

"Where's Leo?" I asked as we got our trays and our usual Friday night special of overcooked spaghetti and gargantuan meatballs.

I saw Alicia give Lally a sideways glance.

Lally replied, "I don't know. He was kind of vague about meeting us here."

"Oh." I waited until we got to our table and sat down before I said as nonchalantly as possible, "I saw him earlier with that girl, um, what's her name? Nancy? Natty?"

They both said, "Natalie."

There was that ache again, as I remembered the first dinner I had with the three of them. I had sat next to Leo. He pinched my cheek and called me "*bellina*" right in the middle of arguing about what kind of music he wanted to play at the toga party. While Perry was in Kurtzman with Suzie and Pepa. While Perry was still here.

I couldn't stop myself from saying, "Isn't she supposed to be some really good athlete?" The minute the words fell out of my mouth, my stomach turned cold. The same competition with an athlete, the same outgoing, pretty athlete. *She's another person,* I told myself.

Alicia furrowed her brows as she cut into a very soft meatball.

Lally swirled spaghetti around her fork. "I guess. I don't know what he's doing with her."

Alicia replied, "She's not his type, and I don't know why he does this. I mean, I thought he liked you, but he's so touchy."

"*I* know what it is," Lally said. She always did. "He's scared how much he likes you. That's why he's being all weird. It's a guy thing."

Well, not just a guy thing, since I had been doing the same thing.

"Especially with guys who are kind of run-arounds like him," she continued. "Suddenly they see someone they like, and they're like, 'Uh oh.' I know so many guys like that." She shook her head and then pointed her fork at me. "He *really* likes you, Jess."

Got it, Lally. Got the message loud and clear. I felt both scared and relieved.

She continued, "I give them until Sunday."

"For what?" I asked, knowing perfectly well what the answer was going to be.

"For Leo and Natalie to remain an item." Her words hit me like the sound of a heavy stone plunking through the surface of a still lake.

"They're an *item*?" The words sounded much more panicky than I had intended them to be. I wanted to be calm, of course.

Alicia sighed, "Whatever they are."

"Is she nice?" I sounded shrill.

Lally regarded me and said, "Jess. I wouldn't let it get to you."

And that's all we said on that subject for the rest of the very, very long weekend.

CHAPTER 19

God Only Knows

Sitting in the chapel that hot Sunday afternoon, I was completely alone despite sitting sandwiched in between Lally and Alicia and, although I hadn't seen him since Friday, Leo, who sat between Lally and Natalie. I watched them and noticed Natalie not paying much attention to him. He gave me a solemn glance as if to acknowledge something, but I didn't know what. We all sat lined up in a row, silent.

The preoccupations I had about Leo and Natalie were pushed out of my head when I stepped into the chapel. In fact, whatever I had been protecting myself with that week had disappeared, and I now felt surrounded by Perry. Although I had been hearing story after story about how she died and why, the sad trajectory from straight girl to the abyss of substance abuse, I had been able to close myself off from all of that when I felt I'd had enough. But once inside the chapel, I felt Perry's presence all around me.

I glanced over at Pepa and Suzie, who were whispering with Perry's sister, Alison. Part of me wanted them to turn around and see me, but part of me didn't. I didn't want to see them grieving.

The stained-glass windows shed a dusky yellow light onto the heads of all the students sitting in the obscenely straight-backed wooden pews. The chapel retained the smell of incense left over from years of Sunday services. My head started to throb.

Perry's parents and her sister sat in the front row, along with Pepa and Suzie. I could barely make out her father's wild, fuzzy, reddish hair and the tip of her mother's gray-blond bun. I wondered what their faces looked like close up since I only managed to get a glimpse of them earlier from my window when they arrived. Yet the thought of coming face to face with Perry's parents, to be confronted with the clear echoes of a face that was now gone forever, only made more blood pulse through my forehead.

I thought about all the bits and pieces of conversations I had heard that previous week, and how badly I wanted to listen to each and every one of them to learn what others knew about Perry. Were their feelings the same? Aside from that first day when all the old students came back, and Perry seemed surrounded by friends, she rarely went beyond the bounds of our group to be with anyone else. But then, after she died, it seemed everyone knew her, knew what she did. *What* did she do? I wanted to know. Lally commented about the rumors that were floating around about Perry, "People are blowing her drug thing totally out of proportion. It's like they have to blame every weird Perry incident on drugs. It's so sad." But I wanted to hear these stories, whether they were drug linked or not. It was like this grim fascination took over every time I heard someone talk about her. But at the same time, guilt held me back from going over and listening to these conversations. And the funny thing was, no one asked me about her. I saw Pepa and Suzie around campus nodding their heads in front of inquiring students, their faces a mix of shock and resignation. And I listened to the rumors about how Pepa had gone on a drinking binge with Suzie and Hassan, and that she now bordered on a nervous collapse.

My sit bones were killing me, and I shifted myself on the ancient velveteen cushion that was there to give me some semblance of comfort. I thought churches were supposed to be places of solace, warmth, and peace. Right now I was feeling nausea, aching bones, and a rising something in me that wanted to get out. Was I going to throw up? Scream? Stand up and shout to the whole school what really happened between us? The air in the chapel felt stagnant, and a few people waved their programs in front of their faces to circulate the air. I thought of those stories I heard about the Puritans, my ancestors, in Massachusetts and here in Connecticut, who would spend all Sunday sitting in these straight-back pews, and if anyone nodded off, *rap, rap, rap!* went the cane on their shoulders to wake them up. I wondered if Perry was here in spirit, standing by my pew, cane in hand, ready to whop me a good one to get me to smarten up.

Mitch Greene gave the eulogy. Certainly any hard feelings he may have had towards her, especially during the last few weeks when she kept missing meetings, had disappeared. There he was, up in the pulpit talking about one of his "closest friends." I didn't even know they were friends, and I felt both a heavy poignancy in this as well as nagging hypocrisy. His normally cherubic, rosy cheeks were now replaced by a pale, hollowed out face. Even as stocky as he was, he managed to look thin. His voice warbled, sounding odd and foreign. I didn't know what was going to come out of me. I was afraid that if I sniffled, everyone would look at me because mine would be the loudest. I chose silence. I tried to stare straight ahead, focusing on the choir of the chapel. I wouldn't look at the girls. I wouldn't look at Mitch or the Wagners.

When the madrigal group sang Handel's "Where 'ere You Walk," a trickle of relief went through me, and I knew the service would be over soon. The harmonies and the lightness of the voices reminded me of the harmonies from *Pet Sounds* and how in "Caroline No" Brian took a note and traveled with it, conveying his sorrow. I thought of that afternoon in Leo's room when we listened to the album, an afternoon that felt like it was ages ago.

I looked at Suzie, doubled over in sobs while Pepa did the same on top of her, a huddled mass of jerking bodies. Alison soon joined them, and then I heard one particularly loud sob. I thought it may have been Suzie.

As everyone got up to leave to the sounds of the organ playing some more Handel, I tried to exit, to lose myself in the mass of the other students shuffling out. I didn't want to be caught and trapped by the girls. But somehow, everyone else's bodies were making an arc around me, like I was a high-voltage electric field.

The first person I saw as I got out into the close haziness of the day was Marcus, in a dark jacket and tie, under the big oak tree. He quickly stubbed out a cigarette before any faculty could catch him, which seemed kind of stupid since he was no longer a student here. His head jerked up and a forelock of wavy, dark blond hair momentarily got caught in his brows. Brushing it aside, his eyes met mine, and then he looked over my head to see if there was anyone else he knew. Then he turned his head toward the haze-covered blue hills in the distance and put his hands in his pants pockets.

I stayed where I was, near the large wooden door with its great iron locks and bolts. Lally and Alicia were behind me, both speaking in muffled tones about the studying they had to do for finals that were coming up. I spied Perry's parents. I knew I had to go talk to them. I thought I'd look like a wimp if I just ran away, and I was not going to tarnish my reputation further. Pushing my way across the flagstones, past grunts, murmurs, and a "Tch! A little more rude, darling?" from a girl in my biology class, who never liked me to begin with, I approached Perry's family.

"I'm Jessica Thurwell," I stuck my hand out to Perry's father. The spring breeze made his hair dance about his head. His eyes, though, were sunken and his mouth tiny under a reddish-gray mustache. He had Perry's eyes, big and green, the same almond shape with the long lashes. I winced.

He gave me a squinty, confused look as though it took an enormous effort to move his face. I felt Perry's mother and Alison gaze at me, her mother nodding with a strained smile on her face. "Oh, yes," she finally said. "Your brother is in one of my classes." She turned to her husband. "You remember Tom."

I could see him nodding slightly from my peripheral vision. I couldn't look straight at them because I sensed a similarity, the same jaw line, mouth. And then I would have to see their eyes, which I already knew were haunted by a dense sadness. They lost a daughter, something unimaginable. They brought her up all those years, and in an instant she was gone. I lost my grandmother but she was in her eighties. That was expected. This was something else entirely, and seeing the Wagners' dulled, drawn faces, made me realize it was something one could never begin to comprehend until it happened to them.

"I'm so sorry." I could barely get the words out before my throat closed itself off. I heard footsteps behind me come to a shuffling halt. A sniffle, a cleared throat. Pepa and Suzie.

"Pepa," Perry's mom gasped, and then I looked at her, a small, relieved smile on her lips, the exact same lips as Perry's. She stretched her arms out to Pepa, who came up next to me and leaned over to hug her. They both shut their eyes as they embraced, and a chilly warm discomfort went down my spine. I tried looking away at the large fir tree by the chapel through which the warm wind blew with deep hushing sounds, and then I glanced at the crowd coming out of the chapel.

Suzie approached and she and Perry's sister, Alison, started crying together. A few erstwhile friends of Perry's had gathered close by waiting their turn.

Suddenly I started to gag. I tried to breathe deeply to relax my throat muscles, but every time I took a deep breath, the gagging only got worse. My mouth excreted an enormous amount of saliva, and I ran off to a bush around the corner of the chapel and threw up. Actually, I just dry heaved since my breakfast had consisted of water and one tater tot.

As if I were a magnet, Pepa and Suzie followed me to the spiky green bush I was hunched over. When I looked up, wiped my mouth, and sniffed back sour bile, I saw Pepa's face vibrating and twitching with what? Anger? Disgust?

I could feel the two of them lean into me, their breathing slow and steady like hibernating bears.

Tiny Suzie came forward, all myopic brown eyes.

"Here's something more for you to puke up," she said and spat clammy saliva in my direction.

I wiped off whatever had hit me, shaking, as they walked away. Icy claws bore down on my chest, and my heart started to race. My head felt light, everything looked wavy, and dark spots entered my vision. *I'm going to leave, I'm going to run away and forget about this.* My brain scrambled around with these and other thoughts of fleeing so furiously I could almost see the neurons flashing out of control. The ground appeared closer. And then everything went black.

I came to in the infirmary in one of those high, comfortable beds with the kind of freshly starched sheets that you would find only in a place like that. The school doctor stood looking down at me.

"Here she is," she smiled, her gray eyes matching her short curly hair. Her voice was as sweet and resonant as a viola.

"I'm OK?" I whispered. Why was I in here? The bush. Suzie's spit. Leaving the school.

She nodded, still smiling. "You're fine. You passed out. Probably from the heat. Did you have breakfast?"

My mouth felt thick and my throat like dry Kleenex. I had never fainted before. Where did I collapse? On the bush? How did I get here? Someone came over to me and helped me. Someone helped me.

"Who brought me here?"

"Some boy." She raised the head of the bed to help me sit up.

"Wh-what did he look like?"

The doctor poured water into a paper cup and had me drink it. It tasted metallic, but the Kleenex feeling dissolved.

"Tall, dark hair. You know, that senior from Italy."

I listened to myself breathe, trying to imagine Leo carrying me. Were Lally and Alicia with him? "I want to stay here." I managed to say.

"You can, dear." The doctor smiled and brushed her soft, wrinkled hand against my forehead. I caught a sweet whiff of Jergen's hand lotion, the kind Mom always used before she switched to more expensive brands, and my body felt a warm glow.

The doctor left the room, and I lay in bed staring at the off-white cinder block wall in front of me. I kept feeling the soft caress of her hand, like some kind of reassurance that everything was going to be fine; that what happened this past week, this past year, would all be a memory, gone with a brush of the hand.

It was then that I decided not to come back to Fieldings. I would have a long, leisurely summer at home with my parents and my brother, and then a trip to Italy to stay in a big, airy villa that smelled of lavender, boxwood, and garlic. A long, lazy summer in a place where there would be no memories of Perry.

CHAPTER 20

She's Leaving Home

I had a heavy, solid sleep, filled with wispy dreams about the incidents of the day before. There were images of the chapel, the sense of being swallowed up by the Gothic arches, and the smell of incense. The glimpses of the Wagners, Alison in tears with Suzie and Pepa, and Suzie's inky yet fiery eyes as they cornered me near the bush. Then Leo carrying me to the infirmary, but all I could do with that part was imagine his long arms under me.

When I got back to my room the next day, Suzie's pillows, books, toiletries, and some of her clothes that usually lay about, were gone. The Wagners had moved everything out of Perry's room, and I was relieved to have missed what must have been a heavy, quiet drama. I took a shower, got dressed, and headed off to my classes but not before stopping in the dining hall for a cup of coffee to take me out of my still groggy state. There were a couple of students remaining, procrastinating the walk to class, and they looked me over, paused, and then continued on. I wondered how many people thought I was still the guilty one about the notes.

Somehow I made it through the morning although my concentration powers weren't at their best and of course, given this, I was greeted by two quizzes, one in geometry and one in bio. I had a sort of vague feeling that as I was writing down the theorems and functions of the cilia of this and the valve of that, that I wasn't entirely clear as to what I was saying. It was as if I had come for a visit to these classes and took the quizzes just to see what I knew. My mind was too taken up with where Leo was, would I see him later that day, would I see Lally and Alicia at lunch, and if not, what was I going to do? And then of course there was Perry, although every time her face came into my mind, the wide-eyed, open-mouthed fear illuminated by the headlights of an oncoming car, I managed to push it away. But it kept returning, kept harassing me no matter how hard I tried to concentrate on the questions in front of me and the cold, logical facts I had worked so hard to memorize. No one spoke to me that morning, even the teachers avoided addressing me, giving me only nervous glances.

Fortunately, Lally and Alicia were waiting for me in the Fletcher commons room for lunch. They hugged me and asked me how I was feeling.

"Weird," I replied.

"We tried visiting you in the infirmary, but Leo said you were asleep," Alicia said.

"I passed out," I said.

Lally said, "Yeah, we know. But he told us you came to, and he tried talking to you, but you fell asleep."

It was all so fuzzy, I had no memory, aside from waking up with the nurse next to me later that afternoon. Of Leo carrying me, of me seeing him, I had no memory.

"I don't remember that." My heart raced in fear. "That's something I should remember. How come the nurse never told me I woke up earlier?"

The two girls shrugged. "You were pretty stressed out, you know," Lally said.

"Where's Leo?" I asked.

"He's sleeping. He pulled an all-nighter typing a final paper for his history class," Alicia replied.

"Did he say anything?"

The girls shook their heads in unison. They made me think of a little duo of messengers, or ladies in waiting, the way they sandwiched me at the memorial and were there to greet me with hugs as I entered the dorm. "I teased him about being your knight in shining armor," Lally said, and she gave me a smile that looked as though she were trying to suppress laughter.

My head was swimming. I felt like I had missed out on something big. "He said nothing?"

"Just that you had passed out, which we saw, and he took you to the infirmary. We wanted to go along, but he got all bossy and nervous and barked orders at us to go back to the dorm. Like, what trouble were we going to cause if we stayed with you guys?" Lally rolled her eyes. "He was so nervous that we just let him be."

Alicia finished, "And then he said you came to for about two seconds, and then fell back to sleep again."

I wanted to see him again and left lunch early telling them I had to go back to my dorm. On the way out, I stopped by Leo's window, which was where I really wanted to go, and called out his name. There was no answer, and I went up close to the window and although it was too high for me to see in, I tried to hear his breathing. I heard nothing. *Maybe he's with that Natalie chick,* I thought for one paranoid-stricken moment. I ran to the music building to warm up for my piano lesson. Maybe he was there.

But he wasn't. And I hadn't finished my piece. And I had to tell Mrs. McGowan that I wasn't returning next year, which reminded me that I also had to tell my parents, a task that was much worse. Mrs. McGowan would understand, maybe. My parents? Maybe Dad. Mom? If there had been any hairs on my back, they would have been standing at attention at that point.

It seemed like ages before Mrs. McGowan arrived. The concert was that Saturday, and I had only a half-assed ending that was no more than a "ta-da!" and that was it. And still no title. It was pretty pathetic. The truth was, I could not reach a satisfying end, one that would wrap up all that I wanted to say. It was obvious by the introductory chords, that begging element in the piece, I was asking for something, and when I reached the major chords, it was as if to say, "Something completely new and unexpected has entered my life." And I wondered if it wasn't altogether negative. But my impulse was to immediately reintroduce the minor chords from the beginning. The next section I wrote was another answer to that, slightly echoing the first but only this time a little more forcefully and dramatically, as if this so-called new element was a reality, something I had to face. I had been working on this, refining it for weeks, but now I had to come up with an ending. I fiddled around with the keys in the chord progressions, alternately cracking my knuckles, thinking this would solve all my problems.

"Hello!" Mrs. McGowan's prim voice rang out as she entered the room and closed the door behind her. She didn't ask me how my weekend was, what I got done, or if I finished my piece. She settled right into her spot and had me begin with my exercises. There were times when I was amazed at how easy it was to focus on the task at hand with the piano, something that never happened in my other classes. It seemed the minute Mrs. McGowan started me on my exercises, I had no choice but to place all my energy in my fingers, a steely resolve taking over. *I am the best damn player in the world,* I thought, *and screw everyone else. Screw all those people who think I'm guilty. Screw Pepa, Suzie, and Marcie.* I tried not to think about Perry, because every time she entered my thoughts, my fingers clenched up.

Exercises done with, my announcement of my plans for next year hung in my mind. *Come on*, I told myself, *tell her now, now is the time. No, that would ruin it all, color the lesson. The rest of my piece. Wait.*

"I'm not coming back next year." The words fell out involuntarily.

"What?" Her head jerked back.

I cleared my dry throat. "Yeah. I can't come back here."

She paused. "Why not?"

I couldn't look at her. "I'm not happy. I miss my home, I miss my old friends. I'm not comfortable in this environment. This," I indicated the keys in front of me, "is the only thing that's keeping me going." I sighed. "I'm so sorry."

She looked like she was about to melt to the floor for a moment and then just as quickly, composed herself. "Well, I'm sorry too, but if you're not happy here, then you shouldn't be here." She let out a small chuckle. "How's that for a simplistic statement?" She shook her head. "What I'm trying to say is that your not being happy here will cut into your music, and I, for one, am not a believer in the suffering artist." Her eyes narrowed, "I always wondered if this place was feeding you properly."

"What do you mean?"

"You just seemed lost." *Just like at Katonah.* "I mean, a lot of people your age are, but I think you were really looking for something here that this place couldn't give you."

"I got great piano lessons," I replied in her defense.

She smiled. "I'm glad." She paused for what felt like a few endless seconds. "Well, I will miss you, Jess. You're a good student, and I am going to miss working with you."

"Yeah, I'm going to miss you too," I said amazed that I was A) actually saying this to the teacher I had been so fearful of and B) the level of honesty we had between us. I never recalled saying this to Chris. He said it to me, but for some reason, I was too embarrassed to say it back even though I felt the same way.

"Do you have any idea whom you'll study with?" she asked.

"Nope. My old teacher is happy in L.A. No plans to move back."

"Let me see if I can line someone up for you. In the meantime, let's get back to work." Her voice lost the softness it had before, and she was direct and to the point all over again.

We never talked about Perry and the funeral. I didn't know if she knew about the notes, and I didn't want to know. I felt it was all unnecessary, that it wouldn't help me at that moment, with finishing up what I had written. It was as if she just knew that side of my life had to be left in peace for the moment.

At dinner, I got the call from Tom. He had been home for about two weeks.

"Did you get my message?" he asked. It felt like ages since we last spoke.

"No," I shook my head, imagining Pepa or Suzie answering the phone and nodding with a bunch of "Yeah, yeah, yeahs" and "Sure, I'll leave the message," and then hanging up and forgetting on purpose.

"I tried calling you last week and left you a message." His voice sounded perturbed.

"Who'd you leave it with?"

"I dunno. They didn't say, and I didn't ask. I just wanted to see how you were doing."

"I'm OK." I settled into the wobbly wooden chair next to the phone.

"Yeah?" His voice barged in, reminding me a bit of Mom. "When I found out about it, I tried calling you right away, but the phone was always busy."

"Everything's OK." I didn't know what else to tell him. It felt like anything else I was going to say would sound prosaic.

"I guess you know how it happened," he said, his voice so low I had to press my ear to the phone to hear what he said.

"Car accident. They think she was drinking."

"That's *all* you heard?"

All the air went out of me. "You obviously know more?"

There was silence for a moment, and I knew he was trying to figure out how to tell me whatever it was that needed to be told—the real truth.

"I actually, um," he cleared his throat, "knew someone who was at that party. I figured you knew the whole thing."

"What whole thing?"

"Whoa. You mean—?" His voice broke off. He was making me feel stupid, and I hated it. But before I could answer, he continued. "OK. There's this guy in my dorm, Peter, who I'm sort of friends with. Anyway, he was at that party with Perry. He's friends with this painter, Joel, whom she had a fling with *apparently*. Who knows? I mean, this is what Peter told me." The way he delivered this reminded me of Grandma Cunningham. The rush of words, the dismissive tone mixed with intensity.

"I know who you're talking about," I responded automatically.

"Oh! OK, so at least you've heard about him." Then the story poured out of him, his words running together as though he were almost embarrassed. "Peter told me that last summer Joel turned her onto coke, along with another girl, this model or something, I dunno. The relationship was really weird. And then he introduced her to his dealer, this total lowlife that she hooked up with. Then she owed him money, and she became heavy in debt because I don't think she had a lot to begin with. I think she started sleeping with him because that was going to pay for everything. Peter was telling me all sorts of stories about her, that she got pregnant by the dealer—"

The words fell out of my mouth. "She got an abortion. I helped pay for it."

"*What?*"

"Yeah. I thought it was the painter guy."

"You *paid* for it?"

"Well, Mom and Dad did." My face turned warm, and I waited for some kind of recrimination from my brother.

"Jesus." He was silent for a moment. "How did you get the money from them?"

"I lied. I told them I needed the money for another piano teacher. And then, I couldn't live with the lie, so I told Dad the truth."

He let out a guffaw in disbelief. "You *lied* to them? Oh my god, *you* actually lied to Mom and Dad?"

"Yeah, yeah." I wanted to forget about that, it was too long ago. "Are you sure it was the dealer?"

"Positive," he announced. "Joel told Peter." The tone in his voice made it clear that there was no use doubting him any further. "Jess, I'm sorry. It thought you knew all about this. I mean she was your friend. Or, you hung out with her and stuff, although I could never understand why. It always seemed really weird because she was so different—"

"Well," I started to say, like I was now beginning to ponder a million times, *I had no idea what she was to me.*

"It's funny," he said, "because based on what I had heard about her at Connecticut, I always thought it a little odd you were friends with her."

I was in no mood to discuss that with him, but I had to ask, "How long did you know about this whole thing?"

"Since the accident, when Peter said that there had been this accident at a party he went to someplace on Long Island, and he mentioned that it involved Professor Wagner's daughter. I told him she was a friend of yours, and that's when he told me the whole story about what happened at the party. You know, this guy Peter is like this—"

"What happened?" It came out sounding like a demand, and I twisted the black telephone cord around my forefinger, tightening it and then loosening it again, watching my finger go from purpley red to normal beigey pink. Plus, I really had no interest in hearing about Peter, whoever the hell he was.

"He said that she was so wasted. I mean, she wasn't just drunk, she did a lot of coke that night. Her dealer had been threatening her for a while, and so when she saw him at the party, she apparently grabbed her friend's, that model chick's, car keys, and this girl was just as fucked up as Perry, and didn't do anything. But I think that's pretty typical for models because they're such airheads. *Anyway,* Perry got in the car 'cause she was running away from her dealer. Maybe the accident had something to do with the weather, but it wasn't that bad there. She just lost control."

I felt like my brother had thrown a boulder right in my lap. In some ways, it only made sense that she'd have a dealer. All that coke couldn't just magically appear. But I always imagined her getting it through a friend. A dealer sounded so old, someone people in college know even though I knew it was incredibly naïve to think this. But at the same time, I felt relief that it wasn't suicide, and that it wasn't caused by the events going on at school. That it was something completely different.

"And that guy she was seeing at school?" Tom's voice sounded like it was coming from the far end of a tunnel.

"Marcus Feld," I managed to say, although he name felt foreign on my tongue.

"Yeah, he was in on the whole thing, too. He wasn't as bad an addict as she was, but he was helping to pay for her coke as long as he got a bit of it. Codependant hell."

I sat there, letting my brother rattle on, while I breathed slowly into the phone. I wondered if Pepa and Suzie knew about this. But then again, was it even worth asking them? How many people knew about this, aside from Marcus? Hassan, obviously. And if Hassan knew, then Pepa would know (unless, of course, he was keeping secrets from her), and then she would tell Suzie. They wouldn't tell me because they didn't trust me. But they kept me close to them. I recalled that line from *The Godfather* where Al Pacino grumbled advice to someone, "Keep your friends close, but your enemies closer." And that's exactly what Perry tried to do.

I heard my brother's voice again. "I'm sorry, Jess. I thought you knew."

"I had an inkling. I knew she had a drug problem. She had been making it kind of obvious." It was as if I was defending her. That when I met her, she was only just beginning her descent, and it didn't become full-blown until the spring. Or so I thought. Quite frankly, I didn't know what to think any more. I just felt stupid and innocent and naïve and ignorant and a whole slew of demeaning adjectives.

Why didn't I see this? In retrospect, it was obvious. I had known for a while she was doing drugs, but out of some sort of self-protection, I pretended it wasn't so bad. All this time, my gut told me there was something really wrong with Perry and her crowd. The way she took me under her wing immediately as if to say, "She's *mine*." I must have seemed so out of it, so innocent and harmless, that I was an easy target. But I wondered, had I not roomed with Suzie, would the same thing have happened? And despite the warning signs, I stayed, just to see what it was like to be with her. To be with someone who appeared so much less isolated than myself. Older and cooler and all that crap that makes you want to see what it's like to be a part of a popular crowd. Or a crowd that is somehow or other revered. At least that's what I thought of them. That's how I thought they were perceived. But hanging out with Lally and Alicia proved that wrong. It occurred to me that Perry, Pepa, and Suzie had no friends other than each other. Perry may have held some kind of upper status what with her being an over-achiever and being with Marcus. But the fact of the matter was the group didn't want anyone else. For all of Perry's talk about how she went out and grabbed life whereas I was just scared and hibernated with my music, I realized she was just as isolated as I was, if not more, living in her own world (as were Suzie and Pepa) with this thought that she was much bigger than the rest of them.

I got phone calls from Dad every day to see how I was doing. Mom was some-times there and sometimes not, and I noticed I was always a bit more relaxed when she wasn't. My head was swimming. *Should I tell him about the notes*, I wondered, *or was that better left unsaid, like some sort of blip in the whole drama?*

"I finally spoke to Tom," I said to Dad Tuesday evening.

"Good, I'm glad he got in touch with you. I know he was trying."

I swallowed. "Yeah. He knew someone who was at the party." I waited to hear Dad's response.

"Yeah, so he said."

I shut my eyes tightly. "Did he say anything else?"

"No, just that she had a bit too much to drink." He said something about how tragic it was, clearly trying to give me the message not to drink and drive, but at the same time he didn't want to be preachy. But in something like this, it's unavoidable. A parent could just sigh or remain silent and the message would come bounding over the wires and hit you in the face full force.

"Right." I was at least relieved that was all Tom had said.

But Dad didn't want to talk about Perry, he wanted to talk about me, how I was, what was going on with Suzie and Pepa.

"I'm not that close with them. They're just off together a lot. It's OK. I don't have anything in common with them." The words struck me with a finality that should have occurred to me before, but never had. I was so far off on fantasy land, even though the whole thing was staring me in the face.

"Dad," I took a deep breath and continued. "I don't want to come back next year. I hate this place." It may have sounded whiny and petulant and maybe it did to him, but it came out, and I didn't care any more.

I heard him let out a breath. "I had a feeling."

"You did?"

"Yeah. You've had a bit of a rough time."

"I miss home, I miss going to the city. I want to be with Kim. I mean, even her classes seem so much more interesting than the other ones here. I don't know, like there's more imagination. And this place is so small."

"Sure you wouldn't want to try a larger place?"

"No." I barely let him finish the sentence.

"OK, I'll discuss it with your mother."

"No," I almost shouted into the receiver but didn't. I sounded forceful and almost authoritative. "Dad, I do not want to go to another school. Katonah will be fine. Really."

"OK. But I do have to let your mother know."

"OK."

The whole week, I locked myself away in Bartlett finishing up my piece and trying to do as much work as was possible without having to go to the library. The ending finally came. I did bring up the begging, minor chords from the beginning but only briefly before switching over to a major scale that ended on a high note, with a light touch. I wondered at first if placing a scale at the end wasn't some sort of cop out, but it felt satisfying as long as I kept the touch on that last note light, giving the piece a sense of hope.

The other reason why I was remaining in Bartlett for so long was that I wanted to run into Leo. And I did, but it was always anticlimactic. He would give me a brief wave and ask me how I was and then scurry away like he was embarrassed or something. I couldn't understand why he was being so weird.

"I know why," Lally announced at lunch on Friday when I told her and Alicia this. "OK, Jess, I gotta be honest with you. He really liked you, and I think he felt like you were jerking him around—"

I let out a groan. It's awful hearing your crimes repeated back to you.

"I know. I'm just saying that's probably what he was feeling. You know? Like what he was perceiving. Sorry to drag this all up again, he was really upset about the whole Marcus thing, which I know is totally stupid since he was with Natalie even though she was basically using him to get to this other guy. And then after-wards, with the notes and stuff, he really tried to reach out to you, but you were always backing off."

"I didn't know who to trust, Lally."

"No kidding," Alicia echoed.

"I know, I'm sorry. You're right," Lally continued pushing on. "But he really likes you, which is why he carried you over to the infirmary that day." I noticed how she didn't say, "The day of the memorial service." She added, "But he thinks you don't feel the same way about him, so he doesn't want to get hurt."

A force welled up inside of me that made me realize I had to do something about this now. I couldn't wait any longer, particularly since school was almost over. I wanted to jump up from my seat and run to his room, or wherever he was. I didn't know how I felt about him, whether I liked him as a friend or more than that since my feelings seemed to change all the time. But what I did know was that I didn't want to lose him, which probably meant that I really liked him. But the thought of kissing him struck the fear of God in me for some reason. That I couldn't figure it out, and if I couldn't imagine kissing him, maybe he wasn't boyfriend material, but who was I to choose? And look what fantasizing about kissing Marcus led to.

I had my last lesson with Mrs. McGowan that afternoon. I played my finished piece and then looked up to her, and she gave me what I had been seeing in my mind all week.

"OooK," she nodded, her eyes half shut, her fingers playing with her jade necklace. Once again, I thought of the mother raccoon in *Wait Til the Moon Is Full*, who smiles down at her son, his baseball bat and glove in hand as he's trot-ting out the door, and she tells him that he can finally go outside.

"So what are you going to call it? What is this piece saying to you?"

I thought about the past year. How during each term, something distinctive happened to me that woke me up, somehow changed me. How what we studied in English seemed to correspond or contradict so strongly to what was going on in my life, it was a little uncanny. But something new had entered. I thought back on the person I was when I first came here in the late summer and who I had become now in the late spring. I didn't exactly know who it was, but it was completely brand-new and unexpected, like I had just entered a new season of my life. Summer, fall, winter, spring.

"The Fifth Season," I finally said. She gazed at me for a bit, and I added, "It's about my life. What I went through this year, through each season, and how I've found myself in a completely different one."

She smiled. "Good, that's good."

"So I'm done, right?"

"No. Maybe for now. But I think this is something you can continue to work on and refine. Don't overdo it. You've gotten off to a really good start, and when you learn a little more about composition, you can go back to it and refine it. Speaking of which, I found a teacher for you who I think is going to work out well. George Kaplan."

She looked at me as though I should have known his name. The name had so many hard consonants, already he sounded like a ball buster. There was something about the name Kaplan that connoted a tall, overbearing, and loud teacher.

"Where is he?"

"At Mannes. He's wonderful. He'll really help you with your technique, which is what you need, but he's also a terrific composition teacher."

"Does he like melodies?" I gave her a wary look. I imagined learning serious, unmelodic music and getting a migraine.

She laughed, and I realized I had never heard her laugh this loudly. *Wow*, I thought. *I'm getting to be like Leo.*

"Obviously I wouldn't line you up with someone who isn't right for you. Trust me, this guys knows his way around a melody."

"OK."

She whispered to me, "Think of this as another adventure, Jess. Just like in your piece. Don't be so scared."

I looked out the window next to me, and it was as if Mrs. McGowan had parted the curtains for me to take a look at a world I hadn't seen.

It was late afternoon when I finally left Bartlett. I didn't exactly know where to go. Mom, Dad, and Tom were arriving the next morning. Kim and Andy couldn't make it since both of them had a big English paper due. As I wandered the campus, up the hill, and into the large quad that was surrounded by Fletcher, the marble and yellow-brick administration building, two other dorms, the tall, brick math and science building with its marble columns, I fantasized that once I was home and playing my piece for Kim and Andy they'd be so impressed with me that he'd ask me to write the songs and be the keyboardist for their new band. Then I imagined a new life where I'd be in college, living in the Lower East Side of Manhattan, playing in a band at CBGB's, sort of like the next Talking Heads or Blondie or something. I sat on a stone bench in the center of the quad and eased my knapsack off my shoulders. I was looking forward to the week after next. Exams. It meant I would get out of here soon. I felt a small surge of confidence, knowing that whatever came about, I could handle.

I looked over where the large elm fell during Hurricane Gloria and thought of that warm rain splashing on my face, the wind raging from Long Island Sound blasting at us that jittery afternoon. When I thought of myself then, gaping at Marcus, laughing hysterically with Perry and Suzie as we spun around in the storm, I recalled a quote by Shirley Temple from a biography of her I read when I was a little kid. It was one of the first real chapter books I read that was geared for adults, or at least movie buffs, who wanted a quick look at a star's life. She talked about how, as an adult and no longer in the movies, watching herself in her films made her feel like she wasn't so much watching herself but some distant relative. And that's how I felt at that moment, sitting on the stone bench that June afternoon.

I stood up. I decided to go to Fletcher to see if Lally and Alicia were around. I wanted to run into Leo, but was so afraid I would come upon the same scene with him and maybe some other girl in the commons room, that I pushed that thought away.

I headed up to the entrance of their dorm and glanced over at Leo's window, as I always did, and then immediately averted my glance to Lally and Alicia's window.

"Jess." The word was so faint, it was as if he were reluctant to say my name.

I stopped and turned to look at his window. He seemed faded a bit by the screen in front of him.

I took a deep breath and walked over. "Hi," I announced, dropping my knapsack to the ground, and put my hands on my hips.

"Where have you been?" he asked while chomping on his gum. He was chewing with his mouth open, which I thought was totally annoying, his face was serious and his eyes a bit dull. *Isn't that what I should be asking you?* I thought.

"Working. For the concert tomorrow. Remember? There's a concert?" I felt the sarcasm grow in my voice.

"You don't have to get so obnoxious with me. I just asked."

I know, I thought. *I'm just angry about Natalie and everything.* "That's where I was. You've seen me. In fact, every time I try to say hello to you and thank you for what you did last week, you act like I'm about to kill you."

"No, I just had a lot of work to do."

"Oh, come on! Everyone does! But you make all these nice gestures to me and then back off." I paused. "Like what I've been doing."

He raised his voice. "Yeah! I know! Why are you always doing these things?"

"OK, look, I was scared. After all that happened to me, I was really freaked out. Like you were."

"I wasn't scared." He sounded like an eight-year-old saying, "Wasn't my fault."

I stared hard at him. "Oh, yes you were, OK? I'm the daughter of a psychiatrist. I know these things."

He snorted as he leaned on his elbows and looked down at the windowsill. He must not have been that pissed off at me, or else he would have slammed the window shut. He continued to stay there, twitching his mouth, chomping on his gum, and then he mumbled, "OK, whatever."

We both stayed rooted in place, me staring at him, hands on my hips, knapsack at my feet, him pouting by the windowsill, chewing with his mouth open. Finally he said, "You wanna come in? I'll meet you in the commons room."

My stomach flipped over, and I nodded and trotted into the dorm.

He greeted me, still chewing, although this time more furiously, and I signed in. He took my hand, his was big and warm, and led me down the hallway of the boys' side and into his room. "Wanna listen to *Pet Sounds*?" he asked. His face still sullen.

"Yeah," I replied and plunked myself down on his bed like it was my own.

The tinkling harp came out over the speakers, and he turned to look at me. His face had softened a bit, and I hoped mine had done the same. He spit out his gum in the trash can, walked over to the bed, sat down, put a hand to my face, and started to kiss me. He tasted like mint and tobacco, and it was absolutely delicious. I felt as though I wanted to crawl inside him the more I kissed him. He caressed my face, and I pulled him as close to me as possible. It was as though we couldn't get close enough, but the more we kissed, the more likely it seemed. Although the volume wasn't very high, I could still make out the large symphony of the album in the background. It was like being in the corner of an enormous room, with the band playing at the other end. Brian Wilson and Mike Love's high voices came through clear and bittersweet.

I had always heard sex described as this unifying experience between two people; that old corny chestnut, "when two become one." I never bought it. I always thought it was wishful thinking on the part of the songwriter. Leo and I didn't have sex; we didn't even fool around. All we did was make out. When I later compared it to what happened with Marcus, technically it was pretty chaste. But the experience with Leo was so intense, I felt like everything around us had disappeared, except for the Beach Boys' harmonies. His lips and his tongue became these soft, moist petals that I wanted to keep with me forever. His hands, large and muscular, held me just firmly enough without feeling gropey and possessive. He caressed my hair with such tenderness and gentleness I wanted to cry.

I didn't really know how long we remained like that. Leo got up a couple of times to change the sides of the record. The soft sounds, the close harmonies, the unpredictable turns of the melodies hung in the background. We ended up lying down on his bed, and at one point, I looked out the window to see that it had become significantly darker than it was earlier. The lyrics of the song, "I Just Wasn't Made for These Times" came out canonlike as Leo reached over to the bedside table and turned on his small metal lamp. After gazing at each other with big grins on our faces, he sat up and told me he had to go to the bathroom. As he was leaving the room, he gestured to his record collection. "Play what you want, OK?"

I wanted to listen to something similar, something with that same wistful, hazy feeling that I got from *Pet Sounds*. And I found it, a Velvet Underground with Nico album that had a banana on the cover. The song, "Sunday Morning," I had only heard once about a year earlier, but it made such a huge impression on me, I wanted to go out and buy the album. When I put the record on, I closed my eyes to listen to the xylophone in the introduction, followed by the bass and strings.

The song faded with Lou Reed's voice echoed by a distant piano chord. The door opened, and Leo came in, looking relaxed and happy. He clapped his hands together and bellowed, "I love this song!"

He pulled out his bottle of Absolut vodka from a duffle bag under his bed, along with tonic water, and then a lime that sat near the window. We drank vodka tonic from two mugs. Not only did the buzz come quickly, but I didn't do much to slow it down. We didn't talk about what had happened earlier. We talked about music. He went through his record collection and played me songs that I had never heard before.

When he finally put on the Style Council's *Café Bleu*, it sent me into floods of tears. The peppy sounding "You're the Best Thing," had such a sweet joyfulness to it. The simple guitar passages in the chorus that made me already miss Leo and having this kind of time to sit on the floor with him, the smell of his cologne, cigarettes, and peppermint gum, illicitly drinking vodka tonics after an amazing make-out session.

He started to laugh and took me in his arms as I sobbed. "We will see each other on vacations!" He kissed my forehead.

And just like that, the tears subsided. "Oh! Wait a sec! I'm not coming back to Fieldings!" Even in my somewhat drunken state, I realized I said this a lot more easily than I had planned.

His eyes became huge, and then he jumped to his feet, practically sloshing my drink. "That's incredible!" It came out sounding, *Dat's incredible!* "When did you decide?"

"I think a while ago. I hate it here."

"Wow! Do you know what this means?"

"I know!" I nodded even though the answer wasn't very clear to me. I knew I wanted to see him, but I wasn't quite sure if this meant he wanted us to be boyfriend and girlfriend. It sounded like a pretty cool idea, though.

CHAPTER 21

I Know There's an Answer

I woke up starving from lack of food and hung over from too much vodka. I remembered that Leo accompanied me back to Kurtzman where he gave me a long, drawn-out kiss, and then I floated upstairs to bed, not even caring if I ran into Suzie or Pepa, or even a faculty member, for that matter. Thinking about the kiss caused a light, dancing feeling in me that also made me feel like I was about to splinter off into a million different pieces, and I wasted no time calling Leo after I inhaled a breakfast of Eggo waffles, swimming in butter and fake maple syrup.

"Heyyy," he said when he got to the phone.

"Hi!" I felt like a bottle of seltzer water that had just been shaken.

"Are you ready for the concert?"

"As ready as I'll ever be," I replied. My chest tightened in panic as the thought of all those tricky syncopations I had put in made me wonder why I had to make my piece so damn hard. Right now my hands, as they clutched the receiver and the phone cord, were not only far from awake but seemed to not be a part of my body. I was splintering off except not in the way I wanted to.

"When are your parents coming?" he asked.

"Around noon," I said, anticipating the sight of my mother walking toward me, a thin, stretched-out smile on her face, eyes gleaming blue, blue, blue, her hair blond and pulled so far back, keeping everything under control. Then I thought of my dad, of Tom. But the thought of Mom hung over me. She knew I wasn't coming back, and I knew she wasn't going to take the news well. She wanted to get her kids out of the house, off her hands, have Dad to herself, have all the attention. But there was Dad, and he was a warm comfort. She wasn't going to react well to Leo, either—this big, tall, threatening Italian with whom I was probably going to spend the vacation in Italy. Or maybe next year. But quite frankly I wasn't ready to think about that.

"And yours?" I asked.

"They just called me. Woke me up. They'll be here right before the concert. Around 12:30 or something."

"I can't wait to meet them," I said, thinking I actually could wait. Meeting his parents would be like seeing an extension of him, of who he really was in a way that I wasn't prepared for, like weird facial similarities and how Leo himself would behave because everyone behaves differently around their parents. It was going to be so bizarre, so *Twilight Zone*-y. And then having my parents meet his parents, and then the subject of this summer coming up, and there would be all this awkward conversation. And then hearing his parents' foreign accents in comparison with Leo's Americanized one, which would make him look more pulled together and secure than they were, and that wasn't right. It was supposed to be the other way around.

Leo and I met up later that morning in front of Kurtzman after I fidgeted and fussed over what I was going to wear, how my half empty room would look to my family, and then having to explain that. My mind jumped from one thing to another, the nerves in my body standing on end. And when Leo planted a big kiss on my lips that I wasn't expecting, my stomach flipped over, and I thought I was going to collapse. I asked where Lally and Alicia were, and he just shrugged and said, "Around." Part of me wanted them right here with us, and another part of me was grateful at the thought that Leo wanted to be alone with me. I started to feel the Eggos revolt a bit, but I knew it was just nerves. I didn't know whether I would feel better warming up at the piano or walking around. As noon approached, I got jumpier and jumpier. I wished my body could settle on one feeling.

The dark blue Volvo drove up, making crackling noises on the driveway. Three people got out, and I involuntarily ran over to them, Mom feeling like a sharp light. Dad already had his arms open to take me in, and we hugged each other hard. All of a sudden, that first day came back to me—the sun, the constant thirst, Perry in front of me, Dad behind me as we headed into Kurtzman. I squeezed him hard, trying to simultaneously hold onto the memory while at the same time trying to release everything else. I thought of Perry's father and the hair that blew around his head that sad, windy afternoon. *No, not now. I cannot think about it now.* I sniffed in Dad's pipe tobacco smell.

"Hi, Mom," I said, my voice unusually high, and my eyes squinting back at her smile.

"Hi, sweetie." She gave me a bony hug that was hard and brief. The sinking feeling from lunch last spring came back, but surprisingly, only for a second.

Tom gave me a hug not dissimilar to Dad's. And then I introduced Leo, hoping my face didn't betray signs of anything that happened the night before. Tom looked at him as though he knew absolutely everything, this sort of knowing smile on his lips. He didn't make things obvious though, by looking back at me with a "what-else-did-he-introduce-you-to-aside-from-cigarettes?" kind of look. But I knew he knew, and I wondered, therefore, if my parents knew. My mind spun as Leo shook my parents' hands, and Mom gave him her quick, bright smile. There was some conversation I couldn't pay attention to about Italy, about where he lived, a jaw-dropping moment on his behalf when he discovered that he knew my grandmother's villa. "Wow!" he looked at me wide-eyed. It was just up the hill from his house.

The sunlight hit my head hard, and everything looked dewy and light green. It was like a 1950s Technicolor film, all romantic and idyllic. Everything just blurred over and I hoped we wouldn't be having any awkward encounters with Suzie or Pepa as we headed over to Kurtzman. Leo looked at his watch and announced he had to go back to his dorm because his family was showing up at any moment.

There wasn't much to see in my room, aside from the fact that it was almost half empty, which probably looked odd to them, but fortunately, no one said anything. I gave my parents a few things, like winter clothes, to take back home. Giving them the duffel bag caused a huge weight to lift from my chest. No mention was made yet of next year, probably because my parents didn't want to make a scene before the concert. Tom and Mom were also too busy looking at some of the remaining pictures on Suzie's bulletin board and making comments. "Did you know him?" Tom would ask, pointing to various actors pictured next to Suzie's dad. "Oh my God, she looks so young! I thought she was, like, dead!"

"She's had lots of work done," Mom replied in her lock-jawed voice which caused all of us to burst out laughing, the ice finally broken.

As I got my staff sheets together, Tom asked if he could have a look.

"Nooo!" I squealed.

"Nervous?"

"Duh," I replied with a snort and a roll of the eyes.

"Good," Mom said. "It's a really good sign."

It was quiet for a few moments as I wondered whether Mom wanted to discuss my not coming back. I wanted to be alone with Dad for that, but I knew that was going to be an impossibility. We filled up the space with talk about the drive, the weather, who was performing, and what they were doing, what Leo was playing, the fact that he was going to NYU next year (I didn't look at Mom, but I just knew her eyebrows were raised) and then, Thank God, I had to go warm up. I went to Bartlett, trying to calm myself down by breathing deeply.

My hands were so light over the keys, I wondered if I was going to be able to hit the notes correctly and with the right accents. When Mrs. McGowan came by, it was all I could do to keep the headiness that was in me under control. I purposefully slowed down my triads and felt self-conscious when I started going over my piece. I flubbed a section in the middle, but decided to move on. "Go back and repeat the phrase," she declared, gazing down at a notebook that was placed on the piano. She was strict and unsmiling, which sent me plunging down to earth, and I thought she was mad at me, like she knew what I had done the night before.

She looked over at me as I repeated it, to no avail. "Focus. Ignore everything else in your head. This is all that matters now. It's normal to be nervous, but use it to focus."

I swallowed and returned to it. It became clearer, better.

"Good," she said and turned her head back to her notebook.

When I finished warming up before the concert began, she rubbed her spindly, ring-covered hand on my back and told me I'd be fine. Her voice still had that red-wine sound. She then turned around and grinned at Leo, who did the same, and I thought I was going to jump out of my skin with nerves.

In the concert hall, we sat by the windows, catty corner to the audience, the rustling programs and whispers filling the room, which felt unusually warm, and I smelled a mixture of different perfumes and body odors. I changed the room in my head, imagining it to be someplace else that was not a part of Fieldings.

The choir sang, their voices rising and falling with the conductor's hands. They sang something that was very modern and had to do with prophetic joys, realizing space, and flying clouds. A tiny girl, a senior, came forward and in her soprano voice sang a solo, hitting a note towards the end that sounded a bit flatter than it should have. But the whole piece was lovely with its complicated harmonies, changing melody, and tempo.

And then I went on. I sat down at the piano and tried not to see my family as I gave a prim smile to the audience. But there they were. I told myself not to search for Leo's parents, but I immediately saw his brothers Tiziano and Pietro and the two parents next to them. His father looked like Santa Claus, a big mop of white hair on his head and around his mouth, and little, wire-rimmed glasses around his eyes. His mother was dark, dark eyes, short, dark hair, and a long mouth. I couldn't tell, in that brief moment, which one Leo resembled most. My nerves stood on end as I told myself to focus. I noticed Mrs. McGowan sitting by one of the long windows with its mustard-colored curtains behind her like a dramatic backdrop. I started "The Fifth Season." Thank God it started slow and meditative.

I played as well as I could. I had played better, with more feeling and more correct notes. The syncopation worked this time, even if it was a bit exaggerated. I lost track of some of the notes toward the end and did a little improvisation, that, in a normal practice session I would have disregarded and changed. But I got through the piece without vomiting, although my stomach made a few threats. My thighs were glued to the bench. I kept the touch light on that last note of the last scale. The applause that greeted me at the end sounded muffled, although when I looked at the audience everyone was clapping, people were smiling as though they had enjoyed it, and I realized the whole thing was over.

A fullness and excitement rose up in me, coupled with a numbness that was still left over from the shock of a few weeks ago. It was there, and I realized it had to be there, that this was normal. I was a bit bummed that I messed up my piece, but it wasn't like anyone would know. I looked over at Mrs. McGowan, and she smiled, her eyes doing more of the work than her mouth, but I knew that was a good sign. Lally and Alicia gave me excited hand waves and thumbs-ups.

And in the back, I saw Suzie. I couldn't believe I missed her before when I half-heartedly scanned the audience. The bright brown eyes and dark brown mop of hair on her head seemed to jump out at me at that point. She had been there the entire time, and now she was clapping and almost smiling. But Pepa was missing, something that didn't surprise me at all. I smiled back at Suzie.

And I could feel Perry. It wasn't like I saw her watching, but I felt her presence in the background, angry, upset, and confused. She clutched at something in me, and then she went away. That was the way it had always been and would remain for a while—clutching, leaving, clutching, leaving.

I didn't look at Leo until I got back to my seat. Then I turned to him. He smiled at me with that gaze he gave me during those embarrassing lunches. Only this time, I wasn't embarrassed.

It was his turn next, and if he was nervous, he showed no sign of it, gliding over to the bench, looking as though he commanded the whole room. He had this aristocratic air to him that I had never seen before, and I wondered if it wasn't because he was nervous. He played the first movement of the Beethoven Sonata Number 31 with just the right nuances. My parents gave me a tape of it for my birthday three years ago, and given the number of times I listened to it, I knew Leo was hitting the keys correctly. Yet, only part of my attention was devoted to his performance, because watching him made me think of the night before and that big kiss he gave me that morning. I felt hyperaware of my body, how I was sitting, the curtains draped behind me. I hoped my parents would be impressed with him, and when he finished, I glanced over at them for a split second to see their reactions. Smiles, fast clapping, along with everyone else. *OK, it's going to be fine,* I thought.

Leo returned to his seat, and we looked at each other as he made a "whew" motion with his hand across his forehead, sticking out his tongue. He sat down and squeezed my leg. *Oh my God, my family* must *have seen that.*

"Hey!" Dad almost bellowed at the end of the concert as he threw his arms around me. It was the most excited I had ever seen him. "That was terrific!"

"Thanks!"

Tom gave me a hug and kissed me on the head, which immediately made me feel a bit embarrassed but warm at the same time.

"That was wonderful, honey!" Mom squeezed my shoulders, gazed down at me, and then stretched her neck out to look around the room.

"Thank you," I replied and searched the room for Suzie. Never before had I wanted to see her so badly, just one last time. I spied her heading for the exit, and I excused myself.

"Suzie," I said when I reached her. She turned around and looked at me with worn and tired eyes. "Thank you for coming."

Again it looked like she was trying to smile, her mouth not knowing what to do. "That was really good. You're really good."

"Thanks," I said, wanting to say more yet feeling mute.

"Sorry," she half whispered. "I'm sorry about what we did to you." She couldn't look at me.

"It's OK. I'm sorry about Perry. I mean it sounds so ..."

Suzie shrugged but the small gesture did nothing to cover up a heaviness that seemed to be pushing down on her without any respite. "Whatever. She had a lot going on. Too much."

"Yeah."

"I'm not coming back next year," she grimaced.

"Neither am I."

"I figured. We're not right for this place, or it's not right for us or whatever."
I nodded.

We stood silently listening to the commotion of laughs, introductions, and congratulations. People pushed passed us.

Suzie let out a sigh. "I should go. You were really great. Please forgive us." And with that, she rushed out the door.

I made my way through the blur of handshakes and nervous giggles, to my parents, who were talking to Mrs. McGowan. I got hugs, and they all said, "We're so proud of you," while I wondered if they saw me with Suzie. If they did, they didn't say anything. Mrs. McGowan mentioned George Kaplan, and I wanted to bolt out of the auditorium. It wasn't how I had anticipated introducing the subject of next year, but better her than me. And plus, she was talking about a good piano teacher, so that was at least a positive thing for my parents to hear. I saw Mom's neck tighten a bit as Mrs. McGowan explained that she was sorry I wasn't coming back next year, but that George Kaplan would work out quite well for me. And she listed the reasons why, but I paid no attention. My eyes searched the room for Leo; he was nowhere to be seen. *Oh no*, I thought with panic, *had they all left already?*

When we made our way outside to eat a picnic lunch that my parents had brought, Tom said to me, "It must be quite a compliment to have your teacher ask you to compose something. I mean, everyone else has to play other people's stuff, but she clearly pointed you out as being different."

Yeah, I am different, I thought wearily. I needed to eat something greasy, and I saw some cold chicken waiting for me.

Tom read my face. "Well, Jess, duh."

"I—," Mom and I started together.

"She *is* different," Mom said, her whole face squinching up into a smile, and something else, like a curious thought had just dawned on her. Maybe she was beginning to figure me out.

"Yeah, thank goodness," Dad replied, brushing my cheek. "So Mrs. McGowan had some pretty good things to say about this new teacher."

"Yeah." I looked at Dad when I said this.

"Do you really want to go back to Katonah?" Mom asked, still squinting and squinching.

I grabbed the chicken while my stomach made some noises, and then I nodded slowly at her. "I really do, Mom. I don't like it here."

"Well, your father and I have discussed it, and we know this year hasn't been easy on you—"

"Mom, I don't like it here. It's too small. It's too … formal. I miss Kim, and I miss going to New York."

"She wants to be a suburbanite," Tom chuckled and winked at me.

"Like my brother," I said between mouthfuls. It felt good to get something into my hungover stomach.

Mom looked at him and then back at me. "You sure you don't want to try another school?"

I looked at her, knots developing in my back.

"I think she knows. I think you can trust her." Dad rubbed her back.

"No, I'm just saying!" Mom shook her head, and I could just detect the defensive rise in her voice. "I mean, of course, it's your decision. We're certainly not trying to force you, you know that!"

Yes, you are. "Yeah, I know. And I know what I want."

"Good!" For a moment, she sounded like Mrs. McGowan, those quick compliments she gave me, short and to the point, as if to say, "Got that finished, now let's move on!"

Lally and Alicia rushed over to hug me, and then I introduced them to everyone. And then right behind them was Leo, bashfully smiling at me, surrounded by his family. The brothers kissed me on each cheek, saying, "Ciao, bella," making me feel very European, and congratulating me. Leo and I hugged one another, but it felt jerky and tense.

"Congratulations!" His dad almost broke my bones when shaking my hand, a curly tuft of white hair bouncing on his head as he did so. His mother did the same, although in a quieter way. I noticed the same nose and mouth on her; it was like seeing an older, female version of Leo. They both had the accent, but the ease with which the words flowed out indicated that their English was pretty good.

There were more introductions, and I noticed Dad was much more relaxed than Mom. That was always the case; it wasn't a new observation. But for the first time I saw something guarded in Mom, like she had a little wall around her to protect her from threatening outside influences. There was something too prim, too held back in the way she greeted them, but I didn't think it was readily apparent to the Borghis. At the outset, it was all twinkling sapphire eyes and what I once saw as elegance. But I saw her tense shoulders, the immediacy and quickness of the way the smile was put on. It was Perry greeting Dad on that first day I arrived. It was funny, because I wasn't creeped out like I felt like I should have been. I just felt kind of distanced from her. Not in the devastating way of that lunch we had at the Saloon. She didn't feel like a part of me, and I suddenly realized that although it felt odd, it was OK. She was Mom, but compared to the tug I always got when I saw Dad, when he hugged me, there was nothing with my Mom. It was both unsettling and a relief when I realized I wasn't that upset by her distance.

Mom and Dad found Mrs. McGowan again and decided to go talk to her about next year and, I was sure, my performance this past year. I trusted her with them and wanted to be alone with my brother.

He lay back on the grass. "Mom and Dad mentioned something about you finding other friends. Were they those girls?"

I nodded.

"Well, you've made some friends here."

"They're all seniors."

He narrowed his eyes at me. "And uh, Leo? Nice squeeze he gave you at the concert!"

I playfully hit him on the shoulder. "Stop it! It's nothing."

He gave a laugh that came out of his nose as a snort. "Oooh, Jess and her Italian stallion!"

"Shut up," I replied, trying to suppress a giggle, thereby giving myself completely away.

I wanted him to say something more about Leo, but instead he said, "I hope our last conversation didn't upset you too much."

I tugged at the grass, some blades slipping through my fingers. "Well, I didn't want to tell you over the phone, and I never told Mom and Dad, but things were really ugly for a while between Perry and me."

"I kind of noticed over Christmas," he started.

I wanted to tell him everything. "No, it was more than that. I was pretty aware she had a drug problem. And then she broke up with her boyfriend. And a few months afterwards, I kissed him." Why was it, every time I told this story, it sounded like a laundry list?

"You're kidding!" Tom's eyebrows lifted for a moment, and he had a huge grin on his face. "First you lie to Mom and Dad and now this? What happened to the little mouse we knew and loved?" Little mouse, *topolino*.

I knew he was trying to humor me, and part of me wanted to give in, but I couldn't. "No, it was really bad. I mean, it was only like this one evening." The whole story came out, and I couldn't look at my brother as I was telling it. I continued to tug at the grass as though with each tug, I was letting go of something. But there was something about telling someone not associated with the school at all that validated the whole experience, that made it real, that made me step away from it and gain perspective.

"That's pretty messed up." Tom pulled at the grass with me. We were making a communal pile.

"Yeah." I felt frozen in place, the memory of the whole evening cloaking me.

His voice was uncharacteristically quiet and gentle. "Did everyone actually think you did it?"

"No, but there was gossip for awhile. I'm sure some people still think I'm guilty."

"What about those two girls, you know, your roommate?"

"Suzie showed up at the concert."

Tom jerked his head back.

"She apologized. I told her it was OK, even though I still feel messed up about it. She looked pretty wiped out. She's not coming back either."

"I wonder if they know what actually happened at the party."

"It's funny, but I honestly don't care. I mean, I did right after you told me, but now I just think it's no longer important."

"You know Dad's going to throw you into therapy."

I had a vision of my father tossing me into an office in one of those palatial turn-of-the-century apartment buildings on the Upper West Side, and then me spending the summer in this dimly lit, soft-toned room, a noise maker whirring in the hallway, and a woman looking at me enquiringly, hands on her lap.

I fluttered my eyes heavenward and sighed. Maybe I had to do it, maybe it'd be good for me. I just didn't want to think about it at that moment. "I want to go to Italy first."

"And ride around Florence on the back of Leo's Vespa." Tom gave me a sly grin.

"Shut *up*," I giggled and threw the pile of grass we'd made at him.

After it was all done, after everyone had left, we had to think about finals, the seniors about graduation, and there were the yearbooks. I took mine, knowing it was important to take it, that this was an important year that I couldn't let slide by. But I couldn't look at it. I didn't open the pages, I had no one sign it, and when I did sign others' I tried to avoid looking at the pictures. Lally mentioned that I was in two pictures, but I wasn't anxious to see them. I remember when one photo was taken. We were walking across the quad, books in hand, Suzie, Perry, Pepa, and I on our way to class on a winter afternoon, all of us grinning and trying to look pretty as this guy with a camera told us to smile. Another one was of the four of us sitting in the butt room late at night. It would have been like looking at me yet looking at someone else—that Shirley Temple thing.

I couldn't wait to leave. Kurtzman felt haunted and cold, despite the late spring outside. I got whiffs of Perry every now and then, the Obsession perfume, the smell of Bazooka gum, and I would freeze for a moment, everything in me block up. It was all old and morbid. Pepa never spoke to me, never looked at me directly. Marcie avoided me with brief smiles. Suzie and I didn't do much talking, but we exchanged shy smiles when we saw each other, and that was about all that was necessary at that point. But seeing them together at the dinner table like that, alone, sometimes with Hassan, I saw that that was what we were like all year, this little isolated unit that never mingled with anyone else, never let anyone else in, and seemed to live in a separate world with a completely disengaged view of the rest of the school, thinking everyone looked up to us, when that was hardly the case. It wasn't like I could ignore the past year because it was still too close. Yet there was something old and foreign about it as well. I wanted so badly to move on.

I studied for my finals while wondering about the summer and the future back at home, at times recalling the poem I started over spring break. I wasn't fantasizing about the summer ahead of me or what life would be like going back to Katonah as the new and improved Jess. It was tempting, no question about it. But it just lay there—the future, unexpected. I could smell the flowers in the dry Mediterranean heat, hear the rain on the sidewalks of lower Broadway near NYU, the sound of banging lockers in the hallways at Katonah. I didn't want to think too much about what could be because I didn't want to let myself down like that again. But I focused on the curtains parting, giving me a glimpse of the future, and it would be up to me to live it.

My last exam was English, and when I was done scribbling my essay in my blue book about finding common ground in Romance, Tragedy, and Comedy, I ripped out the last page which was empty. The year was over with what felt like a flick of a pen, not only for me but for everyone else. I looked at all the bodies ahead of me in the gym, hunched over their books, and wrote the rest of the words to my song/poem that I would later set to my composition:

> *You find yourself an open road*
> *With nothing left for you to hold,*
> *A season's cycle come gone,*
> *A fifth one now where we belong.*

THE END

978-0-595-40429-2
0-595-40429-4